HIGH PR

ONE-THIRTY IN THE MORNING...

The bus was lit with pink lights like the lobby of a peepshow. A Saturday evening's trash lay scattered on the floor, including two complete copies of the Sunday newspaper. There were three passengers when we got on, smiled at the bus driver, and sat down without paying. One rider, a thickset Hispanic man with close-cropped hair, began shouting at us. "Hey, y'all don't get to ride without payin'! I paid my money!"

"Shut up, dude," said another rider, a lanky, pale man with glasses, wearing some cobbled-together ensemble of black clothes, leather boots, leather jacket. The female version of him was seated beside him. She had the waxy complexion of someone who had had too much to drink.

"No, *you* shut up!" screamed the Latino.

I stepped over to the Latino man and brought my joined fingers across his neck. Just testing; just seeing what such a thing would do. My claws severed his windpipe and unleashed a bright spray of blood across the seats in front of him.

He put his hands up to his neck in a vain attempt to stop the blood, and he tried to scream, but I had cut him just below the Adam's apple, and his voicebox now had nothing to work with but fluid.

The girl screamed instead....

Other books by Jemiah Jefferson:

FIEND
WOUNDS
VOICE OF THE BLOOD

A DROP OF SCARLET

JEMIAH JEFFERSON

LEISURE BOOKS NEW YORK CITY

A LEISURE BOOK®

January 2007

Published by

Dorchester Publishing Co., Inc.
200 Madison Avenue
New York, NY 10016

Copyright © 2007 by Jemiah Jefferson

ISBN 0-8439-5724-7

Printed in the United States of America.

Visit us on the web at www.dorchesterpub.com.

ACKNOWLEDGMENTS

Wholly inadequate thanks go out to Cecilia Cannon for her invaluable insights, suggestions, encouragement, and countless nights of elegant fun; to Myrlin Hermes for her editing expertise, sympathy, and all those awesome dinners; to Celeste Ramsay for her enduring friendship and support; to Terri Kelly and Autumn Dawley, for believing in me from the beginning; to my editor, Don D'Auria, for his continued enthusiasm and sanity; to Davey and Shawna at Dark Horse, for making me feel at home; to the Vaults of Erowid, for its enormous research resources; to my family, for demonstrating the eternal bonds of love; and to all my friends and fans who always believed that I could do it again.

PROLOGUE: LOSING

ARIANE DEMPSEY

Don't get me wrong; there *were* good moments.

There were together moments, denial moments, lying in bed with limbs braided together, silent and cool, undisturbed but for the slow, silent rise and fall of breathing.

I could pretend we were just ordinary lovers, just Ariane and John, almost married but still, deliciously, not, snoozing in the beauty of a spectacular Portland spring sunset.

For a little while, I could forget what I was.

I could pretend that he had forgotten what he was. Or maybe, that he had suddenly accepted it.

But the moment was always too brief. Time moved forward, and the sky's blush began to recede. In the sinking light, I would notice the luminescent, eggshell whiteness of John's neck, the slight flutter of a pulse visible alongside his dusty curtain of dark hair.

Blood in him, blood that could be in my mouth, inside my body.

I tried to resist noticing, knowing that if I felt it, he would get hungry, too. He would, no matter what I did. Like a yawn, the blood hunger was contagious, and nearly impossible to resist.

I struggled against the urge until it burned through my core like an electric current, running from my mouth through my throat and into the core of my spine, slowly spreading, until my entire body quivered with red-hot electric need.

Night had fallen, and I needed blood. In a minute, John would too, and nothing would be safe.

John didn't think to resist the hunger. He answered his need with the blind desire of a nursing infant. The silk-soft tip of his nose grazed along my arm, joined by the coolness of his lips and his tongue. I tensed in anticipation, and yet still, the stinging, erotic surprise of the points of his teeth piercing my skin made me twitch.

I tried to block out the bloodlust, replace it with sexual lust. *I always twitch when you penetrate me, baby.*

Unfortunately, the two were far too similar.

We both opened our eyes at once, and there was no mistaking, no disguising, no hiding the thin trickle of dark blood running down my skin. His pupils contracted into tiny deep voids, focusing intently on the sight of the peculiar, inhuman blood. His cheeks moved at the sizzling sensation produced by my blood, his tongue sweeping his suddenly scarlet lips.

I couldn't stop my own body's response of stomach-clenching desire. I wanted to see tides of bright red animal blood, pouring out, pouring into me, leavening my own blood, feeding me.

I tried not to let the desire overpower me. He'd recognize it, and I wanted us to stay as we were, lying together on the smooth, cool bedsheets.

But it could never happen, not when blood had been spilled.

"No," he whispered, jagged and shaky with voiceless horror. He tore himself away from me, his red lips drawn back from his teeth, the fangs gleaming. I reached out my hands to him, sending him calming thoughts. John clapped his hands over his ears and clenched his eyes shut, shaking his head. Sweat suddenly dampened the hair at his temples. "I can see something—feel something that shouldn't be there—something not me. Oh, dreadful—I—dreadful! Dreadful!" He clapped his hands to the sides of his neck, thumbs down against his collarbones, like he was trying to hold his head onto his body.

I watched his agitation helplessly. Even though he had sometimes panicked before at the sight of my blood, or his own, this fear was far more intense than usual. This was different; this was a new form of hell.

Yes—dreadful!

An astonishing, searing pain, horrific in its brevity, flickered like lightning through all my nerves, burning away even the thirst for blood.

Instantly, I was less than I had been. Something had been taken from me, all at once.

Daniel . . .

My progenitor. My ex. My enemy. My eternal love.

His blood in my veins.

Daniel Blum, dead for real, gone forever. It violated everything that made sense to me. Vampires weren't *supposed* to die. I'd always known, in the back of my mind, that it was possible; I had been told that they could. Until that moment, though, I hadn't really, truly believed it.

I felt ill. I felt like screaming.

When I opened my eyes, John wore a vicious grin, his eyes dilated again, and as fathomlessly black as a tar pit. He laughed soundlessly, his bare white chest sinking and expanding. With his long hair hanging down into his face, he looked like the bloodthirsty psychopath that he had become.

"Is it true?" he whispered, unable to keep the glee from his voice.

I had to turn my face away.

I struggled not to hate John for being so fucking happy. He couldn't help it, and I really couldn't blame him. Daniel had casually torn out John's throat, just to inconvenience me. I'd be pissed off, too, if I was John. If it wasn't for Daniel, John would still be sane and human.

But it wasn't all Daniel's fault.

It was also, and mostly, mine. I was the one who led John into Daniel's path, and no one was safe in Daniel's path.

But somebody had finally gotten the upper hand, and the nasty cur had given up his eternal life. Daniel would never have died by accident; a vampire's death, just like his birth, had such specific conditions that it couldn't *just happen.*

It could only be murder, suicide, or, of course, the wretched combination of both.

John leaped off the bed and let his laughter loose, ugly peals of nasty cackling. "He's gone!" he crowed. "We did it! We've killed him!"

"He did it himself—don't flatter yourself," I said, lightheaded now that the pain had passed, and with it, the living vibration of Daniel Blum, which I had always felt, even thousands of miles apart, with an entire country between us.

At least, I thought, *he didn't suffer long.*

John curled into a small knot in a corner of the bedroom, underneath the dark wood shelving, his laughter silent now, his smile dissolving, his words degenerating into grunts and moans. He was overwhelmed, churning between the two poles of my pain and grief, and his own vengeful delight. His ability to use verbal language had left him. I had seen this symptom before, almost always triggered by intense feelings of fear, and both blessed and cursed my ability to share his thoughts. Sometimes, I didn't want to share thoughts.

Too bad for us both. My blood ran in his veins.

He rocked himself with his arms clenched around his knees, keening softly to himself.

I needed a drink, badly.

I uncapped one of the plastic bottles of blood in the kitchen fridge, and gulped hungrily at the cold fluid. I went into the parlor, an oasis of carpet, hardwoods, and near-total darkness, sat cross-legged on the floor, and pushed my fingers against my temples.

Orfeo, please come to me. I need you.

There was, of course, no answer.

I put on some clothes and shoes, and went to my job. For a few hours, anyway, I could pretend that I was just a bioscience postdoc doing leukemia research, just an ordinary human being with a car and a house and weekend plans. I could pretend that there wasn't a schizophrenic vampire on my bedroom floor, and that the leukemia research wasn't just a front for finding something, anything in the world, that could help him put his shattered mind back together.

I

No Delight and No Mathematics

<u>John Thurbis</u>

This and not this.

Someone else driving. Night without morning. A color not right, a spectrum of dark, darker, more dark, never the ultimate, never getting there.

Brickwork, broken cobblestones, a crisps packet. A T-shirt and a glance, an inrushing of air, and not this, but this.

That's right. It can't be right. It can't be actual.

Screaming and moaning. My hands dripping blood and slimy green shreds of stomach contents, the moaning coming from me and the screaming coming from some other throat. The electric beast, the heartless white stag, looming above my head, ready to cleave my skull with its hooves, then continuing down, splitting the earth in two like a machete halving a coconut. The earth is like a jawbreaker inside.

Town. Metal bands linking the halves, a street dividing that, up a hill, a park for the dead. Sometimes a waxed rock.

There must have been something before this. Someone else driving; we never get to where we're going.

"I know you remember. I know you can't help it."

Her soft fingertips caressing my temples, skimming along my sandpaper jaw, light from a candle, the smell of ginger and honey. Who was she, where was I, when was now and then.

It came apart.

I had the two ends but I could not put them together. The torn edges would fray and slip apart, and in the scrambling to recover one end, the other would escape . . . gyromagnetic ratio a positive 8.6, but that wasn't all, I was missing some bits, and then what?

Annihilation was in there somewhere.

Licked my fingers, felt stable for a moment.

Outside the Greyhound bus terminal, watching the moon set over the tree-spiky hills, hidden in the shadows in the parking lot. Ignored the luggage jockeys who yelled at me. They spoke in backwards hieroglyphics, currents of voices broken by the crash and squeak of their carts, the screams and grumbles of the blue whale buses, constantly refreshed, coming and going, swimming into their slots, opening rectangular mouths to consume and disgorge streams of people, baggage, sucking down tangy cola streams of gasoline.

I would happily drink. Gasoline, coffee, river water, anything. I could eat a crisps packet.

So thirsty, so hungry, I was sick. Gagging up shreds

of plastic. That horrible lack inside me, a fetal tiger, gestating. Waiting it out.

The tiger would soon be born, leap out of me fully formed, jaws slavering, and I would step aside. Not yet.

Now was later and before and always.

The moon had gone and a bright yellow star hung in its place. Mars. Thirty-five million miles away, but I held it between my thumb and forefinger like a shuddering fly. Around me, the metal animals dove and swam smoothly through the concrete ocean, eyes bright or dangerously dim, but all of them blind to the planets above, ignorant of the weak force holding them to the surface of the planet they were on, ignorant of the creature with a tiger growing inside him, tucked away in the ravine between the bridge entrance and the bus station.

Where the moon dropped away, I knew my wife was there. West. Where the sky was gold and pink and jumbled with clouds and faint stars when I woke up. There was a house of white angles, brown velvet, framed dull prints of green-feathered tropical birds, and it wasn't my house at all. My house was a narrow dark thing, semi-detached, with a triangular cupboard piled with old newspapers under the stairs. That's where Mum and Dad and I lived. And then suddenly not Dad. My house was a flat on the third story with books stacked against the walls and a tiny stained glass panel in the kitchen window that spilled a psychedelic pattern of red, blue, and orange across the coffee stains on top of the cooker. That's where Dr. John the physicist lived. And then suddenly not Dr. John. Dr. John was killed. He wasn't there anymore. The tiger ate him.

My wife's house was in Portland, Oregon, but it was

not my house, and she was not my wife. But she *was*. Dr. John the physicist loved Ariane the biologist. And Ariane loved Dr. John, with a force as omnipresent (and feeling so strong, though it was so weak) as gravity. I could say it or sing it or carve it into someone's face or into the living skin of an oak, but it would never be enough, because I knew that though what dwelt in that house *looked* like Ariane, it was not Ariane, the girl I loved. I had fallen in love with a *girl*—an extraordinary girl, an argumentative spitfire, a dimpled distraction, so infuriatingly literal at times, so unsentimental, always focusing on transcendence, on the impossible. But human. And that human was dead, and a changeling monster had taken its place, with the sheer gall to wear my Ariane's adorable face and walk about in her kissable body.

And then there was me, and who was I to talk? I was just as dead as she was, walking around in a body that resembled the brilliant professor, but absolutely wasn't it. This body, this me, had hands like white spiders and no smell but what I put onto it and eyes that could see the heat rising from living things and skin that fixed itself when I cut it.

Maybe only the human Dr. John the physicist loved the human Ariane the biologist, and the gestating tiger, now kicking roughly against my throat, had no love for anything.

I would have to step aside soon and let the tiger tear its way out. It wouldn't hurt as long as I paid no attention to what it did.

Snap to attention, utter clarity.

A plump girl in a lavender tank top with a backpack walked out of the bus terminal, heading away from the brighter and denser lights and the heavy smell of humans, turning a few times, pausing, bemused by the yellow-gold street lamps, obviously not familiar with the layout of the city, sandals clapping against her bare soles.

Lost and vulnerable. The tiger struggled, preparing to tear its way free.

I could always just leave. Go home. Work on my lesson plans. But the mesons and fermions slipped through my fingers and left me with a head full of static. Chaos. Someone else would have to drive.

Lavender girl stumbled into the paws of the tiger in the darkness under the curving bridge on-ramp and gave a quick "Oh!"

"Are you trying to get downtown?"

It sounded like my voice, but I hadn't said anything, and I couldn't decide which class to concentrate on, couldn't remember what we'd done last week, or even where we were in the semester, and I couldn't get home. And the tiger was out, so I had to step aside, quickly.

Someone else should drive.

There was still darkness—darkness and crying and the hot reek of spilt blood—but I was elsewhere.

In the garden, the long narrow strip of the back garden of the house in Boldon Colliery, the soot-coated bricks and the stunted weeds breaking through cracks in the pavement. Cold—no time to grab a coat or hat or anything—secret mission, outside without permission, Mum gone to the chemist's to get more of those horrid pills for me to choke down. My throat would just close up on the dry lozenges and I couldn't swallow, and by now, six months later, Mum got cross when I coughed and gagged. I didn't *ask* to be ill, I

shouted at her, and she gave me a smack and went out.
I hadn't been in the garden for a long lifetime of
sweaty sheets, and went out with my head uncovered,
my heart pounding with excitement. I had to make it
quick; the chemist's was only a short distance away by
bicycle.

But then—my hands cold and sticky, the stench of
blood and fresh shit, my rabbit's dashed brains leaking
all over my trembling, skeletal hands.

No, wait. Lavender darkening to deep violet. That
wasn't all of it.

I hadn't seen my bunny since my uncle Iaun bought
her for me, and they brought her to my bed, and I lay,
roasting with fever, and stroked the lush black-white-
black fur, the softest and most lovely thing I'd ever
touched, and she sniffed me and wasn't afraid and I
couldn't keep myself from weeping. I blinked out, and
when I woke up, they told me they'd put her in a lovely
hutch down in the garden, and I must get better soon,
so I could see her again. But I didn't get better for the
longest time, and Mum didn't care for animals, and
Dad absolutely could not be arsed to feed and muck
out a rabbit, no matter how lush its fur.

Rhombus the rabbit had grown up while I'd lain
groaning in bed, and she was no longer a tiny, fluffy
Easter bunny, but now a ten-pound, mottled, rheumy-
eyed October monster with nuggets of dung clinging
to her fur. I determined not to be frightened by my precious bun, my little darling, no matter what she looked
like now. I opened the wire cage and tried to feed her a
thick blade of grass. She lashed out with her streaky
brown incisors and bit the nail on my forefinger clean
off and blood went everywhere. And without even
thinking, almost without feeling the sword of rage that

cut through my senses, I shouted and grabbed the rabbit by the ears and swung her against the bricks.

And she didn't die at first—oh, no sir.

First, she screamed.

under the bridge you're under the bridge look at that mess lap up the blood drink it drink it drink it

And I panicked because Mum was coming, I heard the gears of her rusty bicycle, she had to have heard the scream like a siren, eyes flashing red and blue, and I hit the rabbit's head against the pavement, twice, three times, the skull crushing like a smashed orange—

"John! What have you done?"

In my wife's house, sitting on her kitchen floor. The realization was as abrupt as a bucket of cold water thrown on my naked back. My wife's hand hovered above my temple, and blood dotted her fingertips. She had gotten the blood off my face when she touched me. My wife had seen this, the lavender girl, the bloody tiger paws, without having been there. If she was my wife she could not have seen; my wife was a human, and this . . . something else. But, oh, she looked like her, and I wanted her. I wanted to fuck. I wanted to kiss and squeeze. I wanted her to hold me. I wanted the human woman to hold the human man, and it was impossible; only the monsters existed now, only the tiger and the stag and the deep bone chill of the spectrum of darkness.

But my dick was hard, nonetheless.

I needed to be somewhere else.

"Did the cops follow you here?" she asked in a whisper.

"I killed Rhombus, Mum," I said, completing the thought. I was so cold, although I was wearing a coat now, and I clutched it around me with a shudder. "I'm sorry. I didn't *mean* to. She bit me."

Ariane glanced at the black square of the kitchen window. What a beautiful curvature of her neck. The second-softest thing I ever touched. No, that was the inside of her thighs, followed by the backs of her arms, and then, that tendon in her neck that only emerged when her head was turned, perfect for sliding my lips across. She was listening to the street, listening for the soft pick-up of the engines of police cruisers, muffled but distinctive, like a silencer on a gun; she heard those sounds coming from a dozen blocks away or more, and she guessed by their electrochemical properties that several of them were probably taxicabs. I was glad that she could sense that, because I couldn't at the moment; the screaming of the rabbit blotted out everything that I might hear from my environment, and despite everything that I did to try to blot it out, it grew louder and louder. I could see Ariane's thoughts inside my thoughts, very clear and in three dimensions, but off to one side, like a holographic inset on a video screen, one among thousands of others.

"Yes, you did kill her," she said aloud to me. I took a deep breath and held it, and the screaming began to slowly withdraw. "She hurt you. *Rhombus* hurt you. Did the girl hurt you?"

"There's no girl," I said. My voice was deep, and I had the same cold-water shock of understanding that I was an adult, that I was thirty, that I was—

killed killed dead but alive a nightmare a monster

Time to step aside. Reasonable; adult male having slightly confusing conversation with adult female. Nothing funny going on here. "I'm not sure what you mean. There's no girl."

"Well, there's not anymore." Ariane gave a little humorless laugh. Ah yes, I understood; dry Ariane, droll Ariane, Ariane with the superpower of harsh tactlessness. My own superpower was the Singularity Sarcasm; I could make anybody's ego collapse into nothingness. What a great pair of berks we were. Perfect for each other; a couple of ruthless bitches with tongues like scythes. She was talking, didn't care about anything I'd said, that I'd felt, that she'd seen by stealing it from my mind. "You obviously killed her. But were you seen by any cops? Did the police follow you here?"

Fuck it. I didn't *ask* to be ill. "It's all over my hands," I said, holding them up. But all the blood, all the slimy wads of brain matter and fragments of bone, seemed to be gone. Even the blood that had been crammed under my fingernails was gone, absorbed, soaked into my skin like some immensely cruel lotion. "I didn't *mean* to. She bit off my fingernail."

"Your fingernail is still attached, John, see? It grew back." Ariane grasped my left hand and held it in front of my eyes. I needed to be somewhere else immediately, but I couldn't leave; her touch kept me rooted to the spot, slumped on the linoleum floor, quivering in a hundred watts of electric light. "That was a long time ago. You were just a little kid. You're all grown-up now."

Still not listening to me, damn her. Sometimes I hated her chamois-silky Southern accent, hated her turn of phrase. I looked at her, trying to determine if further communication was even desirable, let alone possible, then squeezed my eyes shut against the infernal electric light. There was no way I could make her understand as long as the lights were threatening me.

Too much electric light meant the stag, and I had been trying all night, as hard as I could, not to think about the stag and what it could do. The stag controlled the bridge, not the troll. That bridge was forbidden. The stag could read minds; the wrong thoughts would evoke the cataclysm. Then, of course, the tiger came. I couldn't get away; they had me trapped, Scylla and Charybdis, position and momentum, never knowing, never driving.

Darker and darkest.

I felt myself physically shaken. "John? You have to be here with me now. Do you understand?"

I couldn't speak. I had been muzzled, paralyzed, my mouth useless. I couldn't reach Ariane. I tried to reach out with my hand across an infinite gulf. I could touch Mars; surely I could touch her, hold her, beg her to hold me?

My darling, are you gone forever?

She grabbed my wrists so tightly that my fingers went numb. No communication was possible, and she was hurting me, and she was a monster of the darkness, all tiger, all savagery, all the time, a driver, a commander of metal animals, a butcher of flesh. Yes, gone forever, my girl. Both of us, dead.

I struggled, rolled over her, trying to pin her writhing to the floor, mutely begging her to let me escape. She was easily as strong as I was, maybe even more so. Her inertia carried us over again, her on top of me, and my fingers began to throb. I tried to bite her, but she distracted me with a swift blow of her knee against the space above my own. Oddly enough, the pain cleared my mind, purifying it, bringing me inexorably back into myself. What the hell was I doing, wrestling with my wife on the kitchen floor, with all

our clothes on? And where were my eyeglasses?
"Ow!" I said. Sounded so normal, so human.

"Dammit, John!" Ariane shouted. "I'm trying to
help you! Quit fighting me!" She let me go and sprang
to her feet, her eyes wild and desperate. I had to laugh.
"John? Are you listening to me? Are we in danger?
That's all I need to know."

"I killed her," I admitted. I slowly rose to my feet,
the vague pain in my knee vanishing as soon as I stood.
The darkness outside looked good, clear and perfectly
detailed. I wanted to throw off these stiffening clothes
and go for a swim in the river. "I killed Rhombus.
Sorry. I needed to kill her. The tiger was hungry. You
have a tiger, don't you? Or are you tiger all the time?"

I focused on her as much as I could. Ariane was
thinking of a bottle of blood, hungering for it, but not
in a true way; she just wanted it. It was in her car. I
laughed again, even though there were tears on my
face, knowing that she would have to go and fetch it,
the same way I had to stand aside when my tiger
wanted out. Ariane was not a killer, but there was
something inside her that my tiger recognized as being
similar to himself. "Stay here," she said to me. "I can
help you. Stay here."

"You can't help me," I replied. I was suddenly exhausted. I didn't like the direction her thoughts were
going, and I didn't like how I could see them, no
longer looking in through the window, but being there
inside, with no outside of my own. I needed the river, I
needed the woods, I needed to be out of this house, my
wife's house but not my own, a house for my wife and
another man, and their sexual lusts and their tigers
thirsting for blood. Why blood? Why consume blood?
What kind of creature drank blood?

"I *can* help you," Ariane insisted. "I'm just gonna go out to the car and—"

Not. Listening. Not my wife at all; that skinny monster's monster bride, and me a victim in the middle. Fuck it. I didn't ask to be ill. "Ha ha *ha,*" I responded, raising my head, a ghastly smile stretching my mouth. I stared her full in the face; she was a stranger, with pale skin so unlike the honey cheeks and cinnamon freckles of my Ariane, the stranger's hair in such perfect curls, not the anarchy of my Ariane's obnoxious frizzy mane. This was not my wife. My wife was human. *Was.* Gone forever, my darling. "You won't *help.* You *can't* help. Who the fuck are you, anyway?" I couldn't smile anymore, not even a death's head skull grin. "What are you doing here?"

She paused at the open door, her eyes riveted to mine. "I live here," she said, struggling to keep her voice mild and neutral. I had to laugh again. She would lose! "So do you. You live with me. This is your house." She swallowed, and whispered, "I'm your wife."

"No, you're not," I said, staring over her shoulder at the deep night outside, straining my ears for the faint sounds of electric lights, frogs, traffic on Burnside, anything different from the sounds of screaming, of begging, of gagging. "And you know that as well as I do." I shoved past her through the door, out onto the side porch, my face turned into the rising wind.

I heard her voice catch in a gasp as I dashed into the road, skidding to a stop in the brilliant glare of the lights of an oncoming car. For a moment, I turned back to the house, catching a glimpse of her clutching the doorjamb with her long, sharp fingernails, and as the car's brakes screeched, the car's driver swore, and Ariane gasped, I made a silent leap into the trees, heading towards the cement and scaffolding and the cold snake of the river.

Moments later, I broke the river's surface and took a deep breath of evening sky. Winter was on its way; I could taste it. The water was so cold it was syrupy, and so filthy my hair felt oily and soapy at once. I swam to the east bank, shambling along the road in my heavy, soaked clothes and bare feet, and did not rest until I was secure in the cellar of a house with three newspapers in the front yard and plenty of fallen leaves on the sidewalk. Outside the cars swished by, creating a sound like waves breaking on a nearby shore. The sun was coming, the biggest electric light of them all, so powerful and vicious that it even made the stag stand down.

In the back of my mind I could feel Ariane crying for me, but the brightness of dawn grew to a dazzling intensity, and I crept as far back into the packed dirt and shadows as I could get.

The tiger was quiet, but not silent. It could wait me out. It was always stronger than I was; I was its plaything, just a vessel for it to ride around in, something to make its desires manifest, someone to torture.

I didn't ask for this.

II

ABSTRACTS

ORFEO RICARI

I dreamt of Ariane often. My child, my creature, confused, alone, frustrated, suffering and crying, lost in the pain of her own creation.

It made sense to me; I had wept my share of tears. Indeed, it was a terrible existence at times. It had never really been otherwise, nor would it ever be. Nothing that I thought, said, or did would change that.

The scent of Roman soil assailed my nostrils immediately upon waking, obliterating the sensations from the dream I had just had, where the world's scent was fresher, greener, and altogether American. I was so many thousands of miles away from her, but in my sleep she seemed so close I could reach out and touch her.

In Rome, I had taken lodging near a university campus. Such institutions were a sensible place to settle for a creature such as myself. With many students having reckless first experiences with alcohol, drugs, sex, and motor vehicles, accidents and fatalities were not uncommon. My activities, kept discreet, would not ever be noticed.

I did not have to go more than a street or two past my hotel before my goal was met. I gently grasped the arm of the first student I saw and drew him back into the shadows, cloaking his thoughts as we moved. The young man in short sleeves made no effort to stop me as I drank from his arm, swallowing slowly to minimize his discomfort, the sleek limb warm and tanned and muscled, his armpit smelling of deodorant chemicals. That scent, more than anything else about him, informed me that he was an American. A lot of the students on this campus were American. I had a weakness for the young American students: their accents, priorities, and strange attitudes.

When I had satisfied my urge, I indulged myself by looking over the young man I'd chosen. He was very calm, even wearing a hint of a smile, as if he were assaulted by a vampire every other day and didn't much mind it. I hadn't taken much, just a mouthful or three, just enough to keep the urge at bay for several more nights. His blood was as clean and healthy as a woodland stream in a forgotten forest—no smoking, no alcohol, no drugs, almost no meat. Most extraordinary, a college student with no chemical vices. "Are you all right?" I asked him, even though I knew that he was. In fact, I knew most everything about him.

"Yeah," he said, rubbing the spot on his arm with his thumb.

"There won't be a mark," I said.

"Okay," he said.

"May I go into the library with you?" I asked.

"Sure," he said, checking his watch. "It's open late tonight. Till ten."

"Splendid," I said, and nudged myself out of his memories while I followed, as subtle as a breeze, behind him through the doors of the university library.

As I walked silently along the shelves, I mulled over details from my dream. I had more difficulty focusing my thoughts than usual. I was distracted by the atmosphere of concentrated, silent, urgent energy, all these learning minds surrounding me, trying to cram in a semester's knowledge in a weekend.

Again, my thoughts returned to Ariane.

It was a bitter feeling, to hope for the best, to hope that she was all right, and knowing good and well that she wasn't. Everything that had happened to cause her unhappiness had sprung from my own impulsiveness. It was easy enough for me to see that truth when I was in a dark mood, immediately after awakening, when I could not control those parts of myself that I despised. I had thought that I wanted to be free from her (and I did, certainly), but it was only after I had doomed her to her fate that I realized that I wanted more to be absolved of the guilt of my deeds, of my helplessness and brutality.

Like a child with a broken toy, I wanted her back the way she was before. I wanted her to be restored to her previous state, before I'd awoken after a coffin-contained sleep of but a few months, reduced to a pathetic and vicious monster, and fell insensibly upon the nearest innocent victims. It was a great shame that the only surviving victim was possessed of that infinitely questing mind, and that the victim was a pretty girl, engaged to be married to a man who loved her more than life itself, and who had yet to discover what it was to hate the one you loved.

It would have been kinder simply to kill her and

walk away that night, kinder to merely recreate John Thurbis as a widower, and not as a cuckolded, lunatic vampire.

I knew just how mad he was. I quivered along John's wavelength, too, directly related by blood. Ariane and I created him together, using the same method by which I had been changed, where he received the blood from two separate sources at the same time. But whereas Maria and Georgina successfully mixed their blood in my veins, Ariane and I had not been so skilled or fortunate.

I should have taken the upper hand and given him the entire necessary quantity of blood myself, without trying to pass some of the burden of the task onto someone else. If it had been my sole responsibility, I could have created him correctly, and he would have been a whole and sane person—if any one of us night-crawling bloodsuckers could be considered whole and sane.

I always tried to do the right thing and failed miserably; when I tried to debauch, I was extremely skilled. It gave me no comfort whatsoever to know that I was no exception to the rule.

And then, I so casually left those two young, terrified children that I had orphaned from their humanity. Cruel Orfeo! Cowardly Orfeo! But it had to be done. I reckoned that she would have to experience this pain of figuring out life on her own sooner or later, and make the best of it; it had happened to me, and I was fine!

A long-haired girl in an astonishingly short miniskirt and a pink sweatshirt passed close by me on her way to the journals, and she looked up at me and shook her head. "You're *not* fine," she said to me, all American matter-of-fact.

"I'm sorry, I didn't mean for you to hear that." I forced blood into my cheeks, deliberately blushing. "I must have been talking out loud," I lied. Blessed Virgin, how much more had she overheard? I should have had better self-control.

She looked me up and down and smiled a little. I smiled back. The sweatshirt that draped so nicely against her arms and breasts had a crass, whorish phrase printed on the front. She had a dimple in her cheek that was not as dear as Ariane's, but enough to make my heart beat faster. In her eye I saw a reflection of a thin young man, perhaps twenty, with large gray eyes, prominent ears, stark-white skin and smiling red lips. Inside her thoughts, I brought to mind obscure fantasies, even though I was the antithesis of her "type"—I was at least six inches too short, and those ears . . .

"Actually, I take it back," she said, her smile growing. "You *are* fine."

There were urges I had that I minded a little less than bloodlust upon awakening. All the same, I had no desire to set another catastrophe into motion simply because I felt lustful; it would not be enough, for me, to simply give her a ride on my fingers, and I had never been a fan of French envelopes, and if any wet part of her touched any wet part of me, we would know too much about each other. I wasn't in the market for a slave or a disciple . . . not today.

If nothing else, Ariane had reinforced the lesson that I should have memorized with the case of Daniel Blum. It was a variation on the aphorism concerning the feeding of a stray cat—*Don't fuck 'em unless you want to keep 'em.*

So I gave her the bare suggestion of a wink, then

walked with a student's determination in the other direction. She'd only remember me as some weird-lookin' but totally cute guy she met over by the copy machines, but she would never be able to exactly recall my face or the sound of my voice. I felt regret that I had not paused to watch her walk past so I could see her thighs working against the fabric of her skirt, but I might not have been able to let her go by if I had.

It *had* been a long time.

I resolved to go to the jazz club in Testaccio later in the night, and stimulate different senses till time for midnight Mass.

I didn't deserve more.

Heading down the other path in the journal stacks, I picked up a glossy magazine on the subject of blood science. Ten years ago, Ariane had a paper published in it; I did her a favor and gently excised the pages that held her name. Eventually she would have to disappear, and it was much harder to do these days than when I was being published. I did what I could to erase her at every academic library I visited. I performed the same service for John, whenever I could, but his list of published papers was rather long.

Oh, beautiful John. Clever John. I had been profoundly humbled as I reviewed his research, instinctively grasping what had been written, but having no actual framework in which to place it. He wrote and lectured on two different branches of subatomic physics, as well as mathematical and philosophical theories on the nature of infinity. His science was so far removed from what I understood that I was faced with the immensity of my age, shocked into immobility as I grasped the enormous leaps in human knowledge that had occurred since the date of my birth. I had been more than a hundred years old when Einstein's first physical theories had shaken the foundations of the world, and here was John Thurbis, who regularly opened his lectures with the phrase, "Einstein didn't know everything."

And now, all that had been taken from John, his mind reduced to howling waves of disorder and meaningless symbol. He was in agony. He was terrified. My old blood, older than the city in which they now lived, had done nothing to cure him, and he refused to take it after the first several attempts. That was the limit of my curative knowledge, so I gave up. I fled. I abandoned them. Any philanthropic, Darwinistic nonsense I could tell myself was meaningless. I just couldn't face him. I couldn't face Ariane. I couldn't help.

But I had been deserted, too, and I had endured it, though it took me twenty years of solitude and watercolors; still, I was never completely free of the longing to see my mothers again, whether or not I was immediately conscious of the fact.

It had been a long time since I had last thought of the one who I wished could help me, the one I wanted most to see, but I thought of her more and more all the time, driven into the tightest corners of my own desires by the incessant mental demands of Ariane and the disjointed flashes of John's terror and rage. Sometimes I wanted to be helped, sometimes I felt the crushing solitude, and I thought of my own makers just out of instinct.

I want Mama.

One of my two creators still lived. I had felt it when the being of Maria had ceased, but I had not yet felt the absence of the note played by the soul of my other vampire mother. Indeed, of late, since the time when I had arrived in Rome, I had heard that note more clearly than I had in decades. But I tried not to hope.

My eyes settled upon a picture in the glossy magazine, a magnified image of human blood cells. I had seen my own blood cells under a microscope once, and they did not resemble the blood cells of humans—my blood was altogether darker, more dense, more bizarre. I could not look at the image of my own lifeblood for more than a moment, and turned away with a shudder, but I would never forget how alien it seemed, how deeply grotesque and unnatural our bodies were.

I set the magazine back on the rack, my throat aching suddenly as it held down a desolate howl.

I sent out my thoughts, calling to my creator, longing to hear the sound of her voice saying my name, teasing me, to see her face, touch her luminescent pale skin.

Jadzia . . . Georgina . . . George . . . Mother, lover, friend, please answer. I feel you hear me. We are connected. Where are you now? I know that you are near. Please come to me. Here I am. I do not ask you to stay, only to touch me once more.

I felt the echo within me, the same plea, in the cadences of Ariane's thoughts. *Orfeo, I need you. . . . Please help me. . . .*

I shuddered and left the library, slipping back out onto the streets, seeking to lose myself in the chaotic whirlwind of Roman traffic. A little baritone saxophone, a piano, drums with brushes and jazz babies in low-slung blue jeans and stiletto-heeled shoes; perhaps I could forget for a night.

I had stepped into the street to cross, and was nearly run down by a laughing couple straddling a motor scooter, when I felt a ghostly, silky caress on the back of my neck. I whirled to look behind me, seeing only the city lights, but feeling an invisible, disconnected pair of full, soft, feminine lips kissing my ear.

You're reading the wrong magazines.

"Georgina!" I cried aloud. Students walking by me in the street paused to stare, but I couldn't have cared less. When was the last time they had gotten their hearts' desires? Did they not shout with joy?

Look behind you, came the whisper. *Behind you, my Feo. Can you bear to look at yourself, reflected in the water? Reflected in my eyes? Can you bear to look at me? Do you feel now as I felt, deserting you? Do you understand at last? Come to me, if you dare. I will wait for you here.*

I bowed my head like a penitent and rushed to the Fontana della Barcaccia, eager to bathe my face in its waters, to gaze deep into my reflection, happy to accept any consequences.

Ah, my George, my beautiful mistress, my carnal mother, my comrade, my woman, my boy.

I knew before I reached the Piazza di Espagna that there were no others of my kind present. Certainly, the square was heavily populated, Romans and tourists of all ages flocking around the cool, water-splashed stone edges, seeking respite from the still-hot evening, but they were all most certainly human. I found an empty stair with a good view of the merrily burbling waters of the fountain, and resolved to wait for as long as was necessary.

A small child in big shorts came running past me, and as he passed my step, dropped a glossy color magazine into my lap. I stared after him for a long while, deploring the relentless activity of today's candy-crazed children, before I bothered to pick up the magazine. It was a sleek but cheaply printed local circular, advertising the recent collection of some designer or other, identical twig-like women dressed in appalling, frothy, utterly ridiculous clothes, marching like hip-cocked soldiers towards the photographer.

I would have crumpled the circular, just for the sensation of crushing something in my hands, but instead I opened it to the center, where a wire staple neatly bisected the stern, unsmiling face of a most familiar-looking girl.

Oh, the wrappings and ribbons were different from the last time my eyes had met hers; instead of a hoop-skirted gown or a dirty, ink-stained jacket and flannel trousers, she was wearing a garment that looked like splintered pencil lead, through which her rosy nipples were visible. The hair was a thick pouf of bilious blonde, but I could never forget that face, those thin shoulders, the defiant angle of her elbow away from her waist, even those fragile-looking bony ankles, and the torso that simply became hips without acquiring any sort of curve at all.

My George, strutting her stuff on the runway.

It was so perfect, so incomprehensibly hilarious, that I lost myself completely in laughing and did not notice the silent angel settling down beside me on the step.

The sparkling eyes, the bold and knowing smile; the reality of her could not possibly be captured in a photograph. Thank heavens, the yellow poodle-pouf had been a wig, concealing very short, sleek, stylishly cut dark hair. In a gray T-shirt and black tracksuit bottoms, she was a hundred thousand times more beautiful than that awful fashion designer had even attempted to make her.

We did not speak, only touched hands and smiled.

Within moments she held me between her legs, pressing my forehead against her chest, gently rocking me to and fro. I locked my arms around her waist and wet her blouse with my tears.

We sat on the step, clinging together, until nearly sunrise.

III

THE SOUNDS OF SCIENTIST

MARGARET WILLIAMS

I didn't sleep a wink the night before I first went to OMI. I tossed and turned until I had kicked off all the sheets and pillows on the bed in the attic room at Aunt Willoughby's house. It didn't help that it was about 120 degrees in there, even with the fan going; Aunty W. didn't feel the need to air-condition the attic. All of my cousins were visiting right then, too, and they'd taken up all the decent rooms downstairs before I got there.

I could deal with a temporary situation. I'd get my own place soon.

It would be easy to do. I knew my way around the city. Portland was where my brother and sister and I went on summer vacation. Portland was so pretty and idyllic compared to the weird bleakness of Vegas. Even San Francisco was a lot better than Vegas. I mean, I enjoyed my time in S.F., but I didn't interact with the city very much, because my entire life was nothing but school while I was there. I knew I'd still be really busy at OMI, but it wouldn't be like it was at NCIT. Portland still felt like vacation to me. Existence itself was a treat. There were just so many trees, so many flowers, so much moss and clover, and pineapple weed growing in the cracks of the sidewalk and tiny daisies scattered across the grass in the park.

I just couldn't sleep that night. There was too much oxygen and I was too excited.

I would get to work with Ariane Dempsey, whose molecular biology papers and articles I had frequently read and cited when I was an undergrad. I couldn't believe my luck; I had gotten accepted for the position as her assistant at the very last minute, saving me from the drudgery of having to get a lame job in some pharmaceutical company's R&D department while I figured out where I wanted to go for my PhD. I'd applied for the OMI position twice before, just as a lark; I hadn't thought I'd actually get it. It was like, while I'm on my way to apply at Taco Bell, winning Miss America. I hoped to God it wasn't too good to be true.

Dempsey had a reputation as an amazing scientist, but a slightly prickly, impatient one. Some folks at NCIT told me that she was prone to fits of temper, to watch out for her, not to be intimidated by her. I had seen her picture, and I didn't think anybody could be intimidated by her; more than anything she looked like a doll, or a silent movie actress, with big dark eyes, a dimple, freckles on her cheeks, and a pretty, if guarded smile. I knew they were old photos because she looked about the same age as me, and I knew she had to be in her mid-thirties by now. Maybe not; maybe she had some kind of wonderful beauty secret. Maybe she slept a lot or had a perfectly clear conscience. I couldn't find any date information associated with the photo on the college's online faculty guide.

Actually, a lot of that information was pretty spotty.

There was some kind of controversy surrounding her, but nobody could tell me what it was when I asked. Her students had given her good ratings. Most of the faculty she'd researched and taught with had left NCIT, and the ones who were still there didn't know much about why she left.

I knew she hadn't been fired. She just left. She said she was taking some time off, and then disappeared without a word. Then, after about eight months, she popped up at OMI and got a research position.

Too weird.

I gave up trying to sleep and hung out the attic window, put on my new Scientist CD, and watched the streetlight on the corner cycle green, yellow, red. The low pulse of dub soothed me, made my brain flow, and gave me a break from trying to figure out something that probably wasn't even a mystery.

I must have been more tired than I thought, because I imagined that I saw a human figure, with long, bare, very pale arms and long dark hair. The long hair made me think it was a woman at first, but the figure didn't move like a woman; then again, it didn't really move like a man, either. It seemed to crab-walk along the pavement, feet stepping sideways, the arms held out, almost for balance, somehow shambling and graceful at the same time. It came to a stop and lifted its head, and I caught the sparkle of the streetlight on its eyes.

It looked right at me.

The reflection of the streetlight disappeared. The figure seemed to shimmer, and then it vanished altogether.

I guess I'd nodded off. It was a pretty weird hallucination to have, but the combination of brick-heavy dub reggae and staring at the streetlights probably induced a hypnagogic, hyper-suggestible state where I could very easily misinterpret the sight of the limbs of the trees shivering in the wind as a lost, confused person who disappeared as I fell, at last, to sleep.

That had to be it.

I was up at the crack of dawn, the sun breaking through the uncurtained window. None of my cousins were up yet, but the perpetual early riser Aunty W. had already set out some toast, eggs, and sausage links for me on the table by the time I made it downstairs. "Your Uncle Stan just called," she said, pouring a mug full with coffee that looked as dark as river mud. "He wants to know if you want to go to the zoo today."

I blinked. "The zoo?" I echoed. "But I have to go to work today."

"Apparently, you might not be able to meet your new boss until pretty late this evening." Her voice was tight. Aunty W. disapproved of OMI. A friend of hers had died after having a procedure done at the hospital, and it didn't matter that her own brother was a departmental administrator there. She wasn't particularly fond of the sciences in general; she was an expert on John Milton, and thought science was for people who lacked imagination. When she frowned, she looked so much like my mom that you'd think they were twins. "He suggested that you go to the zoo, grab some lunch, then swing by the Institute to fill out your HR paperwork. He'll be by in a little while; he's on a bike ride."

"I guess that'd be fine," I said, tucking into my breakfast. "Looks like it's gonna be a nice day, anyway." Before I finished eating, my uncle announced his presence with a brisk rapping on the front door. Uncle Stan, Aunty W., and my mom all looked incredibly alike—taller than average but not to an extreme, athletic in a wiry way, with the same light brown hair and pronounced cheekbones. He had changed out of his biking clothes into a collared shirt and slacks; obviously going for casual, he had foregone the tie. Still, his hugs were warm, as though he hadn't just seen me the night before. "You look very nice," he said. "Did you sleep well?"

"Eventually," I said. "Bye, Aunty Dub—see you tonight for dinner."

Uncle Stan and I went to the zoo, then to the science and technology museum where I'd spent so many childhood summer days, then had lunch on the patio of a sun-dappled restaurant. He seemed to be in no hurry to get to OMI, and it began to make me wonder just how late was late. Over more coffee, I asked him what he thought of Dr. Dempsey.

My uncle could make that sour face, too. What a family of charmers! I wanted to poke him and make him laugh, because his smile, like my mother's and Aunty W.'s, was really great and made everyone else around him smile, too. "She's good," he said, after taking some time to think about it.

"Is that all you can tell me?"

He scratched his neck a little at the edge of his collar. "Yeah," he said. "Kind of." I was about to either give up or start teasing him when he continued, "She's on kind of a different track from most of our researchers or doctors or instructors. She doesn't teach any classes, and all of her work is privately financed."

"Wow," I said, "she must have a hell of a grant."

He didn't respond to that, staring into the middle distance for a moment before going on. "By the way, that means you're going to be in the HR office for a long time, because you have to fill out different paperwork with Dempsey than you would otherwise, since you get paid out of different funds. I'm not entirely sure what she's working on right now; the last papers she's done were on theoretical pharmacology, really weird stuff. I don't see a lot of application for it, but as long as it's not being financed with the school's money, I guess she can do whatever she wants."

I immediately thought of a thousand questions, but then my uncle stood up and tossed his cloth napkin onto his coffee-stained saucer. "Well, shall we?" he said briskly. "There's a lot of paperwork that needs to get filled out."

The OMI campus crowned one of the hills to the west of downtown. I had to visit two HR departments in totally separate buildings. He left me at the first building, admitting to some administrative work that he would have to do before five, but encouraged me to take a walk around the campus and to meet him at his office in Building A after five. "Then we can go meet your aunts and cousins for dinner," he said with a smile.

"When do I get to—"

"Probably after eight. She told me she'd leave a message letting me know when she'd be in tonight. She keeps very peculiar hours. Here's a map; any of these yellow question marks is a phone, so don't hesitate to call if you run into any trouble."

I began to wonder if Dr. Ariane Dempsey was a legend or an elaborate hoax.

* * *

The sun had settled low in the sky, and my uncle and I'd had dinner with Aunt June, Aunty W., and my cousins Byron and Dylan Willoughby, before I returned to OMI for the actual meeting. I had barely touched my meal, too consumed with anticipation, and the guys teased me. "She's avoiding you already, Mags," Dylan said, and I knew he was kidding, but it still kind of stung. I'd taken astronomy before, so meeting professors after dusk wasn't all that unheard of, but still; this was biology, and that could be done just as well while the sun was up.

"She's very eccentric. What can I say?" Uncle Stan said, trying to be chill, but I could tell he was a little off-balance, too.

At nine o'clock, we went down to the labs in the basement of Building E and went to the door, marked with a simple gray plastic plaque that read ARIANE DEMPSEY, HEMATOLOGY RESEARCH. Uncle Stan knocked on the closed door without enthusiasm. As we paused there, my anticipation reached a fever pitch, and I felt positively lightheaded.

No answer at the door, because Ariane Dempsey was approaching us from the opposite end of the corridor. I felt something like an electric shock seeing her in the flesh, in a terra-cotta-colored suede jacket, plain black twill pants, and black-on-black sneakers, walking down the hall with her intense, liquid, dark eyes directed toward the floor. She wore no jewelry, not even a watch. Besides the preoccupied expression on her face, the thing that struck me most on first glance was her hair—very dark red, thick, incredibly shiny ringlets straining against bone-colored plastic clips anchoring it at her temples. Her complexion was a flawless pale olive, much lighter than I'd guessed, and the freckles that had dominated her cheeks in the photograph were barely visible now. Her hands were in her pockets. Her body was curvy without being voluptuous, neither thin nor overweight. She was an almost mathematically average woman, and yet I'd never seen anyone more fascinating.

"Excuse me—Dr. Dempsey?" said Uncle Stan.

She looked up at him with an expression into which any manner of things might be read; she wasn't smiling, but she did not look particularly annoyed. She looked like she was so far beyond him that nothing he said would have the slightest bearing on her life. It was difficult to imagine anything that might irritate her or cause her any insecurity. She was calm, unruffled, and very beautiful. I couldn't believe that I'd thought she looked cute and sweet; even though she still looked very young, something had happened between then and now that had replaced her impulsive fireworks with iron.

"Glad you could finally make it," my uncle said. "This is your new assistant, right on time."

"Margaret Williams," I said. "It's an honor to meet you." I stuck out my hand and gave her my winningest smile. Dr. Dempsey kept her hands in her pockets and didn't say anything, her eyes focused on something that was close to me, but wasn't me.

After a few seconds of immobile silence, I took back my hand, feeling incredibly stupid, my face going hot. Dr. Dempsey met my eyes then, and smiled just a little. The vague smile didn't really change her expression, just the position of her full, unpainted, rose-colored lips. Then her lips changed again as she spoke. "Any relation?" she said.

My God, her voice. It was amazing. Everything changed. I felt my clothes against my skin, my empty stomach, the tickle of my hair on the back of my neck, my toes next to each other in my socks. I was aware of my physical being in a way that I had rarely experienced; it was like her voice going into my ears had unleashed some chemical in my brain that I had no conscious access to, that I could only witness, allow to flood through me.

Her voice made the tiny question sound like a seduction—a combination of a faint Louisiana drawl, a low register, and a lilt that implied dark mystery. Her eyes, though, remained neutral, even slightly challenging.

Suddenly, I was very thirsty. My mouth had been hanging open, drying my tongue.

Uncle Stan cleared his throat. I hadn't been looking at him, but I wondered if he had a similar, but more male reaction to her, and that was the reason why she made him so uncomfortable. He had been happily married for twenty-one years, but my aunt June could never, ever inspire feelings like the ones I was having. And I was as hetero as they came. "She's my sister's daughter," he admitted, "but nepotism never came into it, if that's what you're thinking. I processed her CV with the same rigorousness as all the others, and your availabilities coincided. You've got to admit, she's a well-qualified candidate."

"I was at NCIT," I explained, "and a lot of your work on the blood-brain barrier was really useful to me for my last couple of papers. I've always planned to come here for my doctorate, since . . ." I shrugged and smiled at my uncle, who wasn't looking at me, but instead was staring at Dr. Dempsey with something closer to shame and sadness than desire. "I have a lot of family here besides him. I've always loved Portland and hoped to get a chance to work at OMI. It was all me, really; I'm just very pleased that you selected me. I'm sure you had a lot of applicants for the position."

I had a small lock of hair that I'd impulsively dyed bright blue the night before I left to come here, braided and discreetly tucked behind my left ear, hoping that no one would notice it. Ariane Dempsey's eyes locked onto it, though, and her smile deepened, the dimple springing up in her right cheek, and then, as if following it like a little sister, a matching dimple on the left. She walked past us to her office door, and paused with her key in the lock. "Well, it's nice to meet you, Margaret—do you go by Margaret? You can call me Ariane. I'm a little in the middle of something right now, but if you've already taken care of your paperwork, why don't you consider it a little extension on your summer vacation, and come back tomorrow at . . . let's say nine?"

"Nine A.M.? That'll work."

"No—nine P.M."

Uncle Stan gave Ariane an exasperated look. I blinked. "Why so late?" I asked.

She looked into me. Not at me—*into* me, her gaze like a black obsidian shard plunging in and then yanking back out. I felt my heart suddenly collapse tight, then expand again, gushing the blood back out through the arteries. I had a brief dizzy spell. I really ought to have eaten more dinner. "Because that's what time I come in," Ariane said, softly and evenly. It occurred to me that she could do whatever the hell she wanted, whenever she wanted, and I felt pretty stupid for questioning that. "I work best at night." She turned her gaze to my uncle, whose face had been pulled into the smile that I liked so much.

"C'mon, Maggie," he said. "Let's go get you home. You do have classes tomorrow, if I recall correctly."

"I do, at eleven," I said, suddenly remembering. "I'm taking a class on the history of physiology."

Ariane Dempsey said politely, "That would be Professor Wayne's class. I sat in last fall. It's fun."

I suddenly wanted to get out of Building E, and be anywhere else. Uncle Stan had begun to fidget, too. "Is it? Awesome. I thought it might be. Thanks, Dr. Dempsey. Oops, I mean Ariane. Nice to meet you, and I look forward to working with you. See you tomorrow."

She gave each of us a nod, and disappeared into her office, locking the door behind her.

I made Uncle Stan take me to get a burrito on the way home, even though he protested that Aunty W. would be more than happy to make me something. I just couldn't wait; I was starving.

I knew I was going to have trouble sleeping that night, too, my back all locked up and stiff. I needed to go dancing. I tried to convince Dyl to go with me, but he refused with the excuse that he had to catch his flight back to Austin the next day. I knew good and well his flight wasn't until three in the afternoon; he was just blowing me off. He looked at me with a funny expression, his eyebrows quirked and his forehead wrinkling with the same creases that had become permanent in Aunty W.'s brow. I wanted suddenly to slap that look off his face before it got stuck like that, but instead I just shrugged and went to go get my shoes on.

My violent thoughts startled me, and I brooded over them for a moment while I drove down to the club. I hadn't had the urge to smack Dyl since we were kids; I didn't usually ever have the urge to hit anyone. It was just the tension of the day. A couple of hours in a place where live music was playing, and a beer or two, would loosen me up enough to at least get to sleep. And Dylan *had* been pretty obnoxious about it.

The Imperial had been designed as a Kingston pub, complete with West Indian flags, darts and dance floor, occupied by a couple dozen white kids bouncing along to a chipper reggae band; the only people of color that I saw in there, besides some of the members of the band, were playing darts and sitting at the bar. It was a typical Monday night crowd. I got a bottle of Rolling Rock beer and drank it too fast, moving onto the dance floor before I'd even finished. The band wasn't all that great, but they were competent, and all I needed was a loping beat and a touch of reverb on the vocals; I wasn't looking for a religious experience.

I was pretty sure I'd already had one today.

My mind kept catching on the moment when Ariane Dempsey had looked into me. I knew that that had been a tipping point, but I couldn't determine exactly what had been exceptional about it; she'd just looked at me, and we'd made that kind of intimate eye contact that can play with the mind. Usually I didn't have that problem, though; I was great with eye contact. I had always had a transparent protective barrier in front of me that nobody could breach. It was like I had been looking at people through sunglasses before, and she had suddenly torn them off me and we really saw one another.

I wasn't sure that I'd actually really seen her, though. I *looked* at her. It wasn't the same at all.

A rational voice came from the back of my mind, velvety and calm. *You're making too much out of this.*

Relax and unwind. You've been seeing things, reading too much into things. It's cool. There's nothing to worry about. Go home and go to sleep. You have class in the morning.

It might have been her voice, maybe not. But it was in my head, so I did as it suggested, knowing that the mind moves in mysterious ways.

IV

SUNDOWNING

ARIANE DEMPSEY

Margaret easily accommodated my schedule. I promised to have her out of the laboratory by one A.M. on Monday and Wednesday nights, so that she could get to her history class Tuesdays and Thursdays at eleven. I gave her Friday nights off. Sometimes I needed my lab to myself.

Within a few weeks she seemed to settle into her new routine. She knew my old papers well, almost as if she had been an actual student of mine when I was a TA. She worked with my equipment with an experienced ease and grace; she had been "slinging slides" since high school, she told me with a grin. As soon as she knew that I didn't mind, she dyed most of her hair blue, with a random streak or three of bright red. Every Portland kid did it eventually. It showed how dedicated to school she had been that she had never actually dyed her hair a strange color before. I felt bad; I had gotten that out of my system by the time I was eighteen, and here she was at twenty-two, grinning her ass off with how bold and daring she finally was.

Poor, ridiculously sheltered child. Her eager mind was almost too easy to play with, and I soon had plenty of practice.

"Why's . . . your computer all wrapped in plastic like that?" she asked.

Rather than explain the truth, about my body's strong bioelectromagnetic properties, and how I could easily destroy the delicate circuitry of a computer if I touched it, I told her that I had allergies, and that I was allergic to any number of things. When I was human I was allergic to bee stings; I related a true story of being stung on the butt sixteen times and having to have an injection of epinephrine to save my life. I practiced my deadpan delivery: "It was in the hospital recovering from that that I learned I was also allergic to soap operas."

Margaret roared with laughter, completely falling for it. It gave me a strange little twiddle of pleasure to make her laugh. Had it been so long since I'd amused anyone? John laughed frequently, but always at the wrong time, when there was nothing funny going on at all. "I'm allergic to bee stings too, but I confess that I used to be a total whore for *Guiding Light*. I actually scheduled my classes around it. I guess I just need the escapist fantasy. You know, I just have to spend an hour every weekday living in the unreal."

"I should try that," I said with a straight face.

"You don't like Uncle Stan much, do you?" Margaret said.

I gave a faint chuckle. Distract, and distract alike. "I'm not the president of his fan club, no. He's just a bureaucrat, and I'm not too crazy about bureaucrats.

I'm glad he mostly just leaves me alone. I'm sure he's a perfectly wonderful guy in his personal life, but I have no particular desire to see or become a part of his personal life—I've got plenty of my own personal life to deal with."

Margaret digested this information, nodding. "If it reassures you in any way, I'm really not like him very much. He's a little too square for my tastes. He's a country club-and-golf kind of guy; I like bourbon and cursing and reggae." I couldn't fight off a smile in response. That did sound familiar. "And staying busy. That's what kept me sane when I was living in Vegas; just staying occupied all the time, as much as possible. I'll do my best to not give you any problems; I'm here to help you have fewer problems. I'm here to help take care of the little dumb stuff, and leave you more mental space to get some actual research done. I'm not one of those girls who'll spend all day talking about the soap story lines or my gas bill. Although, I guess in your case, it'd be all *night*." She gave a little self-conscious chuckle. "Are you married?"

I gave her a look. Had I been thinking out loud? "That's kind of a personal question, isn't it?"

"Is it?" said Margaret, blinking. She shrugged, and returned to the microscope. "Sorry, I didn't mean it like that. I'm not trying to pry . . . it's just small talk."

Surprising myself, I went on. "It's just kind of . . . a complicated answer. And yeah, it is kind of personal. And uh . . . yeah, I am, and no, I'm not."

Margaret grinned. "What does *that* mean?"

"It's complicated, like I said. It's not all diamond rings and roses. Maybe you'll meet him one of these days." I thought, *But, for your sake, I kind of hope not.*

She blinked again as my thought-projection permeated her brain. "Wow. I mean . . . sorry. But I'm just really, incredibly curious about you. You have this kinda very strange reputation. You were at NCIT for two years, right? And then you, like, disappeared, and then suddenly, you were here with a completely different physiological emphasis."

"Life can take a person in strange directions sometimes, Ms. Williams." My smile felt tight. *Get out of it, dear.*

Margaret lightly smacked herself on the side of the head. "Sorry, sorry. Tell me to shut up whenever you need to."

"Okay—shut up. You're asking questions I don't have simple answers for." I kept my voice gentle. "I mean, you stick around long enough, the answers'll probably come. But you know what they say about cats and curiosity."

Margaret worked silently for several minutes. I stared at the computer screen some more, the images of molecular models burning themselves onto my retinas. When I closed my eyes, the shapes appeared, slowly and gradually wisping away into nothingness, only to be replaced by the vapor trails of thoughts that didn't belong to me. Margaret was thinking about her new apartment in the heart of the city, thinking about my hair and wondering how I got it to curl like that, running a favorite song through her mind, wondering what my not-really-husband must look like. I was glad that she hadn't done her research all that thoroughly; John's picture was probably on the NCIT staff directory Web site, and his handsome smirk had sold a lot of "NCIT Science Hunks 1993" novelty calendars.

"Sorry if I went over the line."

"It's all right. You're a good kid," I sighed.

Margaret laughed. "Aw, c'mon, don't call me kid. You're not that much older than me."

"I'm older than I look. Good genes. Everybody in my family tends to look pretty young." I smiled a little. "It's just in our blood."

When I slept that morning, I dreamed of the molecular models, multicolored hydras floating serenely on a field of black. I had spent so many hours building and viewing molecular simulations on the computer that they played in my brain when I closed my eyes.

In my dream I examined the structures, zooming in and out with a thought, rotating, adding spindly benzene rings and soft green nodules of nitrogen to the chemical structures of known antipsychotics. I was trying to find an impossibly intricate puzzle piece for a puzzle I had never seen, about which I had only theorized. I had been testing and re-testing John's and my blood for years, throwing most of the periodic table at the cells, one element at a time. I knew I was closer to a chemical that would help John, although the psychiatric medications that caused drastic changes in the human brain could not cling to the miniscule, hopelessly efficient vampire blood cells for more than a few minutes at a time. It was as if every single cell metabolized and filtered all foreign substances, like a microscopic liver. If only I could arrest that process for long enough to deliver the right drug to the brain and keep it there; I was fairly certain at this point in my research that I would have to interrupt the ability for the blood cells to carry oxygen. That part, at least, was easy. There were any number of chemicals that interfered with oxygen uptake.

But what drug had the right structure to go with it?

Clozapine's not it. Maybe olanzapine . . . but perhaps a more typical antipsychotic . . . haloperidol? No. Poor guy; he's got enough problems without EPS twitching or becoming a knocked-out zombie. Dammit! These are not gonna work! The long, crooked chain of Haldol spitefully blipped out of existence, deserting me in the darkness. *I need help.*

Instantaneously, I was sitting on one of my oversized velour chairs, but rather than the warm and cozy disarray of the study where they belonged, the chairs and I hung in the featureless darkness of the default screen of the molecular graphics program. There was even a menu bar up above in the "sky," which vanished as I glanced at it. On one side of me, a small table was set for tea. On the other, Orfeo Ricari sat in an identical chair, watching me.

What a sight for literally sore eyes! Elfin, boyish despite his already thinning hair, impeccably dressed, he looked the way I remembered him from the last time I saw him in the flesh. He bent to fuss with the disintegrating yarn of his chenille socks, holding the teapot aloft in one hand. "Oh, *thank* you," I gasped, too excited to remember to be angry with him. "Hi. Wow, God, I miss you. I only ever see you in my dreams anymore. Are you here, really? Are you talking to me, or is it just me?"

Ricari arched his eyebrow, and poured a steaming jet of tea into my cup. "Concentrate less on breaking the molecule," he said, "and more on the postsynaptic cell membrane. Remember, we're not like *they* are. We are here, and yet not here. Yet, here we are."

His sweet, husky voice, still lilting with a vague Neapolitan accent, drove me to distraction. "Does he still love me?" I begged. "I gotta know. You can see into his mind, can't you? Better than me? You're ten thousand times more powerful than I am. You're exponentially superior to me with every year you've been alive."

Orfeo spooned sugar from a bowl into my cup and stirred it. "GABA enhancement *would* have been an effective short-term treatment," was all he would say.

"There's only so much Valium can do for him . . ." I sipped from my cup, but the tea tasted foul and metallic. I couldn't spit it out; it was too late. I tried, though. "Ew! What did you *put* in here?"

The old vampire wore an inscrutable smile on his paper-white, boyish face. Without speaking, he turned the sugar bowl to face me. A vivid purple K+ floated on the glossy white finish, no whiter than Orfeo's spidery fingers clasped around the neck of the bowl.

Abruptly Orfeo seized the bowl and dashed it to where the ground should be. The bowl shattered, the crystalline contents exploding into flames. I stared with my mouth open.

"Fix it," said Orfeo flatly.

"But it's not my fault," I protested.

"It doesn't matter anymore. It's *Daniel's* fault. But he's dead; *he* can't fix it. Only you can." His voice dropped to a whisper. "Remember . . . we must breathe."

My consciousness flicked on with the sunset, hunger and thirst punching me in the gut and, more intensely, a lightning-strike idea polarizing my brain. I jumped out of bed and pounced on the cube fridge in my closet, tearing open the door and grabbing the first bottle I saw.

I took a deep breath with the cold, viscous liquid in my belly, slowly relaxing as it dissolved into my veins.

Marvelous oxygen and exquisite hemoglobin; an unbeatable combination. I looked out the kitchen window at the orangeade dusk, and concentrated on sending a thought to Margaret that I would need her in the laboratory an hour early, and bring supper—it would be a long night.

I knew exactly what I had to do now. It would either cure him or it would kill him; either way, the end of John's suffering was in sight.

I sat in my office with Margaret, scarfing down pad thai. I always got a kick out of eating foods made with a lot of garlic; sure, like all food it would pass straight through me, my body whisking it away the same way it did any foreign matter. But it did taste marvelous. "OK, here's a little quiz on your synthesis knowledge. If you made molifaxone with potassium cyanide instead, would the resulting compound still be stable?"

Margaret twirled noodles on her fork for a while. She had added another vivid red streak to her fading indigo hair, and the dye still stained her fingernails like wedding henna. "Yeah," she finally decided, "but it'd be insanely toxic, of course."

"Would it?" I said musingly. "Here's another question for you—do you think we could make it?"

Margaret snorted, then, seeing my completely serious face, shrugged and nodded. "Well, yeah, it's theoretically possible, but why would you want to? Nobody would be able to take it."

"Well, that's not necessarily the point. Mainly, the FDA probably won't be too cool with me making my own molifaxone, but it won't really be molifaxone, will it? It's a theoretical compound. It's uh, an applied theory."

"Yeah, but I thought we were studying histiocytosis. . . ."

I stared deeply into Margaret's eyes, my will firing into Margaret's mind like a bomb blast, opening her doors, her windows, brilliant white light erasing everything. Margaret's voice trailed away. It was simple. The girl had no concept of mental defense, no idea how to protect her thoughts from outside influence, or even a notion that she might need to do so.

"It's just what we have to do," I said.

"It's just what we have to do," Margaret echoed indistinctly. A thin trickle of blood ran from her left nostril.

Damn. Too much. I made a concerned noise and, grimacing, handed Margaret a tissue. Margaret was too easy a target; any more effort and I could have reduced Margaret's brain to mashed turnips. "I mean, what else are you here for, except to help me? You'll understand why, after we've done the synthesis, and then we'll write a paper about it. I assure you, there *will* be applications for the results. And you'll get a great recommendation from me to go do whatever you want to do after you leave here. Or at least, after you don't work for me anymore."

"Yeah, I know—shit, my nose is still bleeding."

"I'm sorry—oh, wow, it's really going. Put pressure on it. Here—tip your head back." I grabbed a can of strawberry soda from the fridge and put it against Margaret's forehead. The girl, pinching the bridge of her nose with one hand and grasping the red-soaked tissue ball with the other, looked miserable.

"All the blood's running down my throat."

"Sometimes you just gotta swallow a little blood," I said. "It's gonna be okay in a little while. Just relax." I handed Margaret a fresh tissue, and while she had her eyes closed, I turned away and, with a shudder, stuffed the bloody one into my mouth.

Sweet, fresh, garlicky blood, with just a little paper fiber in the way. Worth it—absolutely worth it.

Come to the lab, John. I need you. I'm going to help you.

To my surprise, I felt him respond immediately. Though his thoughts were in pieces, he was calm. He could even communicate with me. It was one of his good nights.

Last night, he'd run all over the city, from the motels and strip malls of the far east side to the dollhouse Victorian houses, rose gardens, and cemeteries of the city center, and still more strip malls further west. Still not tired, he walked in circles until the sky went pearly-gray, then as fatigue finally embraced him, he crawled into the dank burrow beneath the spreading roots of a massive tree up in Forest Park. He slept there, and dreamed that he was sleeping next to me, a dream so beautiful and vivid that he cried when he woke up, alone and cold, and realized that it wasn't true. He wanted to touch me again, tuck my head under his chin, hold me and sway to inaudible music.

When I arrived at OMI, John stood waiting for me at the side door to Building E, rubbing the tips of his thumbs and forefingers together, creating a convulsing butterfly with his hands. His clothes and hair were crusted with dried mud. I approached him, slowly, in case he didn't recognize me. He saw me and caught his breath sharply, biting his lip, his eyes bright, suspicious, hopeful all at once. We hadn't seen each other for months, and I felt self-conscious, like meeting a stranger.

"Hi, darling," I said to him.

"Awright then?" he replied, casual, like he always used to.

So beautiful, I could eat him. I stood on tiptoes to kiss his rough, chapped lips. His butterflying hands reached up and twined themselves through my hair.

Yes, that. More, please; more of what I don't get enough of.

We sank into the darkness of the doorway, mouths pressed together, a brief touching of tongues. Marvelous to embrace him, to be this close to his body, our thoughts crashing into each other, then merging and stretching away, only to rise up and interlace again. I still had enough presence of mind to hold his dirty hands away from my light-colored jacket. He pulled his hands back and held them up, laughing a little, surrendering, embarrassed.

"Damn, you need a wash," I said with a smile. "C'mon in, you'll have a chance to get cleaned up." He nodded and tried to smile, so I kissed the corner of his mouth and made his attempt successful.

Ah, my homeless boyfriend. Holding his hand, I led him inside. "Is it better now? Can you talk?" I asked.

After a failed first attempt, he managed, "Yeah. I can talk. We don't *have* to talk."

"No, but I love your accent so much, and I can't hear it when you're just thinking to me. I know it's gotta be hard sometimes. But you're doing okay right now. I know you are. I can feel it." I led him to the bathroom, which had a shower, at the far end of the hall, and closed and locked the door behind us. "Take your clothes off."

John smiled. "You do it," he said.

"Gross," I chuckled, but obligingly began pulling the muddy, stinking layers from his lean body. Underneath the filthy shrouds of Army jacket, unraveling sweater, and river-scummy wool pants, his body was still beautiful, at least to me. Other people might find him too skinny, too pale, too insubstantial, the body of an intellectual who forgot to eat, but found plenty of time to drink and chain-smoke; who wouldn't lift weights to save his life, but who had swum laps for an hour most evenings after classes. I had always adored his lanky legs and veiny wrists, his high-arched feet and the tight curves of his ribs, visible only as he raised his arms to shrug out of the last layer of T-shirt. As I pulled it off, he leaned down and kissed my forehead, stroking the tip of his tongue against my hairline. He held his hand a careful centimeter away from my body, just close enough for me to feel the heat radiating from him. He had fed on fresh blood tonight, though he had no memory of it that he could access, only of the flame-colored cirrus clouds fading to silver, and the brightening of the stars a few degrees above the horizon. He undoubtedly slaughtered someone earlier, but he thought only of the value of the gravitational field surrounding the planet, the concentration of water vapors veiling the starlight.

"You also have to shave," I said.

John gave an impatient groan-sigh. "Why?"

"Because I want to see your pretty face," I replied, stepping back and gazing at him. "You've got mud in your beard . . . and what looks like . . . uh . . . Look, I'll do it, if you want."

"You brought me here to shave me?" John laughed. "You kinky so-and-so."

"If we're going to dance . . ." I held up the electric beard trimmer I kept in that bathroom for this exclusive purpose. "I can't have you scratching me up."

"Okay," John said, nodding slowly. His eyes saddened and lost their focus. "Not that it matters, does it? You'll heal. We'll always heal. We can't die."

I shushed him. We'd had this conversation before, but it still could break my heart. "None of that, okay? We gotta play the cards we're dealt." He held still while I buzzed off most of his scraggly, sparse facial hair. It fell in clumps to the floor, the shorn hairs dissolving into the gray-brown powder that resembled nothing so much as cremains. Intact human hairs were entangled in the muddy dust. "Besides, you and I both know that that's not true. Can I trust you to wash?" I asked. "With soap?"

His voice went from sad to tetchy. "I'm not a baby."

"It's not about that."

"You infantilize me because sometimes I have a hard time . . . ," he fell quiet for a second, searching for the words, "thinking straight."

"I'm sorry. I don't mean to. Sometimes you're . . ." *Mad? Insane? Off your cuckoo rocker?* I brushed the last clump of beard hair from underneath his chin, and watched it dissolve before it ever hit the ground. "Dangerous."

"I did it every day for years," said John. "I shaved every day—or whenever. It's just not important now. And don't say 'dangerous' when you really mean 'off my cuckoo rocker.' Now if you don't mind, I'd like some privacy."

"That was a bad choice of words. I'm sorry, but I can't help what I think, no more than you can. If you don't mind, I'll stay."

"I can't be hurt," he growled, glaring at me. "You think I'll cut myself shaving? Or slit my throat, is it that? You think I'll bleed to death? You know how many times I've tried that? And I'm still here, aren't I?"

I put up my hands. It was best to just back away when he got like this. "I'm sorry. I'm sorry. I forgot. Can you blame me? I'll go grab you some clean clothes, and I'll be right back, okay? Just please stay here; don't go anywhere."

John didn't reply, only turned his back and stepped into the shower stall with an indignant snort of "Shaving!"

I closed and locked the bathroom door behind me to the tune of a blast of water and John yelping as the spray hit his skin. I couldn't resist a giggle. "Unfamiliar sensation, cleanliness," I murmured. It wouldn't make any difference to his health or his smell if he never washed again, but I couldn't yet give up that twentieth-century American affectation, any more than I'd stopped engaging in unnecessary pleasures like eating.

I had learned to keep stashes of clean men's clothing in my car and in my lab, just in case John showed up filthy or, as he had done several times before, naked. He did always come back, no matter how many times he disappeared, for days or weeks or months at a time. Like a feral animal who has been fed, he stayed in my proximity, maybe as a way of retaining some sense of the familiar, some sense of the rational past. Maybe it was just love.

That was my faith. I prayed to that.

Clean shirt, sweater, pants, and socks in one hand and a bath towel in the other, I returned to the bathroom to see him standing there naked, almost exactly like what I remembered—his square jaw clean-shaven, shoulder-length dark hair mixed with random single white strands, rising from a widow's peak on his pale forehead. But his water-beaded skin was waxy-white, and his too-long, skeletal fingers were tipped with thick, keen-edged claws where rounded fingernails should be. His arched feet were better suited for an alabaster gargoyle than a man. What was remarkable was how little he had changed otherwise. His face was still, ten years later, that of a largely healthy thirty-year-old man. He would look like this until the end of time—or *his* time, at least, or of my time, when I would no longer be able to look at him. But I didn't know any more about what happened at the end of my time than I did before I slept through the days.

Perhaps he would be there.

His eyes flicked up at me briefly, then away, catlike, just barely acknowledging my presence. Sublime, arrogant bastard.

I asked, "Better?"

"By whose standards?" he replied sulkily.

I drew the towel around his shoulders. "You used to be such a clean freak," I sighed. "Remember how you used to gush about how great the water pressure is in the U.S.?"

He smiled, still not meeting my eyes. "Better at my place than yours. More hot water, too."

"Well, you could *afford* a better place."

John tugged the towel out of my hands, and finished the drying himself, scrubbing himself briskly. "No—remember, I was just so deep in debt to Barclays I simply reckoned that another thousand dollars a month wasn't going to make things any worse." He paused and grinned. "I remember you screaming at me for about twenty minutes straight when you saw my bank statement. You told me I had to get that sorted out before you married me. 'Honey, you ain't worth no six figures' worth of debt!'" He even punctuated the impersonation with a street-girl's head roll.

I stamped my foot. "Oh, man, I totally didn't do it like that!"

"You *said* that. Precisely." He pulled the T-shirt over his head and then tossed his hair off his forehead, glaring at me.

"I was just trying to see if you remember," I replied in a low voice.

He slid back into his dirt-encrusted boots, instantly besmirching the new, clean white socks. "*I* remember. Do you? I bet you do." His fingers jerked at the muddy bootlaces, snapping them between his fingers. He gave a fed-up sigh. "Eh, I've got an idea. Why don't you stop trying to fuck with my head and just treat me like an adult? What's it matter what I remember? I remember more than I want to. And half of it didn't even happen to *me*."

I struggled to remind myself to be grateful that he was lucid; there was no way that we could fight like this if he weren't. "I'm sick of apologizing, so I won't do it again. I refuse to apologize for checking in on how you're doing. I know you know that you're not all there sometimes."

"I don't know what I am," John murmured.

Down the hall, the door to my office was open, and the lights on. I paused outside the bathroom door,

John halted next to me, his nostrils flaring and his eyes narrowing. "It's just her," he decided, relaxing.

"Can I trust you?" I whispered.

"Of course not," was his reply.

Margaret had tossed her book bag onto the floor next to the door and hung her jacket on the coat rack, softly whistling "The Harder They Come" through her front teeth and bobbing her head slightly in rhythm with her whistling. She wore a bright green T-shirt that rode up a little, exposing a hint of an elaborate tattoo on the peach-tanned skin of her back. She smelled of lemongrass and Red Stripe beer. John and I watched her silently, fascinated, from the doorway. Margaret half-turned to start up one of the computers, caught sight of us, and gave a little hiccupy shriek. "*Hee-eek!* Oh! Jesus fuck! Hi, Ariane! Oh my God. You almost made me wet myself," she gasped.

Margaret continued to stare at John with alarm, and I gave him an appraising glance over my shoulder. His angular face was shockingly white against the worn black fabric of the T-shirt, his fresh-scrubbed lips very red, and his dark eyes uncomfortably intense. I gave Margaret eye contact and a gentle smile, and projected to her, *In this day and age, who can really tell? Lots of people everywhere look like vampires. He's just kinda gothy. Don't mind him.*

"Margaret," I broke the silence, "this is John. He's my . . . uh . . . y'know, my whatever you want to call it . . . my other."

"Her husband," added John, with a hint of condescension. I stared at him. "Don't be self-conscious about it, darling."

Margaret was instantly appeased, and her face broke

into a sunshine smile. "Her husband. Wow . . . awesome . . . Well, it's nice to meet you. Ariane, you shouldn't be self-conscious about it; he's a total fox!"

John grew a big smile on his face. "Thanks," he said.

"Did I say that out loud?" Margaret muttered behind her hand.

"No, I didn't hear anything," said John. Margaret closed her eyes, and held them closed, as though she had gotten distracted in the middle of a blink.

I could perceive John reaching into her, shuffling her mind like a pack of playing cards, like ethereal tongues of vapor flickering over her body and her face. It wasn't something that was visible, per se; I just sensed it in the same way I heard the heating coming on a few floors above, or a car honking in the parking lot of Building A, or the fading scent of temporary hair dye, mixed with sweat, emanating from the collar of Margaret's T-shirt. He wasn't trying to baffle her or make her forget; he was trying to find out who she was, what made a girl like her think that he was a fox.

That was one of the things I liked about him; he genuinely didn't know.

I spoke to Margaret, and her eyes opened, her attention switched to me. "How did those slides go?"

"Fine; results are in hard copy on your desk."

"Good," I said. "Be a babe and type up that request form sitting in your box so we can have it in the mail by tomorrow morning. We're gonna go into the lab and monkey around."

John put on his most roguish smirk. "It's all right. I'm a scientist."

In the lab, behind closed doors, John gently kissed me. "You're a *physicist*, babe," I murmured.

"Physics, physiology; what's it matter?" He sat in one of the swivel chairs. "What did you actually bring me here for?"

"I need some of your blood," I said.

"You can always have it," said John, stretching his long neck, exposing it to me, swallowing a little to make his Adam's apple quiver.

"Not like that," I said, my voice shuddery. "With a needle."

"I don't like that as much."

"Neither do I."

"I don't want you to." John's voice became very quiet, very small and young.

"It won't hurt."

"Yes, it will."

"It's just a little pinch, John. It'll be over in no time. I have to test something in your blood, so I can find out if my theory is right. If it's right, I might be able to help you. I know that's something that *I* want, and I think you do, too."

He sat still and mutely accepted the acute stab into his arm, only groaning when I had to repeat the process again and again as his flesh tried to reject the needle as the blood was being drawn out. "Stop now," he muttered. "Please. I don't feel good. I'm getting hungry."

"I'm done," I said. I slipped the needle out and rushed to the refrigerator to grab the bag of blood with the most recent date on the label. I thrust it into the crook of John's uncompromised arm, then rushed to create slides of drops of John's blood. From experience I knew that I had perhaps ninety seconds in which to make a smear before the blood hardened into black stone.

John stared at the blood pack.

"Drink it," I said over my shoulder, "it's pretty fresh. It was drawn yesterday."

John hesitantly took a swallow from the bag, then gagged and threw the bag against the floor, spattering the tiles red. "No! Gah!" he yelled.

I wanted to stamp my foot, but didn't dare jostle the delicate leaves of glass and blood. "It'll sustain you!"

"It's horrible!"

"It's *necessary!*"

"For *you*, maybe," John snapped. He stood up, rubbing the raw spot on his arm, already sealed. "You got what you need. Now I'm going to go get what I need. Something fresh, not this plastic piss."

"Don't touch Margaret," I warned. "Don't threaten Margaret. Don't even *smell* Margaret."

John's laugh was about as joyful as the whisper of a guillotine. He looked different; his face visibly paler, glistening with cold sweat. His body clamored to replace what had been lost. "I don't need your little girl," he sneered. "I've got all *them* out there. Heh . . . I could take any one of them. Ten of them. You know, I don't like the taste of little girls. I like women who are all grown up. *Fat* women with plenty of blood to spare. Mothers. They taste better. Something about the stress."

I simply had to tune him out. No reasoning with the tiger. I couldn't change his thoughts, I couldn't control him, and I had work to do. It was hard for me, too, when all I wanted was to drop to my knees and lick the floor clean.

John circled me. "Or, I could just have some of yours," he added.

"I *need* mine," I murmured.

"Just like I need mine," he countered. "You can have

your bottled stuff. You don't even remember the taste of fresh blood out of the tap, do you?"

"I can't forget," I said.

He lifted my hand in his, gently kissed the side, then sank his sharp teeth into the meaty base of my thumb. I had to grab the edge of the table to steady myself. It wasn't the pain; the prick of pain was intense, but somehow negligible. It was the vicious intimacy of it, like having my entire circulatory system fucked, my mind in fireworks of excruciating pleasure. He could drain me dry if I let him go on.

But he didn't go on. He loosed his mouth under his own will, kissing the damp wounds, tickling his lips with the electric buzzing of my rapidly healing skin. The skin of his lips bonded briefly to the skin of my thumb, and for a moment, we were physically attached.

It was only a few cells. John pulled his lips away, shearing off the tissue-thin epidermal layer from his lips and my thumb, leaving them bloody with a mixture of his and mine. I slumped dizzily against the table.

John stepped around the spill, unlocked the laboratory door and disappeared.

"Ariane? You okay in there?"

"Yep," I called back, sounding drunk. "You can stay there, I don't need any help, thanks."

"John sure left in a hurry!"

I spoke without even thinking about what I said. "He realized he forgot to set the VCR. Some soccer game or other. English. You know how they are about their footie."

"Oh, he's British? That explains the accent. Just gorgeous. Man, Ariane, if that was my husband, I'd take out billboards going 'Sorry ladies, this one's mine!'"

"Don't really wanna advertise it," I said, staring with dismay at the dreadful mess of a pint of blood leaking onto the floor. "I don't really want other women trying their luck at John Blackjack. Heck, he's so easy he's practically Go Fish."

To the sounds of Margaret's answering giggles, I picked up the discarded bag and found that more than half the pint was still inside. I shrugged sadly for the waste, and sucked down what was left.

I had an adequate sample from John; testing could commence.

V

THE GIRL NOTHING HAPPENS TO

ELISABETA REVIKOFF

"That's the thing, isn't it?" August said, exhaling a bitter cloud of heroin smoke and handing the foil sheet to
Debbie. "You know, it's like . . . when you already own
all this stuff so there's nothing you want to buy, and
you've traveled to all these places, when you've done
all this crazy shit, there's not really all that much else
to *do* but drugs."

His greasy face was still beautiful in that unique
way that disrespected symmetry, forcing the eye to
dance. Star quality, even when he wasn't acting. If I'd
wanted to become a casting director, I'd have been
brilliant. Or terrible; sometimes that particular star
quality was not what they wanted. They sure as hell
didn't want August, that troublemaker, that barely legal waste of potential; in the years since he'd grown
out of his precociously sarcastic, apple-cheeked childhood into a rangy, confrontational adolescence, he
hadn't gotten so much as a walk-on role. Producers

just didn't "see" August Beagle in anything; but they didn't see him in his most profound moments, hunched almost double over a pile of smack, nearly the only way I'd ever seen him.

The money he'd gotten when he was a child was all but gone; he had acquired a habit of decadence early. He was a beautiful bundle of addictions—hookers, gambling, video games, alcohol, marijuana, tattoos, needles, cars that he'd wreck or give away or lose because he was too high to remember where he'd parked.

I didn't mind. I was an addict, too. They chased the dragon, caught it, and brought it to me.

The idea that he and his fair-weather celebrity friends got all of their heroin from a vampire, who drank his smack-saturated blood every night, didn't bother him nearly as much as the idea of doing without the heroin, or worse yet, having to pay for it. Self-destructive, yes; stupid, no.

They thought it was cool that they knew a vampire.

"I mean, you know what I'm talking about," August said. His voice lowered to a silky mumble, his eyes vaguely fixed on Rachell, the model's spindly hand busily scrubbing, wiping his wrist with an alcohol-soaked square of gauze. "I mean, it's gotta be worse for you. You're a vampire. You're an immortal killing machine. You've seen *all* kinda shit. You've probably killed more interesting people than I've ever met. But then what? It's gotta be so boring after a while. I mean, whaddaya *live* for, y'know?"

Rachell was still sober, and she looked at me for a moment, her pointed face searching mine for permission she didn't need. I nodded to her, and she brought the gleaming razor blade across August's wrist in a sharp, quick slash. August moaned, then hissed through his teeth. I would make it quick.

The wrist flooded my mouth with blood, and August relaxed, his eyelids fluttering as the heroin and my saliva slipped into his bloodstream at once. I felt their eyes on me, Rachell, Young Lad, and Debbie, their thoughts prodding at me, wondering if they could be next.

My husband was in the main bedroom of the suite, reading *Le Monde*, down the hall from where the actors, the model, and the disgraced pop singer smoked and snorted and shot their way through their declining days. My husband had the newspaper delivered to our room, along with the *New York Times*, the *L.A. Times*, the *London Times*, and the Johannesburg *Star*, every evening at ten o'clock.

He read each paper cover to cover and was usually finished by midnight. Then, we'd either go out or "order in" from the addicts down the hall.

Rachell was his favorite, since she was the cleanest. She didn't drink alcohol or eat meat, and her drug use was so well-managed that it barely approached addiction. She didn't shoot up, only smoked or snorted. She was a maintenance user and a post-rehab control freak. Her well-kept, fragile skin smelled of rice milk and rosewater. She did not allow cutting, only direct bites, since those healed fastest, without any visible marks at all. Alex was better at that than I; his fangs were thirty years sharper than mine. It barely hurt at all when he bit.

It was hard for me to watch them together, Rachell sitting on his lap with her arms around him as he punctured her neck. There wasn't much I could say, seeing as I kept August and Young Lad and Debbie and Lila at my beck and call. I made them do things a hundred times more depraved than that. But I wouldn't let August or Young Lad sit in my lap. I had no protective feelings toward them, and was not attracted to them except in the most abstract way. I admired their traits the way a breeder admires a stud horse's big balls. If there was an element of the sexual in it, I would never admit it. It seemed far too close to bestiality.

Of course, my husband did not prefer Rachell to me as a woman. Alexander's standards of beauty were purely of the century previous to the one before, and even my body, defined from athletics, had always been a little too skinny for his tastes. Rachell looked like the most beautiful girl in the concentration camp. Lila, who had at one point been the third-most successful model in the world, was slightly more robust, but he too saw her abstractly, a six-foot, tobacco-colored, braided bullwhip of sinew and meanness. Lila couldn't fit into Alexander's lap if she tried—it would be like a giraffe sitting on a sparrow—but I knew that she wished that she could. It seemed so pleasant there.

And Alexander Vassilyevich found it pleasant to feel a girl in his lap. He liked to nuzzle her neck and sip from her slowly, tentatively, a cautious tongue on hot soup. I did not fault Rachell for clinging to him, for writhing a little before her spindly limbs went slack. He smelled of bay rum and new clothes, and he held her gently and savored her. Rachell fit on his lap exactly, and her blood had an elusive, addictive taste. He claimed that he liked Rachell more than he liked Debbie, who was more his physical type, because he preferred to drink his blood from people who hadn't been smoking crack all day.

He could drink my blood, if he wanted to. But he'd lost his taste for vampire blood a long time ago. I didn't blame him; it wasn't the same thing at all.

When I returned to our room, Alexander had just finished with the last newspaper, and he carefully folded the broadsheet and placed it atop the others on the tray. He watched me slump inside and crawl onto the bed by the balcony. I was very high, almost to the point of feeling sick. August, Debbie, and Young Lad were unconscious, but they'd make it, since I had drawn a large fraction of the heroin from their blood-streams. Now it was inside me, softly blunting every-thing. I'd saved their lives once again; Debbie, in particular, had done a few bumps to be able to make it to the hotel, and that, combined with the powder she'd smoked, would have probably led to an overdose if I hadn't stolen some.

"Rachell?" Alexander asked hopefully.

I sighed. "She went to a party instead," I told him. His face fell, and I had to close my eyes. "It's her *job*. She has to be *seen*."

He said, studying the newspaper, "Be careful that you hide the drugs when you're done with them, and try not to spill so much when you drink. I wish you wouldn't use razor blades. The cleaning staff have begun to snoop around. I think those bloody towels alarmed the laundry; I had to pay out quite a bit to keep them quiet."

"Fuck the laundry. You shouldn't have paid them. If anyone talks, just kill him and his family."

"Elisabeta, your sense of humor worries me."

I wasn't trying to be funny. "I'm tired of this hotel," I said. "We should move on to a different one."

"What's wrong with the Turandot? You liked it here fine last week. And you have the children." He called the group encamped down the hall "the children," and as their median age was twenty, he was not far from correct. To me, they were more like exotic, high-maintenance pets, half-wild animals seen out the windows of the safari jeep. "Would they come with us?"

"I don't want them to come with us. I'm not about to have an entourage like Daniel had, especially not one made up of skagheads. They bore me. All junkies are the same everywhere."

"These, at least, are cuter than average. Wealthier, too."

"There'll be another group of them in another hotel," I pointed out. "Nick's, or the Bev, or the Chateau. Clots of former child actors in rooms littered with rolled-up hundred-dollar bills. I'm sick of L.A. altogether. Let's go somewhere far this time. Let's go to Bogotà or Bueños Aires. Or São Paulo."

He laughed. "We've *been* there. You hated São Paulo. Remember? We were there for Christmas in 1968, and I don't know that it's changed except to become more of what you didn't like. You'd probably hate Bueños Aires. And Bogotà? You're not serious." I could tell by the sound of his voice that his eyes were crinkling at the corners. My old man. He'd been forty-five, back then, back in the old country, more than a century and a half ago.

My skin suddenly crawled and tickled; a common side effect of opiates. Young Lad called it "verma-derma" because he couldn't remember the clinical term for it. It happened to me sometimes even when I wasn't high. Usually, thinking of Russia brought it on.

"You're getting too much heroin in the blood, Elisabeta. It's making you sad all the time."

"I'm not sad," I said, wiping my damp face against the pillowcase. "No sadder than I've ever been."

Alexander stood up from his chair and lay alongside me, covering me with half of his body and kissing my hair. "I like your hair long," he murmured. "It's been so many years since you've had long hair, I almost forgot how it looks. It astonishes me to think about it. It's been almost thirty years since I touched your long blond hair."

My skin crawled so much I wanted to tear it off.

June 10 was our eighty-eighth wedding anniversary. Alexander and I went to Venice Beach and sat on a wooden picnic table with our arms around each other, silently watching the sea. There was no moon, and the stars wavered behind a vague mist, much like the night we were married.

That strange ceremony had taken place in darkness, secrecy, and haste. The priest had no idea that he was joining, in the eyes of God, on consecrated ground, a vampire and a human; he never questioned the lateness of the hour or the lack of family. Alexander whisked any questions from the priest's mind with a wave of his hand. No one was there in the lightless stone church but Alexander, the priest, and myself. My human senses saw and heard no one who could have witnessed this. Nonetheless, the next day, my brother Vladimir Pjotrovich shot the officiating priest three times in the head.

Vladimir searched the rest of the day until he found us, an hour before nightfall, too foolish and too crazed with jealousy to stop and realize that there was no way he could meet a vampire in battle armed only with a pistol, a rifle, and a crucifix. He hadn't expected Alexander to be awake before sunset. Vladimir Pjotrovich thought he had the upper hand of righteousness and morality and principle. He believed that, now that our father was dead, he owned me as much as he owned his horses and his dogs and his whimpering, cowering wife; he believed that no marriage between human and not-human could be genuine, that I was deceived and under some kind of an enchantment, and that he could snatch me back and imprison me until I became a lady or shriveled up and died, whichever came first.

When night had fallen, and Alexander was finished with Vladimir Pjotrovich, there wasn't much left of him; certainly nothing that could be recognized as my eldest brother—hardly anything that could be recognized as a man at all.

Even in his unarmed savagery, Alexander did not take Vladimir Pjotrovich's blood. Alexander didn't want to know, even for a few seconds, the parameters of Vladimir's mind, or even briefly to see the world through his eyes.

I loved Alexander for that.

I had always known Alexander as a vampire, and a swift, silent, and efficient one. I had never before seen him angry. But once he had tasted my blood and known, from my own thoughts, the truth of what my brothers had visited upon me, what they had planned for me, their headstrong spinster sister, I saw a fury in him doubly shocking because of its novelty.

All the same, I felt no regret or remorse about what happened to them, or to me. Not really. I loved Alexander more than anything else in the world. He saved me, kept me safe, removed me from the mortal life full of despair and uncertainty and brought me into his twilight world of blood and flight, defending me until I could defend myself. He adored me, appreciated me, knew me. That he could tear my despised brother apart as easily as breaking bread only made me love him more, and commit myself fully to the idea of escaping with him.

If only I could forget the October terror, the November cold, the stabbing agony of my skin torn open and my bones snapping as I was flung to the frozen earth beside the screaming tracks of the train. I still dreamt of it, the world pulled upside down and painted red and white. Sometimes my dreams were accurate memories—running down the aisle of the train with Vladimir Pjotrovich's lieutenant so close behind me that I could smell his breath and the wet oil on his pistol, other passengers crying out in fear and alarm, Alexander far ahead of me, pulling open the door and seizing my arm in his cold fingers, the shriek of the frigid night air ripping my at my hair, the fall, the impact, and stars exploding against my closed eyelids. Sometimes my dreams pushed the lieutenant's rifle against the side of Alexander's face and blew it off, and Alexander still grinned with what was left, the other side shredded and dripping. Sometimes I flew from the open door of the train and never hit the ground, just kept falling, twisting, always steeling myself for the impact that never came. Sometimes the train held, not passengers, but gray and silent corpses, watching Alexander and me with empty expressions.

The dreams happened a lot that summer at the Turandot, until I stumbled across August dipping the flame of his butane lighter against a tiny Fuji of brown-sugar smack. August didn't know anything about the Revolution, couldn't even find Russia on a map, and his past only extended back to the days when *The Cosby Show* was still on TV.

His ignorance alone was an opiate.

"Elisabeta," Alexander whispered to me. He shook my shoulder. "Don't fall asleep. It's too early. We should go out. Follow Rachell to her party."

I don't know why I agreed, but I did. I put on a black silk paisley Anna Sui camisole and Hudson jeans so low-rise that they exposed my hip bones, and slid my feet into custom-made poison green lizard stiletto heels. I added the usual shiny rocks and pretty wires. A quick pass with the ion brush restored my tangled hair to shine and straightness. Alex wore his usual charcoal gray Hugo Boss suit trousers and a plain white shirt that made him look bigger than he was. The right look for a Hollywood party. Obvious money; but who *were* we?

He called Varlet to bring the car around to meet us.

While we were in the lobby, we ran into Young Lad, hitting his bullet in a phone kiosk. He had been there for almost an hour, knocking back bump after bump of pure Columbia flake. When he saw us, he skittered out and fell into step beside us. "Where ya headed?" he asked. His eyes nervously sought paparazzi who weren't there, and even if they had been there, wouldn't have bothered wasting film on him. He wasn't even a subject of scandal; he was just yesterday's sweetheart, his face forever consigned to moldering heaps of teen magazines in landfills. Still, a one-hit platinum album eight years ago had been enough to keep him in blow and Kangols.

"To Studio Six," I said to him. "That party that Rachell went to."

"She's not there anymore," Young Lad said. My eyes caught Alexander's sad face, despite trying to look elsewhere. "She just called me. She's on her way back here. I guess she wants to see August."

"August doesn't have anything for her," I informed him. "Only I've got it, and I'm going out. Call her back and tell her to meet us back there."

"You can't do that," Young Lad said, still with us as we went out the doors. "You can't go back to a party you've already *left*."

"I have the heroin," I said, watching Varlet driving up in the Lincoln. "If she wants it, she'll do it. Coming?"

As soon as we were in the car, Alexander grabbed Young Lad by the sides of his head and took a mouthful of the boy's neck. Young Lad dropped his bullet on the floor, but there was nothing he could do. Young Lad's famous blue eyes rolled back into his head. I picked up the bullet. "Idiot," I said. "I can't stand this guy. Why don't we put him on the front page?"

Alex gave me a quick wink of understanding, not moving his mouth away from the boy's neck. I reached forward and gave Varlet the bullet.

Varlet lifted his chin proudly. "Thank you, ma'am, but I don't do white powder drugs."

"Shoot it up, then," I said, and he laughed and shook his head.

We tossed Young Lad out of the car outside a popular strip club. As far as I know, he was dead by the time he hit the pavement.

Studio Six was half-full of unimportant Industry types; not the faces, but the backbones, the supporting struts.

Up-and-coming musicians schmoozed as desperately as they dared. Makeup artists spread gossip about the plastic surgery scars they were paid to paint over, the coke-fueled tantrums they witnessed, and the rare, unexpected kindnesses received from high-strung actors. It was a good environment for me, with the heroin finally dissipating away into fond memories, and for Alexander surfing his wave of heavily coked blood. It was fun to watch every face in the room snap up expectantly when we came in, then return to their companions, or search again for someone actually famous or powerful.

We walked to the bar, and the bartender set down two vodka Gibsons with four onions each. The man standing next to us, who had been trying to flag down the bartender with a twenty-dollar bill, stared at me, his angry expression melting away into slackjawed astonishment as I showed him my fangs.

That's right, darling, we don't pay.

In the back of the club, I shared a thought with Alex. *I miss Daniel. Once upon a time I could have called him and had him meet us here, liven things up a little. Why did he have to get himself killed?*

Alex chewed a cocktail onion, his face dark and intense. The cocaine made him tremble slightly. *He couldn't stop thinking about the past,* he mused.

I distracted him, and myself, by sending over a young woman whose ensemble screamed "assistant" and having her ask him if he was that one ballet dancer. By the time he'd smirked and told her no, but that he got that all the time, I had finished my martini and gone to fetch another one. When I returned, I asked him aloud, "Do you remember Ariane?"

"I think on her now and again," Alex replied, blinking in surprise. "I hear her voice when I am falling asleep. She is crying out for the one who created Daniel. The Italian. Orfeo Ricari," he remembered. "And Ricari is ignoring her. That poor child."

"I hear her too. It's awful. She's lost, with the one she made. She didn't know what she was doing."

"She did it to save him," Alex said with a sad smile. "As I did for you."

"I don't think I could keep going if I lost you," I said.

Alex pulled his handkerchief from his pocket and gently blotted the tears that wet my face. I was grateful once again that I had no need to wear makeup; I wasn't one for a poetic tear streaking down my cheek. My eyes were made to weep like tidal waves.

"You won't lose me," he promised, and kissed the wet handkerchief, and then my lips.

The faces of the room snapped up and pointed at the door, and an immense hubbub swept over them all as Rachell Reed walked through the crowd, tapping along on her spike heels as delicately and nervously as an adolescent gazelle, tossing her hair as she searched the crowd. Her eyes lit upon Alex and I, standing at the back of the room, and she broke into the kind of toothy, humorless grin that spoke of a vicious jones with the end in sight.

I saw the same smile on my husband's face.

"Did you hear about Young Lad?" asked August, solemnly chopping ketamine chunks with a rusty old blade.

"Don't do that K yet," I said. He blinked at me. "Yeah, I heard. Heart attack, I guess."

"He musta done a lot of blow."

"He did," I said. "He stole it from me."

"What? Holy shit . . ."

"I had Alex kill him." I smiled.

This news bothered him, though he tried not to show it. Even with his thoughts fogged by smack, he saw the truth. I gently stroked his bent back. "It's for the best," I said. "It put his last album back on the charts, you'll notice. But don't worry about him." I stroked him some more, and his posture unknotted itself and his brow cleared. He even smiled back. "I need you to do me a favor."

"What could *I* do for *you?*" He gazed at the finely minced ketamine wistfully.

"Can you use the Internet?"

"Yeah," he said with the kind of half-laugh that showed he thought that it was like asking, "Do you know how to walk?" He rubbed his nose and sniffled, dredging out the last micrograms of cocaine trapped in his nose hairs. "I've got it on my phone."

"Do a search on a name for me. Search for Ariane Dempsey. Dr. Ariane Dempsey."

He obligingly fetched the electronic device from the pocket of his leather jacket. It was the size of a small sandwich, and could not only telephone without wires, it played music, showed video on its tiny screen, and could also apparently access the Internet. Obsessed with its rounded-edged silver cuteness, I had bought one a few months ago, and promptly fried its impossibly delicate magnetic circuitry by merely holding it in my hand and thinking about sex.

"Ariane Dempsey," he said after a few minutes. "One hit for a Dr. Ariane Dempsey. It's on somebody's blog—some Margaret Williams . . . she's got on here that she works for Dr. Dempsey. And she says she's, uh, 'so amazing.' That's it, though. That's weird that there's nothing else on this person."

"There shouldn't even be that," I said.

"If it's ever been online, ever, it can be found again."

That was valuable information to have, even if it was bad news. "Where is this Margaret Williams?"

August poked at the device with his grubby, blunt but surprisingly adroit fingertip. "Oregon Medical Institute, Portland, Oregon. Do you know this person?"

"Dr. Dempsey is an old friend of mine," I said, scribbling the address that I saw on the tiny screen onto a pad of hotel stationery. "I fell out of touch with her, but I think I'd like to pay her a visit. She's been through some hard times recently."

"You'd leave me?" August whispered.

"Do you believe that you mean something to me?" I asked.

He averted his eyes, and then remembered the ketamine. He bent his head and snorted up a line of the powder, rocking back and blinking hard. "You mean a lot to *me*," he said.

"How much does your life mean? Do you want to go out like Young Lad? Do you want to be remembered as a beautiful, tragic fool, or do you want to get bloated and terrifying?"

Another line. "I was hoping for a comeback. . . ."

"You're never going to get clean, Auggie." I smiled sadly at him. "I know you. You're never going to make a comeback unless you really commit yourself to getting clean, and being deeply ashamed of what you are now. Look at you; you've got a drinking straw up your nose. And your girlfriend Debbie's an even more hopeless case than you are. You're never going to make an-

other film and you know it. There's only so much luck
in one lifetime; you burned all you had by the time you
were fourteen. Just be grateful for that."

"Goddamn it." August chopped another line, and up
it went. "You're right. But I love you for real." His eyelids drooped heavily, and his words came out in a
gummy mumble as his lips went numb.

"I won't leave you here to live," I promised him,
gently stroking his hair as he slipped out of the conscious world. His thoughts folded in on themselves
like an origami box. "If I leave, you leave, too—I'll
need to be fed before I travel."

I carried the hotel notepad back to the main suite.
Seated at the desk, Alex curled around Rachell, not
drinking from her, only rocking her unconscious body
back and forth in his arms. He looked up at me and
carried Rachell into the end room, settling her gently
on the couch next to August.

We returned to our room and shut and locked the
door, shutting the human world outside.

13 September
This will find you—I know it will. Your little
assistant has let slip that she belongs to you. I do
so love Internet search engines—everyone is the
secret police. Still, that means that your time as
Dr. Ariane Dempsey is limited; I'd have another
name and destination lined up sooner rather
than later, if I were you. If you need assistance in
this matter, you can ask me and A. about it—by
this time, we are experts.

Ah, my friend, I can see you before me, curled
like a pastry, unglazed—no tears were shed. Yet

*you are not physically there for me to see. I can
hear you in the next room, screaming and tearing the wallpaper with your nails, crying not to
God but to us. And yet you are not there around
the corner or behind the door. I can smell you as
surely as I smell the artificial smell of new cars
that is sprayed on the hallway carpets to make
the guests feel powerful and wealthy as soon as
they step out of their rooms. This is not my place;
this is the decision of my husband, of his love of
luxury. I would as soon join your offspring in the
sewer pipes of an unknown city.*

*And not only your offspring—I know this! He
is one of the blessed ones, one with two parents.
You know well how rare this is, especially in today's society!*

*Orfeo Ricari hears you. There is no way that he
cannot. There is no way that anyone of our kind
on the planet cannot hear you. They may not
know the specifics of your plea, but the blood
they drink tastes flat, and their dreams are filled
with remorse, terror, and flight. You too have felt
this from others, even if you didn't know the
cause! There are untold thousands of us on the
planet, all of who endure moments of self-torture.
Not all of them feel as strongly as you, not all of
them scream as loudly as you. Not all of them
love as you do. But they are cursed, and you are
cursed.*

*And I am cursed, with 500-thread-count sheets
and icy buckets of Blanc de Blancs, and no crystal flutes or silk-gauze curtains can possibly re-
solve my unease. I have convinced A. to leave*

Los Angeles. A. thinks I am simply bored, as I have been before. What of it, if I am? Fifty years in a single city is enough to bore anyone. I am young yet—young enough to tire of this isolation, of this gilded cage perched on the edge of a quivering precipice. There is no permanence, but just try convincing the wealthy of this fact. Thoughts like this cause me to commit reckless acts. The sensible thing is to pack up and find another place to explore together. A. has agreed, but only by small steps—hence this ridiculously opulent, secretive hotel, full of movie stars and boy band survivors all screwing each other and smoking crack, where even the press photographers can't find them. I know it is time for me to leave L.A. when I start to envy the powder-nosed supermodels their foul-smelling, infernal death wish.

At least they are iconoclasts, destroying the images of themselves. What am I but an appendage?

Do you think there is room in the northwestern sewers for a foolish Russian girl? I have heard that the rains never stop in Portland, and the trees are green all year round—real trees, not these manicured absurdities planted in sand. I long to be outdoors, alive as part of Nature's immensity, an organism, a thinker, a hunter, at one with the elements.

I await your immediate reply; we shall remain here at the Turandot for another month (as much as I hate it here, there are amenities). I look forward to hearing from you, and I hope, <u>seeing</u> you again, in the flesh, and not simply in my hallucinations.

Always sincerely yours,
Elisabeta Hanya Revikova
P.S. Call me El. That's how lazy we've gotten.
I've lived too long.

VI

DOSING

ARIANE DEMPSEY

The days never ended soon enough.

It wasn't as if I needed to be particularly worried about the sunlight. A heavy, monochromatic cloud blanket had enfolded the city since an hour before the past dawn, and by the end of the day, the solar radiation wouldn't do more than pleasantly warm my skin, like sitting under a heat lamp.

Still, I didn't feel like getting out of bed before it got properly dark. Something about this evening reminded me of the last day I'd spent as a human, trying to enjoy mundane things like snack food and movies, all the time knowing I was going to die before the sun came up again, that I'd never be able to just stand out on the pavement and stare up into it, blinking and averting my eyes and feeling freckles spring up on my skin. I knew it was my last day, but of course I had no idea what that meant.

I missed the sun.

I had stupidly thought changing would make life easier. Orfeo and Daniel—especially Daniel—and Risa and Alex Revikoff made their vampire lives look so easy, so calm, so beautiful. Of course it looked easy to my limited human senses, to my young human's naiveté, impressed with the healing power, the outlandish physical strength, the ability to become invisible to human eyes, and of course, the ability to read minds, to make anybody do what they wanted them to just by thinking of it.

Of course it looked beautiful, when my existence wasn't steeped in blood and desperation and insanity.

I woke up at 4:45 P.M. and drank a pint of cold, bitter blood out of the mini-fridge in the closet; but before I'd even finished swallowing, I rushed back to bed and crawled under the covers, hiding in blanket darkness. Delaying the inevitable.

Relaxed by the drink, I lay there for hours, drifting as in half-sleep, reading my memories like a book, watching them like TV. I could turn my memories over and over like a piece of hard candy in my mouth, one which never got any smaller. It was the ultimate snooze, one that, if I wasn't careful, could last all night.

I did have control over it. I mostly concentrated on the good memories of John before the transformations. I could relive strolls along Haight Street on rainy, frigid winter evenings, takeout and a video rental and the many sexual positions that could be accomplished on a sofa. I lingered on the first time I saw him lecture at NCIT. He'd had to borrow a T-shirt from me because I'd torn the buttons from the shirt he'd been wearing the night before, and as he moved across the podium, rapidly scribbling equations on the whiteboard, I caught glimpses of his deer-like figure encased in a Talking Heads T-shirt a size too small, peeking from underneath his suit jacket. I got a thrill of girlish excitement every time he had to push up his glasses, astonished at his total lack of stammering, at how he never looked at his notes because he knew all the complex gravitational equations by heart. And I thought to myself, *I can't believe I've had this freakishly sexy genius. I can't believe I get to have him again. Tonight can't happen soon enough. Stupid time! Hurry up!* And, like he'd read my mind (a good two years before he actually had that ability) he looked over at me, and a sly smile bloomed on his face like the first spring flowers through snow.

My mind was snatched back to my bedroom by the blare of a car horn and a shriek of brake pads outside the house. The night now fully upon me, I was out of bed and crouching on the floor, my body coiled to strike, before the sound died away.

I opened the curtains. The car had disappeared down the hill toward the city, and a stray cat crawled deep into the underbrush. A heavy fog had rolled in, and the bedroom window showed a chilly and smudged darkness, pulsing with subsonic menace.

I slowly let out my breath. I said to myself, "Well, that's it."

On the bedside table, a prepared syringe of the drug lay atop a folded white face towel. We had finished the synthesis and washing of the analyte the night before. After I'd sent Margaret home, wishing her a good weekend, I spent the next several hours testing the compound's solubility in water, ethyl alcohol, acetone, human blood plasma, and human blood serum. The analyte, a chunky, pale-lavender powder in its pure form, dissolved most readily in serum, turning the liquid a moody black-crimson that bore an uncanny resemblance to vampire blood, and remained in a liquid state, which the whole plasma refused to do. I drew five milliliters of the fluid into a bottle and brought it home, then prepped a syringe.

Then I just set it down and stared at it.

I hadn't been able bring myself to do it the night before, so late it was early, the sky already starting to lighten. Sure, I had blackout curtains, but I was so tired (no—that was a lie—so scared) that I decided to get some sleep instead, and try it when I got up that Friday evening.

My methodology wasn't crazy. I couldn't administer an untested drug to John. I had no idea if the substance was poisonous, or inert, or otherwise dangerous; and there weren't any other appropriate test subjects. I had to take it myself, with only theory to guide dosage or toxicity or administration. If my guesses were wrong . . . well, I knew what it would do to an ordinary animal— lactic acidosis, delirium, seizures, coma. But I was pretty sure my guesses were right. *Pretty* sure.

"I'm a scientist, goddammit," I told myself. "I know what I'm doing."

I had no fear of needles. Those slender, slanted, hollow silver points were just another tool to me, and I knew, better than I knew anything else in my life, the sensation of being punctured by something sharp and pointed. But as I picked up the syringe and gazed at the dark liquid inside, a cold knot of ice rested where my stomach should have been. I shrugged it off, justifying the sensation as being caused by the drink of cold blood hours ago. I glanced at the clock on the wall, and said aloud, "The time is eight twenty-two P.M. Dosage at point oh-oh-two milligrams active, serum solution."

Just a drop of scarlet.

I lightly clenched my right fist until the blue-green vein swelled against the skin in the crook of my elbow. I'd never given myself an intravenous injection before, but I'd seen it done enough times to know how. I paused with the tip of the needle against my skin, but not penetrating it, breathing deeply and slowly, struggling to remind myself of the sensuality of it, trying to reach that mental landscape of lying with a lover, with his member poised to slide into me, but holding it there for as long as he could bear the wanting.

I got shivers.

Think like a junkie. It'll be easier.

Not a pinch, as nurses so incorrectly describe it. Much more of a violation—the surrender of the skin to the needle's metal fang, a slow stabbing pain that flows through one's arm. With shaking fingers, I depressed the plunger on the tiny syringe, pulled the foreign object from the flesh already trying to heal around it, and set it down on the towel on the bedside table. I clutched the sore right arm to my breasts and sank back down onto the chilly tangle of pillows and bedspread, wishing there was a warm hollow that I could crawl into, a warm arm to enfold me, warm lips to kiss my forehead and a soft voice to whisper, *There, that wasn't so bad, was it?*

And there it was.

Warmth flowed through me, not all at once, but a spreading tingle that swept through my chest, to my scalp, and then washed over me like the inexorable atomic glow from a sunrise, the swift and glorious oneness that I had once associated with orgasm, and over the last ten years, had come to associate with the nourishing rush of drinking blood.

I was floating, lighter than a wisp of milkweed, and weighted down with millstones at the bottom of a hundred fathoms of clear ocean. As if stepping into a perfumery or a bakery, my head was crowded with a sweet, intimate, comforting scent.

"Oh, *vanilla!*" I whispered aloud. "Orchid vanilla!"

I could see the sound of my voice. Even in the darkness behind my eyelids, I could perceive the outlines of every object in the room, as if I were a bat. "Bad ass," I whispered again, "I've got sonar!" I giggled, and the sound-images grew stronger and more solid, then danced away into nothingness.

Fabulous. But still . . .

This new sense was interesting, but I waited patiently, grinning, eyes still closed, for my body to assimilate it, get used to it, make it mundane. Even through human blood, drugs never felt *real*, like something actually happening to *me*. They were experienced, but at a distance, seen through another's eyes and sensed through another's skin. A dress worn by someone else; an accident happening to the car in front. It had never been genuine, personal, immediate before.

This was definitely personal.

The cotton sheets underneath me melted into a slippery pool, as if oiled. Startled, I swung my arms outward and heard/saw the shushing sound of skin and hair on woven cloth, and my hiss as my wrist jolted against the corner of the bedside table. It hurt so much that it almost brought me down. "Ow," I groaned, rolling over and involuntarily opening my eyes.

The fog had crept into the room.

Everything was fuzzy and vague. I pulled myself upward, laboriously, gazing at my misty reflection in the mirror. My screwed-up hair stood out from my head in a wild, tangled mane, one lock, at my temple, apparently trying to escape the rest of it. When I blinked, my hazy vision cleared. I was sitting splay-legged on the bed in panties and a T-shirt, jaw hanging open. The fog remained outside, pressed against the window like a hungry dog, the whining grown soft, scratching forlornly at the windowsill with the tip of a windwhipped branch. I burst out laughing, the sound of it strange, foreign, insane to me.

"Oh God," I murmured, sliding back down until my head reached the pillows, "this is crazy. I hope this stuff isn't lethal."

It didn't *feel* lethal. It felt wonderful. I felt no distress whatsoever. Even the bumped wrist throbbed in a friendly way, as if to remind me of my physicality. The injection site in the crook of my elbow had vanished, as was usual and good; the drug had no effect on my body's ability to heal itself. But my blood hadn't swept the foreign molecules away, and the drug washed through and against and over my body like an incoming tide. It was a very pleasant, though intense, sort of vertigo.

When my eyes drooped closed, I was suddenly somewhere else.

There was sunshine, brilliantly glaring down onto the ravenous green of a grassy meadow. I turned around and stared at it all, trying to adjust to the overwhelming brightness, breathless at the sight of tiny white daisies growing shyly in the midst of the infinity of verdant blades, the hot, living perfection of the deep blue sky.

I hadn't been in the sun for ten years. I'd forgotten how enormous it was, how all-encompassing, how all life seemed to bend to it, absorb its energy, then diffuse it outward, back into the world. This was not any actual place that I had ever been, and yet I felt that I knew it, as I felt that I would know Heaven if I saw it.

I wasn't entirely sure that this wasn't it.

Glorious sunlight! Hot and pure on my tingling skin, in my astonished eyes. And I could stand in the warmth and the deep, satiny grass and stare right into the burning white eye of the star without pain, without blindness. I felt that nothing bad could ever happen again.

"This isn't *real*. . . . " I crumpled to my knees in the soft grass and abruptly began to sob, and as suddenly, began to laugh again, like a madwoman, a tripper far out on too many doses, out of control. Tears poured over my face. "When *is* this gonna wear off?" I wondered aloud. My voice painted the details of the bedroom over the sight of the bright field, the edges of the standing mirror and bureau and open closet door, flickering in colorless precision, then shimmering off as the echoes decayed. Disappointment and relief battled within me. The sunlight, the green meadow, the daisies, were a hallucination, and I wasn't in Heaven, and I hadn't really been staring directly into the sun. I was simply under the influence of a drug so powerful that it dragged me to another plane of existence entirely, and I had to remember that, as marvelous as it would be, to forget it.

It was time to touch base with reality. I'd make it quick.

I opened my eyes and struggled to focus on the clock face. The hands now marked a quarter to nine. "Wow," I breathed. I wished for a moment that I had thought to prepare a tape recorder, but I didn't need it. I wouldn't ever be able to forget this. And it wouldn't be as if I would be able to share the results with anyone. Anyone human, anyway.

Poor, dear Margaret. Maybe she would understand this.

Maybe . . . but I won't ever know. That's not my world anymore.

I couldn't hold on to such a melancholy and dangerous thought, steeped as I was in this vast cup of lazy warmth and pleasure. In fact, I couldn't hold on to any thought at all for more than a few instants. I relaxed and let myself be pulled back into the vision. When I closed my eyes, I lay in the warm grass, contemplating the sharp, white-hot boundary of the sun. I stilled my body and turned my breath into a silent loop so that the world of the meadow attained a kind of perfection, so intense, so hyper-real, hyper-genuine.

Suddenly, the outlines of the bedroom glittered across the deep blue sky, the green periphery, the intense white sphere overhead. I wasn't conscious of having heard anything, only "seeing" it. But there was no mistake; a tapping and rustling, very faint, painted on the mirror and the bureau.

I groaned as I opened my eyes and rolled over, annoyed at the possibility of having to sober up and deal with whoever happened to have the bad luck to invade my house. I'd neglected to lock the side door that morning before I went to sleep. I smirked at the thought that it might be a hapless transient, and wondered greedily how taking more blood would affect the course of the experience. I was shocked to see that the clock read ten minutes till midnight; no time seemed to have passed at all, or else all of it.

The smell—dirt and trash and worn, tattered cloth with no human sweat binding it together—told me definitively that my own dear John was that hapless transient. I made out the fractionated parameters of his mind, trickling into mine much more slowly than usual. He had never surprised me before; usually, I could sense his approach when he was still miles away. Relief and dismay came at once; I hadn't felt him at all, and thank God it was he, and not someone more dangerous.

Because we *could* die; we *could* be killed. Fortunately, that wasn't what he had in mind.

With my eyes open, I watched him creeping into my bedroom. By the time he was inside, he was already undressed, and he crawled onto the bed beside me, tossing his hair aside and laying a kiss on my bare thigh. The sudden touch of his chapped-rough lips sent heavy waves of velvety sensation over me. I moaned and pulled him up to me by his hair. His eyes were distant. Through his skin I felt flutters of worry mixed with lust, combined with the ever-present desire to be somewhere else.

I didn't care about anything but the lust. Instead of kissing his lips, I licked them, sucked them into my mouth and stroked my tongue over them until the ragged dry edges were smoothed and healed. He bit the inside of my lower lip with a light touch of his fangs, and furled my tongue back into my mouth with his, sliding my panties down with his hands.

I pushed him slightly away, breaking the kiss, still holding onto his hair, gazing into his eyes. He grimaced, almost as if I'd hurt him. "Hi," I murmured.

He blinked at me, unsmiling. "Are you all right? I can't see you," he whispered.

I realized that I didn't perceive myself in his mind; touching him when he was beside me, looking at me, was usually almost like looking into a mirror, or more properly, seeing a hologram of myself. It had been extremely disorienting before I got used to it. In fact, I couldn't 'see' into him very well at all right now; everything was muted, soft focus, indistinct, and I surmised that it might go both ways. "You can't see *into* me?" I clarified.

"Right—that's what I mean. I was scared." He gently pulled me upright, and pulled the T-shirt over my head. "I had to touch you." He nuzzled his stubbled face against my breasts, under my arms, and I sizzled, hissing softly through my teeth. I might not have been able to see much, but my tactile senses were in great shape. My feet wrapped around the small of his back and I curled my toes together, locking him momentarily in place. Before he could settle there, with his face against my chest, I used my heels to push down on the firm shelf of his pelvic bone.

"You need to make me happy," I murmured. Even my voice was in soft focus. I wanted so badly to close my eyes, to return to the light. "Now. I *need* you to."

John chuckled and shrugged a little, pretending to be embarrassed, but obligingly slid down through the loop of my legs. Even in his state, he always remembered our euphemisms. "You want to see into me, you need to make me happy," I whispered. "I want you to come with me. I'm in a beautiful place."

He pushed my legs apart, holding my feet up on a level with his ears, kissing each ankle, kissing the soles of my feet. "You gonna make me happy, too?" he asked, pressing his lips up each leg, closing the distance. "I want to get happy." His breath blew hot and damp against the backs of my knees.

I didn't reply until his kisses reached their goal. I was as wet as if I'd been toying with herself for hours, and he added moisture with his tongue, hooking my knees over his shoulders, opening me up, putting me off balance, relying on him to hold me up. He was *just so good at this*. "Oh, yeah, I'll make you happy," I said, my fingertips tingling. "I'll do anything to make you happy. I'll do whatever you want. I've done it all for you. All of it—it's yours. Take it, please. . . ."

He slid underneath me, turning us both over, pulling me to a sitting position on top of him, and used his hands to guide himself into me. I closed my eyes, wordlessly urging him to join me in that sun-soaked field, now a broken, wavering kaleidoscope of echo-images of the room, of the sparkling grass, of our bodies together, drenched and bound in light. If I could have stayed there forever, I would have.

John gasped and began tearlessly sobbing, rocking up against me, then clutching me and holding me closer and closer until I could barely move, our movements no larger than deep, sighing breaths. "My God . . . What is it?" he pleaded.

"Can you see it? Come with me," I whispered, clutching his right hand in my left. "Close your eyes."

"I can't come with you," he protested. His eyelashes swept against my damp forehead, and his body twitched, startled by the change between what his eyes saw and what his mind painted.

I held tight to his hand. His stomach did a little flip of vertigo, and his hand clenched back. "You can—it's all right—it's the sun. . . ."

He was breathing hard and fast. "I can't—what the! Oh, God . . . oh, it's amazing . . ."

"Don't be afraid," I said, kissing his temple, pushing back his hair. I opened my eyes and watched him. His eyes were closed now, his face glistening with sweat. I smiled and brushed the back of my hand against the dark beard growth on his cheek. He opened his eyes and pressed his lips to our joined hands.

"What is this?" he asked. "What am I feeling?"

"It's the sunlight," I grinned. I knew I wasn't exactly answering his question in a way that he could understand, but I hoped he'd get the true sense somehow.

His face wanted to be cynical, but couldn't quite manage it. "Are you on something? You feel . . . I feel . . . different."

I couldn't resist a laugh. "Just *come* with me," I said, kissing his mouth. He pushed me off him onto the bed, and turned me over onto my face, entering me again with a salacious grunt. I had to laugh, even as I wanted to just scream and moan. This was so exactly what I needed, what made everything perfect, that the only proper response was a laugh. "Poor boy—my poor hungry boy. Can you smell the vanilla?"

He didn't answer, concentrating on ravishing me, one hand between my legs and the other on my lower back. I pressed my face into the pillow and felt the orgasm that had been building up in me—since the moment the needle left my arm in fact—crest and smash down like a massive wave, listening with satisfaction to John's helpless yelps of pleasure as my vaginal walls briefly gripped his cock like a fist.

As my orgasm fluttered away into nostalgia, his abruptly kicked in. He fell silent, which was rare for him; his abdomen went rigid and his toe-claws tore the sheets as he struggled and failed to keep it from happening. It wasn't that he worried about not gratifying me; he'd felt me come. He was trying to make it last, so that he could figure out what was going on, since nothing I said had made any sense.

He lay on his side against my back, breathing into my hair. "There's magic in you . . ." I was about to tell him "thanks," but he went on. "Witchcraft . . . fucking witchcraft, this. It's not real. It can't be."

He pulled me closer, resting against me with his arms curled against my belly, the way I loved the best. His damp fingertips stroked my breasts, his rough thumbs circling my nipples. "I feel strange," he whispered. When I closed my eyes this time, I was no longer in the sunlit meadow, but in a velvety featureless darkness, a nothingness as beautiful as the sunlit field. I perceived John's mind, but no one else's, and his was the essence of soft-edged silence. For all the extrasensory perception I had right then, I might as well have been human.

How peaceful.

In a very human way, John had begun to fall asleep, but unlike the warm human lover's, his vampire sleep mimicked the chill stillness of death. Already his body was growing cold. I wanted to draw away from him, but found my own muscles and joints stiffening, my mind growing dull. I had to make a gigantic effort just to grab the wadded blankets from the side of the bed and draw them over us. Once that had been accomplished, I sighed, and surrendered to the leaden fatigue that was only partially mine.

We woke together, in dark gray mid-afternoon.

I felt freeze-dried and hollow, a sensation that had

once been familiar to me in my days of Tulane microdot and margaritas-to-go, but which I now hardly recognized. I groaned my way to the mini-fridge and collected a liter IV bottle, returning to bed even before opening it.

John lay on his side, propped up on one elbow, with his long hair pushed back from his face, calmly watching me uncap the bottle and drink. "Give us a bit, then," he murmured.

I handed him the bottle, and he finished it with just a shadow of a grimace. "This isn't going to be enough, you know," he said.

"That's the last bottle I have at home," I grunted, sinking back into the bedding, mentally kicking myself for being so excited about the compound that I forgot that I might need blood when I woke up. Still, that one bottle would have been adequate if John hadn't decided to show up and make sweet love to me. It was too fucking early for me to want to deal with this shit.

"You know that doesn't have to stop us," he said.

"We should be fine for now, John."

"We *should* go out soon, though," he said.

I opened my eyes and gave him a solid look. He was still fairly grubby, but other than his dirty and unshaven state, he seemed perfectly reasonable. His eyes were clear and direct. His voice was his own, not his mum's, not his lecturers', not that of his broken, bitter, savage childhood self. He sounded like John Thurbis, a thinker, a physicist, a man of thirty, who should have been forty, if he hadn't been savagely murdered and just as savagely resurrected.

He continued, "I know a place we can go find some people who'd be willing to let us . . ."

I blinked. "Willing to let us kill them?"

John shrugged. "We don't *have* to kill them. They might not like that. But taking their blood? Yeah, no problem."

I sat all the way up and stared at him. "Are you feeling okay?" I asked carefully.

John shrugged. "I feel fine," he said.

"You feel *fine?*"

"Yes, Ariane, that's what I said, didn't I?"

"It's just that you haven't felt 'fine' in . . . I mean . . ."

"What were you doing last night?" he asked, angling his head towards the bedside table, the empty syringe still resting on the towel. "Has it come to gear? It wouldn't be like that, though, would it?"

"I made a . . . I did a . . ." A slow smile spread across my face, even though it made my head hurt to squish my cheeks like that. It wasn't such a gray day after all. "I made something for you. I made a drug. A new psychoactive; one that's never been synthesized before."

"So what? I know a dozen undergrads who whip up a batch of MDMA every weekend." He sadly sucked at the neck of the empty bottle.

"John, think about what you've just said. You don't. You don't anymore. You don't know anybody anymore. Remember?"

His face fell a little, considering.

"I made a drug that *we* can take. I made a drug to make you feel better. I took it last night, and you must have gotten some through me—enough to make you feel 'fine' today. Enough to make you seem more 'fine' than I've seen you since—"

"Since Daniel killed me," John finished quietly.

"Since Daniel killed you," I agreed, "and I brought

you back." I didn't think it would be very nice of me to mention Orfeo Ricari's assistance at that moment.

John rubbed his eyes with the sides of his hands for a long time. "So, you took this ... substance you created—"

"Would you be willing to take it yourself?" I jumped in.

John frowned, and I forged ahead, gripping his hand in mine. "It can't hurt you. I took it last night and it was—it was amazing. It was awesome. I feel a little strung-out today, but maybe I mixed it too strong or maybe it shouldn't be IV or something, but it works, I'm telling you. And I think it's gonna help you. For real." I bit my lips together, but still, tears prickled up in my eyes, and it was simply easier to let them happen. "Will you take it?"

He stared at me for a moment, mulling it over. I sniffled and wiped the tears off my chin with my free hand. "What if it doesn't work the same way for me?" he asked worriedly.

"It should. I need a control. Will you trust me? I mean, seriously, how much worse can it get? You can remember how it was before last night, can't you?"

John didn't say anything, but I could see his memory flickering back. I knew he could remember; he couldn't help it. It was unpleasant sometimes, but it was just a fact of life.

"I took it, and if you want, I can give you half the dose I did last night just in case. Please. Help me test my theory. Because if I'm right . . ."

"I saw the sun," John murmured thoughtfully. "It looked so real. It was so bright I wanted to close my eyes, but they were already closed. . . ."

"I saw it, too," I said. "If someone had told me about it, I wouldn't believe them, but I know what I saw. I know where I went. Don't you want to go back there again?"

John shook his head, but not in denial. His eyes had filled with tears, too. "I don't know what this is. I don't know what you've done, I'm not sure how to describe how I feel right now. . . ."

"Do you love me?"

He made a quiet scoffing noise. "If you don't know that by now . . ." He chuckled at my reaction, which, seen through his eyes, resembled a kitsch painting of a sad-eyed puppy. His expression sobered, and he lifted my chin with his forefinger. "Never doubt it," he said, looking into my eyes, brushing my eyebrow with the forefinger of the other hand. "All right?"

Flickering across his thoughts, more swiftly than he could ever conceal, was *But if this stuff kills me, I hope it kills you, too.*

VII

In a Rested Development

John Thurbis

What had I experienced?

I thought it over while I was in the shower with Ariane. I had been in the woods, listening for her, caught up in her thoughts, unsure of why she was recalling my opening lecture on the Higgs boson, why it was making her get all heated up like that. Then it didn't matter why; she was all tangled up in bed wanting to shag me. Then it took me forever to get there, as I kept forgetting where I was going, I kept getting scared out of my wits, I kept stumbling and doubling back to make sure I wasn't being followed. I kept losing the thread that connected me to Ariane; it wavered in and out of my perception, and inside me the fear mounted until I was choking on it. But then I found the house, purely by sense of smell, as the sky was fluffy and gray and low, the fog blotting out the stars. From outdoors I could hear her talking. I paused on the threshold and listened for another voice, but it never came; she was alone, and talking, giggling, moaning to herself.

I thought I'd better give her someone to talk to, maybe join her in a little moaning, see if her body could cleanse some of the horror from inside my head.

I got in there and saw her works, and thought *morphine*. As far as I knew, she'd never touched it before; it didn't seem like her thing. So be it. I wasn't averse to a narcotic now and again; if I got high by fucking her, I'd get high, because I was most definitely going to fuck her. I'd come from miles away, from relative safety, where the leaves on the trees never strobed with the lights of passing cars, where there was absolutely no music, only the sweet, intricate voice of the mossy darkness, for the express purpose of having one with my wife, or the next best thing.

And I got high, all right. And it wasn't morphine.

At first I wondered if it might be, because I felt so marvelous as soon as I'd gotten a taste of her. She didn't taste the way she ordinarily did, which is to say, barely of anything at all; this night her juices had a very faint mineral aftertaste. Not in a bad way; actually she tasted of avocado. I thought it was a nice touch.

Then I started to become very relaxed; the whole world became so soft, so warm, and everything felt lovely against my skin. I fought it; I didn't want to do any passing out while I had Ariane naked and horny at hand. I actually began to worry that I might not make it at all. She was so far gone that nothing she said made any sense, and I soon felt my own coherency slipping away, unimportant. It was just so warm and lovely in bed. I began to see things—not hallucinating specifically, and not really *seeing* things with my eyes, but perceiving things that I never could before, developing new senses, while others were refined, smoothed, made linear.

I saw the sun and felt its unmistakable heat on my skin. It was too much; I could go blind.

It was definitely not morphine.

After our shower, I made Ariane have a walk and talk with me so she could explain herself. She was all too happy to do so; so proud of herself, treading the fine line between dedicated and insufferable as always.

When we set out, afternoon was still going on, and the sun, though barely a degree above the horizon, remained in the sky. She kept staring at me, occasionally prodding me with questions. I didn't particularly want to revisit the bad feelings from the earlier part of the night before, and although half eaten up with curiosity about what had happened, I felt perfectly all right. I wanted to go somewhere and have a proper drink of blood, and thought of a young girl who I frequently saw in the shadows under one of the bridges; she was wondering where I'd been. It had to have been at least two weeks, likely more, since I'd seen her. I hoped she was all right. She usually got to the Rock by sundown, and I didn't like to think of her being out all night. She was crazy, like me. She was just a kid, though, and I had never been able to bring myself to harm her.

Ariane and I held hands as we walked, and without speaking, she transmitted the information about the drug she had created. There was a lot to take in, and there was only so far I could truly understand her theoretical process, lacking her background in microbiology, but I got all that was necessary and would probably be able to describe the process if I had to. I was fairly well floored that she would dare to try taking that stuff herself; how far gone does someone have to be before she'll inject potassium cyanide into her vein? There was absolutely nothing in my line of science that carried such a terrible personal risk—the worst I had to worry about was catching a buzz off my whiteboard markers. She had to have been out of her mind. The important thing was that it hadn't killed her, or me, though at moments I'd wondered if I could die from sheer pleasure.

When we had reached the steel and concrete of downtown, I spotted an abandoned umbrella in the gutter and I swooped over to get it. Ariane recoiled from the mud-encrusted thing, but I shook it out and opened it. "What are you afraid of—germs?" I teased her. "You know they won't hurt us. And we need something to give us some shade over the bridge. Look at the world—it's full of everything you need. You just have to keep your eyes open."

I shocked her again before we got to the bridge by pausing for a moment to capture and snack on an adolescent raccoon which was drooling and shivering under a bush as the flush of rabies turned its nerves to fire. It amused me to see how repulsed Ariane was; she really was a high-maintenance city girl, completely unfit for life on the streets. I had never even stopped to think that I oughtn't do as I pleased. Who was stopping me? Who cared what I did? The police? The neighbors? I was already dead. I had no reputation to uphold, no burden of good citizenship. For all intents and purposes, I didn't exist.

But I did exist to Ariane. I still had emotional and physical needs. I even had a friend. I did exist. I was alive. It was just different now, was all.

And different again, after last night.

On the crest of the bridge, with the traffic groaning and flashing behind us, I paused and turned fully to the amber west. The clouds were all curled, tangled, translucent, orange and red where the sun was just giving up on the hilly horizon. I thought of Jupiter and Saturn, supermassive storms on their surfaces, any one of them immense enough to engulf this whole little planet. I was overwhelmed with a sense of cosmic fragility. "We won't see the sun again, not really," I murmured.

"No, not really . . ." She sighed. "I can't explain the hallucination. It was really intense, and it never changed. It was like I'd literally gone somewhere else."

"My guess is that it's wish fulfillment. Your mind shows you what you most want to see."

"I'm interested in finding out whether or not it's consistent among subjects. I'm interested in how dosage affects the specifics of the hallucination."

"Maybe it's purely subjective?"

"But you saw it, too."

"Wouldn't that lead you to believe that it might not have anything to do with dosage, then, and everything to do with the particular experience? I saw it because you saw it and I was there. You saw what I saw, am I correct?"

"There wasn't much going on with yours," she said.

It was a hell of a sight better than my usual existence. "Maybe all I want is a moment's fuckin' peace."

"Yeah," she replied, her voice faint. "I hear that."

"You've got peace to spare," I said. For a second I felt dizzy. My voice sounded odd to my ears, and she grimaced a little, and I saw that I was gripping her hand, as if trying to hold on to her to keep from being blown away.

Ariane sighed. "That hurts, John," she said. "Remember to control yourself. You still have a lot to learn."

I had so many indignant retorts that they all got bottled up in the doorway and I just grunted with my tongue stuck to the roof of my mouth. I felt bad enough about it as it was, without her slamming me right back into sixth form. I let go of her hand, although it pained me to do so; it was painful to be physically separate from her after such a long, delicious time of touching, letting our feelings flow through to the other without trying to find words to define them. Still, if she considered me so immature and unformed, I'd spare her the discomfort of having to share mental space with me.

Shaking my head, I walked away, down the bridge's curve toward the other face of the city. She followed close behind, trying to stay in the shadow of the umbrella, even though the sun was all gone.

Now the streetlights were coming on, and I wanted to be on the other side before they all lit up.

"Let's get off this bridge," I murmured, already casting my thoughts forward, searching for a human presence, maybe one of the messed-up teenagers who liked to hide on the rock under the bridge as much as I did.

On the east side of the river, where the buildings and big empty lots gave way to chunky, steep cliffs sloping down to the water, I led Ariane down the familiar flights of concrete stairs, then lightly jumped over the rails into the silt and weeds near the water's edge. Ah, the sweet east side under bridges, the water's edge, the pure heart of town, even the garbage forming an essential part of it, a protective outer skin, composed of superthin plastic packets and broken

brown beer bottles. I tossed the umbrella onto the
ground beside a scrub of blackberry, fixing its location
in my mind. Ariane grinned at me. "You gonna pick it
up later?" she teased.

I just smiled at her. "Not tonight, but maybe some-
time. Some morning I'm caught unawares. Always
pick up umbrellas, Ariane . . . remember, the sun's our
enemy. Or did you not learn that?" She said nothing,
concentrating on keeping her footing on the mud-
slick, slanting earth.

The Rock hadn't changed much since I was last
there. It was still graffiti-stained and covered in layers
of melted candle wax and cigarette butts. Someone
had left a bouquet of roses, half-rotted now, tied with a
grimy white ribbon that read "R.I.P. Elliott, the beautiful loser." My hiding place, shared with generations of
others.

The young girl was there, huddled in the shadows
under the bridge, where she couldn't be seen until you
were right next to her. Yes, it came back to me; we had
history, sharing this space, sharing thoughts of pain.
Psychward. All in black, reeking of black hair dye, taking concentrated pulls on a bottle sloshing with brown
liquid. By the scent, it was bottom-shelf blended
whisky, an alcoholic's drink; an alcoholic father's drink.

"He's not my fucking father," came the girl's voice
from the darkness. "He's just fucking the woman who
was married to my father."

"That's . . . enormously complicated," Ariane murmured.

Psychward sniffled and took another hit off the bottle. She was hitting her stride, only grimacing slightly
as the alcohol hit her tongue. "Hey, John," she mut-

tered, curling her lip in a practiced Johnny Rotten sneer. "Who's this?"

Poor kid; she was all scraped up with longing and confusion and jealousy, missing me even though she barely knew me, suspicious to the point of violence at the sight of Ariane, but too depressed to bother to take action. I sank down next to Psych, pushing her black hood back all the way and running my fingers comfortingly through her greasy India-ink hair, exposing her rounded face, black eyeliner smudged halfway down her cheeks. I wanted so much for her to not cry any more, to not feel so horrible, at least for a moment, if there was anything I could do. All her hostility melted away. She relaxed with a quiet moan, her head drooping back.

"She's my wife," I said quietly.

"Oh, okay, cool. . . ." She was hypnotized. I hadn't even really had to do anything; I could hypnotize her just by being there. She wouldn't cry any more tonight.

"You know her?" Ariane asked, her voice neutral.

"This is Psychward," I told her, sitting beside the girl and taking one of her small, warm, dimpled hands in mine and rubbing it gently. "We've spent some time being crazy together."

"Psychward, huh?" Ariane chuckled, sinking down next to us, closing the circle. She immediately grasped the girl's real name, but respectfully said nothing aloud. I had never called Psych by that other name, and I never would; she had no identity, only a selfhood, and I knew that self, as battered and fractured as it was.

Psych looked up, her sneer struggling to return. "I've seen enough of 'em to know," she hissed, attempting bitterness, but the gentle pressure of my hands against hers defused her hostility. Her eyes went soft, unfocused, gazing inward. "You're Ariane," she whispered. "He didn't really talk about you, but I could see you through him. Like a picture in his mind—I'd see little bits of you, I could feel how he felt about you . . . sometimes you were all he could think about. You're really beautiful."

"Thank you," said Ariane, as sincere as I'd ever heard her. "So are you."

"Will you do me a favor tonight?" I asked Psych, angling up her chin and looking into her eyes. They were the kind of hazel color that's nearly iridescent, holding onto so many different shades at once, refusing to commit to any one of them.

"You know what I want you to do," Psychward mumbled.

"I won't do it," Ariane broke in. "She's thirteen."

I looked over my shoulder at Ariane. "No," I said, "you won't have to. That's not what this is about." I said to Psych, "If I thought you'd be better off dead, you'd be dead. And why would I think that? No, tonight we need your strength. And I know you've got that."

"My *strength?* I don't have any strength. I'm a fat, retarded fuckup," said Psychward, but she didn't sound convinced.

"Nonsense," I said. "No, you're looking out at a beautiful view of a city on the water and getting hammered; that's a great way to live." I laughed. "I like that one myself. It's better than death, any day."

"Is it, though?" She sighed and set the bottle down. "You can take whatever you want, however much you need. Both of you. I really don't care."

I held her hand lightly, firmly in my fingers, the skin

surging gently with her pulse. "We specifically *don't* want to kill you, okay? Now tell me. Where will it hurt the least?"

"My neck," Psychward whispered, with a kind of erotic urgency.

"Ah, ah, ah, you know I can't do that." I stroked my claws against her neck anyway, chuckling. I was torturing Ariane, making her listen to me using a voice that she'd only heard done just for her on someone else. I wanted to tell her that it was just business, but it would have been a lie; taking blood is never just business. I couldn't help winding Psych up. She was just so weird and exotic to me. I'd no real idea that thirteen-year-old girls could be so silly and melodramatic, but with steel underneath. And if it gave her something nice to think about, where was the harm? "There's too much blood coming too fast, and I might make a mistake."

"It wouldn't be a mistake."

"Don't contradict me, Psych. I've got you beat in the tragic and useless department."

"Have you noticed that he's different?" Ariane interjected.

Psychward opened her eyes fully and gave me a thorough look. "He is talking a lot more than he usually does," she said. "But I think I thought it was because you were here."

"Ariane, please keep your mind on what we're doing here," I said, unable to keep impatience from my voice. "You still haven't said where, kiddo."

"Don't call me kiddo," Psychward said, lying back and hiking up the fabric at her ankles until her legs were exposed to the dark saddle of the crotch of her tights. She poked her finger through a rip in the knee of the tights until she had opened an eight-inch tear to mid-thigh. She pointed to a dark bruise on her pale skin, an inch or so above the knee. "Right there," she said, "it already hurts."

It wasn't my first choice, but it would have to do. Bruise blood was like overripe fruit, or meat a day past fresh. "It also won't taste very good." Before anyone could say more, I bent my head to the velvety white strip of inner thigh.

Pierce and draw. Pure elegant instinct. The alcohol hadn't made it into the bruise yet, but I sucked until the dark sludge had been pulled out and fresh blood swelled up in its place. Psych gasped in a way that I don't like to associate with kids, but at least she was enjoying herself.

At any rate, the headache that had been threatening all day disappeared, and I felt my body and my mind expand their capabilities, with a wavery top note of Canadian whiskey and the odd bottom twiddlings of the medications they had Psych on. She hadn't taken them that day because she hadn't been home; she'd been wandering about, hopping from bus to bus to train and back, trying to get through the day without making eye contact with anyone, without speaking to anyone, or having anyone speak to her. She was afraid to go home because she hadn't been back the night before, afraid to even imagine what punishments she would have to endure.

I knew that terror well.

I raised my head after five small swallows, wanting more, as always. Ariane took her turn, puncturing the skin a few centimeters away from where the holes left by my teeth had begun to close up. The girl slipped into unconsciousness. Ariane sat up and pressed the last drops of blood into her lips with her tongue, shaking her head against the onslaught of cheap alcohol. "So have you fucked her?" she asked, false-casual.

"*Her?*" I gave Ariane a look. "How diabolical do you think I am? She's barely old enough to bleed. That's the kind of shit your Daniel would've done."

"She's crazy in love with you," Ariane pointed out. "I know a lot of guys who would take the opportunity to get into something that young."

I wasn't surprised by this viewpoint; Ariane was a student of the everyday grotesque. But I could also tell that she believed me. "That's disgusting." I pulled Psych's skirt back down as far as it would go without it slipping off her waist. My face was hot, but I always felt flushed after a drink. "I wouldn't do that. I don't feel that way about her—she still draws on herself with Biro, for God's sake."

Ariane wouldn't let it drop. Argumentative thing, her. "I mean, are you protecting her future? She's on a dose of psych meds that would knock out a horse, and she's out here, after dark, where meth freaks carve up and rape little goth girls like her. She needs professional help if she's going to make it at all. What are *you* going to do with her?"

I looked over at Psych's slack face, a hank of black hair sliding down into her open mouth, and wished I could cry about it. I couldn't, though. This was a sadness that made your eyes dry and prickly, and no amount of blinking could clear it up. I turned the girl onto her side, arranging her garments until she was all covered except for her nose and lips poking out from under her hood. "I'll probably kill her eventually," I answered. "I guess I'll have to. She's gonna push me into it, or I'll make a mistake, or I'll just suddenly realize that it's kinder to do that than to let her go on like this. It's what she wants, anyway, and what else can I do? I won't do what you did to me, and I *sure* won't do what Ricari did to you."

"What, almost kill me and dump me off on someone else, hoping he'd finish the job?" She laughed without smiling. "Yeah, that was pretty lame."

"I don't know what you see in that little nelly," I muttered.

Her smile caught up with her laugh. "Hey! Don't talk that way about your dad."

"He's not my fuckin' *dad!* I never asked to be born!" I shot out, then began to laugh when I thought about what old James no-middle-name Thurbis would have thought of fancy-pants Signor Ricari. They did share a certain distasteful distance from the troublesome result of their peccadilloes. I can't say I really blamed them. "Either time," I added. I sighed, patting the rising and falling mound of black clothes. "I understand where she's coming from."

"Self-pity doesn't look good on you," Ariane said, wagging her finger. "On either of you, really. On anyone. And at least *your* 'dad' Orfeo isn't a tin-plated asshole."

"Neither is yours, anymore," I said. "He's dead, thank God." I clapped my palm against my forehead. "I can't tell you how relieved I was when that happened! I mean, the proof that we can die. You know how freeing that is? The idea that there is an escape, eventually—that *this* isn't forever." I pricked the tip of my tongue with one of my fangs and felt my mouth spring into life. Ariane was holding herself, gently shaking her head. I held out my hands and stared in distress at how freakish they were, long and skeletal and glowing a faint blue-white, with those horrible, sharp, gray claw-like nails that were as tough as hardened leather. *"That's* what suicidal thoughts are all about, in my mind. Just the thought that you can end it all, and you don't have to be stuck in the hell you're currently in—sometimes it's the only comfort that I have. For a long time, it was all she had, as well. But I showed her that there was something else. I'm kind of a symbol to her that this horrible life she's in isn't all there is. That there's magic, still; that there are things that the world of hospitals and stepparents still don't know about."

"That's a lot of power to have over someone," Ariane said.

"Yeah," I said, "you're right."

After a moment of silence, Ariane shook herself and stood up. "Do you want to take some more Orchid?"

"Eh?"

She smiled modestly. "'Orchid.' That's kind of what I've named it. Because it smells like vanilla. In your mind, I mean. In its normal state it smells more almondy—"

"Yeah. Right. That. Orchid. I get it." I glanced over at Psych, who was coming round. "Yes, but I should get her home."

"You're going to take her home?" Ariane arched her eyebrow. "How? Are you going to spring for her bus fare?"

"Self-pity doesn't suit *you,* either." I placed my hand against Psych's dirty cheek, and whispered to her, "Go back to sleep." Her hazel eyes met mine for a second, then dropped closed. "Wait here," I told Ariane. "I'll be back in a jiff."

For all of Psychward's constant declarations of how

fat she was, it took almost no effort to carry her. I positioned her carefully, holding her arms locked lightly over my collarbone and her body draped down my back. Even carrying her, I easily skimmed up the side of the cliff and up past the road, avoiding the bright streets. I had always thought that it would be nice to be able to fly, but this was the next best thing—only occasionally acknowledging gravity and inertia, never touching more than the balls of my feet against the ground. I could traverse half of the city in ten minutes on foot and never be seen by human eyes, even the startled barks of nervous dogs coming to me from far behind.

Some bits of this life were all right.

I settled the girl gently on a rain-dusted plastic chair next to a barbecue grill, on the concrete square in her family's back garden. She'd be all right there until she woke up. I looked up at the light on in an upstairs bedroom and hoped I was doing the right thing; at least she'd sleep someplace warm and indoors. Whatever thoughtless jerks these people were, I didn't imagine that they'd kill her, whereas the desperate types who skulked under the bridges might very well consider it.

I should know; I was one of those desperate types.

Returning took even less time. I dropped silently onto the Rock next to Ariane. "There, she'll be all right at home," I said. Ariane just stared at me and smiled, her eyes wide. "She won't be pleased to be back there, but I really think she's better there than right here. Now. Home and hard drugs, then, darling?"

I never took my eyes away from Ariane's face as she administered the injection. "I'm wondering if I can make a compound that can be taken orally," she mut-

tered half to herself, "but for now, this'll have to be it."
I felt the cold fluid rush through my arm, and instantly,
her voice sounded blurry, almost underwater. "This is
point zero-zero-two milligrams of Orchid, in point
two-five milligrams of total solution, the same dose as
I gave myself. Just tell me when you can smell the
vanilla."

It was a useless effort to keep my eyes open. Ariane
rubbed the injection site with her fingertip. Suddenly I
felt very warm. I collapsed onto my side on her bed,
curling my arm underneath me and tucking my knees
into my chest. The vertigo was momentarily intense;
then, just as suddenly gone, replaced by calm stability.

I was just *all right,* like the relief that comes when
the fever finally breaks. Feeling that things were getting better at last. It was glorious.

Ariane combed her fingers through my hair. "John,
you okay?" she whispered.

"This . . . is . . . nice . . ." I replied.

"I'm right here. Tell me if you're not doing all right."

"And then you'll do what?" I opened my eyes and
smiled at her. "Is there an antidote to your pretty poison . . . or did you not think that far ahead?"

She gave a dry laugh. No antidote. "Just tell me if
you need blood," she clarified.

I pulled her down beside me and wrapped my lax
arms around her. "I need blood," I murmured, giggling, kissing her, "all the time." I kissed her harder,
for the sheer pleasure of it. "Ah yes, this is great. This
is really nice. Oh, and the vanilla. I understand what
you're saying now, yeah . . . it's like walking into a
sweet shop. Very . . . sweet. Like cakes topped with
spun sugar and angels made of marzipan."

I lost interest in speaking. I didn't fall asleep, but lay

there without moving, letting go of everything. Ariane curled up next to me, my arms around her, her ear pressed against my neck listening to my pulse, eavesdropping in my brain.

I wondered if it was boring, utterly dark, simple, comfortable, and quiet. It was just peace, really. A release. If I didn't want to hear what Ariane was thinking, I didn't have to. I had this warm blanket of darkness and privacy to draw around me. I let her see in, though; there was nothing she hadn't already seen, and she still wanted to lie next to me, so I guess she was able to tolerate it. For a moment I was stricken with remorse for what I'd put her through, but I put that aside, too, because she was still with me, no matter how much I screeched and whinged and bled all over her hardwood floors. I held her as close as I could and kissed her hair.

"No wonder you're so crazy," Ariane murmured against my shirt. "I hope you sleep well tonight. I hope I've done that, at least."

"You've done a lot for me," I said. "This is just the latest. Thank you, for just this moment."

And I had, for the second day in a row, a sleep as blank and gentle as the interior of a cloud.

VIII

THE HEART OF A DOG

ELISABETA REVIKOFF

Debbie and Rachell handled the news of Young Lad's death with surfaces of calm indifference, but August was hit harder than he could fake away. I hadn't thought that the two of them were very good friends, but I supposed the two of them had formed a strange bond forged from their mutual status as has-beens who were barely old enough to legally drink, with six-hundred-dollar-a-day drug habits. Now August was a lonely boy. He eschewed chasing the dragon for inject-ing it directly into his bloodstream. His blood tasted even more sweetly poisonous.

He wasn't going to be around much longer. Neither was Debbie. Debbie looked terrible, lips blistered from the pipe, eyes sunk into purple hollows in her skull. And she hadn't been a particularly pretty girl to begin with. Her relationships with August and Young Lad hadn't ever been more than ostensibly sexual; they were more like siblings or members of the same secret

society, the same gang of wannabe hardcore kids
grown up too fast and yet too slow.

The *children*. Was I supposed to feel sorry for them?
God, I was so sick of their thoughts and their experiences, always swirling around inside my head. Sometimes I had to take a moment to separate my thoughts
from theirs, remember what I had done myself, what I
was myself. Some nights I went without blood rather
than polluting my mind by dipping into their pools. But
I always came back, longing for that laser-beam rush of
blow, the seasick swirl of Red Bull and vodka, the bliss
and terror of diacetylmorphine cut with God knew
what else. And the children could not do without us;
they phoned incessantly, played John Bonham drum so-
los on the door to our suite, moaning pitifully until one
of us let them in. Half the time they didn't even want to
do our drugs. They wanted to be bitten, cut into,
drained. They wanted to sit at our feet and zone out in
adoration, and all I wanted was to kick them away.

It was clear that something drastic would have to
be done.

"Are you going to get out of bed?" Alex asked me.

I shook my head and thrust my face deep into the
pillow. I heard him chuckle and turn away, going to the
toilet, shaving, rubbing bay rum over his neck and
cheeks before dressing. Inside me there was a hunger
for blood, but I set it aside, trying unsuccessfully to go
back to sleep.

A dream had been troubling me for the last two days.
It wasn't an unpleasant dream; to the contrary, it was
almost painfully wonderful, like hearing a favorite
childhood song for the first time in decades, but being

unable to remember more than a few words of what had been a favorite lyric. In the dream, I was taking a stroll along a sunny country lane, the sky a silky-pale springtime blue, the road ahead of me thickly strewn with apple and cherry blossoms, and the trees in half-full adolescent leaf. In the shadows between the trees I passed I saw movement, perhaps an ambiguous glimpse of a grinning face, and heard faint giggling and sighing, as though I were being followed by a troop of amorous fairies trying not to be seen. The very best part of the dream was the scent in the air; it was not the fruity sweetness of blooming apple trees, but rather a warm, buttery vanilla, like baking madeleines. At the edge of the path, a brightly colored flower caught my eye, and I bent down to pick it; but before I could grasp it, I woke up. It was maddening to have the same dream twice in a row, and to be equally unsuccessful at getting the flower, or even really getting a good enough look at it to tell what kind of flower it was, or what color— orange, violet, red, I could not recall.

Alex had not had such pleasant dreams. His were filled with diamond-sharp memories of the scores of men he had destroyed to make our escape from Russia. I caught the barest glimpse of crushed jawbones and blood-choked begs for mercy, and retreated into myself. I could tell myself, or tell him, that avoiding the thoughts myself might help to draw his attention from them, but we both knew that I just didn't want to see it. Those were things that he had done, that he had on his conscience, not I.

I heard the room service cart being wheeled up the hallway to our room and the faint knock announcing its arrival. Alex poured himself a cup of steaming hot black tea and rustled the newspapers. "'Sbeta," he said, "are you sure you won't get out of bed?"

"Alexander Vassilyevich, please, I'm trying to think."

My sweet husband only chuckled at me. "Oh, get up, you lazy cow, you've got a letter. Or I could gladly throw it in the shredder if you don't care about it. . . ."

I was up like a flash, dragging most of the blankets with me. "What is it? Give it here!" I snatched the large cardboard envelope from his fingers and tore it open. Inside was another, standard-sized envelope, very plain, boring white, addressed to "Mrs. E. Revikoff, Turandot Hotel" in terse block capitals, containing a single sheet of plain white unlined paper, inscribed with the same brisk handwriting.

9/27

Dear El (it suits you),

It was a surprise and a pleasure to get a letter from you after all these years. Even though I'm not thrilled about the way you were able to find me, I'm glad you did, because you're not one of the people who I'd ever want to lose touch with. Even though our only connection was through our mutual acquaintance with Daniel, I'd like to start out on new footing without him being the only thing that links us. I'm sure you're aware of the bad history between us—since it's pretty hard for folks like us to hide something that has such an unpleasantly intense emotional signature— and I don't imagine you had very many illusions about what he was really like. You knew Daniel for much longer than I did; you and he were lovers for fifteen years (I don't know how you stood it—he probably showed you a lot more respect than he did me, since you were already changed when he met you), whereas I only had to be subjected to him for a matter of months. (I do remember that we had some good times together, but almost everything else he did negated that.) To me it seems like he and I shared a lifetime, but then again, he made me, and his blood is still in my veins, even though the man himself—the living individual organism—is gone.

Anyway, I'm not writing to bitch about our dearly departed mutual ex (as much as I could go on for hundreds of pages on the subject). I am hoping that you and A. will at least make a visit here to our wet but lovely city and have a chance to stop by and say hello—and I can share my most recent discovery with you.

I'm sure you've felt it. I've done something extraordinary. Not only does it benefit J., but it's pretty fun and beautiful and profound for me, too. The best thing about it is that it can be taken directly—no human intercessor necessary.

I'm working on a second batch as we speak.

Do visit; I'd love to see you.

From up here, Ariane

"Pack your bags," I said to Alex, "we're leaving town tonight. I'll call Varlet. He can drive us."

"So we're going to Portland, are we?" Alex asked, taking a casual sip of his still steaming tea. "What do you want to do about the children?"

I grimaced. "We'll have to kill them. We can do it on the way. Come on, now; you don't have to read the paper." I had already set out something to wear, and began laying out the clothes I wanted to take with me. There were surprisingly few, considering how much money I had spent on these garments, but they had been camouflage, and absurdly impractical at that. Who the hell needed sheepskin-lined boots in Los Angeles?

"We won't make it to Portland tonight," he said, raising his eyebrows as his eyes skimmed the letter. He had read it along with me, his mind delicately sweeping through mine, but he wanted to touch it himself and gather what subtle vibrations of the writer remained in the fibers of the paper. "Oh, my, what *is* she up to? A drug, is it . . . indeed. Anyway, it's too late."

"So we'll get a hotel room at sunup. Call the kids; tell them to meet me at the Top Layer in an hour." I glanced at him, still sitting there, sipping his tea, gazing mournfully out the window. "Do you want to kill Rachell yourself?" I offered. "I know she means a lot to you."

He gave a little start, as if the thought had never occurred to him. "I—no, you do it. And she doesn't mean as much to me as you seem to think she does; she's just an interesting grotesquerie, a perverted human expression in the form of a girl. She is very famous, though. This is going to be a massive scandal, all three of them at once; we'll have to be careful about this. Are you capable of doing whatever needs to be done?"

I shrugged into my blue Jil Sander minidress and zipped up the back, catching a strand of hair in the zipper. "I am always capable of doing what is necessary," I told him, and ripped the hairs free from my scalp.

I never even felt a pang as I chopped a generous amount of swimming pool cleaning powder into a gram of high-grade Columbian flake cocaine, an exceptional sample that I had hoarded for months in anticipation of a special occasion. Rachell took her gift with a plastic-pretty smile, and the skagged-out Debbie could barely even open her eyes or her mouth to thank me. I will admit that I was unable to meet August's eyes as I slid a wrap into his pocket, following it with a gentle kiss on his ear. "Your day will come," I said to him, holding his hand. "It's just around the corner, I promise. Now wait to hit this until after I've gone, and—don't share it with anybody, okay? This one's all for you." Not that I particularly cared if anyone else happened to dip into it, but a gentle stroke of the ego has never gone amiss.

"You're good to me," he said with the intensity that should have gotten him a dozen movie roles, but instead made producers uneasy. He was too feral, too close to the real intensity of the rough life, too involved to ever dial it down or contain it long enough to perform a scene. I had to kiss him one last time, a brief meeting of the mouths, so that I could memorize him as he was, before the sodium hypochlorite ate oozing ulcers through the interior of his face.

But it had to be done; and by midnight, Alex, Varlet, and I were on the highway, slicing through the black, yellow-striped night.

I had never been to the northwestern United States before, and after more than fifty years of California winds and sunshine, the change in climate was alarming and delightful. The rains began almost precisely at the California-Oregon border, making all three of us laugh. "Good thing you bought that umbrella," Varlet commented.

"Oh, who's afraid of a little rain?" I declared. "Does it snow here?"

"Only in the mountains, and Portland isn't in the mountains."

"Oh, drat," I said. "I want to see snow. It's been years." Amazing how absence made the heart grow fonder; in 1917 I never wanted to see a single flake of the stuff ever again. It would be different here; American snow, playful and clean, not a half-frozen, blood-spattered, blackened Russian slush.

Alex kissed me on the cheek. "If you like, we can go to the mountains. Whatever you want to do. Adventure agrees with you," he said. "You've looked so beautiful the last few days."

"I told you how tired of the place I was," I said, lightly pinching his cheek. "I know I loved it once, but enough was enough. We stayed too long, that's all. Promise me we'll never stay in one place for so long again."

"I promise," Alex said. Adventure seemed to have no effect on his looks; he was beautiful to me as always, so calm and steady, even with memories of slaughter bucking behind his eyes. I had heard about him from my brother's fellow soldiers; they called him the Borzoi, the wolfhound, quietly smiling, but with a bite that would take off a finger if you petted him at the wrong time. They described him so accurately for having never known his true nature.

I glanced at Varlet in the rearview mirror. Poor Varlet; what would become of him? He was a good man, dedicated, loyal, unflappable, nearly inscrutable; he had gone from valet parking in high school to taxi driver, to diplomatic chauffeur, to 24-hour, on-call driver for a pair of ridiculously wealthy bloodsuckers.

I wondered if he could ever be induced to betray us; but why give up three hundred large a year to be an accessory to inhuman murder?

Still, I thought to myself, Portland would have to be the end of the line for him. Then I caught Alexander looking at me in the mirror, his expression resigned and distant, so I rubbed his hand and kissed him again, and he wrapped his arms around me and buried his face in my hair.

Varlet drove on, none the wiser.

As we approached the city, which was much farther north than I had realized by just glancing at a map, neither Alex nor I had much to say aloud. Our thoughts were consumed with Ariane, with our separate but conjoined memories of her, more than ten years previous, when she was still Daniel Blum's human companion. I had said some things to her when he had not been present and not paying attention, and vice versa, but we had not seen separate sides of her. I wished that I had a bond to her by blood; as I approached I was able to get an ever clearer impression of her mind and her movements, but it remained frustratingly vague and elusive.

"Which exit should I take?" Varlet's voice broke through my concentration.

"One–B," said Alex, as if in his sleep. "Follow the signs to I–405."

There was Ariane, as if the presence of her mind was bounded by city limits. Her presence solidified and images of the area where she lived leapt suddenly to mind, like the afterimage left after a photographer's flashbulb. She heard us; she awaited us; she showed me her neighborhood again, through the memory of having driven these streets. I had forgotten the pleasures of this experience, as a similar mind came suddenly into plain view. Of course, old Alexander Vassilyevich had gotten the contact first. "Take a left," I said. "Up . . . twenty-nine blocks. And then a right, and up the hill, and right again . . ." I turned to Alex, and he was gazing at me and beaming, sharing the pleasure.

That other mind, though . . . that John . . . his mind was much harder to access, guarded, shuttered; but through the cracks I got a glimpse of incomprehensible complexity. Nonetheless, he did not seem insane to me.

We pulled up to the quaint little white house, almost entirely surrounded by massive trees, with a wild, neglected garden, stones edging the leaf-covered walk up to the front door. A standing cement birdbath, crowned with a sinuous-necked swan, bore a thick coating of moss, and the water of the bath was choked with fallen leaves. But for the soft glow of candlelight coming from some of the windows, the house looked abandoned. Varlet drove up the gravel driveway and pulled in next to a grimy white car that showed evidence of exactly as much attention as the house; I would bet that the car had never once been washed.

The two of them stood at the side door under a gentle yellow porch light, waiting for us. Ariane looked much the same; small of stature, well-proportioned, a riot of red hair and her hands in her pockets. Her stance was challenging, trying to look tough, but why? Perhaps it was out of protectiveness for her gentleman, John, who stood close by her, but not so close as to give her comfort. He just stared at me as I opened the car door and stepped out onto the gravel. He had a pretty face, if a little on the long, horsey, and feminine side, his body was nothing to write home about, and his blank-eyed glare did nothing for his looks. Ariane was too much woman for him.

As suddenly as the sunrise, a welcoming joy abruptly shone out through her. "Risa!" Ariane called, grinning, half-anxious, half-delighted. "I mean . . . El. I'll get it eventually, I promise."

My hard shell disintegrated, too. Poor kitten! So young, without anyone to guide her! No wonder she was afraid all the time, even though it was high time she learned to trust herself, even if she was wrong most of the time—the only other option was paralysis. "That's all right, my darling. It's just a label; you know what's inside." I clutched Ariane in a warm embrace and kissed her on both cheeks, and then on the lips.

John gave an audible swallow.

"You must be John," I surmised, extending my hand to him.

John glanced at the rings glimmering on my fingers, then held his head up straighter, but he did not take my hand. "You . . . must be . . . El," he replied, a tinge of unease in his voice.

Up closer, I supposed his face did have something. Pretty lips, mink eyelashes, but an expression that delivered on Ariane's promise of toughness. A very appealing, stark defiance. This was one who had learned to trust himself, who had never not done so, even when he was crazy and terrified of his reality. His eyes said, *Fuck you and your sparkling carbon; I know what you've come for.*

"It's a pleasure," I said, taking my hand back and smiling *I am not a threat to you* into those coffee-brown eyes. I had gathered reams of information from Ariane in those three kisses; clarifying the way John had been before a few nights ago, before she'd given him the miraculous anodyne, unable to keep his thoughts to himself, terrified of street signs, and sleeping in holes dug in the ground. I had heard his nightmares like a cloud of white noise in the background of my thoughts for more than ten years, but over the last week, that static of chaos had quieted, all but disappeared, replaced by this guarded coolness and logic. It all made sense. His expression softened, collapsed slightly, as he felt that I had figured him out, that I understood, but he shook his head, thinking that I could never understand.

Alexander Vassilyevich emerged from the other side of the car, bundled in his gunmetal Gaultier trench coat, which matched my buttercream one, and a green cashmere scarf around his neck. Ariane embraced him just as eagerly. "It's good to see you, Alex," she said.

"You are even more radiant than I remember," he replied. "But then again, you were only human then."

Alex, Ariane, and I engaged in some cheerful half-fake laughter, which John only acknowledged with a long-suffering sneer. Ariane's smile could not entirely be wiped away. "Well, come in, come in . . ." Ariane glanced back at the car. "What about your driver?"

"Ah, yes . . ." Alex turned his eyes toward the driver's seat of the town car; Varlet, his eyes barely visible underneath the brim of his cap, gave a slight nod and put the car into gear. The car backed down out of the drive and disappeared up the road, swallowed by the dark shadows of the trees. "He's in my service," Alex sighed. "I told him to get us some rooms at a downtown hotel, and get some sleep while he has a chance. He'll return when I call for him. You should have a retainer, too, Ariane; it does make life a great deal easier, having someone to look after the mundane details for you."

Ariane laughed faintly. "I kinda like the mundane details," she shrugged, holding open the kitchen door. John nodded to me; I felt he was not so much being chivalrous as not wishing to have me at his back. Such distrust! I rolled my eyes at him and proceeded inside; Ariane followed, then Alex, and John closed and double-locked the door behind all of us.

Her kitchen was almost appallingly modest after what I had grown used to. There was dust; there were cheap, mismatched kitchen towels; there were flecks of old, dry blood worked into the white paint of the built-in cabinets. She lived like an academic, one who forgot her undoubtedly enormous wealth. I knew Daniel had left her everything, and I knew how much money Daniel had been worth. Why would she not retain someone to come in and dust the windowsills? On the other hand, I should have to get used to rough living now and again, now that Alexander Vassilyevich and I were on our adventure.

"Can I get you anything?" Ariane offered shyly.

I laughed. "You've never had guests here before, have you?" I surmised.

"I don't have much company," Ariane mumbled. "I kinda like being alone. Helps me concentrate."

John gave her a searching look, then walked toward a doorway leading to a hall. Ariane extended her hand after him, indicating that we should follow him.

"Do you have anything to drink?" I asked in the hallway.

"Uh, like what?" Ariane meandered into the study, and busied herself lighting a second candle on the mantel above the unused fireplace. The study was much more well kept; she obviously spent a great deal of time here, reading and thinking and sometimes even sleeping. There was hardly any dust on any of the surfaces. I pictured Ariane on her hands and knees, cleaning it all herself. Monstrous. "I haven't got much . . . ," she mumbled.

"Uh, like *vodka*," I said. "What do you think I meant? Ah." I smiled. Her face took on a blank look of embarrassment. "You don't entertain, so nothing to drink. Nothing except your treated blood in a bottle, am I right? Please don't be insulted, but I think I'll take a pass on that, if you don't mind. Oh, poor Ariane." I rested my palm gently against Ariane's cheek. She was cold, barely warmer than room temperature, and I felt terrible for her, drinking that cold stuff out of plastic, never feeling the fresh living warmth surging through her. I could never be so cruel to myself. "Don't be uptight. I'm your friend. Alex is your friend. You invited us. You haven't got anything to be afraid of. Come on; let's sit, and you can tell me all about your new creation."

She and I sat in the two brown plush chairs, while John sat on the floor at Ariane's feet and Alex perused the bookshelves, his blunt-cut claws gently clicking against the spines of bound journals, textbooks, leather-bound novels, and cheap, thumbed-over paperbacks.

"I call it Orchid," said Ariane, "and I made it for John, but I also took it myself." She placed her palm against mine, lacing our fingers together. Even though her flesh was chilly, her buzzing energy deeply impressed me. Despite only having been changed eleven years ago, her strength and power approached my own levels. Intriguing; a rich gift from Orfeo Ricari, and more power than she knew what to do with. Did he really see so much potential in her, or had he been swayed by lust? I hoped to meet this fool Ricari. "Allow me to show you what it's about," Ariane murmured to me.

Ariane mentally revisited the theory and practice of the compound, the information of her thoughts sliding into my brain like so many razors into slots. I was no scientist, but it didn't matter; I knew it as well as she did, saw it as she did, followed every step of the process along with her nearly instantaneous memories. It almost hurt to learn so much of something so foreign so quickly, but that which did not *quite* hurt always gave me enormous pleasure. "Potassium cyanide," I said to her, taking my hand back, the palm slightly dampened with sweat, and laying it against the side of my neck. "Affecting oxygen uptake. And quantum dots of potassium, at that. Incredible. It would figure that we would need something utterly unnatural to get through our blood. Yes, I never would have thought of it myself."

"That's the way it works, isn't it?" John piped up from the floor. "That's science for you. It's the stuff we hadn't thought of as being possible—or wouldn't let ourselves think of as being possible—that changes things."

"So, did you assist in the theory—" I began to ask.

John cut me off with a wave of his hand. "No. No, that's all her. If she got help, it wasn't from me."

Somewhere in the back of her mind, Ariane thought of a polished sugar bowl shattering into pieces. This made no sense to me, and she hid the details, trying to keep them from John, but also shutting me out. I wondered what these two could possibly have to hide from each other.

John spoke again. "Besides, physics and bioscience only tangentially have anything to do with each other;

nanotech medicine would never have been possible without Heisenberg's equations, but—no offense, Ariane—physics is way ahead of biochem on that score."

"Dude, don't even start." Ariane and John shared a grin. "Science is science."

"Anyway, it's all mathematics in the end," John drawled, lacing his fingers behind his neck.

"I don't understand," Alex broke in, much to my relief. "You have created a therapeutic drug based on a poison?"

"Aren't they all?" said John.

"It all makes sense on the microscopic scale. Our blood is obviously structured differently from human blood," Ariane explained, "and the blood of those who aren't created properly, but manage to survive the process, have yet another different structure. Something like cyanide won't hurt us, but if the compound is unstable, it does affect the way our blood works—hence, the way our minds work. Basic neurochemistry."

Alex sank slowly down onto an empty chair opposite Ariane and me. "I might need a drink after all," he murmured. "I'm a soldier, not a scientist."

I laughed. "Well, I want to try it," I said. "You said it was fun. What's it like? Do you have any?"

"I don't know if I can describe what it's like," Ariane said, flustered. "I believe that it's different for each person who takes it—and it might very likely be different every time. All my experiences have been . . . well, extremely pleasant . . . but it's different every time."

I clapped my hands and bounced in my seat, quite unable to contain myself. "That sounds great! I want to try it! Now!"

Ariane continued to drone on uncertainly. Now that

she had my interest, she was going to draw it out for as long as possible. "It's best if you do it right before bedtime, just in case you fall asleep—"

I was beginning to lose my patience. We had been driving for a night and a half, I had given August Beagle pool cleaner to stick up his nose, and I wasn't about to take no for an answer from barely-a-vampire Ariane. "Do you have any? Please, Ariane!"

"Steady on, now, kitten," Alexander said. "Don't be pushy."

"You ask me not to be pushy? I'm always pushy. It gets results." I shrugged. "You haven't answered my question. You *do* want me to try it, don't you? You need more subjects."

"I've got about . . . six more doses at what's been demonstrated as a therapeutic amount for John. I think it's really up to him . . . ," Ariane evaded.

John made a scoffing noise. "You just started on a truckload more. I'll be all right until tomorrow, you know."

"I'll look after her, Ariane," Alexander offered. "I don't want to take it. Not tonight, anyway."

We all stared at Ariane until she dropped her eyes to the floor and mumbled, "All right, I'll get the works. . . ."

"Hurrah!" I crowed.

"Not much to do down in L.A., is there?" John said quietly.

I gave him a carefully measured smile. He didn't flinch. I began to like him more and more all the time. "There's never been anything to *do* anywhere, but bloody murder," I pointed out. "Till now. And I'm not about to miss it."

* * *

"I haven't done this in a long time," I said as Ariane set up the works, lightly tying off my arm, unwrapping a fresh blue cap insulin syringe. The drug itself was a dark, viscous liquid in a sealed bottle. Eyeing the syringe carefully, Ariane withdrew a few ticks. This whole process, the ceremony of it, made my mouth water and my head go foggy.

"Drugs?" Ariane said mildly.

"Needles," I clarified. The sharp prick of the tiny needle was so minimally painful that it felt good, with a promise of glories to come. Already I was speaking freely, untangling the associated memories. "There hasn't been much need for the last ninety years. But before . . . oh, God, yes. It became a pleasure, the needle. I did a lot of morphine on our journey out of Russia, didn't I, Sasha?"

Alex said nothing and looked away. He might have felt me slowly moving away from him as the cool stream of the drug entered my vein; the room became like a soft, enfolding brown velvet blanket. I couldn't stop talking—my tongue had a will of its own. "I left everything I knew as it was being destroyed by people I barely knew existed. All I knew was that I was getting away from my family, from my brother, from the priests and the tax collector and the empty stone rooms . . . and going on an adventure with the one I loved." In my view, Alexander, standing anxiously by the bookshelves, grew blurry and impressionistic. "There was a train accident on the first night."

"There was no accident," Alex said.

I heard him, but I was off, riding a rapidly swelling wave of heightened sensation, soft and gentle, but thrilling at the same time. I could not have told you which direction was up or down; it was all the same beautiful dimension. I closed my eyes and began to drift. "I was . . . badly injured, falling from the train. Because I could still walk, we didn't stop to get the damage fixed. We splinted and bandaged as best we could, but I was in so much pain I kept losing consciousness. Morphine was the only thing that got us out of Russia. I needed massive quantities to sustain me. Alexander cleared out an entire Moscow pharmacist's stock."

"And an entire Moscow pharmacist," Alex murmured.

"You needed his blood. There's no sin in that. I begged him," I said. My voice was so heavy, slow, and thick that I wondered if I could even still be heard, or if the words were just unfurling, bubbling up inside my mind. "I begged him to end the pain. I begged him to make me like him. . . ."

I was swimming in warm brandy, as far away as it was possible to get from that frozen plain, from those frigid stables, the iced-over stations that I had been trying to describe. I wanted to discuss the contrast between the two, but no sounds came out when I tried to speak.

"Is she all right?" That would be my husband.

"Yeah, yeah . . . El, you okay?"

I waved my hand to assure them and found my voice again, though when I heard it, it didn't sound like me at all. "Better than. Please . . . silence . . . please," I sighed. "Come here. Alex, come and hold my hand; let's please not talk. I can see every word we say like it's been stitched onto the world. And that's a shame. I'll tell you later what it's like, the enormity of it."

Alex settled onto the floor beside me and cradled my head in his lap, gently stroking my hair. Next to us, Ariane and John held their positions at the chair, Ariane seated on it and John at her feet. I could hear the quiet, crisp sound of his fingers stroking the fine hairs on her bare ankle. We all lapsed into a warm and quiet peace, loosed, for a change, from the strictures of time and released into an infinite *now*.

How could I be selfish? Under the influence of the drug, I felt all my selfishness vanish, and I wanted nothing more than to share my happiness with those who I loved best, and even those who I had not previously loved, those who I didn't even know. Every creature deserved to experience this bliss.

After a while, I had an odd feeling; a mounting excitement, a purposeful movement in the world, toward me, toward this soft, dim room. My call of joy had been received. I decided to say something. "Do you feel them? They heard me. They're coming."

Ariane said, "Who?"

Her voice bothered me; it was far too hard-edged, too paranoid for how good we had all been feeling. "Can't you feel them?" I asked. "Can't you hear them? I hear them. You hear them, don't you, Alexander?"

My husband gave a sigh of acknowledgment.

"Who?" Ariane demanded. "Who is coming?"

"They heard me," I said, my voice a low subsonic throb. "And they are curious. Samuel Rifkin. And Leland! Leland Quary—I've not seen him for so long! Oh, I'm so glad he still thinks of me. They overheard . . ." I paused, listening to the wordless, staggered little moan of anxiety that Ariane had made. "You've got to understand, the way I feel . . . I felt you, too, Ariane. You were in my dreams. I felt your ecstasy without understanding it—but now I do! It's like having a gigantic, screaming orgasm, and it's not until later that you realize that the neighbors could hear. But in a way, you're not sorry—"

"So they're on their way here," Ariane said, "and they want to take Orchid. Do I have that right?"

"Looks that way," came John's dry voice. "Good thing you started on another batch, pet."

Perhaps it was wrong of me to laugh right then, but I couldn't help it; it would be so good to see Leland again. And already, even though I hadn't started to come down yet, I wanted to take more Orchid.

I truly had been waiting for it all my life.

IX

BOLD IN HER BREECHES

JADZIA KOPERNIK

In all this time of being alive, I hadn't ever found much that was better than lying naked on a disarrayed bed as the sky purpled at the horizon, my naked boy splayed out next to me, his eyes squeezed shut in ecstasy as we listened to the same Diana Ross song for the tenth time in a row. I was pleased that my boy shared my appreciation for the operatic drama of that particular strain of late 1960s/early 1970s pop music; the Supremes, Ronnie Spector, Tina Turner, Donna Summer—women with voices strained to the limit with existential terror and worse, hope. He had never listened closely to that music before, and I writhed with glee watching him experience it, eyes rolling back in bliss, as helplessly transported as I had been when I first heard it, twenty or more years ago, when it was already ten years out of style. The right albums transcended fashion and would always be exactly right for someone at some time in her life. Orfeo and I gorged ourselves on it. I had been carrying my record collection around with me, and on that first night when we came together again, we bought—from a desperate, recently evicted artist on the street—a dusty, dinged-up old player that looked like it was a good sneeze away from total collapse. It still transmitted the music, though, through a filter of faint static that enfolded us in a perfect, gauzy, Neverland fantasy.

I literally worried that I might die from joy; I had never felt it so strongly before.

Truthfully, it was pure ecstasy to see Orfeo again, to spend days at a time in bed, fucking and talking to each other like we'd never get another chance, pausing only to light another candle or flip over the record so that we could hear "I Hear a Symphony" one more time. It was eerily like old times, as if no time at all had passed between 1848 and now, except that we had music in the bedroom with us, something we had always wistfully longed for in those dusty, drafty Parisian apartments. He had not changed—of course not!—except that, of course, he had. So much had happened to him since we had last been together; over one hundred fifty years that had stiffened him, hardened him, polished him to an impenetrable mirror finish, like a bit of petrified willow. So heavily armored against emotion! I took even greater delight in seeing how quickly and completely I swept aside that protective shell and began gorging myself on the soft underbelly of his subconscious. This often took the form of tickling him until he shrieked with laughter, tears pouring from his eyes onto my waiting tongue. I licked his salty emotions away and savored the sweetness underneath.

"You needed this," I told him. And he agreed.

I'd needed this, too.

"So you're a model," he said during our first break from shagging. The sunrise had already come, and a painful glow assailed my eyes from underneath the hems of the velvet curtains at his windows. I resolved to put something in front of that leak as soon as I was able to tear myself away from him.

"I *was* a model," I corrected him with a yawn. "I got scouted, hanging out in a nightclub with some girls who I'd just met. I think it was because I was about half a meter taller than all the other girls, and I was wearing this pink leather jacket I found in Amsterdam, so I was rather visible from across the room. And no, I don't still have the jacket. Get over it."

"I didn't say anything," he grinned, and squeezed my breast. "Why would you want to be a model, though?"

"I felt like making a little money. It's actually quite a bit more difficult than I had anticipated. Mostly it's holding very still, or walking ridiculously and holding the same dying fish expression on your face. In ridiculously high heels. I tried it as a joke. But I was good at it, and it was a fun physical challenge. I got asked back. I was even treated quite well for what I was. Money was good, but it wasn't everything. When it stopped being fun, I took off."

"So what's this?" He glanced over the wrinkled, creased pamphlet that had signaled my presence to him over on the Spanish Steps. At last, I had found a justification for my sentimental attachment to the stupid flier; I looked laughably absurd, as did all the other girls, and the clothes were awful, but still, it was in print, a concrete proof that I existed.

"That was from last season. I paid the kid ten lire to drop it in your lap. I've probably done ten shows for that same design group since that one. I did three shows last week in Milan. Easy, small-stakes stuff, made in Milan for the consumption of the Milanese. But as soon as that one was finished, I left without even bothering with a good-bye. The great thing is, I'm probably already forgotten." I smiled and touched his chest with my palm. "They won't find out anything. Name, residence, country of origin—they think I'm a Kazakh named Anna. One of those tall skinny girls who ran away, who keeps her identity a secret because she's on the run."

"You were always a master of invention," Orfeo said with a smile.

"It's fun to pretend. They don't need to know more than my measurements, my shoe size, and whether or not I'm psychotically evil. I took my payments in cash; it's not that unusual."

"You ought to be careful how much of yourself ends up in the magazines, my dear Georgie."

"I am not particularly memorable," I said. "There are so many thousands of faces in magazines, who could possibly remember them? Any particular woman's appearance is a disposable commodity, and the world takes no notice of it if it's not explicitly told to do so. It's no longer anything to do with talent. I was curious about this process, and also just bored and susceptible to flattery." He trailed his finger across my neck, stroking the short edges of my hair at the temples. "It was something to do, you know. Something I hadn't done before. And you?"

"I am extremely dull—I only ever do the same things," Orfeo said.

"There is no shame in consistency. You still paint? Write poems?" I asked him, and he nodded. "And I am doing the same thing, too. I do something different constantly. It's how I get over being disappointed. I wouldn't stop if I could. Oh, Orfeo, I've done so many things; I've seen so many things."

"As have I," he said, still smiling, "without making any particular effort."

"Ah, but how much have you enjoyed what you've done and seen, in this life where you seek no variety?" I parried.

"And how much have you?"

At such an impasse I would kiss him into silence.

He would discover all in time, and the more I kissed him, the sooner he could know. Of course, this let him in to me, too. I tried to prepare myself for the opening of the floodgates of his memories, but I found that I was helpless against his pain, his rage, and his shame. At least one aspect of him had changed in the intervening years: his sense of personal terror and uncertainty had become so muted that I could barely perceive it, and it was no longer his own safety he feared. I had felt all of this in him, distant and vague inside me all this time, but I found it more convenient to classify it as a feature of my past, and try to ignore it and continue on with the specifics of daily life. But Orfeo was not in the past; he existed in the present, in my own world, a part of my body and soul, retaining his attachment through the physical distance of thousands of miles. I knew about his Berlin, I knew about his Hong Kong (and resolved to share some of my own stories of that place), I knew about his repeated attempts to return to the earth for a final sleep, all of which had been thwarted by the clumsy meddling of human hands. I knew that he had created offspring, one of whom had gotten himself killed, one of which was broken and mad.

What was strange to him was that I wouldn't judge him for anything he had done. He had to relearn that. I had never judged him before—why would I begin now? He was my creation and I loved him unconditionally. As long as he forgave me for walking out on him—and I knew immediately that he had—there was nothing to be concerned about, and we could loll around in bed, working through all the ways that we could remember to make each other come.

Unfortunately, no lovers can stay in bed forever, else I am confident that Orfeo and I would still be there. Eventually hunger kicked us out of bed. We went through the same decision-making process as human newlyweds—just a quick bite on the corner, or a leisurely meal in a chic atmosphere?

Orfeo chose the latter, his desires continuing to run concurrently with mine. I chose some fresh clothing from my knapsack and pretended not to notice as he gazed longingly at me as I dressed. "What are you staring at?" I asked him.

"Oh—you," he answered. "Your style. You do wear clothes very well."

"Yes, and I only had to wait two hundred years to get a pair of trousers that fit."

He was staring at me and thinking jealously of all the women I'd had in my lifetime. The number of women Orfeo Ricari had ever fucked could be counted on one hand, without bothering to involve the thumb. It was slightly stupid; he could have any woman he wanted, quite a few of them without having to resort to hypnotism, but his inner core of faith prevented him from following through on his carnal desires toward women, or even taking them particularly seriously. Of course, he had no such moral barrier separating him from his desire for men. Again, nothing that I could really comprehend, as I had no moral barrier between me and anything, or any one, that I wanted. I had always loved his contradictions.

We went together to a nightclub that neither of us had ever visited before, and to which we would never come again. We drifted gently through a crowd of limousines and half-dressed, eager people until we reached the front of the line.

"Does this place have a VIP area?" I asked the doorman in a gritty Detroit drawl, cocking my hip and doing my best to resemble the models who had so recently been my comrades. It wasn't so much for the doorman's benefit—he was trapped between my will and Orfeo's, and he would do whatever we suggested to him—but for the benefit of those still standing in line waiting to get inside. I had long ago learned that if I wanted to steal something, it was best to look utterly confident and relaxed, as though what was happening was the most natural thing in the world.

The doorman nodded numbly, let us pass by, and tapped the shoulder of another hulking guard. "Show these good people to the back," he said to the guard.

Once in back, Orfeo and I split up, made rapid acquaintances, and took our time satisfying ourselves with the blood of the Very Important People. It tasted exactly like the blood of the Less Important, just with different chemicals and a different flavor of stress byproducts.

Shortly, Orfeo and I found ourselves back together again, leaning against each other on a gray velvet sofa. "I wish I could enjoy this even more," he sighed heavily. "I can't stop thinking about her."

"Yes," I agreed reluctantly, "I can hear her, too. She's feeling an increasing sense of panic—it's as if she doesn't care who hears her. Someone should probably assist her soon, or someone else, someone without any emotional investment whatsoever, is going to silence her."

His shocked expression told me all I needed to know. *"Silence her?"*

"Orfeo, think of how grumpy you are when her unhappiness disturbs your sleep—and *you* love her. There are others, you know—so many others, ones we have never known. As it was, in those first few years after I left you, I met several, previously unknown to me, whom I had to persuade against tracking you down and chopping your head off, so they would be spared the perception of your grief." I squeezed his hands to take away some of the sting of my words. "There are many. Some of them ancient and sensitive. Some of them botched and psychotic and unable to protect their own minds against those of others. As it is, you have left her in danger. You have no idea of the other vampires surrounding her, or of their levels of restraint."

"But . . . but she's formulating something to help the mad ones," he said. "If it's even possible, she'll be the one to do it. Perhaps she can redeem herself."

"Oh, her usefulness was never in question. Her discretion . . . her self-restraint, her maturity, another matter entirely. I'm just telling you that she is at risk. She wants your help."

"I don't want to go," he murmured. "I don't want to see her. I don't want to see John."

I grinned and stroked his hair back from his brow. "I didn't want to see you, either," I informed him. "I didn't ever want to see you again. Not because of what you are, but because of what you symbolized. I can never see you without also seeing Maria, without grieving for Maria, without feeling betrayed by Maria. And yet I would not now trade the sight of you for—" I stopped short, unable to think of anything else that would compare.

"For a swift and easy death?" he suggested, smiling vaguely.

I averted my eyes. "I don't long for death," I said. "You and I are different in that way."

"Haven't you ever?"

"Oh, of course I have. But not to any practical extent. I realized that my wishes were childish, just a wish to get out of doing something that I didn't want to do, something I didn't want to acknowledge or take responsibility for."

"I understand the true meaning of your words," he said stiffly.

I had to laugh. "Oh, Feo, everything is about you, isn't it?"

He gave me the kind of look that meant that he wished he had a drink to throw in my face. The only thing I could do was kiss him, because the expression was adorable and made my heart swell enormously with love. He squirmed away from the touch of my lips, his face burning hot scarlet like he had been slapped on both cheeks, in the same places where he blushed when he was a young human barely old enough to be called a man. I grabbed his wrists, held him still, and gave him another kiss. "Stop being such a girl," I said.

"Someone has to be the girl," he sniped, "and we all know it won't be you, *George*."

I moved one of his hands to my breast and the other to my crotch. "You're mean," I purred. "Nobody has to be the girl. We can both just be people. I am not condemning you, don't you understand?"

He kissed me on his own then, his fingers gently clasping my erogenous zones. "Would you be willing to go?" he asked.

"Go? To Ariane?" I laughed. Now I wished *I* had a drink to throw into *his* face. "She doesn't know me from Adam."

"She knows you," he insisted. "She has seen you in my mind. You are my maman, and her great-grandmaman." I shrugged a little, not caring for the terminology, and he lightly brushed his lips against mine. "You are related, and she knows that you are beloved to me. Go to her. Comfort her. Let her know that my heart is with her—and find out for me what's really going on there. You'll be so much better at it than I. You are such a good detective."

And, yes, I have been known to be susceptible to flattery.

The next night, we went to yet another new nightclub with a VIP section, this one in the penthouse of a high-rise hotel. The restricted section was crowded with French and Italian film stars, models, and third-tier idle rich. It amused me no end to spend time in places such as these, dressed as I was, with my unstyled haircut, my rubber-soled running shoes, no makeup, no jewelry, no mobile phone, and yet to be gazed at and envied specifically because I was so minimal, so original, so simply chic. It was a joke that I could continue to laugh at, at least for right now. I had been dressing almost exactly like this for the better part of a hundred years, but until recently I was considered a transvestite, and, with a baggy jacket to hide my modest but unmistakable breasts, usually passed as a man. Of course, I turned this misunderstanding to fuel for my adventures.

How strange that in this day and age, I was considered a beauty without having to alter my appearance at all!

As I was moving on to my fifth blood donor of the night, I felt a sweaty hand settle on my shoulder. Under different circumstances, the owner of the hand would not have survived his next breath, but I already knew before I turned around that I had simply been spotted by someone that I knew.

"Anna! Oh my God! How fabulous! How have you been?"

It was Lila Jacobs. I was shocked and dismayed to think that she remembered me; I had assumed that since her thoughts were mostly concerned with herself, she wouldn't need any psychic promptings to put little old me out of her mind. I had underestimated my own charisma, apparently—I hadn't seen Lila for almost a year, since fashion week last September. I saw her in the house when I walked for Prinzi, or she saw me on the runway, and she'd barged backstage to harass Giotto Prinzi, and we'd gotten to talking. Then, in one of the makeshift dressing rooms, she let me finger-fuck her, and I was so pleased to have the opportunity that I'd forgotten to take her blood. She was a terrible person, but she was also a luscious dark goddess, and it wasn't as though I was interested in talking with her. We duplicated the experiment twice more that week and then she disappeared, to Tibet or Phuket or something like that; I finished my work and took my money and went to check out the ladies in Stockholm.

I could have just silenced Lila Jacobs, but too many people were paying attention to us right now, and I didn't feel up to the effort of wiping the minds of thirty people.

"Good, good," I said, slipping back into my Russian accent as if donning a dirty silk robe. "And where have you been?"

"Oh, darling, everywhere really. I've been in *Paris* for the last week. I *was* in L.A. before that." She leaned in close to me. "Isn't it terrible what happened to Rachell?"

It took me a moment to determine who she was talking about. Lila assumed that I knew every single person involved in the fashion industry on a first-name basis, just because she did. Still, if there was a single vague first name that I could twig, it was that of dainty drug diva Rachell Reed. "Oh, I have been in a sex cave for the last few weeks," I said. "What happened?"

"Oh my God—oh my God, you don't know? It was everywhere in the news. You really were in a cave. Or dead." She actually looked slightly green. "I don't know how you could have missed that. Ugh."

I pushed the hangers-on away from us and led her over to the entrance to the service hallway. I felt Orfeo creeping up on us, listening hard with those big rabbit ears of his. Lila glanced around the room, her blue contact lenses clicking against her expansive false eyelashes. "It was horrible," she whispered. "There was a bad batch of ching they got hold of. It wasn't just her—it also killed August Beagle and Debbie Hayes and a couple of total strangers."

"Killed?" I said. "That bad?"

Lila suddenly gave a gigantic sniff, as if being reminded of cocaine immediately made her want some.

It was strange; it didn't smell like she'd had any at all recently, unheard of for Lila. She had been doing plenty of chain-smoking, though. "There was something like . . . like Drain-X in it," she said, still whispering. "Some kind of nasty industrial chemical. They were all dead within minutes. It's crazy. I don't know what was going on there. All of a sudden, a lot of kids I used to hang out with started OD'ing and turning up dead."

This immediately piqued my interest. "Who else did you hang out with?"

For a moment, I saw the person, the apprehensive young woman, underneath Lila's façade of bitchery and wealth and taste. "You might think this is crazy," she said.

I grasped her shoulder and stared into the black circles in the center of the bright-blue plastic disks on her eyes. "You can trust me," I said. "I won't think it's crazy."

She swallowed, her eyelids fluttering as she tried to keep me out of her mind. There could only be one reason why she was able to keep me out of her head: something or someone had put up a barrier between a truth inside her and her ability to verbally express it.

"They're vampires," I said on her behalf.

Lila nodded.

"They drink your blood," I said. "And it's all right, isn't it? It doesn't hurt or anything, does it?"

With difficulty, her tongue curved and lifted. "They're real," she said.

"They didn't get you," I guessed, talking mostly to myself. "They got everybody else, but they missed you."

Lila shook her head, breaking eye contact with me. I didn't need it anymore; she wouldn't keep anything from me. "Yeah," she agreed, too shocked yet to be frightened. "I guess so. I just got lucky. I happened to not be there. And it's enough to make me wonder about Young Lad. They say he died of a stroke, but that *is* odd. It's too soon. They were really the only connection we all had."

"Are they still there?" Orfeo asked, gazing at her. He was an even bigger fool for bombastic, artificial beauty than I was. It almost made me laugh; the top of his head barely reached her shoulder. She looked over at him, her forehead wrinkling a little as if in confusion.

"I don't know," Lila said in a small voice.

"What are their names? Maybe we know them," he said.

"We?" I asked crisply, staring at him.

"Oh, come on," he said, rolling his eyes at me. "It doesn't matter in the end. I want to know who it is."

"El and Alex," Lila said. "Some Russian last name; I can't remember it now."

These names meant nothing to me, but Orfeo frowned. "Alexander and Elisabeta," he said slowly, "Revikoff." I arched my eyebrow at this revelation, and he clarified, "Friends of Daniel's. This is knowledge I got from Ariane—Daniel never told me about it, obviously, but he told her everything. Daniel was having an affair with Elisabeta back in the fifties, living in the house with her and Alexander, her husband. They were all quite fond of each other, but they turned their backs on him with the whole Ariane business. Very protective of their privacy, which makes me wonder how they could stand Daniel. . . ."

"They had great blow, great brown, K, everything," Lila said. "And El's got mad style. Rich as fuck. They were, uh . . . diamond mine billionaires or something."

"No, they were vampires," I corrected her softly. "Well, I guess they could be both."

"I imagine that the Revikoffs are not there anymore," said Orfeo, "if bridges were burned so completely."

Lila struggled to keep the fear from her face. "Are you going to have to bump me off?" she asked, voice trembling. "Am I a bridge that has to be burnt?"

I put my arm around her shoulders. "No, Li," I said soothingly, "you are *the* supermodel. You are now, especially. You won't tell anybody anything, because there's nothing to tell. It's a shame about Rachell Reed, but you're glad to have done with it. You've really moved on with your life, and you realize that drugs are the wrong solution. Am I right?"

"Well," Lila said, with a slight smile, "everything but that last part."

I had done well; she was relaxed, and wouldn't question the last five minutes of her memory simply disappearing. "Living on the edge, dying young. The only thing that means anything to you kids these days. What are you waiting for?" I kissed the side of her face and pushed her gently back toward her entourage.

Orfeo stared after her. "I feel very apprehensive," he said.

I did too, but I just shrugged. "Why? It's just some dead actors."

"I think I know where the Russians went," he said.

Our party mood died a violent death. We went back to Orfeo's room and got undressed and lay on the bed with a zinc-white splash of moonlight illuminating our nude bodies, but he was so preoccupied that he didn't even squirm or protest when I kissed him, only lay there, his mind wrapped in opaque thought.

He was listening across the world, really listening

instead of passively hearing for the first time in many years, focusing on Ariane. I could not take precedence in his mind, so I settled for clinging to him, my fingertips splayed over his chest, pulsing faintly with his strong, blood-fueled heartbeat, lending my concentration to his, focusing him like a lens.

This also allowed me to hear what he received; unfortunately I could not make sense of what I perceived. I picked up on a strong, bizarre, transcendent muddle of ecstatic impulses interlaced with fear and uncertainty.

Orfeo, please hear me. This is real and we're doing it and it's amazing but I don't know what to do next and they're all here and there's more coming and I wish the night would come. Orfeo, please hear me.

"What does she mean, there's more coming?" I whispered.

"Ssh," Orfeo said, but without conviction. "They all want it. Do you understand? How many times have you sought out drunkards so that you could be drunk too? How many times have you cursed when the morphine wore off too quickly?" I had to nod. "This is something we can take that they can't. This is ours. And it heals the sick in mind. I just realized I haven't heard John since I saw you. At first I thought I was just too distracted and he slipped from my mind, but we both know that should be impossible. And yet I know he's not dead, which means that he now has control over what comes into or goes out of his mind."

"Without dexterity, perhaps?" I suggested. "Everyone out?"

"Better than the alternative," Orfeo said, opening his eyes and gazing at me. "Please, will you go to her for me? As my ambassador? I don't know these Revikoffs, nor do I trust them. I am suspicious of any 'friends' of Daniel's, particularly ones with a tangled and sordid history. And I don't know what John is like now, but if I know him at all, he has stepped aside from Ariane and is unwilling to provide her support. I think she needs you. She needs a friend."

"You really love her."

The moonlight gleamed across his open eyes again. He looked impatient and stern. "Yes," he said. "I really love her. Just because I left doesn't mean I don't love her."

"That's right," I said, and took the advantage of his attention to kiss him. A few moments later I put the needle onto the record and whispered to him, "Yes, I'll go."

Intercontinental airline travel, for the sunlight-averse among us, could only be accomplished in a series of short hops and overnight flights. Again, an adventure.

In Newark, New Jersey, I changed into my costume as a modest Muslim in floor-length skirt and long sleeves, with a yashmak over my face, dark sunglasses, and gloves to cover my arms and wrists. It was secretly hilarious to note the reactions garnered by my change of clothing—it was as if the veil had struck me blind, the Americans gaped at me so openly. Then again, perhaps that was simply how Americans were; under the right circumstances, they were charmingly childlike instead of rude, gawking village idiots.

Before arriving in Portland, I slipped to the rear lavatory and changed back into my usual clothes. The expressions on the faces of my fellow passengers suddenly made the whole trip worth it; so many conflicting emotions flowed through them, especially the ones who, for a moment, mistook me for a man. Still, I turned their attention away from me, filling them with embarrassment for staring. I turned to my sleeping neighbor to replenish my exhausted, depleted blood, draping a blanket over us as I gently nicked and sucked at the young boy's thumb. I had not been very aware of my weakening state, mentally absorbed as I was in the details of travel with counterfeit identity documents, but as I swallowed the child's blood leaking from the puncture wounds, I felt a vicious punch of oxygen that made me so dizzy I moaned out loud and slid out from under the blanket. A flight attendant asked me anxiously if I was all right, and I told him I was just worn out from my flight from Kraków. It was only partially a lie; I had been fleeing Kraków for almost two hundred years now.

The climate in Oregon was mild, still warm, but with a threat of colder weather so far underneath that the human population probably couldn't sense it. I knew I would not be recovering from the mild, drunkish disorientation caused by the sweetness of the air for some time, so I resolved to enjoy it while I could, before my body became acclimated to it. I staggered cheerfully outdoors to the loading lanes and the taxi rank, and began scanning for an available car, struggling to keep my eyes open. The violet of the sky had begun to warm, stir, fatten itself on the coming sun. What a beautiful horizon, bumpy with trees.

Despite the ungodly hour, I was not alone. The humans passed, swirled, jumped into cars, traded embraces; but I was not alone.

"Would you like to share a taxi?"

A nice-looking man in an overcoat too warm for the weather, hat in hand, brown eyes, perhaps forty, badly thinning hair and a smile that managed to be apologetic and wicked at the same time; he looked as though he had stepped into the wrong time, but that he was correct in and of himself, that it was the slick contours of the twenty-first century that were unnatural. Only he would be able to sneak up on me without my noticing; only he would make me feel that sweet pang of happiness. He grinned at me and the yellow streetlights glittered on his fangs.

"Arthur Chicot, my old friend," I said in French, "are we going to the same place?"

"I was hoping you knew where it was, my dear Lady Georgina," said Arthur.

I glanced over at the lacy horizon. "We're going to terrify the poor girl," I ventured.

"Yes, most probably. Shall we give her until tomorrow? I don't know about you," he said, "but I'm used up and worn out." A taxicab swung in to meet us. "Shall we get a room?"

"Yes, that'll be just the thing." I leaned forward into the driver's seat, holding out the sheet of paper upon which Orfeo had written the address of the house that he had bought in this city to provide Ariane and John with a home. "Do you think you can recommend a hotel that's pretty near to this address?" I asked the driver. At his assent, I sat back, grinned at Arthur for a good long time, then took him into my arms. "It's been years, my darling!"

"Any excuse for a party," was his response.

X

HUNTING

<u>ARIANE DEMPSEY</u>

At least I got them all to agree to meet me outside my house, practically spraining my brain envisioning the Greenhills cemetery until I sensed acknowledgment. I didn't want them all crowding into my kitchen, grinning demands at me. Maybe it was primitive of me, but I wanted to preserve some illusion of sanctuary, wanted to exist here for just a little bit longer without the opinions of others making me see my place in a different light.

After getting home from OMI, I lay in bed with John until the sun came up, knowing I'd have my illusions for at least another day. Even so, I was too anxious to sleep, even stretched out in bed with John; just lying in bed with him used to be an instant source of comfort and relaxation, but tonight it just wouldn't work. He drifted off, and I moved away from him and stared at the shadow-coated walls.

I wanted badly to open up the blinds and see what

must have been a clear, idyllic blue autumn morning sky, maybe a tiny cloud fragmenting into cotton candy spun from gold.

Beside me, John's corpselike sleeping body weighted and chilled the bed. I took some macabre comfort in his utter stillness, with no outward indications of life whatsoever, not even a perceptible flicker from his mind to inform me that he was dreaming. He'd told me earlier that night that he realized he wasn't dreaming since taking Orchid—not just blind to the dreams and memories of other people and other vampires, but not even perceiving his own dreams. Perhaps he wasn't dreaming at all; I had no idea if dream-state sleep was as essential for vampires as it was for humans, but we all processed information, including receiving messages, when we slept. He claimed to be glad to be rid of dreaming, but to me it sounded like being grateful to have a sore limb amputated; I resolved to experiment with his dose and bring his dreams back.

I had been experimenting with dosage and administration myself over the last several days. If I ingested the serum solution, it took effect even more quickly than by injection. Our physiology was designed with extremely absorbent qualities of the mucous membranes of the mouth. I could not hold a mouthful of blood in my mouth for more than a few seconds before it simply soaked into me; the same was true for Orchid, but with an extra delight added to the pleasure of nourishment.

An oral dose of .0004 milligrams—twenty percent of my first test dose—had a pleasingly mild sedative effect, accompanied by a warm, trembly, sensual feeling in my limbs and a corresponding emotional lift, but I didn't slip into an entirely separate mental state or become drowsy. Ingesting less than that had barely any noticeable effect; it might have a therapeutic use if taken regularly. John had responded best to the same .002 as I'd first given him. After the first night, his euphoria, disorientation, and the overwhelming urge to sleep considerably lessened, but eventually Orchid still knocked him out.

By 9:30 in the morning, half-delirious from fatigue and sick of my racing thoughts, I took twice the minimum effective dose and lay on the farthest edge of the bed from John's rigid, livid body until I drifted softly away.

The next I knew, I was bolt awake, every vein in my body raw and ravenous. John stood naked before the unshuttered window, an empty blood bag in his hand, staring out at the twilight.

"They'll be in the cemetery in thirty minutes," he said.

I nearly tore the door off the cube fridge, and desperately gulped down a bottle, then a second one. I could be greedy; both the cube fridge and the large-capacity one in the kitchen were completely packed. I had a full bar—whole blood, fresh-frozen plasma, RBCs, washed RBCs, leukoreduced—nearly all the products that were delivered to me once a week for my research purposes, except for several pints of whole blood and all of the serum, which I'd set aside.

I got a sudden craving for the luke, and staggered to the kitchen. There were only two packs—it was expensive—but I was damned if I wasn't going to have one of them right now and remind myself of the taste of it.

John followed me. "What are you doing?" he asked curiously.

I was standing in front of the open fridge door, guzzling the luke out of the foil packet like a TV teenager with a carton of milk. I couldn't answer him for a while, even after I'd emptied the packet, closed the fridge, and stepped away.

"Are you all right?" he asked dubiously. "You're really red in the face."

I felt heavy, grounded, and thoroughly chilled, and when I looked down at my arm, I saw it robustly flushed, like I'd just been working out. That was more than I usually ever drank all at once like that. "I think I'm feeling their hunger," I said, my tongue thick in my mouth.

His eyes went momentarily distant, then became fully alert again, as though he had peeked out and then thought better of it and gone back inside. "Come on," he said. "As much as I'd love to have you naked for the rest of the night, it's going to be a bit brisk out. Should be gorgeous, though . . . clear as a bell, Mars up, Orion rising . . ."

Back in the bedroom, we pulled on the same clothes we'd been wearing for the last few days—his ancient, half-bald corduroys and D.A.R.E. T-shirt, my drawstring velour pants and clingy silk sweater. There was a dark droplet stain on the sleeve of my top; when I squeezed it, it crumbled, so it was not my blood or John's blood. It had to be Orchid, spilled from the tip of the syringe.

I felt a sudden spike of rage at wasting even a drop of Orchid, because there was so little of it in existence. Then I remembered that I was already making more of it; I had the raw materials and the clearance to obtain more, a nice, clean, private laboratory, and an assistant.

I could be greedy.

"What's that smile for?" John asked suddenly.

"Do you want to do a triple-ought four?" I asked, just as suddenly.

His eyes darted back and forth, and a smile quivered at the left corner of his mouth. "You mean . . . get high before we go?"

"I don't see why not." Already I was scrambling back to the cube fridge, John close behind. "I can't imagine that it could do anything harmful. Chances are it'll wear off subjectively before we even get there."

"As long as you're not driving," he said, deadpan.

"No, no, officer, we'll walk." I drew down a miniscule amount of the fluid into a syringe. "Open wide . . ."

I squirted the tiny dose into his mouth. John couldn't resist flinching as the jet of fluid shot out of the needle and hit his tongue. "Dear God, why would anyone ever let a man do this?" he snickered, then broke into convulsive laughter.

"I dunno, there's a certain pleasure involved." I gave myself a squirt, also, and felt the spark of the drug flowing into my bloodstream, carried throughout my entire body with a single heartbeat. It all happened so quickly that I never tasted it; the cyanide should have made it virulently bitter.

We stood there for a moment, making ambiguous sounds and smiling suggestively at each other.

"I guess we should go do that thing," I said.

"It's a beautiful night out," he said by way of agreement.

"I should bring some Orchid with us," I said.

"I think that's a fine idea."

I hastily prepped another, larger syringe, and drew

up half a mill, capping the needle and sliding it into the pocket of my pants. "You okay?" I asked him.

"I'm great," he said.

We walked side by side along the shoulder of the road toward the cemeteries that crowned the west hills nearest my house. The moon was in competition with the streetlights to produce the brightest glow; I could barely make out the stars through all the light-noise. The traffic was still steady at that hour when people were returning from dinner or late shopping, or heading out to parties or clubs. At first I wanted to walk slowly, to savor the gentle warmth of the Orchid, but as the sidewalks ended, John said, "Bugger this creeping; I want to meet them," and flicked away up around a corner. I discovered in catching up with him that it was just as pleasant to rush as to meander, to run on the balls of my feet, to put distance behind me in a blink.

At once the hill before us was dotted with pale tombstones, gold and beige in the streetlights. John did not pause for reverence; he approached the high stone fence, jumped to the top of it, and disappeared over the edge. I scaled the wall more slowly, not as familiar with what was on the other side. A thick, immaculately manicured lawn rose up like a wave flecked with marble spray.

As soon as I had cleared the wall, my head began to swim. So many minds so close to the surface; I couldn't shut them out as easily as I could human minds. John had paused, too, his expression suddenly unsure. I took his hand and we went up the hill together.

Over the rise of that hill, the lawn began to descend again and the gravestones became denser and more varied. Five figures stood in silence beside a massive, sprawling elm. Not a single voice could be heard with the ear, but my head felt like a busy newsroom of criss-crossing data.

All at once, the five turned and looked at me and John. I almost turned around and ran back home, but John gripped my hand tightly and strode toward them, holding his head up.

El and Alex stood in their matching dyed-leather trench coats. Next to them, a gangly, blond-haired teenage boy in straight-leg jeans, canvas sneakers, a thick green hoodie and jean jacket gave me a friendly smile of recognition, and I remembered meeting Leland Quary all those years before in Hollywood, rolling myself a cigarette out of Leland's tobacco. With my new perceptions, he looked even younger to me than he had then; he was just a weedy country kid who should have been ditching wood shop to hang around the Dairy Queen parking lot. At the edge of his smile, his fangs were dangerously long, startlingly sharp.

The fourth and fifth vampires, a man and a woman, I didn't know.

The man, apparently of an age similar to Alex's, was slightly taller than me and wearing a battered fedora hat and shapeless overcoat that effectively hid his body type completely. Judging by his face, he was extremely thin by late twenty-first century Western standards, but by no means unhealthy. He smiled at me, too, knowingly, as though he'd just been told some good ones about me.

The female of the two was John's height, around a hundred and twenty pounds, flat-chested, narrow-hipped, impossibly long-legged, with cleverly cut, short, shiny black hair and expressive dark eyes. She wore brown pants with pinstripes that made her Thoroughbred legs look even longer, a tiny black T-shirt, and a red, black, and silver promotorcyclist's jacket. I felt like I might have seen her somewhere before; her face seemed achingly familiar.

Without further ado, she broke away from the group and held out her hand to me. "Hi," she said, her voice low and husky, with an ineffable pan-European accent. "I'm George."

"George . . . ?" I repeated, taking her proffered hand. *"Georgina?"*

Jadzia Kopernik, aka the Lady Georgina Grise, aka Georgie, aka Jerzy, aka Zia, aka Georgie Girl, aka Anna, but mostly just George. Just a quick injection of factual knowledge, and she took her hand back. To break the transmission was almost painful; I felt sick with curiosity. I had heard so much about Orfeo's love for Georgina, about his life with her and Maria and the Bohemians in Paris. She had created him, and Orfeo had created Daniel, and Daniel had created me. Of course I had seen her, in my dreams, in the back of my mind, without understanding the significance.

"Orfeo sends his love," said George, without a hint of irony. She extended her hand to John, but he shook his head.

"I don't shake hands," he said.

"You must be John," George said with the same knowing smile.

The man I didn't know stepped forward. He didn't put out his hand. "My name is Arthur Chicot," he said with a strong Parisian accent. "I am a physician and an herbalist, so I am very interested in seeing what you've made."

"I'm Ariane Dempsey," I replied out of habit. To their credit, no one said, "We know," but I saw Chicot glance at George, then back at me with his eyebrows raised.

"Arthur has known me for a very long time," George said, throwing her arm around the man and hugging his shoulders, bending her head down to touch it to his. "And Orfeo, as well. He was with us in Paris; Feo and Maria and me."

"But mostly with Orfeo," Chicot explained. "After *she* left." He gave her a mock-disapproving glance, and she tore his hat off and put it on her own head. Underneath the hat, his muddy-brown hair was thin and his hairline high. He just shook his head and kept the same smile on his face, letting her keep the hat.

"Yeah, you did run off on him, didn't you?" I recalled. "When he needed you most?"

George didn't rise to my bait. "We all have to do what we need to do," she said. "We all have to get away from our parents eventually, don't you think? And we all certainly need to get away from our children, if they won't leave on their own."

I introduced John and Leland. John was visibly shocked at how young Leland looked, but he still wouldn't shake hands with him; they might have been mentally communicating between the two of them, because John suddenly looked away and shuddered, and Leland shook his head a little, regretfully. But then Leland reached into one of the pockets of his jean jacket and withdrew a hand-rolled cigarette. "I rolled you a butt of the Virginia flake," he said almost shyly, "since I remembered how much you liked it."

"Even though it does me no damn good," I said, blushing.

"The point is the pleasure of the smoke," Leland admonished me, sounding eerily like a crusty old southern gentleman of quality. "Besides, sounds like what you've got's way better than any ol' nicotine."

Oh, yeah, that. Everyone's eyes lit up, and I changed the subject. "But isn't Samuel Rifkin supposed to be here?"

El said, "He's just arrived in town a short while ago. He wants to meet us later; decide where you want to go and we can direct him there. He's very eager to see you again, and to meet you, too, John. He's very interested in seeing the effects of the Orchid. And speaking of which, can I get some more from you right now?"

"I figured you would ask," I said. "I've got a couple doses that are on the smaller side than what you had before, but they are still pretty nice. And it works great taking it orally; I can save on needles. I warn you, though, if you haven't taken this before, it might not have the same effects on everyone."

"Eh," shrugged El, "give me one."

They crowded around me in the shadow cast by the huge tree, and I administered triple-ought-four squirts, one after another into their open mouths, like feeding baby birds. El, George, and Leland laughed as soon as the liquid hit their mouths; Alex and Chicot grimaced, obviously able to taste Orchid's repugnant bitterness. Those grimaces quickly melted away, replaced with misty, sloppy smiles.

"Do you smell vanilla?" I demanded.

"Is that what that is?" George said.

"I like it," decided Leland. He closed his eyes, smiling, and took a deep breath, savoring the air he drew in.

"I need another one," said El. "I can barely feel it at all."

I gave her another squirt. "We're down to four doses," I said.

GET UP TO 4 FREE BOOKS!

You can have the best fiction delivered to your door for less than what you'd pay in a bookstore or online—only $4.25 a book! Sign up for our book clubs today, and we'll send you **FREE* BOOKS** just for trying it out...**with no obligation to buy, ever!**

LEISURE HORROR BOOK CLUB

With more award-winning horror authors than any other publisher, it's easy to see why CNN.com says "Leisure Books has been leading the way in paperback horror novels." Your shipments will include authors such as RICHARD LAYMON, DOUGLAS CLEGG, JACK KETCHUM, MARY ANN MITCHELL, and many more.

LEISURE THRILLER BOOK CLUB

If you love fast-paced page-turners, you won't want to miss any of the books in Leisure's thriller line. Filled with gripping tension and edge-of-your-seat excitement, these titles feature everything from psychological suspense to legal thrillers to police procedurals and more!

As a book club member you also receive the following special benefits:

- **30% OFF all orders through our website & telecenter!**
- **Exclusive access to special discounts!**
- **Convenient home delivery and 10 days to return any books you don't want to keep.**

There is no minimum number of books to buy, and you may cancel membership at any time. See back to sign up!

*Please include $2.00 for shipping and handling.

YES! ☐

Sign me up for the Leisure Horror Book Club and send my TWO FREE BOOKS! If I choose to stay in the club, I will pay only $8.50* each month, a savings of $5.48!

YES! ☐

Sign me up for the Leisure Thriller Book Club and send my TWO FREE BOOKS! If I choose to stay in the club, I will pay only $8.50* each month, a savings of $5.48!

NAME: _____

ADDRESS: _____

_____

TELEPHONE: _____

E-MAIL: _____

☐ **I WANT TO PAY BY CREDIT CARD.**

☐ VISA   ☐ MasterCard.   ☐ DISCOVER

ACCOUNT #: _____

EXPIRATION DATE: _____

SIGNATURE: _____

Send this card along with $2.00 shipping & handling for each club you wish to join, to:

Horror/Thriller Book Clubs
1 Mechanic Street
Norwalk, CT 06850-3431

Or fax (must include credit card information!) to: 610.995.9274. You can also sign up online at www.dorchesterpub.com.

*Plus $2.00 for shipping. Offer open to residents of the U.S. and Canada only. Canadian residents please call 1.800.481.9191 for pricing information.

If under 18, a parent or guardian must sign. Terms, prices and conditions subject to change. Subscription subject to acceptance. Dorchester Publishing reserves the right to reject any order or cancel any subscription.

"That's okay," El murmured. "I think I'm good."

Nice night for it. The moon swung higher in the sky, creating multiple shadows from every headstone, tree, and blade of grass, rendering the world in wheat-gold velvet. We wandered over the hills, past mausoleums and mirror-polished black granite shields inscribed in Chinese, granite markers no larger than a brick, half overgrown with dry yellow grass. John walked with George and Chicot, and I walked with Leland, smoking our rollies. I saw the flicker of a security truck's headlights once or twice, but no vehicle ever turned down a road toward us; we were, all of us, transmitting vibes of *stay away*.

"You know Daniel's dead, don't you?" I said to Leland.

"You know I do," he said. "And I know you're glad."

"I'm not glad," I said. "I mean, I am. But on the other hand, it doesn't make up for any of the shit he pulled . . . but you probably wouldn't know as much about that."

"Of course I know," Leland said. "Just because we were friends didn't mean I approved of everything he did. Hell, I didn't approve of almost *anything* he did. I could never stand to be around him for very long, but we'd have a good time when I happened to be in town."

"Where are you usually?"

"I never stay anywhere for very long," he said. "Never more than a few weeks at most. I'm like a shark; I gotta keep moving. It's always been like that. I ran away when I was twelve years old, trying to avoid getting my face cut off by some Indians, and just never went back home. Then it was those same damn Indians that kept my ass alive for another couple years.

They were good to me, taught me to use and respect
the earth, how to be wild and how to stay lost. But I
just couldn't stay away from white folks; I got so
homesick for a white face that I went into the wrong
damn town, hoping to have a conversation in the
King's English and ran into the wrong kind of white
face. That ol' Fox Madder, though . . . sometimes I
damn well wish I had stayed at home. That ol' Fox
Madder, that rogue, he made me what I am. That ol'
bastard come all the way over here from England and
made a bunch like him. Indian girls, mostly. I don't
think most of them survived; but then again, I don't
know, even a little girl'll kill you to keep from being
killed."

"And what happened to him?" I asked.

"I killed him," Leland said. "Soon as I came back to
myself, I found him and I sucked the life out of him
and mashed his head in with a rock. That ol' bastard.
Wish somebody'd done it before he got to me." He
glanced over at me, and answered my unspoken question. "Hell, no, I didn't ask for this. I was bedeviled by
him and I had no control over what I did. But it's what
happened and it's what I am, and I do what I can with
it. It's easier if I don't stop moving; I don't look like
much, I can disappear, and folks just die, all the time.
They can't pin it on me—I never existed."

I was quiet for a while. We were approaching the
far gate, leading to a different road down out of the
hills. Ahead of us, John and George were laughing. "I
wish you had another cigarette," I said, just to say
something.

Leland grinned. "Well, look at what I've got here.
Another one."

I laughed and took it, and he deployed his lighter.

"You're so sweet," I told him. "I'm touched that you remember."

"You know I can't forget anything," he replied, his voice suddenly flat and stern. "I remember your dress and your hair and how you were looking for food all night. I remember your friend Lovely and he was barefoot and he had his nipples pierced and I remember wondering what was going to happen to those after he got made."

"Lovely's dead, too," I said.

"Good for him," Leland said, and I knew he was sincere.

I led the group out of the cemetery and through downtown, heading for a bar that I knew of but had never gone to. It had the added bonus of being across the river, so we all got the pleasure of walking over a bridge with the moon and all the city lights shining on the water. At the halfway point, John suddenly stopped and looked back; overhead to our right rose the massive green neon sign with the rampant buck in white, flashing and coruscating, one green word at a time lighting up, then all of them, then going momentarily dark, leaving only the white stag. From here, the sign looked oddly small, but even through the sounds of the traffic, I could hear the electrical chattering of the lightbulbs being fed and coming to life. "It doesn't make sense now," John muttered softly, wringing his hands. "This is just a *symbol* of terror. Something that was alive and yet not alive, and yet alive. It's me; the white stag, existing artificially. The stag is in charge of that bridge; I'm not allowed to set foot on it. The terror's still real. Symbols are hollow; they blink on and off. Position and momentum. I don't know . . . I don't know."

I struggled to find the right thing to say, but George just patted John on the shoulder. "Never mind," she said, not unkindly. "Let's go. I want a vodka and Coke." It seemed to be enough for John; his face cleared, and he smiled and walked in step with her, ahead of the rest of us on the narrow walkway. I looked at the sign for a few moments longer, suddenly able to understand how John had spent entire nights of his life just staring at it, paralyzed with a wordless, incomprehensible fear.

But he was better now.

Before we left the bridge, I gave myself another shot of Orchid. This time I tasted it; it was terrible, like rotten avocado. Leland saw my face and laughed. "Looks like you could use a drink yourself," he said.

That additional dose of Orchid, taken approximately an hour after the first one, had a most interesting effect. By the time we reached the bar and went in and got drinks handed to us, I felt almost completely disconnected from my body; I could still control it, but it was all automatic, from downing the drink to sitting down in a booth next to Chicot and scooting aside to make room for El. Her eyes were slightly glazed, and her hair had been disheveled by the wind on the bridge. She hadn't touched her own drink. "I wouldn't drink that, if I were you," I heard myself say. "It seems to have a synergistic effect. Momentary, but still."

"You sound *really* trashed," El slurred.

"I am," I told her, looking around us at the other people in the bar. The place was mostly full, most of the people wearing every shade of black, jostling for drinks at the bar, dancing wherever they could find space in the tight corridors between tables and people. Some of them were staring at us, transfixed, longing and suspicious. These darkness-obsessed kids knew there was something different about us. When I met their eyes they looked away, gathered their things, and walked upstairs to leave. I was bemused; even my mind-changing impulses had become automatic. I wanted to tell John that he should bring his friend Psychward here as a treat, but he was locked in conversation with George at the other end of the booth and I just didn't have the will to get his attention. He seemed to be having a good time; I would leave him to it.

El tugged my sleeve. "Look, Sam's here."

My strongest memory of Samuel Rifkin was that he scared the hell out of me. I found it a wonder that he could mix in human society at all; he was over six feet tall, his skin a surreal, glossy light-mahogany shade that no human ever bore, with dull black hair hanging down to his waist, fastened at the back with a series of thin silver bands. His features were narrow and imperious, the nose, brow, and chin of an arrogant British colonialist on his dark face, eyes like two cruel black holes, and dark, narrow lips. Now, he just looked fabulous to me; no less dangerous, but vastly impressive, in a knee-length black cassock with silver toggles that matched the bands in his hair, and tall, gleaming black riding boots. I could absolutely understand why he had come in surrounded by attractive young women, and more approached and more glanced and whispered behind their hands.

"Ariane," he said, "how beautiful you've become."

El sprung up from the booth and embraced him with far more warmth than I'd ever dare, even now. Rifkin himself seemed slightly taken aback, and he held her away from him and gazed deeply into her eyes. She threw back her head and laughed, a good, solid, hearty, drunken laugh. "You've gotta have some," she said to him.

Rifkin regarded me with one eyebrow arched. "I intend to do so," he said imperiously.

I felt for the syringe in my jacket pocket, uncapped the needle, and shot a dose into El's ignored vodka shot. I handed it up to him without rising from my seat. "Bottoms up," I said.

Rifkin stared at the glass of now-purplish, cloudy fluid, and I saw a flicker of what might have been fear cross his face. I couldn't resist a laugh—Samuel Rifkin, afraid of me and my little Orchid!—and glanced over at John again, interested in his reaction to Rifkin. John watched, but he didn't even seem tense. And it looked like he and George were holding hands.

What the hell was that about?

Rifkin bolted the shot and slammed the empty glass back onto the table in a very manly fashion. El disappeared into the other room and began to dance, and George tore herself away from John—they *had* been holding hands—and joined El on the dance floor, around the corner, out of our sight. Rifkin sat next to me in the booth. He and Chicot stared at each other, and it might have been hostile in another situation, but with the dose of Orchid sinking in to Rifkin, neither of them could focus very effectively.

"Ah, the apothecary," said Rifkin, his voice infinitely softer than I'd ever heard it.

"Ah, the lothario," replied Chicot, less softly.

"Have you guys met?" I asked.

"Never," said Chicot. "But I have eyes that see." He turned his glance to the gaggle of pretty young things standing around awkwardly without purpose now that Rifkin had sat down at a full booth.

Rifkin looked up at the women and waved his hand, dismissing them with a "Pah!" The women obediently made themselves scarce, joining the three-deep throng at the bar.

"Do you smell the vanilla?" I asked Rifkin.

At the end of the booth, John abruptly stood up and went into the other room, where George and El were. Now exposed, Alex looked up at one of Rifkin's girls and held out his hand. "Yes," Rifkin said suddenly, "most extraordinary. How can it be?" He rubbed his hand against the back of his neck, underneath his thick queue of hair, and took the same kind of deep breaths as I'd seen Leland taking earlier. "I feel as though I'm drowning . . . but it is not unpleasant." He looked at me as though he'd never seen me before. "You have quieted your child's mind, though not your own."

"What do you mean?"

"You could not sleep this morning, am I correct?"

"Right . . ."

"You telegraph your emotions across the world. I saw you lying awake in my dreams."

"You would have come here to kill me," I said.

"I *would* have," he agreed. "I have often thought of it. And do not let your friend Elisabeta tell you differently; she had thought of it as well, but her Alexander urged compassion."

I stared at Alex, who now had the girl on his lap and was nuzzling her graceful neck as she giggled. Leland was watching him like a hawk, as was Chicot; like a pack of wolves, waiting for the moment to strike.

I watched, too. His strong Russian nose stroked

against the girl's smooth pale skin, his lips grazing the swell of delicate musculature. I saw her pulse fluttering through her skin, then heard the deep, regular throbs of her aortal valve opening and closing. Rifkin followed my line of sight, and I heard him hiss softly through his teeth when he saw them.

We sat like that for what seemed like an eternity, only interrupted by the return of El to our table. She glanced at Alex, then tossed her hair and put her hand on my wrist. "Come with," she murmured to me, and Rifkin politely stood up and let me pass. "You, too," El said to him.

The dim hallway leading to the restrooms was illuminated with only a feeble blue rope light on the floor. I stared at the rope light, fascinated at how dusty it was, considering that to be a good enough reason to leave my seat, but then Alex came back with the girl in tow, and he pressed her against the wall and leaned in against her.

The girl threw back her head, offering her neck, trembling a little when Alex's teeth sliced into her, opening that vein that had so fascinated us. Crimson rivulets tracked down to her collarbone. El stepped up to the girl and began to drink, then Rifkin after her. By the time she got to me, I could taste the girl's shock, her body helpless to reverse the slide downward into death. Sweet thing; high school dropout, sewed her own clothes, loved fantasy novels and big trucks. Michelle. Nineteen. Unable to resist Rifkin's lethal charisma and infinite rolls of verdant cash. It was a fucking shame, and yet how beautifully her blood tumbled into my mouth, so willing to accommodate me even as her life slipped away.

The problem was, it wasn't quite enough and now we were all hungry.

El half-carried the girl into one of the two bathrooms, and said, "Bring them in here when you're done. It'll be fine."

Rifkin fetched the next, then Alex. By then Chicot had caught on to us and stood with me, waiting for the unfortunates to be brought to us, and Leland played point, standing before the hallway herding victims with full bladders toward us. Unfortunately, this scheme backfired quickly; Chicot jumped back with a curse when a young man suddenly lost consciousness and unleashed a flood-tide of urine down his pants and onto the floor. I hammered on the bathroom door. "El! C'mon! Code yellow! We're leaving!" I shouted.

We left the kid sprawled on the floor with his cheek soaking in his own piss—maybe he'd live—and bolted up the stairs and outside. There was no time to spare actually fetching John and George, but they followed right behind us, laughing. "Oh dear, Arthur, oh dear," George sang. "Looks like you could use a trip to the laundry."

Chicot cursed at the dark stain on the hem of his pants. "It wasn't the first time," he said. "Smelling like piss is far from the worst thing that could ever happen to me."

"This is Burnside," said John, pointing out our surroundings to our guests. Or perhaps just to George. "If the river is the X axis, Burnside is the Y axis." If he hadn't been talking just to George, you'd never know it, because George laughed like it was the best thing she'd ever heard. "We're at negative five, zero. What we want to get to is twenty-nine, four."

"And that's where you live?" said George.

"I don't live anywhere, really . . . I sleep where I feel like it," John replied.

My stomach clenched hard inside me. "Oh, look," I cut in, "it's the bus. Wanna take it across? If you're on a bus over the bridge, it doesn't count, John."

One-thirty in the morning, and the bus was lit with pink lights like the lobby of a peepshow. A Saturday evening's trash lay scattered on the floor, including two complete copies of the Sunday newspaper. There were three passengers when we got on, smiled at the bus driver, and sat down without paying. One rider, a thickset Hispanic man with close-cropped hair like mold growing on his skull, began shouting at us. "Hey, y'all don't get to ride without payin'! I paid my money! That's fucked-up, man! These people ain't paid and we ain't fareless yet!"

"Shut up, dude," said another rider, a lanky, pale man with glasses, wearing some cobbled-together ensemble of black clothes, leather boots, leather jacket, black tusks shoved through holes in his dangling earlobes. The female version of him was seated beside him, her hands shoved into the pockets of his leather jacket as she half-sprawled against him. She had the waxy complexion of someone who had had too much to drink.

"No, *you* shut up!" screamed the Latino.

"Both of you shut up," said the driver through a loudspeaker, his distorted voice crackled through the air. We were driving over the bridge, going fast, the wind whistling through a cracked window, the newspapers rustling along the floor. John and George were staring deeply into each other's eyes, unblinking, sharing God knew what. Everything, I supposed.

Great.

I stepped over to the Latino man and brought my joined fingers across his neck. Just testing; just seeing what such a thing would do. My claws severed his windpipe and unleashed a bright spray of blood across the seats in front of him, the ones set aside for "honored citizens." He put his hands up to his neck in a vain attempt to stop the blood, and he tried to scream, but I had cut him just below the Adam's apple and his voicebox now had nothing to work with but fluid.

The girl screamed instead. Rifkin swiftly clambered over the tops of the seats, giving her skull a good, solid kick with his riding boots; she slumped silently in her boyfriend's arms.

"Thanks," Leland said. His close-cropped gingery hair and the hood of his sweatshirt got soaked with blood from the Latino man's neck, but it didn't seem to bother him.

"I was trying to keep her from throwing up," Rifkin explained, which made me laugh, because of course she'd lost control of her bladder and bowels at the instant of brain-death, and I couldn't say I thought that was any better.

The driver and the boyfriend screamed, too. The driver hadn't taken his foot off the accelerator yet; we screamed across the bridge and into downtown, running a red light at a good fifty-five, sixty miles per hour. George stood beside him and told him gently and reasonably to slow down for the next light. Somehow we came to a stop beside a brightly lit car wash. George very delicately broke the driver's neck, and slid him out of the seat.

"Oh my God," said the survivor. "Oh my God."

Chicot flicked drops of urine off the driver's seat, then sat down. "It can't get any worse," he said cheer-

fully. "Get rid of him, would you?" He opened the
front door of the bus; George shoved the driver's body
down the steps and onto the side of the road, followed
by the larger, slower body of the Latino man. His eyes
were still open, but they weren't focused, so I could
tell myself that he wasn't looking at me.

I stared down at myself. My pale sweater and my
precious suede jacket had caught some of the blood
spray. Beside me, Leland's face was a red mask, wearing a sad, resigned smile. Farther back, John was gently removing the dead woman from her lover's grasp,
then leaning in close to him, toying curiously with the
bone ornaments in his ears. Rifkin sat across from
them, his head nodding heavily. The Orchid was
knocking him out; he wasn't used to it. I watched John
slide the bone tusks out of the man's earlobes and put
them into his coat pocket. Divested of his jewelry, the
man seemed deflated; he blinked sharply once, then
stared off into the middle distance, and blood coursed
down from both nostrils, coating the silver ring piercing his septum with a crimson veil. John set his mouth
against the man's neck, draining him before his body
had a chance to realize that his brain was no longer
functioning.

Chicot drove the bus, smoothly and easily, as though
he'd been doing it for years. I began to feel something
akin to feeling hungover while I was still drinking.
There was one dose of Orchid left; I reached into my
pocket for the syringe, staining my hand and wrist
with the blood that had dripped down onto the
pocket's edge, and wrapped my lips around the needle
as I pressed the plunger.

Better; now none of this seemed real.

The pervasive smell of shit, the quiet stop at the

next bus shelter, and the crunch of the pierced man's skull against the unyielding pavement, the moonlight gleaming off the brass hide of a giant sculpture of a seal on the roof of a building. Screaming from somewhere outside. A rising howl of sirens, like the night gathering its breath, Rifkin, a sleeping tiger in the form of a man, blood flecking the silver buttons on his jacket.

Orion, risen through the trees.

Not real; a movie, projected on thick, cuddly white velvet.

"Take a right," John's voice seeped into my consciousness. "Stop just ahead; there, where the trees come together. Forest Park. Just vanish. Now."

I drifted out through the rear door, Leland half-pulling me along with him; John and Rifkin came after, John bright and mysterious and determined, Rifkin as clumsy as a sleepy boy on a cold morning. El, George, Alex, Chicot—where were they? Already gone. "Scatter," said John, a little sternly, as if we should know this and he was tired of doing all the thinking. Of course; he was the most sober one of us.

Leland kept pulling me, and together we plunged into the bushes, across a small creek, into a copse of trees, and up the stoutest one until we were lost among the heavy foliage. He climbed out on a solid limb and stared out into the darkness, listening, a little wildcat with blood drying in his hair and on the white rubber toes of his sneakers.

Do you have a place to sleep? he wanted to know.

I have home, I thought.

May I stay there? And not like that.

I smirked. *Aren't I pretty? Or are you desperate for a white face?*

I almost made him laugh out loud. *It don't matter who your daddy was, you've got a white face now, white as death, just like mine. Hell, I'll fuck you, if that's what you want, but you and I both know that it isn't.*

He was right, but damned if I could tell him what it was that I did want. Once upon a time, I knew, but it got lost somewhere in the cemetery.

XI

SPOOKY ACTION AT A DISTANCE

MARGARET WILLIAMS

Aunty W. wouldn't strike you as the kind of person who would go nuts with the holiday decorations, but when I was still a block away I could see the front porch of the house strung with thick white fake cobwebs, and the steps and porch railing precisely lined with jack-o'lanterns of every conceivable kind. They were carved out of big orange pumpkins, little orange pumpkins, big white pumpkins, striped squashes, even a couple of tall, curved zucchinis, their expertly cut faces long and distorted, as if seen in a funhouse mirror. Aunty W. took it very seriously, since it was her only artistic outlet, and she was incredibly good at it. She was the undisputed queen of squash-carving, spending an entire day attacking the poor veggies with blunt blades and razor-sharp X-acto knives, slicing out dozens of varied and grotesque expressions. I guess reading all that Dante stimulated her imagination, what with all those shades and lost souls in the multiple levels of hell.

In the foyer, the walls sported paper witches on broomsticks, grinning black cats, tombstones, and cheerful-looking ghosts, and the requisite bright-orange and black HAPPY HALLOWEEN! banner. Aunty W. always gave a Halloween party for her students—bobbing for apples and candlelight readings of Edgar Allan Poe stories, translated into Latin, of course. It was actually pretty fun, and very popular for a bunch of undergrad kids. I had been lucky enough to attend one of these parties when I was fifteen, and ended up French-kissing some PSU freshman out in the backyard. My first real kiss—great at first, but then he had put his hand down my shirt and I'd freaked, shoved him away, and ran back inside. Minutes later I saw him making out with some other, older girl, and then Aunty W. had politely but firmly told them both to leave. I never told anybody about the kiss, even though I'd stayed up all night thinking about it, wondering what would have happened if I hadn't stopped him. Wishing to God I hadn't stopped him.

I was glad to be indoors, away from the pumpkins, and took my jacket and hat off with a sigh of relief. I'd gotten barely four hours of sleep, and I tossed and turned the whole time, waking up even more tired than before. The damp, moody weather didn't help, either. Uncle Stan raised his eyebrow at me as I slid myself heavily into the chair next to him. "Look what the cat dragged in," he said, trying to be funny, I guess.

"I'm not used to being up this early anymore," I explained, pouring myself a cup of coffee. As soon as I had sipped it, I found that I didn't really want to eat, even though Aunty W. was as skilled at breakfast as she was at . . . well, everything she did, pretty much. Damn her. I just needed coffee; something to help me get through this friendly, catching-up breakfast, and then I'd go home and catch a few winks before doing some paperwork for Ariane. We were going to need more heavy potassium; she was ordering five times as much as she had the first time. My special project was making sure that we could retain our authorization to request such exotic material. Fortunately for us, money still talked pretty loud, and wherever Ariane's private foundation had gotten its money, it was as good as anyone's.

"I guess not," said my uncle. "Having problems getting up in the morning? Looks like you've been missing a lot of class lately. Dr. Wayne asked me about you yesterday."

Ugh, that damn class. I'd actually *gone* to class that week. Why the hell had he been spying on me? Didn't he know how much work was involved with assisting Ariane? Didn't he believe I could do it? Did he think my coming here was a waste of time? I put some sugar into my coffee; I guess too much, because they all looked at me funny. I felt funny myself, and it was too much sugar. I wished desperately that I'd gotten some more sleep, called and told them I couldn't make it.

"It's not early," said Aunty W., putting a plate down in front of me. "It's nine o'clock. It's practically time for brunch. I already ate hours ago."

There was nowhere safe for me to look; on the plate, the yolks of a couple of over easy eggs quivered wetly next to a stack of wheat toast that looked as coarse as brick, and across the table, Aunty W. and Aunt June were nodding self-importantly at each other. I ran my hand through my hair and focused my eyes on the salt and pepper shakers, festively shaped like little pumpkins. "My *job* . . ." I began to say, but my stomach gave a little lurch. Really too much sugar, enough sugar for a very sweet whole cup, and I only had half a cup left. I tried to complete my sentence, but my jaw just went numb, like I'd had a Novocain shot. I took a deep breath and started over again with something different. "I usually try to catch up on sleep on the weekends, but I was up late again last night. It's hard to try to convince yourself to go to sleep at the same time as you usually begin work."

"Well, *that's* strange," said Aunt June.

"How are *you*, Aunt June?" I broke in, plastering a smile onto my face. I even picked up my napkin and spread it on my lap, though I still couldn't bring myself to pick up my fork. "How's work going in your back garden? Did you ever get that leaf fungus problem licked?"

That deflected her; she could talk for hours about water features and soil acidity. Aunt June didn't have kids; she had delphiniums. Good old Aunty June, always so sweet and steady, unlike nosy Uncle Stan or paragon-of-perfection Aunty Wanda Williams Willoughby, Widow. It had to be because June wasn't related to the rest of us—she had married her way into this kitchen. There was something inherently screwed up about us Williamses. All of a sudden I was hungry, and I attacked my eggs, nodding and giggling at Aunt June like she was the most fascinating thing in the world.

"But how are *you*, Margaret?" Aunty W. cut in, topping off my coffee mug. "I just haven't seen much of you since you moved here. I was really hoping we'd be able to get together more often, now that you're around, but I haven't seen you since I helped you move. What was that—more than a month ago?"

My appetite vanished while my mouth was still full. I tried to moisten the huge mouthful of toast with coffee, and swallowed it all whole. I stalled under the pretense of washing it down. I mean, what could I say to that? I didn't feel like spending time with the family. I felt different. I was growing up. I was spending all my free time alone. I didn't seem to be able to talk to anybody anymore. I looked in the mirror and didn't recognize myself. I had dreams about stuff I'd never done, never seen, never thought about before. Everything was shitty except for those times when I was in the lab with Ariane; then I felt healthy, energetic, calm, alive.

"Your hair . . . it's . . . it's really pretty," Aunt June said to me in a strained voice, her smile brittle, ready to fall apart at any second. She sounded like she was trying to convince the others so she could believe it herself. "It's so red, it's like a traffic light! I think it's lovely. What is that hair color called?"

I still had a little blue piece, the same lock that had been blue for the last three months, but I'd refreshed the rest of it with red the night before, staying up way too late combing the sticky gel through, staring out the textured glass window; I couldn't really see anything out there, but it felt like I could see the street, interpret the quiet nighttime sounds as shapes, creatures, personalities. I did this every Friday night, on my night off from work—staying up too late, dyeing my hair redder and redder. The color was way too dark to be a traffic light. "It's called Red Velvet Cake," I told them. "It's a temporary color."

"Well, *that's* good," said Uncle Stan.

I really wanted to hurt him right then. I never

wanted to hurt him before in my life; violence wasn't my style at all. And I loved Uncle Stan—he was my favorite relative and a pretty awesome guy, but right then I wanted to take my eggy fork and shove it into his neck and watch his eyes bug out in shock. Instead I just mumbled and poked at the scraps on my plate. "There's not really much going on, Aunty Dub. All I really do is go to work, go to class, and sleep. Every once in a while I'll go out for a drink. Like tonight." I sat back and smiled at my aunts and uncle, grateful to have some opportunity to present myself as normal. "Tonight I'm going out with some folks I know from Hissy-Fizz. History of Physiology, one-twenty-four," I clarified.

Aunty W. visibly relaxed. Did I look that bad? "Well, that's nice," she said, leaning over to the kitchen shelf and touching the slightly rumpled front page of a newspaper. "Looks like it's going to be chilly and rainy tonight, in the low forties. Good autumn holiday weather, since it's so nice to be indoors. Are you going to a Halloween party?"

"No, we're going barhopping."

"Oh, that sounds fun!" Aunt June enthused, a little too excited, and I wondered if she'd ever been barhopping in her life. Maybe thirty years ago, before I was even born, she and Uncle Stan had gone to a discotheque, did the Hully-Gully, and then gone to—oh wait, don't tell me—*another bar.*

When had I become such a jerk? Was it the sleep deprivation? It was their fault for making me come to breakfast.

"Friends of yours?" asked Uncle Stan, crossing his fork and knife over his plate.

"Well . . . not really friends, I guess. I just know

Joanie and Ashley, because sometimes we trade study notes, and they invited me to go along with them. They're all right, though."

"Do you have a costume?" Aunty W. asked.

"Uh . . . no. I don't think we need them. We're just going to a couple of clubs."

She made an impatient sound. "How can you waste great hair like that and not wear a costume? Imagine if you wanted to be Raggedy Ann—you'd be perfect!"

"You guys, seriously, enough with the hair, okay?" I snapped. "I don't even know why I do it. Maybe I just see too much blood all the time."

Aunty W. actually looked contrite. It wasn't an expression that I'd ever seen on her face. "I'm sorry, honey. I didn't mean anything by it; I think your hair is beautiful. *You're* beautiful, Margaret. I just love you, that's all, and I want you to have fun." She reached across the table and took my hand. Uncle Stan was staring off into the corner as though he'd never been looking anywhere else.

I took some more deep breaths. "I'm sorry I blew up," I said. "Everything's fine, really. I'm just a little stressed out. Everything's really new, and even though I feel like I should be totally familiar with all of it, it's still harder than I thought it would be."

They all threw up their hands with the same gesture of "Is *that* it!" It was funny to watch; it was like they were going to burst into song. They nearly did. I was in a room with three people with postgraduate degrees, and two of them with PhDs; the agonies of graduate studies gave them ample opportunities for pep talks and sympathy and "I remember . . ."—I was grateful for it; I just wanted to sink into my chair and not talk any more for a while. They even talked among themselves after I'd given them an adequate amount of smiling and nodding, and I picked up the newspaper myself, wondering exactly how cold and rainy it would be, what shoes I was going to need to wear.

It didn't look too bad; more or less just like now, except with a light rain. I'd have to wear my hair up, and under a hat, so red dye wouldn't leak all over my face if it got wet, and make it look like I'd gotten a nasty head wound. Then again, it *was* Halloween.

I hadn't read a newspaper in a long time, and I got sucked in, chugging down coffee and leafing through the pages. The murmur of conversation didn't die down around me; they were talking about property taxes or property values or something, and I was trying, not very insistently, to find my horoscope. My eye caught an item well-buried at the bottom of a page that listed cross-streets only two blocks away from my apartment building.

JOYRIDING SPREE KILLS 4. Outside of the Tru Love Car Wash at Southwest 19th and Burnside. Two deaths by stabbing, one, possibly two, by blunt force trauma. The details were vague.

Next to it, AREA NIGHTSPOT SHUTTERED. FOOD POISONING SUSPECTED. Seven people were still in critical condition, one upgraded to stable.

I felt my jaw go numb again, and I dribbled coffee down my blouse out of the corner of my mouth. Instantly Aunty W. was on her feet, waving her napkin at me, like I'd just gotten a stain on something of hers. "I'm fine, I'm fine," I protested, dabbing my shirt dry. "It's just a couple of drops. And I'm pretty bored with this shirt anyway." I spread my hands and laughed. "I'm fine. Seriously. Don't worry about me; I'm great."

I brought the paper home with me, and lay in bed

studying the two articles. The killings had happened right down the street. I'd been warned that Burnside was a rough street, but I hadn't seen anything worse than a crank-jonesing prostitute trying to hail a cab just by screaming for one. This was a different matter altogether.

The funny thing was, I didn't feel any less safe. I just felt interested.

Out of six of us who went on the crawl, three were wearing costumes. I supposed it was a good mix; nobody looked completely out of place. Ashley, Kevin, and Josh were in costume. Joanie, Sam, and I were not. Ashley and Kevin were a tandem costume as Miss Right and Mr. Wrong; Josh had a robot costume made out of cardboard and aluminum foil. He was interested more in putting on a show than hanging out with us, which was fine; his costume was great and he didn't have to buy a drink all night.

I did make the concession to Halloween by dressing all in black, with my hair up and mostly hidden under a black bowler hat. I also just felt like wearing black, and disappearing into the corners of the room, watching other people. Ashley kept trying to talk me up, get me out of my shell, but I just didn't have anything to say, and she always had Kevin to talk to.

We started out at the Oceanside Shack, an east side bar with the reputation of having some of the strongest drinks in town and a great jukebox. It was already packed by the time we got there at nine. It was fun to watch Josh try to play pinball in his robot costume, but I felt tired already after having had only one drink, and I knew I wasn't being very much fun. These people weren't my friends yet, and I wasn't sure that

they would ever be my friends, especially not with me
acting so weird and quiet.

We moved on after all of us had gotten one drink,
and progressed past a huge, noisy, raucous karaoke
bar. "We are *definitely* going there later," said Sam
fervently.

"Yeah, it's a shame that we can't go to the Sunspot,"
Joanie piped up, linking arms with Sam. They looked
nice together, well-matched, well-proportioned, two
animals of the same breed. "Did you guys hear? A
whole bunch of people *died* there last night."

"Really?" said Kevin. "*Died?* I thought they just got
sick."

Joanie shook her head. "No, a friend of mine works
down at Providence and she told me that a couple of
the people they brought in died earlier this evening.
She was really kind of freaked out—she says it wasn't
poison."

"It was that crappy food they serve there," Ashley
said hopefully.

Joanie shook her head again. "Heather told me there
was no evidence of *any* kind of toxic substance in their
blood, except for alcohol, and none of them drank
enough for it to kill them."

"Did she say anything else about them?" I asked, trying to sound casual, but it sounded strangled instead.

"No," Joanie said. "She was on her coffee break. I
think she was just trying to give me a spooky story for
Halloween. She's got one for every occasion. I remember the one about the guy who came in with his cell
phone up his butt, which he'd put there on purpose so
he could call himself and it would vibrate."

The ladies screamed, the guys guffawed; and we
were off to the next place, a cozy little strip joint,

where Josh knew all the ladies and all the ladies knew Josh. We all got to drink for free there until Josh tried to mount the stage to do a pole dance and we all got eighty-sixed.

"Way to go, man," said Sam bitterly, leading us a few doors down and past a big, gruff doorman and then up a few flights of stairs. If I wasn't tipsy by the time I started climbing the stairs, I was by the time I got to the top, and my fatigue was slowly ebbing away, replaced with a nihilistic excitement. Halloween wasn't so bad, as long as you embraced the absurd and grotesque, and at least my hair dye hadn't started to run yet. I was even considering taking a turn on the packed dance floor.

These Portlanders took their Halloween pretty seriously; almost everyone in this bar was in costume— everything from exquisite brocade and lace to a bikini made out of duct tape and beer bottle caps to ripped acid-wash jeans, day-glo baseball cap, and T-shirt with "1988" printed on it. I had begun to have a great time somehow, even not really talking all night, just observing and laughing and recognizing, shaking my head at the startling inventiveness of regular people. I'd had two shots of 151 rum and lime, two beers, and no dinner. I thought a piña colada sounded like the stupidest, most hedonistic drink I could have, so I strode up to the bar to order one, grateful that there were so many people to steady myself against. If I looked over at the dance floor behind me, I could see the silvery form of Josh pogoing—and was that another aluminum foil robot that he was dancing with?

The world couldn't be more right.

While I was waiting in line at the bar, I bummed a cigarette from the man dressed up as Dolly Parton (or was it Grand Ol' Opry Barbie?) standing in front of me, and almost didn't cough at all as I lit it up. I'd been quit for nine months, but what the fuck, it was Halloween, and I was having a good time for the first time in ages . . . except hadn't I had a good time Thursday night with Ariane? Yes, that was good, but it wasn't a *good time*. Ariane had gone from being really uptight and suspicious to softer and more open, but recently she was back to being uptight, but not really toward me. Something else was bothering the hell out of her. I couldn't figure out what that could be. We'd synthesized the drug, successfully, which was amazing in and of itself. I knew that John was happy, because he'd come down to pick up Ariane at the end of the night last week, and he looked fantastic, amazing, wonderful, almost handsome enough to be a model. He had a twinkle in his eye as he said hello to me, and at first I thought he was just gloating that he got to go home and fuck Ariane. Then I realized that he looked completely better, his hair neater, wearing clean clothes, and his smile seemed like it was coming from someplace real.

But Ariane wasn't smiling at all; she looked everywhere but at John, and barely even said good-bye to me as she left. It had to be something about him.

Barbie Parton ordered a drink with the bark of a trained drill sergeant, and I looked up, blinking, amazed at how drunk I was. Behind me, the club was raging. I wanted to turn around, but didn't dare, this close to the bar. I looked past it to the booths on the side, across a narrow path clogged with people ignoring the desperate shouts of the woman trying to leave the kitchen with clean pint glasses. In the very back booth, two tall dark-haired boys bracketed a shorter, pale-haired girl, holding her steady with their hands lightly balanced on her shoulders. The dark-haired boys were kissing the blonde's neck, but the blonde didn't seem to be all a-twitter with delight, like I would have been in that situation; instead, her eyes were vague, pointed at the slowly revolving disco ball and the flecks of light swimming around the room.

The neater hair . . . that was John all right, even though he had gotten his hair cut even shorter than I'd seen it the other week. And the other boy was a *girl*, someone I'd never seen before, younger than me, with hair so short I totally thought it was a guy at first. But it was a really skinny girl, wearing a red tuxedo shirt, who looked freakishly tall even sitting down.

A dark line appeared on the blonde girl's neck. If I angled my head I saw the dark line glisten wetly, and John held his thumb over the spot where his lips had been, and he licked at the dark line, smudging it, bringing out its color as if with a paintbrush, a startling, deep scarlet, the same color as my hair, exactly.

I decided to hell with the piña colada. I needed to go home. It took an agonizing eternity to fight my way through the dancing people back to the table where we'd all been sitting, only to find all of them gone except Josh, who was slumped at the table with his cardboard head sitting next to him on the floor. I shook him into bleary alertness. "Tell Joanie I had to go home," I screamed over the music, and he might have nodded, or he might have just gotten tired of holding his head up straight. Either way, I grabbed my jacket and my hat and barreled out the door.

By the time I managed to hail a taxi, I was practically sobbing from frustration and desperation. The driver didn't ask me if I was all right, and I was so grateful for that that I gave him a hundred percent tip (well, that was partially by accident, but he deserved it, absolutely). I staggered out of the taxi and fumbled my way into my apartment.

No lights. I tore off my hat and coat and shoes in the doorway, and the top and jeans in the bathroom. I sat there on the toilet seat for a while, just hyperventilating a little, trying to regain some kind of control.

What the fuck?

What the fuck just happened there?

Was that *blood*?

John? But why . . . ? And who was that girl? And who was that other girl? And where the hell was Ariane while all this was going on?

I was at the lab office for more than an hour, uploading the request files from my laptop onto the server, before Ariane arrived on Monday night. She muttered a hello as she hung up a really nice, tailored, dark-brown belted jacket that I'd never seen before. "Is that a new coat?" I asked.

"Yeah," she said slowly, "the weather changed and I figured it was time to break out the rain gear." She smiled ruefully, rubbing the material of the lapel between her thumb and forefinger. Looked like she'd had her nails done, too; they were shorter, painted a shiny dark brown that matched the shade of her coat exactly. Maybe a haircut as well. I wasn't sure why her freckles were shading back in; if there'd been any sunshine, I hadn't seen it. "How was your pre-Halloween weekend?" she asked.

"It was, um . . ."

"It was *um,* huh? Well, let me take a look over the request paperwork and we can probably get that sent in tonight, and hopefully the shipment won't take more than a few weeks to arrive. The order we placed on the fifteenth should be coming in tomorrow, so be sure to be here at quarter of six, and I'll try to do the same. I'm not a fan of getting up early, either." Ariane sat in the chair in front of the main monitor and fastened the grounding strap onto her wrist before she touched the keyboard. "You did a great job of receiving the shipment last time, so if I can't make it, I know you can be trusted."

"Thanks," I said. We were both silent for a moment, only the faint sound of the printer chipping away at the stillness in the room. "My weekend was pretty interesting, actually. Well, my Saturday. I pretty much spent Sunday either asleep or at the grocery store. But Saturday night, I went out barhopping with some friends of mine from Hissy-Fizz."

Ariane actually looked up at me with interest then. Even after all this time, her eyes still startled me—they shouldn't have been that engaging. But they were. I could see the blackness of her pupils inside her irises and the faint shadows cast by her eyelashes onto her cheekbones. "Yeah? Where did you go?"

"Ah, just a couple of bars down in inner southeast."

"Really." She looked away again, and I was suddenly able to breathe. "Sounds fun. Tell me more."

"I saw something at the Hobbs Ballroom that I'm not sure what to make of," I said. "I saw . . . John. Your husband."

Ariane still focused her eyes on the computer screen, bringing up more documents, sending them to the printer. "Mmm-hmm?"

"He was there with these two other girls. A blonde and a brunette. The brunette totally looked like a guy at first, until I looked at her again. The blonde girl, though, definitely a girl. The weirdest thing was that the blonde girl was in the middle between John and that other girl, and they were both kissing her. Like, on the neck. And it—I'm not one hundred percent sure, but it looked like they were drinking her blood. I mean, I saw blood."

Ariane slid the grounding strap off, and got up and walked over the printer. She briskly stacked and straightened the printed pages, separating them into their separate documents, fastening them together with sharp snaps of the stapler. "The brunette's name is George," Ariane said, still not looking at me, her voice quietly neutral. "She's a distant cousin of his."

"Really? But who was the blonde girl?"

"Who knows," Ariane said. "Some little piece they picked up."

"Oh," I said. "Were they really drinking her blood?"

"I doubt it," said Ariane. "I think they were just pretending. It's Halloween; sometimes people act out little weird bits of theater when they go out on that night. And the Hobbs Ballroom, you say?" She waited for my nod. "Yeah, it was probably just a little bit of gothic playacting fun. I wouldn't worry about it if I were you."

"So you let John see other women?" I asked.

"Well, no," said Ariane, and her voice held a quivering edge of impatience like a violin's vibrato, but I couldn't tell if the impatience was directed at me or at the situation. "But I also don't force him to do anything. John's his own creature; he does what he wants to do. If what he wants to do includes me, then I'm glad. And besides, George is his cousin."

"Distant cousin," I repeated.

"Still." Ariane smiled. "Thanks for telling me, but I don't think it's anything to get upset about. I was out that night, too, with people other than John, and I don't think he would get upset about that. We know where we stand with each other."

It was so strange to watch her lie so transparently, like even she didn't know she was lying, but it was plainly obvious to me. How could Ariane lie? Why would she ever feel the need to? She was such a perfect being, it was almost sickening to see that she had her delusions, just like the rest of us. But who wouldn't, finding out about your husband cheating on you? It was like finding out that there is no Santa Claus. I wanted to throw my arms around her and comfort her, but you couldn't do something like that to someone like Ariane Dempsey. She was just too dangerous. Sure, I was a couple of inches taller than her, and I knew some aikido, but I'd still have been willing to bet money that she could kick my ass into next Sunday. I settled for saying, "I'm sorry if I misinterpreted things. I just thought it was really weird. And we *were* going to go to the Sunspot, but you know."

"Yeah, I heard," said Ariane. "Awful."

"If there's anything I can do for you—"

"Thanks, Margaret," Ariane said, with a gentle sincerity I hadn't heard from her before. "I'll let you know, but I think it's just a boring old 'between us' kind of deal."

We put in a couple of conversation-free hours of initial synthesis, then called it a night around 2:30. I watched her pulling on her fabulous coat, dying inside, wishing that I knew if she was going home to John, to talk it out, to try to save things between them, or whether she was just giving up, walking away, letting him go. Her face was hidden under the heavy cowl of her red-brown hair, a more beautiful color than I could ever get out of a jar, but I could feel her sadness from across the room. "I'll see you tomorrow night at six?" I said hopefully.

"Yeah, I'll probably be here. Thanks again, Margaret."

"It's my pleasure, Ariane," I said.

The drive home seemed horribly long and lonely, although it was less than fifteen minutes from door to door. I didn't turn on the car stereo or listen to the radio; it was just me and my heartbeat and the wet swish of tires on pavement. My apartment still smelled like the incense I had been burning the night before, but I lit some more, just to have something to watch.

Vanilla spice smoke, rising in lazy coils to the ceiling.

I put some King Tubby on the stereo in the living room, very quietly, and lay on top of the covers in bed, watching the smoke. I thought about John and that androgynous girl named, of all things, George. What a name for a girl. She had skinny wrists and a milky-pale face . . . but, then again, so did John; actually, they looked like a well-matched set, in the same way that Joanie and Sam were a well-matched set. It was a horrible thought, Ariane's husband with someone else. It was wrong. He was hers, goddammit. She'd been through a lot for him and with him and she deserved to keep him, even if she wasn't as skinny, even if she didn't go for threesomes. Then again, I didn't know whether or not Ariane did go in for threesomes. Maybe I had this all wrong. Maybe nothing I saw had any basis in fact whatsoever.

I rolled over and went to sleep.

XII

CHARM AND STRANGE

JOHN THURBIS

The weather reminded me bittersweetly of England—a dense fog that was really a cloud sitting on your face, and a listless, intermittent drizzle, just cold enough to justify a coat and scarf. George disagreed with me about the Englishness of it. "Too wild," she said, "too warm. I know it's the same planet, but the whole world seems newer here; younger. Perhaps it's only human civilization that ages the world and puts wrinkles on its face."

That George. She was a talker, that one. At first we didn't talk much at all, mostly because I didn't physically feel like speaking, but after I'd opened up my mind just a bit to suss her out and see if she was lying to us, she'd snuck in and established residence with a wave and a grin. To my surprise, it didn't bother me to have a connection with George, even though I'd initially drawn back even from connection with Ariane, as soon as I'd had the choice to do so. George had a different mind altogether; definitely honest and well-intentioned, sharp as a razor, just really refreshing. She also had a wonderful, silly, laddish voice that was fun to listen to, and she loved to talk, the way a dancer loves to dance. She constantly said things that delighted me.

And fortunately for me, poor socially sandblasted me, one of the things she loved to talk about, had apparently been dying to talk about as badly as I had, was mathematics.

I had completely and utterly underestimated George. I started out trying to impress her with all of my physics and mathematical knowledge; to her credit, she didn't point out that I was being an infantile twat, but instead started reminiscing about giving her father suggestions on attempting to deduce Euclid's fifth postulate while they sat at dinner. "In those days, women weren't really allowed to study at Jagiellonian University, even though my father was a professor there. But my father knew that I had a mind, and made sure it was not wasted. He taught me until I knew everything he knew, and then I had to figure out things on my own. If he had a mathematical problem that he struggled to solve or to explain, he'd work it out with me, and usually we could come to the right conclusion." She spoke with the kind of steely calm of someone who'd been wounded, and healed, but the scars still ached. And I just sat there, silenced, letting her living history sink into me, and in comparison to that, all the plaques and medals I'd ever won crumbled into utter insignificance.

It was so strange to have someone interested in having a conversation with me, instead of just pointing out everything that was wrong with me. I babbled to her, desperately, almost convulsively, like a prisoner just sprung from thirty days in the hole, and she just listened to me, and was interested, and didn't judge.

I even began to try to verbally explain the details of my delusional state, but I just couldn't make it coherent. She told me not to bother. "I already felt it," she said. "It's something best avoided, if possible. Anyway, you're different now." I noticed that she did not say "better," and I appreciated that. My delusions were not founded on nonsense; they came from a different kind of sense, one that didn't reconcile anywhere outside of the back of my own mind. But what I experienced was real, and I hadn't completely given up hope on finding a way to explain it.

"You *could* always decide you're interested in something else," George said, seizing the thought and tossing it out between us. "Then you can just file it away into 'Stuff I Was Thinking About Before But Don't Have to Think About Now.' Maybe you should try that. I think it might save time, if nothing else. Though, of course, you've got as much time as you'd like to have, if you want to spend decades trying to describe what madness feels like. Didn't Antonin Artaud try that? Still, it's best to leave it be for, oh, I don't know, a hundred years or so—the rough edges get smoothed off pretty well by then."

I smiled to her that it sounded as if she spoke from experience.

"You haven't lost a maker yet, have you?" she said.

I wasn't sure what she meant at first. Then it came back to me, clearer than I'd ever realized before— passing out, waking up to punishing vertigo and searing pain in my bitten neck, the sea-salty syrup of Ariane's blood in my mouth, and Ricari bending over me, shoving his ripped wrist between my lips and commanding me to swallow.

She sighed with a sagging smile. "Both Ariane and Orfeo are still with us, and you were sparked with a combination of their blood. I only had one source. Maria." Her voice softened when she said that name. "In my opinion, that's best; less chance of a slip-up. But when she died, I lost my mind, almost as surely as you lost yours. But, of course, it's not the same at all, and it would be very different for you if the same thing happened to you. For me, it was temporary—an emotional lack. What happened to you is supposed to be irreversible. But it wasn't, and this is the mind you have now, and the reality you have now. Why struggle to define your unhappiness while you're happy? I say kick it into a ditch. It's not gone; it'll never be gone. But at least when it's there, it can't overwhelm you anymore. Now, I've heard a rumor that you have a place on the river that you like to go to. We've got four hours till dawn. Can I see it?"

If she were beside me, I could even cross the Burnside Bridge, as long as I was heading east, so that the white stag would be at my back and I could only see its reflection on the wet pavement. She wasn't afraid, and she didn't think I was nuts. It was just ordinary to her. Maybe it could become ordinary for me, eventually.

It wasn't unusual for us to stay out all night, seeking refuge at daybreak in her rooms. She switched hotel rooms every night, everything from the cheapest, dirtiest, noisiest inner-city no-tells to a nice little room in the same posh, wishing-it-was-L.A. luxury high-rise where the Russians were staying. We met with them in the sushi restaurant on the ground floor of the hotel, and El's expression spoke volumes about what she thought George and I were up to together.

Afterwards, up in George's room while she stuffed all of her things into her big, square, dark-brown leather messenger bag, I said, "I'm not sure I want to be best mates with the Revikoffs."

"Oh, good Lord, who does?" said George. "Their lifestyle costs too much."

"I thought you knew them well," I said.

"No, they are friends of Ariane's, aren't they?"

"Ariane hasn't *got* any friends." I punctuated that with a laugh, but still, the realization that it was true shot through me like an arrow. She hadn't had friends back in San Francisco much, either; it wasn't that she was unlikable, but she was so hyper-focused on her studies that she always kept everyone at arm's length. If I'd gotten to know her first, I might not have had the stones to actually ask her out, but on the day I met her at NCIT, I was so annoyed after my first administrative review that I just grabbed the first fit girl I saw so I wouldn't have to get bladdered by myself. I don't think anyone had ever just barged into her world like that and snatched her out. Cluelessness and ferocious alcohol cravings worked to my advantage that day.

"You shouldn't be so neglectful of Ariane," George said gently.

That might have been true. On the other hand, I didn't like to be told. "Am I being neglectful? I thought I was living my life. Finally. I've been in a box for so long. A cave, a cage. Prison. I'm just taking a few deep breaths. Besides, it's not like I've deserted her—she's always down at the labs with that girl, Margaret, playing with test tubes. She left *me* alone. I think she thinks I'm in good hands with you."

She sat on the edge of the bed opposite me. "She doesn't know me from Adam," she said. "She only knows me from Orfeo's legends and from what she's seen since I've been here. She's avoiding me. As far she knows, I'm just some supermodel come to take her drugs."

"Well, aren't you?" I teased.

"I'm not a supermodel." She rolled her eyes, then winked at me. "C'mon, let's get out of here and go to a nice crack den."

"I have to go to the house to get my Orchid," I said. "Will that do?"

We were silent until we had put the hotel a mile behind us, walking through the university district toward where the highways tangled. "I understand that she makes you unhappy," she said. "You can either choose to forgive her, or not."

"And I haven't decided yet."

"You don't *have* to forgive her, John," said George. "No one is forcing you to feel anything. Or to do anything. You're free to go at any time. You can always just leave, you know."

Another arrow hit me, stinging deeply in my solar plexus. It hadn't hit me in the heart yet, so I figured I was safe. "Just take off, you mean."

"I did," said George. "I left Orfeo. It was a very cruel thing to do, but it was what I needed to do right then, and I trusted that he would be all right without me. On the other hand, I didn't really care if he would or not. I just needed to be away, and if he came to a bad end because I wasn't there, then so be it. I could live with that." She chuckled. "Like I told you, I was crazy. But I can be cold like that. I think everyone can, when the chips are down. *You* can be cold like that. I think Ariane would be fine without you."

"Are you proposing we run away together?" I asked, trying to be roguish, instead coming off like a flamingo with its beak caught in a drainpipe.

She laughed so loud, I saw the drivers of cars going past turning to stare. "Uh, not exactly," she said, then surprised me with, "I think I would drive you straight back to crazy town, express, no stops."

I weakly laughed a little myself; monkey see, monkey do. "Why?"

"Because I'd never fuck you, and you wouldn't be able to think about anything else."

"Oh, flatter yourself!" I admonished.

"I'm not. Of course you don't fancy me now, but you're a man; you're still a man. With men, whatever they see that they can never have, they soon want more than anything in the world. It's ridiculous. Don't get me wrong—you're a brilliant, passionate man with a great look and a really stimulating sense of humor. But in general, I don't fuck men. I'm certainly not attracted to them. And I am most definitely not attracted to you."

"Uh, cheers, I guess . . ."

"I'm not asking you to hook up with me. I'm telling you that you have choices. You don't have to stay here trying to recapture the past. You can go off on adventures—see the world! You can do whatever you want." She gave me a big, seductive, wide-mouthed grin.

"Maybe I want to be a pirate," I shrugged.

She nodded emphatically. "You can become a pirate if you want, though I actually can't recommend it; it's not as fun as it's cracked up to be. If I were you, I'd go to Monte Carlo and break the bank; I bet you'd be an ace at counting cards. It's a great way to make a lot of money quickly. I try to go at least once every twenty years. Easier than modeling, let me tell you."

I laughed. "You were *not* ever a pirate."

She winked. "Can you prove it?"

Ariane had not yet returned when George and I reached the house. "See?" I fumed. "It's three-thirty in the morning. Why isn't she here?"

George's eyes glazed over for a split second. "She's putting together the potassium cyanide."

"I didn't mean *literally*. . . . " I poked around in the refrigerator in the kitchen, pulled out a pack of red blood cells, and swallowed it all without even thinking about it. It was a strange, pleasant sensation, like gulping down a ball of frozen champagne, effervescing in my stomach as it dissolved and the cells were split and instantly consumed.

George looked askance. "You *voluntarily* drink that stuff?"

I glanced down at the empty pack in my hand. "RBCs are kind of fun. I mean, sure, it tastes like a bin bag, but nobody drinks Martinis for the flavor, now, do they?"

Inevitably, she said, "Well, I do. . . ."

Ariane had set aside my Orchid in the crisper drawer, all nice and lined up, already measured into syringes. I had three left. I noticed George looking with longing down into the crisper. "Would you like some?"

"I don't want to deprive you of something you need."

"Of course you don't. So, would you like some?

There's more besides this, of course. The next batch should be ready by night after tomorrow."

"Let's go down to the rock on the river," she said. "I'd rather take it there. I don't want to be too near to humans when I'm on this stuff—it has a way of lowering inhibitions a little lower than they ought to be."

"My friend might be there," I warned. "She's just a kid—try not to kill her, all right?"

Psychward was not there, but she'd left me a six-page note explaining how she *really* felt about me, apparently written over the course of a day at school and a night sitting on the Rock. The note didn't make a great deal of sense, but her "forever dedication to the darkness" came through loud and clear. I gave George a few droplets from one of the syringes, and let the remainder dissolve on my tongue while George read the note. "This is dangerous," she concluded, handing it back to me.

"What, the kid? She's a thirteen-year-old, schizophrenic goth—you think anyone is going to take what she says seriously?"

"But what if someone does? Would you be able to do what needs to be done?"

"Of course," I said uncomfortably.

"Orfeo thought that about Ariane, too, and when the time came, he couldn't do it. He'd planned to kill her . . . of course he had. But then they became friends. It's very dangerous to befriend a human who you don't intend to bring with you into the other life, especially these days. I mean, the nice thing is that even if our existence is discovered, nobody will be moved to do much about it, but if you value your continued safety, I would discourage you."

"So I ought to take her out next time I see her? A little kid?"

"She's thirteen—she's a woman, whether or not she realizes it. She says here that she knows where you and Ariane live. She's a loaded gun, and I'm not sure you know what you're doing."

"You *are* rather cold when it comes to it, aren't you?"

"Or so I claim to be." We were smiling stupidly at each other across the Rock, with the condensation dribbling onto our heads from the bridge overhang above. "I don't want to talk about this any more."

"Me neither."

"Tell me more about your lattice computations," she whispered, extending her long white hand to me. I took it in my own, our dark claws clicking together. "Forget the human world and all the awards and the prestige. Show me the elegance of your mathematics. Draw me a portrait of quark-gluon plasma, and help me see it as you see it. I'm starving to see something I've never seen before."

That, oddly, at last got me in the heart. *Forget the human world.* I could continue my computational research, but I could never share it with my colleagues, because they were a different species now and I could never show my face to them again. To them, I had been dead for ten years, cut to ribbons in a hotel bathtub by assailant or assailants unknown; whether I was brilliant or not, whether or not I was onto something, it would be in an enclosed system of one.

Perhaps two, now.

It made me look at why I had been doing physics in the first place, why I had driven myself to succeed, to publish incessantly, to impress students with how *cool* I was. I had been telling myself all that time that I was above reputation, above attention-seeking, above exterior validation; but I had combined blindness and dishonesty. Why did I still think of physics, when it wouldn't do me or the world any good, when it was purer and more honest just to be an animal?

It wasn't my world any longer. I could see it and touch it, but I could never again be a part of it. I was part of the twilight now. Psych had been my friend when I had no other, and because of that, she was doomed.

"Don't hate Orfeo," George's voice shimmered against the nightfall inside my closed eyelids. "Or hate him less, now that you have something in common with him. It is only emotions like this, like the ones you have for your friend, that have brought us to where we are—all of us, including me. If you truly love her, make her; or, if you truly love her, spare her the nightmare that comes from loving one of us. But decide."

Somehow she dragged me up to the street and flagged down a taxi, pulling me in next to her and mentally commanding the driver to take us to the little house in the hills. I don't remember our arrival—I had already nodded off—but I woke up in bed next to Ariane, awake and watching me. Without a word, she pressed a lukewarm blood pack into my hand.

I sat up and drank the freshly drawn blood, probably extracted last night. It had an aftertaste of bitter almond; strange longings, twitchy anxiety. It was from the girl, Ariane's assistant. Margaret. It was cyanide I tasted in the blood.

"If you weren't here," Ariane said in a low voice, "I was going to have it myself. She just sat there and let me take it. She didn't even ask me what it was for."

I slid off the bed, grateful that I was still fully clothed except for my boots. I found the boots next to the bedside table, and slid them on. I wanted to say something to her, but too many impulses happened at once and I kept silent, knowing she could probably see into my head, she being my maker and all. She could probably see through any barriers I put up. I hoped that she knew how I felt, because I sure as hell didn't.

I pulled on my Army surplus jacket and left. I kept my attention focused on the road ahead of me, not daring to listen to what Ariane might be thinking. My mind was too full as it was; there wasn't room in there for her, too.

I sat in a greasy spoon full of punk rockers and junkies all night, transcribing equations onto a series of napkins as I filled an ashtray with Camel butts and my coffee cup was refilled again and again. The lights were too bright and I gave away twice as many cigarettes as I smoked. I was glad for the distraction and the annoyance; anything to avoid thinking about having to kill Psychward.

XIII

THE DAY THE WORLD WENT AWAY

ELISABETA REVIKOFF

"I'm tired of lying low," I said to Alexander Vassilyevich, who was restlessly holding out the television remote control at arm's length, flipping through the channels without giving any of them two full seconds. I could barely stand television at the very best of times, and this strobe of greasy, glittery noise was almost more than I could bear. "Look at the rotten habits you're picking up. Can't we at least go out tonight? Varlet has started to fray at the edges—we can't keep him much longer."

"You can go out if you like, as long as you're hidden." He paused on the station that showed the television schedule, sharing the screen with a shrill game show. The current presenter was a dead ringer for Rachell Reed, enough to startle me for a moment before I determined that it could never be her; imagine, Rachell Reed as an announcer on the program guide channel. It would be like Marlene Dietrich doing a commercial for cheese in a can. Rachell had become successful enough to be a "type," and Hollywood had enormous skill in generating clones. As much as I understood Alexander's hesitation, I wanted to make sure that he didn't have time to sink into brooding over Rachell. He had gotten over girls before, with my help; it was both my duty and my pleasure.

I tossed my hair over my shoulder and played with the ends, noting his eyes inexorably drawn to my hands and my hair. "I don't want to go out only to hide. I can't help it if I have social needs. I think Ariane is simply being paranoid. No one is in any danger; no one has taken any particular notice of us."

"Still, anonymity comes at a price. We have already changed hotels three times. It would really be better if we left town altogether," he said. With a sigh of effort, he turned the box off.

"But the Orchid is here," I said.

He laughed. "The Orchid. I am astonished, Elisabeta."

"Oh, come on. No, you're not. Are you trying to tell me that you see it as just another way to get drunk? You aren't made of stone, nor are you stupid. You admit that your experiences have also been profound."

He nodded, but wouldn't meet my eyes. "Yes. But you can't deny that this town's not big enough for us. I feel as constrained as you, but a night out at the titty bars on the east side isn't going to solve that problem. I am restless here. I want greater anonymity; there are only so many people who go out. You've already been recognized, remember, going back into that martini bar a second time, wearing that same pair of green shoes. If you want to be a part of that kind of society, we need a city with more chic places to go, and a larger population to work with. And *I* miss having a house."

"That's my Sasha—live in one house for twenty-one years, leave it, and immediately begin longing for the next one. But yes, it would be nice, wouldn't it? A kind of permanent roost," I mused. I didn't miss the last house we'd had, but I did miss the house before it, the extended bungalow in West Hollywood, where we lived during the sixties, which we ended up having to burn down so that our previous identities could die. We could probably replicate the floor plan and furnishings of that house, at enormous expense, but it would never be the same; it had been Daniel that created that house, that sense of home, for me. Now there was no house, no base camp, nowhere to go and hide and be in a familiar corner, see a familiar view; there was just me and Alex and our ghosts. "Unfortunately, at the moment, I can't picture it."

"We have traveled so little, and I thought that that's what we left L.A. to do," Alexander said. "Shall we continue, while we still can? Already technology exists that can determine one of us from a human from outer space, if only they thought to look for us. It would not be wise for us to be seen too much."

"How can we?" I said, throwing up my hands. "I don't go *out*. And when I do, you want me to disappear! You won't even let me wear the emeralds."

"Therefore, we are in agreement," said Alexander with a smile.

"We have agreed nothing!" A tiny firework of rage went off behind my eyes.

He walked over to me and threw his arms around me, kissing me forcefully on the corner of my mouth. "You creature," he growled, gently tugging on my hair so as to shake my head from side to side. The firework was snuffed out, as though a massive, soft blanket wrapped around it. I giggled like a child. "Go on, get out of my sight. But please, my lovely, steer clear of the cops, or anyone in uniform. You see them, disappear. Better yet, just cloak yourself entirely. Spring up on someone unaware like a tiger in the jungle. In fact," he said thoughtfully, "I think that's what I shall do."

"Without me?" I cried out.

He knew I was teasing. "I am more cruel than Caesar," he said, his hands sliding down to cup my buttocks, then slipping up again into my hair. "Come, let's take care of ourselves—discreetly, mind you—and I'll meet you back here at four-thirty, and we can decide where we want to go. Will that suit?"

"Anything to get you away from the TV," I said, pinching his cheek. His next kiss actually found my lips, and was light and gentle, though his lips had grown thin, cold, and hard. I wished him luck so that I could feel them the way they should be; if he required the blood of three fat men, I wished him luck, and their souls peace.

When he had gone, I lingered behind, first vaguely considering an outfit, which would then determine the destination. While examining my collection to find the dullest clothes I had, my attention drifted toward Orchid, and I played with the thought of another night out under its influence. Halloween weekend had been a blast; I hadn't woken up covered in leaves and mud in the woods in an extremely long time. Besides my husband, that strange ancient Arthur Chicot had been there, too, draining a gigantic opossum for his breakfast. Once I'd caught and drank one, too, we made a beeline to Ariane's house, to catch up and talk about the night before, to congratulate her, and of course to see if she had any more. We all wanted to try it again.

She hadn't that night (and her expression of sheer terror, with half a dozen vampires in her kitchen, making demands and pleas, was priceless), but days later she had produced large amounts of the drug. She parceled it out to us like a pharmacist, boring us half to death droning about dosage, interactions, and neurophysiology. I supposed that Arthur Chicot did care about such dull things; once upon a time he had been some sort of bonesetter himself, and he listened intently, asking all manner of questions—flattery which Ariane drank as a camel drinks water. She had a limitless capacity for having her intelligence validated. I didn't begrudge her it; that next batch of Orchid was stronger, cleaner, more intense, more everything. She gave Alexander and me ten doses, to split between the two of us. Absurd. We did the lot over the course of three nights, enjoying the effects of taking more all at once, instead of in snippets, like on Halloween.

The next week, she gave us ten more, along with a repeat of the lecture on staying hidden. Alexander and I happily stayed put in our new hotel room, taking all of the Orchid at once, drifting among the stars, an interplanetary ocean dotted with diamonds, the cosmos humming softly like a nursing mother to her infant. We made love almost continuously, burning through all of the blood in our veins, but unable, unwilling, to unlock ourselves to seek more. Orchid calmed those aching limbs and throbbing heads.

The next day I called Ariane, but she didn't answer; and when I dropped by her house the next night, she wasn't there.

John and girl George were, though. George gave me

some of her Orchid, which was nice of her. John just gave me a smirk and told me that he "actually needed it," as if I were plundering his vital organs. I slipped the dose into my pocket, nodded at them, and left before I threw him to the ground and drained him dry. He was so young, he was practically still human; it would have been simple to pulverize his bones, keep him paralyzed for a few days, and teach him a lesson about respecting those older and more powerful than he. Still, George was sitting there, and she was as much older than me as I was more than John. I just smiled at them, said nothing, and climbed back into the backseat of the town car.

Girl George had pushed me, nudged me along like a child. It was humiliating. Still, I got the Orchid; the old dyke could have any opinion of me she wanted.

Without really thinking, I grabbed the bottle from the refrigerator in the suite's kitchen, popped the needle into the bottle, drew a triple-ought-four, and jetted it under my tongue, then went back to my clothes closet to look at shoes. Shortly, though, I just lay back on the floor and relaxed. The Orchid's tiny amount of plasma was just enough to take the edge off the blood craving, but nowhere near enough to satisfy it; merely an appetizer. I wished I could just stay there on the ground, but my weak heartbeat was a flutter in my chest, and I felt fragile and insubstantial, isolated, numb. A decision had to be made.

Jeans, long-sleeved silk blouse, light jacket, plain black shoes with hardly any heel to speak of, and a dark scarf to cover my hair. Simple, plain, and basic. Discretion. Alexander had taken Varlet and the car, gone somewhere south and west, already had a companion, though Alex had not yet tasted her. I felt violently jealous.

Rather than leaving through the lobby, I went out the back service entrance, through an alleyway where the garbage containers reeked of rotting parsley, and onto the bright street. A light rain had just ended, and the pavements were still shiny and slick, shreds of black sky and stars showing through the broken clouds. I stood on the corner, fascinated with the slithery sound of traffic, snatches of speech, and the underlying interwoven tapestry of thoughts.

I shuddered, suddenly flushed; Alexander Vassilyevich had taken his bite, and the blood flowed into him, making his skin tingle and his ears ring.

Across the way, standing in a doorway, a fat young girl in a black hoodie and a long black skirt stared at me, breathing uneasily through her mouth; she had been walking for a long time, and had paused there to catch her breath, perhaps. But she stared at me as though she were reading me, gleaning some information from the sight of me. I reflexively took a step back, blurring myself from her view, but instead of shrugging it off, she shook her head and stared at me again, denying my disappearance.

It was an opportunity I decided not to waste.

I beckoned her with a crook of my finger. She stepped into the road without bothering to check for traffic, without acknowledging the angry horn of a car that had just barely missed her. Momentarily she stood before me, gazing up at me, eyes round, but not surprised.

"You're one, too," she said reverently.

"Come upstairs," I replied.

She did not lower her hood even when we went into our rooms. She stared at the furniture, the mirror, the television set, the crystal candlesticks on the mantel. To her, this was a fairytale palace, bedecked with unimaginable luxury; she hadn't the slightest idea that this room only cost two hundred a night. I realized that she was mad, this little girl, still awkward with her big breasts and the ground so suddenly far away, trying to hide her face with thick lines of black makeup around her eyes and mouth.

"You must know John and Ariane." She spoke abruptly, without looking at me.

"Yes," I said. "Tell me your name."

"Psychward," she muttered.

"Tell me your *name*," I insisted.

She fought me. I was amazed; she fought against my search, self-protective and startlingly strong. I stepped up to her and pushed her hood back, staring into her eyes; she trembled and gasped out, "H-H-Heather."

"Heather," I repeated, unable to keep an arch of contempt out of my voice. I let her drop her eyes and she gasped again, this time with relief. "Heather," I said again, "Dandelion, Clover, Barley. Beautiful names that describe beautiful things." I walked over to the bed and stretched out on its surface, sliding up against the headboard. The girl sat on the edge of the bed, staring at me.

"There are so many different vampires," she said wonderingly. "I didn't know."

"There are lots of us," I said. "And it's our business to make sure you don't know. Can you imagine?"

She nodded, sniffed, her hands pausing at the hood that she wanted to pull up again, but I kept her from it. I wanted to look at her face, the skin thrumming softly with life, the soft faint hair at her temples, thickening suddenly into dusty, dirty black shreds, frayed at the edges on one side where she had chewed on it, threadbare on the other where she had pulled at it until it came out. "Do you know where John is?" she asked, tucking the chewed end into her mouth and grinding her teeth against it, three snaps of her bicuspid teeth, a precise and regimented action. "I was looking for John."

I smiled at the girl. "He's around," I said. "I don't know precisely where . . ." Without much effort, I did know exactly where (pacing the noisy walkways under a bridge, with his eyes locked onto that neon sign which held his obsessive interest), but I wasn't about to give up my dinner. "How do you know him?"

"He's my friend," she said. "He's the only one who doesn't mind that I'm crazy."

"Of course," I said. She'd been his feeding trough, his sounding board. The poor mad bastard could only connect with a lunatic child, and had established a bond of addiction and trust. It was saddening, absurd. "And how do you know Ariane?"

"Well, she's John's wife."

"She's not his wife," I said indignantly. "They never married."

"They didn't . . . ?" She looked as though her stomach had just dropped through the floor. "But they said—"

"They are partners, nothing more. If they told you anything different, it was a deception. A fantasy. A delusion, perhaps."

"Yeah, I *know* I'm crazy," said the girl, suddenly prickly.

"I didn't mean you. Of course you would believe them. You have no choice in the matter. We control you. We control your thoughts and your actions, if it serves our purpose or our whims."

"He said he was my friend." Her eyes locked onto the floor. "So he was lying about that."

I shrugged. "Perhaps. Perhaps not. Friendship obeys no logic. Tell me, would you like a drink?" I stood up and went to the refrigerator, and her wide eyes followed me, her mouth slightly open, as though the mere sight of me took her breath away. "I'm going to have one. Do you like vodka?"

"You drink alcohol?"

"A vodka and Coke?" I asked, pouring liquor and soda over ice.

"But I'm thirteen."

"You were drinking earlier," I said, "I can smell it on you."

"It's my empty flask. I *wish* I'd been drinking earlier."

"You can be drinking now," I said.

If you asked me I wouldn't have been able to tell why I did it.

"Do you do drugs?" I asked.

"What? Yeah," said the girl, sounding suddenly much older, more experienced, but that too was a falsehood; it had been mere weeks earlier when she had smoked cannabis for the first time, and then followed it with a handful of Adderall pills given to her by a schoolmate, who traded them for a shoplifted jacket. Still, she was thirteen, and every day lasted for an eternity of painful new experiences.

"There's this one drug that John likes a lot," I said, "and I like it, too, and I was just going to do some more. You want some?"

"Sure," she said.

A triple-ought-four dose sank without a trace into

the dark, fizzling surface of the drink; the ice cubes collapsed with a tinkle and a burst of carbonated applause. I stared at the glass for a while, trying to see the path that the Orchid had taken in the body of the liquid, but it was invisible.

I handed her the glass. "Tell me if you taste vanilla," I said.

She took a big swallow of the vodka and Coke, then another one, almost completely finishing it off. A robust girl, maybe even from Russian stock. "Uh, not really," she said. "Is it vanilla vodka?"

"No, it's plain vodka. . . ."

I let my voice trail away. Her eyes blinked rapidly, and her throat swelled as she swallowed; she grinned, and the expression was strange on her, stretchy, something deeply unfamiliar. "Oh, man, that's . . ." she started to say. Her mind formed, *really bitter,* but her tongue produced no sounds.

She shook her head loosely, not trying to convey anything by it as a gesture, but more reflexively, like she was trying to scratch her ear with her shoulder. Her wet lips had gone bright red underneath the thinning smudge of black lipstick and her heart beat so hard I couldn't hear anything else.

I leaned over her and grasped her neck between my hands, lowering my fangs to the massive, throbbing pulse, and found that my teeth easily punctured the skin and locked onto the artery. I could taste something almond-like in her blood, corrosively bitter and astringent, but it was nothing like the peculiar chemical flavor that I'd come to accept, even crave when I knew it was out of reach. Her heart shoved the blood into my mouth, then, suddenly, slowed to a vague spasm, then stopped altogether. I lifted my head and looked down at her. I had barely bitten her forty seconds ago, but her heart had fallen still, and her eyes rapidly dulled.

I wrapped the wound in her neck with my scarf, and sat on the floor beside her chair, waiting for the secondary build-up of Orchid inside me, but the rush never came, only the same bitter taste in the blood. Even the blood itself was thin and ineffective; it was greasy with adrenaline, but lacking in richness and roundness. What was it that Ariane had said about Orchid and how it interfered with the blood's ability to carry oxygen? I couldn't remember now. I stared at the dead girl, and decided that I ought not to waste the nourishment in her body, even if it was incomplete and foul to the tongue.

While in the midst of draining her still-warm veins, I caught an image of John, still on the bridge, but heading back toward this side of town, his stride first tentative, then determined. *Psych,* he thought, *Psych's gone; something happened to Psych. I've got to get to her.* He locked onto my position, and all sorts of cruel and vicious thoughts crowded into his head.

I directed my thoughts toward both Alexander and Varlet. *Get back here now. Fly if you must, Alexander Vassilyevich, but don't leave me to face the psychotic by myself.*

Unfortunately, my husband was much farther away than John. I was still alone in the suite with the girl's corpse when John appeared on the balcony, staring menacingly through the sliding glass doors. I took my time getting up to let him in, but not through any desire to make him suffer.

"I'm really sorry," I said to him. "I didn't know."

"You," he breathed, not furiously, but sadly, cynically. "You gave her a compound containing potassium cyanide and you claim you didn't know what it would do to her?"

"Orchid . . ." I whispered.

"Yes, I know. It controlled you," he sighed heavily. Turning away from me he knelt in front of the chair where the girl sprawled, boneless but relaxed, like a melancholy rag doll. With most of her blood gone, her skin had the texture of dirty white wax. "I'm sorry, Psych," he whispered to her, grasping her cold hands, rubbing them gently between his palms, trying without hope to warm her again. "I'm so fucking sorry."

I had the strength to resist him if he attacked me, but he never did; he just sat, rubbing her hands and apologizing to her, a tear running from the corner of each eye and coursing down his nose to the slightly upturned tip. He didn't even turn his head when Alexander and Varlet burst in through the front door. They both stared at John, at the girl's immobile, stiffening body, and then at me.

"I made a mistake," I said, and realized that I was weeping, too.

"Yes," said John unexpectedly, "you did. I believe that it would be only right to pay for your damages." He rose from the floor and slowly approached Varlet.

Varlet's face blanched, and he stared in panic at Alexander. "What's he talking about?"

"He's right," I whispered. "I'm sorry."

"Did she suffer?" John demanded, still staring at Varlet. "You'd better hope she didn't."

I shook my head. Alexander came and wrapped his

arms around me, and I didn't know if I was grateful to him for that or not, because with his embrace, and the warmth and strength of his body holding me up, no matter what I'd done, I began to sob.

John sent it to me. I, who was so old and powerful, felt myself blasted by an immense wave of grief and remorse, and I cried so hard I couldn't catch my breath and felt close to fainting. Meanwhile, John gripped Varlet by one shoulder and marched him out of the room, Varlet struck dumb by the force of John's will, held silent by Alexander's control, the leg of his pants soaking wet with terrified piss.

It was some time before I could calm my crying to the point where Alexander and I could take the girl's body out. We brought it to her home (John had burned the location into my mind like a cattle brand as he frog-marched Varlet away) and lay the soft, heavy corpse gently on a woven-plastic lawn chair that already held the shape of her body. I was stricken. I almost wished that her guardians would wake up, catch us, and sound an alarm; but then what would happen to Alexander, who had so patiently handled the girl, driven the car himself though he barely remembered how, and still spared time to kiss the top of my head?

I could be quite certain that Varlet suffered more than the girl; whatever that poor man felt was sent to me, the deep pinch of John's teeth on his neck, the stabbing pains in Varlet's stomach as his blood was sucked away so rapidly that all his muscles cramped, his regrets, his confusion, his resignation.

The worst part, though, the absolute worst, was lying in bed with Alexander, dawn spilling pink and violet all along the edge of the sky, and even though my eyes were closed and I felt sleep closing its claws on me, I knew my husband was gazing down on me and slowly shaking his head.

XIV

A SUBTLE EQUATION

JADZIA KOPERNIK

As soon as Arthur left, I missed him. He was my oldest friend who was still around. Seeing him again after a space of decades had made me giddy with memories of the Paris that no longer existed. His smile shone out from the back window of a taxicab, and then the taxi disappeared up the road, and a part inside me curled up tight like a night-flower at dawn. It was almost as if gravity itself had increased, weighing my shoulders down. I tried to shake it off, trying to wish him well out there on his journey with all that Orchid, but I couldn't keep myself from worrying. There were vampires out there, undoubtedly more than I had imagined, and it was a fairly safe bet that every single one of them now knew of the existence of Orchid, if not its specific effects. And while Arthur Chicot could have shaken the hand of the fifth King Henry of England (if he'd had any desire to do so), there undoubtedly existed creatures older than he, and my mind painted terrible pictures of the kinds of physical and psychic violence that a thousand-year-old vampire might visit upon poor Arthur to seize the drug. Arthur could be killed—killed forever, that timeless fellow. Still, that could have happened at any time, anyway.

The difference was, there had never been any reason to kill him before.

The Virginian and the Indian were leaving, too, as laden with Orchid as Arthur had been. All three of them had been pressed into service, each carrying half a liter of the compound; they were to deliver it to certain interested parties who had been sending Ariane enormous sums of money. As far as I know, she had set no price, but the eager vampires' guesses were outlandish. She didn't specifically tell me how much, but one night, she carelessly handed me a roll of hundred-dollar bills as thick as her fist and mumbled to me to see if I could make some change out of it; if I couldn't, just hang onto it. I tried not to stare at the money. I had been well paid for walking up and down a narrow plank in six-inch heels and a hobble skirt, but this was absurd.

She had no time to spend any of the money that was being sent to her. Her modest kitchen table held piles of currency. The floors were littered with opened cardboard boxes of 5cc insulin syringes and glass sample vials. I tried to do her a favor by tidying up, but the slowly spreading disaster was impossible to contain. It was easier, anyhow, to just shoot down a triple-ought-four or two and chase it with a blood pack, or go downtown and get it hot and on the hoof. The mess wasn't going anywhere and there was stuff to do.

I took it upon myself to spend some of Ariane's money buying her a new wardrobe, but without bringing her with me to fit her in anything, I could only buy off the rack, with wild guesses about her exact proportions, how she felt about certain fabrics, and that sort of thing. I imagined that she was very sensitive and loved her comfort, as she seemed to favor things like old jeans and velvet. Her clothes didn't pinch her body; at best they cuddled it, holding it tightly and gently. I looked all over for a duplicate of her pinkish suede jacket, but came up empty-handed, coming back with nothing other than the wrong thing. I was certain that she didn't notice my efforts, locked inside her own head as she was.

It was strange to be at her house without John being there. I always dropped by in the early evening, just out of habit, but John hadn't been around for a while. I couldn't understand it; upon the untimely death of a friend, I'd want to spend as much time in bed with my lover as possible. Then again, perhaps he was wise to isolate himself. With the help of the Orchid, his mind was absolutely opaque. He had effectively vanished. But I could still feel him, his presence coming through strong, so he couldn't have been very far away. I wished that I could have been there to warn him not to get too attached to people, especially not very young people, especially not children, *especially* not troubled children, and absolutely not little girls. He was a man of strange, deep attachments, which offended his sense of innate British stoicism. That led to an open rebellion against that stoicism, the symbol of old men, old sexist England. But emotional distance wasn't always such a bad thing.

Still, his situation was complex and heartbreaking, and no amount of stiff upper lip could prepare a man for that—only experience. If he lived through the next year, he'd survive. The fact that he was still alive at all gave me hope every night I woke up. I had no desire to lose any more friends.

With both of them gone so much, I spent a lot of time at the house by myself, or talking with Leland Quary, who delivered ten hand-rolled cigarettes to Ariane every night. The Virginian was an odd one—on the one hand filled with a kind of Buddhist calm, and on the other, full of superstitions so ancient I didn't understand most of them. He never stayed long, never wanting to "impose" his presence, only to touch his hat and deliver the cigarettes, and make a polite amount of small talk.

While everyone was gone, I went into her bedroom closet and found a couple of pairs of her trousers, so I could more accurately size the clothes I wanted to buy for her. I was distracted by the disheveled bed. The image of Ariane and John locked together there, clutched in the height of passion, flashed in my thoughts, and I dropped the pants and hurried from the room as fast as I could. The hallway wasn't much better, nor was the study; they had really fucked all over this house.

Ariane and Ricari had, too.

I staggered over to one of the chairs in the study and seated myself on it. I usually didn't get impressions of the past from places, but at times it was overwhelming, especially if someone else happened to be thinking of that place at the same time, their minds tugged along by my visual journey. It was an alarming phenomenon, hard to fake my way through, that projected déjà vu that wasn't mine. So many vampire minds all gathered so closely together, all our minds, all of us so close to Ariane, had an amplifying effect. That was why we isolated ourselves. After a while the vampire may learn to despise even her most beloved, as she always feels what the beloved feels, and that is a weapon that no love can withstand forever.

Not without a break. A hundred years was good.

I was still in the study musing when Ariane returned home at 3:15. There was plenty of darkness still left in the night; the winter nights were long. In fact, this was an early return for her. I wondered guiltily if she'd caught me peeking and come home to give me a piece of her mind.

Nothing of the sort registered when I popped my head into the kitchen to inform her of my continued presence. "You wanna help me get some things out of the car?" she asked, setting down a pair of fiberglass-and-metal boxes onto the kitchen counter. "I want this to happen fast."

Between the two of us we got the other eight enormously heavy boxes in one trip. "Ten days of whole blood, six liters of plasma, and five liters of Orchid," Ariane described, already sliding the bags into their racks in the refrigerator.

"Five liters? Jesus."

"I've got a lot to send."

"You're like Superfly," I said with a laugh. "You should get a massive gold goblet studded with diamonds to drink your blood from."

"And take away the pleasure of drinking it straight from the bag? Please." She laughed, too, but uneasily. "Has John been around since I left?" I shook my head no, with a rueful grimace. She bit her lip, murmuring, "I just hope he has enough Orchid. I really don't want him to stop taking it just yet. I don't know yet if he *can* ever stop." She put the Orchid into the bottom of the refrigerator, five slim, shiny vacuum bottles, then paused with the door open and her hand on the cap of one bottle. "Well, I'd like to have some, since I've actually got a couple of hours to relax. Would you like some of the new batch?"

"Is it a different formulation?"

"No, the same as last time."

"Good; I liked the last batch a lot."

"Me too."

We each took a double dose. I had come to enjoy the poisonous flavor of it under my tongue. Of course we didn't have to put it under our tongues; all of the tissue lining our mouths was as permeable as the rest. Still, it was ritualistic. Ariane offered me a bag of blood, but I demurred, not wanting to add bitterness to bitterness.

We went to the study and sat on the rug side by side, sighing to ourselves.

"I was in your room earlier," I suddenly confessed. "I'm sorry. I've been trying to buy you some new clothes, but I wasn't sure what size you wore."

Her eyes were soft and hazy, shining a little in the darkness. "Well, that's okay. I wear size ten most of the time. And, like, a medium shirt. But it really depends."

I burst out, "I couldn't stop thinking about you and Orfeo. You know. Fucking. Is there anywhere in this house where you didn't do it with him?"

She blinked, a bit shocked, and I sensed that she was thinking of Orfeo, too, thinking of the similarities between Daniel and me. "We never did it in the kitchen," she said after a moment's reflection. "But . . . yeah."

"I don't blame you," I said, "I used to bang him like crazy when we were together. That's what he was for in the first place. That's why he was brought to me. He was supposed to be a quick cock fix, then breakfast. But then I liked him."

"He didn't talk about you a whole lot," Ariane said with a rusty, disbelieving laugh. "It was like it hurt him to talk about you. When he did, though, I could tell that he never stopped loving you, even though he tried to deny it."

"That little liar." I gave into my lassitude, and lay back against the carpet, sighing with pleasure as I relaxed completely. It was infectious, as I'd hoped, and Ariane soon followed suit, actually moaning a little, giggling at herself. I turned onto my side, facing her, and she faced back, her fingers massaging and plucking at the nap of the carpet. She wanted to touch me, but couldn't allow herself to do it.

I made the move for her. Just a slow, snaking slide of my arm across the rug toward her, my fingers making contact with the inside of her wrist, my touch featherlight, almost tickling her milk-soft skin. The fine hairs on her arms drew up, causing a cascade of goose pimples to run over her, and her cheeks blushed a very faint peach-rose, like the first definite sign of dawn.

When our skin made contact, I realized that I had not ever really known her, only the surface of her, only other's impressions of her, including her own. She did not know herself at all. She was much more fragile than I imagined, a frightened, delicate creature, imbued with whole dimensions of power that overwhelmed her with their intensity, and without providing answers to any of her dilemmas. Her mind was not well insulated against others, and she could easily be carried away and made to feel things from a source outside herself. She was also much stronger than I had imagined, tough and resilient at the core, but she didn't yet trust herself, not enough to relax.

And I? I was starving for a kiss.

It didn't mean anything. I just liked her.

Her mouth made no resistance against mine; she didn't stiffen or try to move away. Her voluptuous lips were as dry and yielding as silk velvet. I slid my fingers up her arm and moved closer against her, almost dizzy myself at the feel of her breasts pressing against mine, and opened her lips with mine, wetting those dry lips with my tongue, then pressing forward, hungry.

Her arms stayed where they were, even when I lay my hand against her shirted belly, and edged up the hem of her blouse so that I could stroke the bare skin of her torso. She was thinking of Orfeo, clasping Orfeo's backside to draw him deeper into her, as we were on the rug in the darkness, with the sound of the rain starting up again, heavy and noisy against the water in the fountain outside. I thought of Orfeo, too, but briefly; Ariane was here, and she was new. Her mouth was still cold from the blood she had drunk. Her breasts heaved a little as my hand passed over them. She wore no bra under her ruby-colored top, and her nipple quickly became erect under my fingertips. My claws snagged against the fabric, and I wanted to take her shirt off and really see the beautiful breasts I was touching, but to do that I would have had to break the kiss, and I was not yet willing to do that. My blood thrummed heavily between my legs. I wanted to take off my pants before I got the crotch all sticky. Again, I resisted. I hadn't gotten enough of the kiss yet.

Momentarily, I felt sorry for Ariane; soon she would be a victim of all of my banked passion, and I'd eat her raw and probably carve up her back with my claws, forcing that magnificent auburn head between my legs. But I'd make it worth it for her. I would bring her to heights of ecstasy that she had never imagined before, over and over again, taking her there with me and trapping her there until we both collapsed. I would get her to relax and know herself and add a new layer of memory onto this room, onto this rug.

Under my mouth, hers was gasping, and the sound went straight to the heart of me, and I actually took my hand back for a moment to clutch my pubic bone and hold my orgasm in the palm of my hand. So much for protecting my pants; I could feel a bolt of wetness seep through the fabric. I lifted my lips away from hers before I bit through them. Now that I had come, I wanted to taste her blood. That was sex, too, a deeper, wilder, illogical version, one that we both knew. I wanted to taste her blood and come again, but first I wanted to make her come, because it would make her blood taste better. I took my hand off my mound and slid it onto hers, and hers was as different from mine as her lips were different, her pubis as soft and plump as her lips were. I grasped her, wishing that she was warm with fresh blood so that I could feel her heat up under my hand.

But it wasn't going to happen.

Ariane tore away from me violently, pushing me away so hard that I slid across the rug and hit the back of my head against the bookshelf. Books fell off and hit me in the face, in the breasts, in the shoulders, a small, sharp-edged rain of blows. "What are you doing, what are you doing, *what are you doing?*" she shrieked at me.

"I'm trying to fuck you," I groaned, sitting up and holding my head. The skin had been broken, and a little smudge of blood came away on the damp palm of my hand. It was almost funny, the simultaneous throbbing in my head and in my vagina.

"No—I don't—you've been trying to—you've been slutting around with John all this time and now you want to seduce me too? What the fuck is wrong with you?" Ariane was over in the corner of the room, clasping herself desperately, like she'd just had her bodice ripped. I suppose I *had* ravished her. I kissed her like a maniac and then proceeded to come just from the sound of her gasps, which I now realized must have been in protest and confusion. Still, how stupid; and I began to feel angry myself. Was I blind and deaf? It wasn't my style to throw myself at women who weren't interested in reciprocating.

I rolled my eyes at her. "I've never touched John. I don't fuck men. I fuck girls."

"But Orfeo!"

There'd been a handful of others, too, but that was none of her business. "Orfeo's special. John is my friend. It's not like that between us. We discuss *mathematics*, for God's sake. You don't even understand how much he needs that, do you? Do you even *know* this man you profess to call your husband? If you think John would ever want me, you're a fucking idiot."

"You're still a slut and you know it." Her voice was damp and quavery, on the verge of tears.

I didn't have time for sentimentality. My cunt was done thrumming, leaving just the pounding of my head. "Fuck you, Ariane. And fuck me, for wanting to bring you a moment's joy. You don't give it a moment's thought when Orfeo does nothing but love other men, but if a girl tries to get to know you better, you throw her across the room. Classic."

"Oh, you think I'm prejudiced?"

"I just think you're full of shit. You're a scared little princess. No wonder Orfeo dumped you. I wouldn't want to have to put up with your adolescent nonsense, either." I wanted to shut myself up so badly, but the beast was out. It was horrific and fascinating to watch myself, the Orchid providing a comfortable layer of emotional distance from the proceedings. I had a flash of scientific insight into the chemical mechanism that might explain that distancing ability that, under different circumstances, I would have loved to present to Ariane, so as to aid in her research and development; but the whole concept of having a friendly scientific discussion at the moment was so absurd that it actually made me laugh.

Her eyes glittered across the room, sparkling with tears, but tears of rage, not grief or embarrassment. I remembered this from the quarrels that I had with Maria, especially toward the end of her life, with her irrational and me savage, saying things I didn't even believe, using whatever weapon was at hand to devastate my opponent.

Ariane's mind was flicking through some options, as well. I could see them all playing out, the Orchid blurring them, but not obscuring them. All of them involved grievous bodily harm against me. The damn young fool didn't even think to hide her thoughts! I'd be able to anticipate any attack she might think to launch and either step out of the way or use the force of the attack against her. If she rushed me I could trip her, then tear out her spine. If I wanted to keep her alive I could just rip open her throat and bleed her out. I could swipe her feet from under her and let her fall flat on her face, then laugh at her, if I didn't think that further humiliating the girl would only increase her anger. She would never get tired, and never give up. It would be kindest, then, perhaps, to just kill her, quickly and efficiently, if messily. I imagined that John would forgive me in time.

I saw, spiraling through Ariane's mind like a falling filament of a dandelion clock, her body arching through the air at me, twisting in midair like a diver, her arms outstretched; a really beautiful move, which I had to be sure not to allow. I let my eyes go out of focus and memorized where all my bones were. It was best not to overthink it. All I had to do was elude and subdue. She was a whelp; I could crush her skull with my little finger, and would if I had to.

Her leap was attempted, and interrupted—but not by me. Almost invisibly a figure inserted itself in her path and caught the force of her hands in its chest, but did not fall. Ariane crashed to the bare floor and the wind was knocked from her with a *whump*. I got to my feet, not believing my eyes.

"Orfeo?" I said.

My beloved Orfeo Ricari stared at me with a very severe expression. He wore the extreme paleness of skin that spoke of weeks since his last drink of blood, and the arid look of someone who had been traveling for a long time. His voice was booming inside my head so loud that I had to shut my eyes. The Orchid didn't protect me at all from this.

WHAT. ARE. YOU. DOING.

On the floor, Ariane cringed. "I'm . . . trying to kill George," she whimpered.

"And you?" Compared to his inner authoritarian, his throat's voice was as husky and soft as a wood flute.

"I'm trying to keep her from killing me," I said.

Orfeo bent down and gave Ariane a hand up, even brushing off the dust from her top and brusquely wiping away her tears with his thumb, like a furious little mother. "Take a good look at yourself. Do you like what you see there?" He turned to me. "Why would you do that when you knew I was coming?"

"I *didn't* know you were coming," I said.

"Don't you find that extraordinary, Jadzia Vilma Kopernik?" he snapped.

I smiled at him. "Don't call me that. You're not my father. I made *you,* not the other way around."

"But you're acting like a child, nonetheless. I'm not afraid of telling you the truth, because I love you and I know that you love me. So listen to what I say, set aside your anger, and think clearly. You had no idea I was en route?"

I shook my head. Ariane, when glanced at, did the same. And yes, it was extraordinary, we both realized. "I never even had a flicker," I said. "I wasn't listening for you, but—"

"You shouldn't have any choice *except* to notice," Orfeo said. "No matter what else was happening."

"It must have been the Orchid," Ariane spoke softly.

"This wondrous drug?" he scoffed. He wrapped his arms around Ariane's shoulders, squeezing his eyes shut as if he were in pain. Ariane trembled in shock, as if the last twenty minutes had just been illuminated for her. "What I don't understand is that I set out to come here five nights ago, and I have been traveling toward you, with you in my thoughts, for five nights, and you didn't even feel a flicker of awareness. How is this possible? Are you on the drug all the time?"

Ariane and I stared guiltily at the floor. Orfeo raised his eyebrows. "Even while you sleep? Did you never even dream of me?"

"I dreamed about you," said Ariane.

"As did I," I said. "In fact you haven't been far from my mind all night."

"Oh, really?" Orfeo inquired, his voice oily with sarcasm. "Yes, yes, I see that. Could you not possibly make the connection?"

"I think of you all the time," Ariane claimed, her voice rising in intensity. "Constantly. Twenty-four hours a day, I'm thinking of you and calling you. And *now* you're here." She gave a short, dry laugh. "Now."

"I just saved your life, you idiot. She would have cut you into a thousand pieces and then mocked every one of them individually." Orfeo kept his arms around her as he spoke, holding her tightly. "Show some proper gratitude or I'll regret having stayed her hand. You have only just tasted the nature of true combat, and it was only because *I* fought Daniel so many times before that you were able to better him. You took my knowledge of how to gain the advantage of him, but you have no such knowledge of George; I have never fought her, and I hope that I never have reason to. I've seen her work—it made my blood run cold."

"Thanks," I said.

"Now apologize to her," he said to Ariane.

Ariane pushed away from him, her eyes lighting up again. "Me? Apologize to *her*? For what?"

"For insulting her," said Orfeo, a puzzled note in his voice.

"*Me* insulting *her*?" Ariane gave another coughing laugh, like a lioness. "Oh, my God. I can't believe you would say that. Did you even hear what she said to me?"

Orfeo raised his head so that he could look down his nose at her. "Yes, I did. Every single word. And I don't disagree with any of it." Ariane laughed again, her voice so strangled with fury that I could only guess that was what the sound was. "You rudely refused her when you could have taken a more diplomatic approach, and called her a name which does not suit her. Promiscuity does not a slut make."

"Oh, *thanks*," I said.

"Fuck you *and* your mama," Ariane cut in. "I don't have to stay here for this. I could . . . I could . . ."

"You call me, I come, and then you leave?" Orfeo said petulantly.

"I can't deal with this right now," said Ariane distantly. "I'm going for a walk." Her mental landscape was chaos. I stepped aside as she walked past me, out of the room, and out the rarely used front door. Her footsteps squished into the soaked lawn, then, splashing faintly on the rain-wet pavement, slowly receded into the distance, down the hill, toward the city.

Orfeo stared at me.

"I'm sorry, rabbit," I said to him. "Wait. John is coming."

"I'm glad to see that I've helped to clear your senses," Orfeo sneered. "I am appalled. How could you let yourself grow so careless? Do you know what I could have done to you, while you were trying to get into her pants? And *that*—can't you ever leave well enough alone?"

"I just wanted a kiss," I said.

He walked to me, stood on his toes, and kissed me, fiercely and deeply, giving me a mouthful of tongue and saliva, at the same time squeezing my left breast with his hand. I knew it was meant to be a punishment, but coming from him, it still felt good. He pulled away as abruptly. "Why didn't you just ask for one?" he whispered.

"You know Ariane," I said dismissively. "I don't know. I didn't think she would react that way. I wanted to prove to her that I didn't fancy John, because she's been shitting herself with worry about that since the moment she laid eyes on me."

"*Do* you fancy John?" he asked, trying not to smile.

"No," I said with finality. "I don't. He reminds me too much of my brother Jozef. And no matter how promiscuous I might be, I have never had any desire to fuck my sibling. Unlike you."

A testy smile emerged on his face. "I could have let her jump on you," he mused. "She might have been able to get a few good licks in. Sounds like you could use a good kick in the tits."

"Orfeo," I said, fluttering my eyelashes, "I love you."

"And I love you. I brought you your records." He walked around the study, trailing his hand over the chairs and the shelves and the lamp. "Oh! How I loved this room. But, oh, how I never wanted to see it again."

A sudden drop in temperature announced the opening of the side door, admitting a breath of frigid wind and the smell of rotting grass. Orfeo faced the entrance of the study and met John's eyes, and did not waver. John stood in the doorway, holding his dripping umbrella, his dark eyes cold.

"Hello, John," said Orfeo, gently and sadly, but on his guard.

"What are you doing here?" John's voice was much softer than I had anticipated.

"I came because Ariane called me," Orfeo explained, "and I couldn't take it anymore. She is in great peril; I am hoping that I haven't come too late to save her."

John turned his attention to me. "Why'd you do

that?" he asked me. "Why did you try to—she's *my* girl, you know. I take that very seriously. I know this might not make sense to either of you, but I don't want other people to shag my girl. I just don't." He grimaced at Orfeo. "I don't want *you* touching her again. Either of you. You're both just the same. It makes perfect sense that you made him; both of you, absolutely rotten to the core. Selfish and venal. Whatever your danglies tell you to do, you do, when you really ought to just have a wank and try to think about something else."

"I'm sorry, John," I begged. "What I did was stupid and thoughtless. It was a mistake I heartily regret. It's the Orchid. I've been so worried about you—"

"What, since Psych?" John smirked, then sighed. "Yeah. So . . . The way you manage your worry is to grab your fanny at my wife and then get upset when she doesn't want it? Well done. Where did she go?"

"Just listen," said Orfeo to John. "Let her into your thoughts—it won't be difficult to find her, if that's what you want."

"I couldn't tell you anymore what I want," John said. "Wait, no, I do. What I want is for you to get out of my sight and stop reminding me of things I'd sooner forget. Both of you—get away from me."

"I have only just arrived," said Orfeo. His throaty voice was soft and calm, but the echoing voice rang inside my head like Gabriel's trumpet, impossible to ignore or disobey. "And I would like to relax a while. Go find Ariane. She is not your possession; she is a person who means a great deal to you, and you can provide a trusted presence in her time of upheaval. She won't turn you away. Go on—you've got your umbrella."

John frowned, struggling against the stronger will,

but it would not be budged. Slowly, he turned and stepped forward, out of the room, following Ariane's path exactly, through the front door and away through the drizzle.

"You cast him out of his own house," I murmured. "Cold."

"*I* bought this house," said Orfeo irritably.

"But then you gave it away. Feo, please."

"You all need to stop taking this drug so much," he said. "All but John, I suppose. The contrast is amazing. He seems able to reason. Action and clarity will be needed soon, I think. We have to get her away from here."

"Do we? Are we her caretakers now?"

"I love her, and I am responsible for her fate," he replied. "It is because of me that she has this life. I realize that I am not so heartless as to cut her adrift when she needs guidance. I tried to do that, but she was not as mature as I had hoped. She needs to develop a new understanding of how the world works. We have insight that may assist her. Think of how lost you and I would be, if not for Chicot. He remained steadfast for much longer than he had to, until he assured himself that we could no longer benefit from his presence. Why not? Might as well perish defending someone of note. She has so much power, so much genius. She and John both do. We may yet benefit from their intelligence."

"You turn guilt into strategy," I teased.

He sighed ruefully. "I might as well do something useful with it—it is a well that never runs dry."

After a brief respite, during which Orfeo refreshed himself with a well-chilled pint of blood, we went together to the first cemetery on the left up the hilly road leading into the woods. We sat, hands locked together, sharing our thoughts and our recent experiences. Well before dawn, we crawled into the darkness and safety of a small marble crypt with one vacant slot, and lay together on the cold stone. It was only then, in the blind dark, with his head nestled into the curve of my neck, that I allowed myself to cry.

XV

DECIDING

ARIANE DEMPSEY

I was grateful for the fog, the lovely blindness that it provided, the streetlights yellow haloes as distant as UFOs in a blurry photograph. Even the small sounds of morning approaching had to struggle through a wall of water vapor before they could reach my ears. Good. I wanted to be blind, deaf, numb; I wanted a goddamn time-out. My feet carried me forward and my lungs breathed for me and my hands uselessly wiped the rain off my face, over and over again, as the droplets accumulated.

As I kept walking, the fog got denser and denser. I was headed downtown, toward the river, a few hundred feet closer to sea level. I was almost completely sober, and I felt beaten and heavy, though I couldn't tell if I needed sleep or if it was just the aftereffects of shock.

Orfeo Ricari, standing there, unchanged, still reprimanding me, taking sides against me.

I had to stop walking and grab my temples with my fingers. Through the distance, somewhere behind me, to the left, back up in the hills, George was upset and crying. I smiled a terrible smile and concentrated as hard as I could to send her my overwhelming urge to break down in tears. Let Ricari dry her face, if he preferred her to me so much.

All this time, I knew that John was following me, nearby but out of sight, but he never emerged; his thoughts were as veiled as the river underneath the blanket of fog. If he felt sympathy, if he felt fear or anger, he kept it to himself. I didn't want to see him, anyway. I wanted to pretend that there was no such thing as vampires, that none of us *made* anybody else, that these horrible creatures were not related to me because they simply didn't exist, and I was just a regular human suffering from massive, elaborate delusions.

At this time of the morning, the downtown area hadn't yet woken up, and the two or three people I saw seemed to be sleepwalking as much as I was. But farther northeast, I heard a low rattle of radio communication and the sounds of multiple tense voices, too many to be mere building security.

Cops. Red, white, and blue lights reflected off the fog on Broadway, and as I approached, I saw that three police cruisers had blocked off a large section of the street, and uniformed officers busily rolled yellow warning tape around the lampposts. It was the kind of scene usually associated with five-car pileups at a freeway entrance, but even through the thinning fog I could see that there were no cars on that street beside the cruisers. An ambulance siren approached from the west. When I got closer to the cordoned area, I saw four blanket-draped figures lying next to each other on the ground, glowing in the golden streetlight, as still as stones.

One cop was standing aside from the others, having just ended a call on his cell phone, and taking a moment to stare into space and think. He was badly shaken by what he'd just seen; the smell of fear-sweat stank through his wet uniform jacket. I crept closer, my calm-and-conceal instincts taking over. "What happened?" I asked him.

The policeman didn't bother to look at me. "Found 'em in the peep show," he said dully. "In all the little dirty movie jack-off booths. Four men and one woman."

"There's only four here."

"One of the men's too delicate to move; we gotta wait until we can get a body bag or he's just gonna slide apart." The cop shook his head and swallowed hard. "The kid at the counter says he's been here all night, and he IDed all of the victims as having come in, but nobody else has been in, and he hadn't noticed anybody going out. He forgot they went in there; studying, I guess. New customer comes in, kid goes to check, and then . . ." He shrugged. "They've got cameras set up everywhere in there. We'll get whoever it was."

"Does it look as though they lost a lot of blood?" Old instincts kept creeping back; hold the eyes, simultaneously go vague and point needle-sharp into the mind to find the detailed memories they didn't know they had. I had to tug on his sleeve to be able to make eye contact, and I almost regretted it as I saw him react to me. He was shocked almost out of his trance. It wasn't that I looked inhuman, it was the fact that I was completely soaked to the skin, in my shirtsleeves, no coat, no hat, probably blue-white with cold. Once eye contact was established, I helped him to decide that such observations were irrelevant. He almost relaxed, being let off the hook, and his eyes went dead again.

"Sure, they lost a lot of blood," he said. "A lot of it's on the walls and floors in the booths."

"Enough of it?" I asked.

"That's for . . . forensics to decide," he replied numbly. "I don't really know. I've only ever seen a gunshot homicide before. Looks like gallons."

At that point I let him go. I had everything out of him, short of being able to examine the bodies myself, that I needed. He was never going to be able to rid himself of the mental image now seared in his mind; one room after another, filled with the stench of death, the walls painted with arterial spray, bodies with pants unzipped, necks, arms, thighs, wrists slashed through to the bone, with wistful, peaceful expressions on their faces. Enormous amounts of wasted blood; probably the work of one, maybe two reckless vampires working together, having a night out.

I wished that I could have just a little taste of the victims' blood, on the off chance that it held enough of a neurochemical signal that would show me their last moments, so I could figure out who had done this before the police did. The problem was, it could have been anyone. Under the right circumstances, it could have been me.

Still, as a general rule, I didn't do things like that. It was too sloppy. If they were smart, there'd be almost no evidence. Our kind left no fingerprints, no skin cells, and no hairs. Then again, this wasn't an act of intelligence, just vicious greed. Why paint the walls? And why four in the same place? A stray fiber could be traced to a garment, maybe, and a hasty step might have tracked a footprint. It had been a stupid thing to do.

It had Orchid written all over it.

My guts flipped as I realized that it might not have even been a vampire I knew. Chicot had gone away with enough Orchid to poison a small town; what if he'd given a hit to some scruffy acquaintance? Before he left, Chicot told me that he would share some of his blood with me, to help me gain strength and ability, including the ability to look at the city and see the unique electrostatic glow of vampires, so that I could know when they were coming; but he'd left before he ever did that. Did he forget, or just change his mind? Maybe found me unworthy? I wished to God that he'd remembered, because I really needed that advantage now. They could be anywhere; close by, waiting for an ambush.

The ambulances pulled up, and I started walking back the way I'd come, suddenly cold, as wet as though I'd been swimming in my clothes. I wanted to get home and take a very hot bath and take some more Orchid and go to sleep, but the thought brought me up short; hadn't I already done Orchid earlier, and hadn't it not been very enjoyable this time? I could get to sleep without it. At least I hoped so.

I was so exhausted that I wasn't sure if I could perform a swift run there. Margaret's apartment was on the way. I walked there at a normal pace, casting my senses in a wide net, watching and listening behind me for any signs of attack or confrontation. I shrouded myself to the eyes of the humans on the street, heading toward their early shift jobs or just wandering with no place to go, moving to keep warm.

Tucked into a small side street directly off Burnside, Margaret's apartment building had a large, beautiful brick courtyard lined with mossy barrels of drowned petunias and a glass-fronted lobby with a brass chandelier. It had been built before my house, and was probably a hotel before it was residential. Her wing of the building had its own call box, which I wouldn't ordinarily use, but this morning, I felt somehow that I should. An answer came almost instantly. "Yeah?" Her voice was ragged with sleep.

"It's Ariane. Can I come in?"

The buzz of the door unlocking prickled and stung like a tattoo on the inside of my ears. Margaret had stepped out into the lobby, her eyes still mostly closed, wearing a red dye-stained gray sweatshirt and a pair of tiny terrycloth shorts. She had a nice pair of legs, but the fact that I noticed them made the nausea of guilt and confusion come back. *Not me, George, not me. Or maybe just not you.*

Margaret led me through the brightly lit hall to an open door, leading to almost complete darkness. I wouldn't have thought it of her, but Margaret's apartment was a cave. She only had one window in the main room, and this was covered with a long rectangle of opaque brown cloth in lieu of curtains. She seemed to keep all of her clothes, coats, shoes, and papers in a chaotic tangle on the floor. To my surprise, she led me back through the apartment to her bedroom, which was, in contrast, the very soul of simplicity—a low square bed with a white solid frame made of featureless rectangles, like slabs of cream cheese stood on end, and a small white end table of a matching design, with a cheap scented candle in a jar on top. Nothing else at all. The window in here was blocked off, too, with multiple layers of sheer fabric and lace. Even though there was a streetlight almost directly on the other side, it only barely illuminated the lace overlapping the outermost edges.

She lit the candle with a flick of a lighter, and sat down on the edge of the bed. "Are you okay?" she asked listlessly.

"No . . . it's been a horrible night," I said. "I'm sorry to wake you up; I know how tired you must be." Even in the forgiving candlelight, she looked shockingly terrible. Her once glowing, honey-tan skin was as pale and dull as wet concrete. "I don't really want anything. I just wanted to see a friendly face. I left the house in kind of a hurry, in case you couldn't tell."

"I was wondering why you didn't sit down," she said, smiling a little, "and then I was like, oh, yeah, she's soaking wet. You're a really considerate person, Ariane."

"Oh, no, please don't say that. I'm not, I'm not at all." Tears suddenly gushed out of my eyes, as if my face had gotten so used to being rained on that it had to stay moist, like a captured fish. There was no way I could have defended myself out there; if I didn't even know when I was going to start sobbing, how could I possibly anticipate the attacks of some vampire, possibly ancient, possibly out of his mind on Orchid?

Margaret stood up and put her arms around me, and leaned back until we were both sitting on the bed. I cried into the neck of her shirt, not minding the flowery stench of the hair dye soaked into it, and let her hold me and rock me, comfort *me*—me, the monster! The irony sickened me and made me cry harder. I was only grateful that John didn't have to see me like this.

The thought of John, trailing me all night, managed

to sober me up and dry my eyes, though still I clung to Margaret and she to me. The slaughter, the strange lust, and the shock seemed far away, and I understood why Margaret had her bedroom like this. It was a cocoon, a womb, a dark, simple, soft escape, as close to death as she could come, with the ugliness and complexity of the world shut away.

But the sunrise was on its way, and I wanted my own bed and my own dark cocoon.

I leaned out of the embrace, and gave Margaret as much smile as I could make. It wasn't much, and her returning smile wasn't either, but at least we both tried. "I apologize," I said. "And thanks."

She shook her head vaguely. "I'll get back to sleep, don't you worry," she said.

"Might as well now," I replied, and gently settled her head onto the pillows and drew the blankets over her. Margaret fell unconscious instantly, already more than halfway there anyway. I took a moment to look at her more closely in the candlelight. She looked worse than she had even when I left her earlier that night; by the look and smell of her, her thyroid function was beginning to fail.

A quick taste of her blood confirmed it.

I didn't take much, just half a mouthful, just enough so that the blood spread over every surface in my mouth before it was absorbed, and I was able to taste it. Her blood was strange and delicious, healthily fed but also bitter with chemical residue, like an imperfect batch of Orchid.

The surface of her skin tasted of it, too. No wonder her thyroid was breaking down—the cyanide was taking its toll, by tiny degrees.

I tucked her in, blew out the candle, and dug through the piles in the front room until I found a very pretty dark-green raincoat, still stained with Nevada dust, a ticket stub from an Eek-A-Mouse concert from two years ago and a cigarette butt in the pocket. She wouldn't miss this old thing, and I still needed to walk home. With just a tablespoonful of her blood in my veins, I found the strength to double-time it home just as the sun had emerged like an electric stain on the eastern sky.

I gave Margaret her coat back the next night, and she almost shook free of her trance, staring at it with confusion. It was odd that she didn't remember anything about the night before, but on the other hand, it was probably a good thing. I only needed to suggest that she shrug it off before she accepted that everything was as it should be.

Even in her weakened state, she worked like a mule. We didn't even bother pretending to study or experiment in leukemia research anymore; there wasn't time. There was Orchid to make, so as to satisfy the demand and ensure that John would have all that he needed. The process was lengthy, complex, and wasteful. Most of our time in the laboratory, we were cleaning up while waiting for one of the steps in the process to cook, cool, dry, or settle. Gone were the days of her endless prattling and wide-eyed questions; now she kept her head down and her eyes focused on her work, with the occasional shy, devout smile as she brushed past me. Her head was constantly spinning with the same questions, but she no longer gave voice to them. I spared a second to wonder if I'd told her to shut up

once, and she received it like the eleventh command-
ment, because she had no choice in the matter anymore. It would have taken a stronger mind than
Margaret's when I first met her to resist my manipula-
tion, and now with the cyanide levels in her blood
growing by the day, she barely had the strength to deduce that C followed A and B.

Thursday night, we worked for a couple of hours
putting Orchid into liter and half-liter and two hundred milliliter bottles, then packaging them up in re-
frigerated carrying cases. I did most of the work, since
I could do it faster, and I had my back turned when I
heard a slithery thump coming from the sink corner of
the outer lab. I was there in a flash, but I couldn't
catch Margaret before she slumped to the ground, her
hands held out uselessly in front of her when she was
actually falling to the side. I balanced her shoulder
blades against my arm, lifted her, and set her down in
a chair on the other side of the room. The water
trapped in her tissues made her much heavier than she
looked. I rubbed her hands and bent her over, so that
her head was between her knees.

"Hey," I said, and repeated it eight times in the same
tone until she shook her head and mumbled in reply.
"Hey, kid, you passed out. Now, don't sit up yet. Give
it a minute or so."

"I passed out," she echoed, confused. "Wow. That's
crazy." When I did let her sit up, her lips were pale violet, and a blood vessel had broken in her left eye,
crazing the white with tiny red capillaries.

"My God! You're not at all well." Her pulse was still
strong; she was not going to die tonight. We had no
cyanide antidote kit because some Lord-beloved drug
fiend had swiped the amyl nitrite capsule out of it,

probably years ago, without me noticing. "I think we're going to take a little trip over the hill."

"I don't want to go to the hospital," Margaret protested, straightening up and waving her hands around. Immediately her eyes glazed and she began to slide sideways again.

That left eye looked terrible, even though I knew it was only superficial, and I began to worry that she might have had a stroke. I didn't bother to talk her into the trip, just wrapped her coat around her and pulled mine onto my arms, then brought her chin up abruptly, causing her to faint again, this time more deeply.

I shrugged her into a fireman's carry, locked the office behind me, and flickered over the winding pavements till I reached the grounds of the OMI hospital. I slowed only as I approached the brightly lit emergency entrance.

The intake nurse rose out of his chair with his mouth open, watching me carry Margaret in. I belatedly remembered to act like I was out of breath and under tremendous strain, carrying a 150-pound young woman like a backpack.

I gave them Margaret's basic information and one of my credit card numbers, and told them that she needed a cyanide antidote administered. "I'd keep her overnight, if I were you," I said.

"Sure—sure," said the nurse.

I gave him my business card. "If you need me for anything, I can be reached at my office extension, but I would highly discourage you from actually calling that number."

"Got it."

I made it back to the lab before I heard the sounds

of approaching ambulances, and finished the titration and packing by myself. I took only one of the crates, though, leaving the others in the inner laboratory, triple-locked and alarmed. Then again, if someone did break into my lab and steal my drugs, what could I do? File a theft report with the police?

I hoped to God that Margaret wouldn't start babbling when she woke up. Maybe the sodium nitrite, the second step of the antidote, would loosen her tongue like sodium pentothal or single-malt scotch, and she'd tell them that she had felt fine until I started drinking her blood and poisoning her.

I didn't have time for this kind of dead-ended worrying. I had to get home by three to meet the Revikoffs.

Someone had neatened up my kitchen while I was at work; John, George, Orfeo. Any one of them could waltz in here, make themselves at home, help themselves to anything I had. Nothing had been taken, only the boxes and paper wrappers cleared away, the kitchen chairs drawn up to attention at the table's edge, the money in a kitchen drawer, the garbage and sharps disposed of. The cleanliness filled me with surreal dread.

I shook it off and changed into a nice skirt and sweater, preparing myself to view friends, not the enemy.

Fortunately, they were late. Alexander had driven their car. I didn't want to think any more closely about where their handsome young driver had gone. I received them at the front door, and we sat in the study. This room got stranger and stranger to me every time I came into it; the rug remained askew from when I had pushed George away, books still scattered across the floor.

I lit one of Leland's cigarettes, and El smoked a Marlboro Light. Alex folded his hands in his lap and smiled his sad smile.

"Were you guys at the Pleasure Video the other night?" I asked them.

"Where is that?" asked El.

"Broadway, downtown. You can't miss it; big pink neon lips on the front of it."

Alex's eyes went vague. "Ah, yes, there were killings there," he remembered, "I read about it in the paper."

"So you didn't do it?" I asked.

"No," said El, "though, not to say that I wouldn't."

"It was a bad job," I said, relaxing slightly, tense mostly because I didn't know what I'd do if they told me that they had. "I was hoping that you wouldn't do something like that."

"Like what? Like killing them? Of course I would," said El, raising her head regally. "That's my right. But that one was not me. We stayed in that night, making arrangements for our departure. Only Mr. Rifkin can take responsibility."

"He can?"

"That is more his style. He hit the place on his way out of town, knowing he wouldn't be back here. They'll never find him. Even I don't know where he's gone—he's hiding himself now."

"It's the Orchid," I said. "He can just wipe himself off the map." I had the feeling that my buyers in L.A. would not be receiving their full shipment, if they got anything at all. I'd been played.

The Russians stared at the floor. Alex cleared his throat and spoke up. "Yes. We shall attempt to disappear as well. It's not as though we're not happy to be

moving on, since that has always been our plan, and
we've already been here for much longer than we'd
initially thought. I would like for us to part as friends.
On good terms."

I looked at El and remembered how much I'd idol-
ized her when I first met her, before I'd changed, and
she was just so lovely and spunky and free that she
made being a vampire seem to be a wonderful thing,
an elegant, no-compromise way of life. Of course, with
my tiny, dull senses, and my naiveté, I couldn't possibly know what she was actually like. "I just wish that
you'd been more considerate of John," I said at last,
words I'd been hoarding for weeks, swamped with
sudden nauseous relief.

"Yes . . ." El said vaguely, "but I think it's pointless
to apologize any more for it. It's up to you, now, to
come to a final judgment of me—well, final for the moment. I don't think you're that rigidly dogmatic. You
are still so young. You have barely thirty-five years of
experience altogether—"

"Let's not discuss my limitations right now," I came
back, my voice mild. "We have business to attend to,
and we'll all have plenty of decades to quantify all the
things that I am still so ignorant about."

I pulled out a sleek little briefcase from where I'd
stashed it behind the chair, and handed it to Alex.
"This contains five two hundred milliliter bottles, and
twelve milliliters in a twenty-five milliliter bottle. The
twelve is for your personal use."

"Only twelve?" El protested. "That's not enough for
both of us."

"Sure it is," I said, ice cold. "That's six effective
doses, three each. You really don't need any more than
that. This is not a medically necessary drug for you,

and I have no idea what the long-term effects are. But I've gotten an eyeful of the short-term effects, and I'm not enthusiastic about 'em."

"That's ridiculous," El scoffed. "Just because Samuel—"

I looked at Alex, who nodded once, lowering his eyes. El took a deep breath, and struggled to smile. "I'm sorry," she said. "You didn't have to give us any at all. I appreciate it."

"Thank you for your help," I said. "Have a nice trip. It's a beautiful train ride, I've heard—a great view of the northern plains and the Rocky Mountains."

"With snow on the ground, it will look like Russia," El replied, her voice ringing in a thin and twisted version of cheerfulness. "Won't that be splendid, Alexander Vassilyevich?" She spoke the last sentence in Russian, but I understood it perfectly well. "Well, it's time for us to go," El said, in English again. "Good luck, and thank you for your hospitality. It is a beautiful city."

Like I owned the place, or built it myself. "Thanks," I said. "It was good to see you again."

"And you."

I don't know why we hugged; I don't know if I enjoyed it. More than being embraced it felt like I was having an internal organ ripped out. I suddenly loved them both so much, despaired of changing them, and regretted having ever met them. Now I was burdened with this love, whether or not I wanted it. When they broke away I knew they felt the anguish and distaste in my bond to them. I hadn't thought that their faces could get sadder, but I was mistaken. They looked old, brittle, and hollow.

They both kissed me on both cheeks and the lips, then hoisted the briefcase and departed through the front door of the house. The path between the driveway and the front door was almost cleared now, with so many footsteps having trampled and kicked aside the layer of fallen leaves.

XVI

Empire Builder

ELISABETA REVIKOFF

A drop like an icicle's tear fell off the rim of my coat hood and ran down the front of my dress. "Doesn't it *ever* stop raining here?" I said to the taxi driver.

"Sure," he said lightly. "In May."

I groaned, and Alex glanced at me. "We choose the right time to depart, it seems," he said, making his accent particularly thick. "We travel to Las Vegas."

I almost snickered before I caught myself. He knew good and well that Las Vegas hadn't been worth going to since Sinatra married Mia Farrow. Alexander Vassilyevich gently squeezed my hand, and continued, "It is still very warm and sunny there even in December."

"Oh, hey, that's great. That does sound nice, because the weatherman said we might get some snow here this weekend."

I squeezed back, so hard that Alex yelped and flinched. I patted his hand apologetically. "We never did go to the mountains," I said, and my chest felt heavy.

"We'll see mountains on the way there," Alex said to me in Russian, "magnificent, wild, snow-capped mountains." I stared out the window of the taxi as it slowed on approach to the train station, and tried to envision what this wet city would look like under a heavy layer of snow. It would be beautiful, of course, but damp and melancholy because the sun would never come out and dance on the surface of the snow. It would be an enfolding cold whiteness like a wet, rough cotton blanket.

I secured my hood so that it cast a shadow over my face, climbed out of the taxi, and mentally called for a porter to assist us. Two slim young men in uniform, one pale and one dark, exchanging slightly baffled looks, moved immediately to place our luggage onto wheeled carts. I stood staring at them until I felt my skin begin to sting and itch from exposure to the cloud-veiled evening sunlight. Alexander joined me on the curving concrete walkway in front of the station, and I grabbed for his hand, wishing that I could make contact with his skin instead of feeling our gloves slide together. My eyes felt very wide open. It might have been excitement or dread.

We would go by train across the top of America to Chicago and then to New York. Ariane was slightly taken aback that we would travel by rail, but I had no need to explain to her why we had never taken an airplane trip, nor would we ever. Driving was an equally distasteful idea; after stripping the license plates from the town car, and then ensuring that the car itself was stolen, the last thing we wanted was to be burdened with acquiring and maintaining another car. Besides, it had been decades since we had gone on a train journey together. It would be romantic.

The clock inside the marble-lined lobby read 4:30; boarding had already begun. The pudding-faced Asian woman behind the counter checked our luggage and pointed us in the direction of the doors that led out to the platform, then wrinkled her eyebrows in concern. "Were you skiing? That sunburn looks kinda painful."

I stared back at her until she averted her eyes. "Forget about it," I whispered, and turned away before I burned a hole through her mind. Alexander was already hurrying toward the doors, as nimble as a goat, the suitcases held in his hands as effortlessly as though they were empty.

Suddenly I felt giddy, and I sprinted after him, catching up and jumping playfully against his back, using his shoulders as a springboard. A normal man would have been flung to the ground from the force of it, but he just laughed at me. "Knock it off, you silly bitch," he said, and when we had climbed up the aluminum stairs into the train car, he set down the cases and gave me a deep and passionate kiss.

We could barely find our room in time. I was already kicking my shoes off and unzipping my coat before we made it to the door, and when I stumbled inside the little suite, Alex, straightening up from where he'd set down the cases, tore open his belt and seized me. He tossed me down onto the blue upholstered lower berth, made a mock-savage snarl, and paid me back for my silliness by jumping on me.

The fuck was good, but before the train had even made it to the next station, perhaps twenty minutes later, I moved away and put my clothes back on. Alex sighed happily, not minding either the desertion or the cold. "You are better than gold-leaf ice cream," he purred.

I pulled open the window shade, and saw the trees whipping past, dark fans against a washed-out indigo sky. The trees were joined by electricity poles and jaundice-colored streetlights, then by crumbling brick buildings and the filthy detritus of the logging trade. We had come to Washington state just by staggering over the border; I wondered whether it was Portland or Vancouver that was the Tijuana of the two.

"My dear?" Alexander Vassilyevich said, sounding annoyed, or concerned. I wasn't sure which.

"Yes, precious," I answered, and pulled the shade back down.

He smiled a little. "No, no, please, let's have it up. Let's soak up a bit of the evening time, shall we? We can still watch the light die."

"I can't see any light over there," I murmured, and our window faced west.

"I can still see it," he said.

"Well, I am happy for you," I said. I stood up and stretched, then walked the length of the room and back. It was about half the size of Ariane's kitchen. "This *is* luxury," I said.

That made him laugh. "But darling, they make up the beds for us *and* bring us the paper. And look— bottled water. Isn't it just like the Turandot? At least, just like the elevator at the Turandot—this one goes up and down, too."

"Isn't it terrible!" I said, coming back to sit with him again. He picked up my hand and kissed it, then held it between his shapely thighs. "You'd think, it being a railway, that it would be more efficient to make the way smooth."

"It adds romance," he said. "Makes you feel like you're going somewhere."

We both fell silent at the same time. I didn't want to look at his face or his body. Keeping my hand between his legs, I gazed out the window. We could have been seen, if someone stood on the signaling tower five feet away through a muddy, weed-choked field. I tried to get an erotic feeling from that knowledge, but I just wasn't interested in public sex, not with my husband. I had been, and done so, with Daniel Blum, but that had been a long time ago, since before Sinatra married Mia Farrow, when Vegas was still a fun place to go at Christmastime, and a very public place to have public sex. Somehow, with Alexander, it was different. It wasn't that I was ashamed of his older, gray-hair-flecked, wiry body; I felt jealous of it. I didn't want anyone to see him naked but me.

I wished that he had tried to stop me, with Daniel.

Alex swallowed and cleared his throat. "There is also a meal service," he mentioned.

"Fresh linens?" I replied lightly, still unable to turn back.

He squeezed his thighs together on my hand. Like my touch in the taxicab, it was hard enough to make me emit a little squeak. He could crush the bones in my hand with his thighs, if he wished. "Remind me to tell the staff to leave our suite alone during the day," he said, his voice casual, spreading his legs a little so I could take back my hand. "They can change our linens in the evening, with us in the room. Not that they'll need to change our linens, if we just keep on screwing on the couch."

With a grunt of distaste, he got dressed, drawing a fresh shirt from the suitcase. He sat on the bunk next to

me and pulled the other case up onto his lap. His claws
delicately spun the combination lock as though he
were playing a harp. The case opened with the tiniest
click, like the sound of a moth landing on a glass door.

Underneath a brown felt false bottom and a thick,
quilted metallic insulating layer, the brown bottles
were strapped in, their little cousin, the twenty-
milliliter syringe, affixed to the insulation layer with a
rude strip of black electrical tape. The bottles were
nearly opaque, but the syringe was not, and I was
transfixed by Orchid's strange, moody color.

"Just checking on it," said Alex.

"It's barely been out of your sight since we got it.
What could possibly have happened?"

"I don't know," he admitted. "I just wanted to look
at it again, I think. We've several hundred thousand
dollars here."

"Which belong to Ariane, if I understand correctly."

"No, Ariane's made her money already," Alexander
Vassilyevich said, shaking his head. He closed the case
and spun the tumblers on the lock, at random this
time. "What we make from this is ours. I heard her;
she might not have said anything aloud, but I saw the
truth in her heart. The last thing she needs right now is
more money. Though I do wonder if that Italian might
want to take his money back all of a sudden; I didn't
care for the looks of him. He has all the signs of a
highly religious hypocrite."

"Some of her money came from Daniel," I pointed
out, but in the smallest voice possible.

Alex gave a guttural laugh and didn't meet my eyes.
"You know, Elisabeta Hanya, that I'm not usually like
this, but I would thank you to try harder not to think
of him right now. I would like to think that when I am

in the room with you, you are not in another room with someone else. Besides, he is dead—it's time to stop thinking about him."

"I don't stop thinking of people when they're dead," I said shortly.

"Of course you do," he said. "You would go mad otherwise. I did not say you had to *forget* him. I simply want your thoughts focused right now, and your warmer feelings directed toward me. Please?"

I could only promise him with a kiss, not words. Hadn't it always been the way? I didn't lie to Alexander Vassilyevich, including making promises that I could not guarantee. "I'd like a drink," I said. "Let's go to the lounge car. I always find that a glass of vodka really brings out your eyes."

I wanted that Orchid so badly that my tense jaw audibly cracked when I tried to laugh. I knew that he could tell, but he grinned with good humor, obligingly sliding back into his shoes and tidying his mussed hair in the mirror just outside the tiny lavatory. He might have wanted Orchid, too, but I had no clear view of his emotions; his thoughts were lighthearted and logical, but his emotions were tightly tucked away and hidden in the dark.

It wasn't like him to do that.

There had always been a part of him that was private, and I appreciated that; as much as I loved him, I knew that it would not be a good thing to see all of him, all of the time. Eighty-nine years of being together wasn't a trifle. But I couldn't hide anything of substance from him, and I never could. We had fallen in love while I was still human, and my mind was as clear to his gaze as a glass of water. Long before I ever had the inner sight, he had developed strategies for keeping parts of himself hidden from my view. I had simply never really noticed, or cared, before.

The lounge car was mostly full, and noisy with alcohol-raised voices. Alex made a table available for us by convincing the young couple sitting by the window that they had reached a point in their new acquaintance that justified having sex, sending them all of his unsatisfied sexual tension. They hopped up and rushed away. I changed my mind, craving champagne. Although he didn't ordinarily like it, Alex joined me in sharing a bottle.

We both looked everywhere except at each other.

Mostly, I watched the dark scenery go by, and occasionally met the eyes of the men who were looking at me, but not for long enough to show genuine interest. As usual, the men were varied, but none of them were particularly beautiful. Not enough to make me stop searching for those ragged holes in the clouds, with the stars shining out so much more brightly than they ever could in the city. Every time I saw a break in the clouds I took a sip of champagne; an hour passed, and champagne remained in my glass.

"Darling," came Alex's voice, quiet but startling all the same, "look. Doesn't it look like Rachell?"

Leaning against the bar, ordering a cocktail that had been trendy three years previous, wearing a satin skirt too short for the weather and a clingy cardigan sweater, she looked like an anorexic high-school girl, one in the first flushes of food deprivation, before she started missing periods, but after receiving constant praise for her thinness. She did resemble Rachell in that way, and also because of the long, straight brown hair and lost-looking eyes. Somehow, though, she was being served alcohol, so she must have been at least twenty-one; what an enigma. "Yes, it does," I said. "But Rachell was prettier."

"Yes," said Alex, and rose from his chair.

I sat back, sipped my champagne, and watched him approach her, and immediately seize her interest; the man she'd come with, a youth in ill-fitting pants and a baseball cap, stared at their interaction, becoming so incensed that he actually approached Alexander Vassilyevich with the intent of intimidation. With one sharp glance and a snap of Alex's fingers, the man in the cap turned on his heel and left the lounge car altogether. The thin girl was enchanted by this. My husband, the irresistible charmer, and his type of lady. He bought her drinks and I finished the bottle of champagne on my own, pouring the last golden drops into my glass as they left together.

Out the window, snowflakes blurred past.

The lounge car shut down at midnight, and the remaining passengers and I were compelled to leave. I thought about lingering behind, keeping my eyes on the flashing ground that now wore a cloak of white, but I thought about the Orchid back in our room and decided to return, if only to look at the bottles. The champagne hadn't done anything except fill my bladder. Perhaps Alex wouldn't judge me too harshly if I only had a triple-ought-four, just a drop, just enough to relax me. Yes, it was early, but we had woken up early, and gotten sunburned for our trouble. One dose a night; I had no intentions of being greedy. I resolved myself to tell Alex that I would have some, relieving myself in the lavatory in the lounge, ignoring the calls to clear the place out.

When I returned to our berth, I saw the girl slumped against Alex, not unconscious, but rather in that dreamy, untouchable state of calm that our kind can produce, leaving almost no recollection when it ends. He embraced her, holding her securely across his thighs, her slippery skirt threatening to slide off him, his face buried in her hair. He opened his eyes languidly when I entered.

"I was wondering when you would join us," he said, a little bit drunk. Her neck had a bright patch where the blood was close to the surface, but no marks could be seen. "You should have some. She tastes like appletini."

"Appletini, huh," I said, taking the girl's limp form from his arms, and laying her on the bunk next to him. I rolled up the sleeve of her cardigan to expose her narrow arm; it was a wonder she had any blood at all in those fine, weblike veins, spreading over her pale skin like blue-green lace. The girl shifted and moaned faintly when I bit into her forearm, not trusting the fragile crook of her elbow, and the blood poured scalding-hot into my mouth. Silly kid, eighteen with a fake ID, heading home to Kalispell for Christmas break, wondering if she should tell her hick boyfriend that she'd cheated on him in college. Her blood was scanty and had a lingering aftertaste of acetone, because she drank instead of eating, "saving" herself for her mother's cooking. My husband and his kind of lady, proud and sentimental and not too bright.

Alex's fingers clamped against my lower jaw, and he pushed me back against the bunk, blood dribbling through my open lips. Beside me, the girl, Courtney-Ann, slumped over, her arm streaking blood over my pale-blue skirt. I protested, but Alex cut in, "Enough. She's not strong enough—you'll kill her."

"I don't care," I said, staring at my dress in dismay.

"Who'd miss her? Throw her corpse off the train at Kalispell."

"Elisabeta, you know we can't. We oughtn't to be like Rifkin. We are in the service of Ariane; we can't jeopardize our safety, or our anonymity. This goes beyond what we ourselves want. It's not unreasonable for us to feed, but please, while we're on the train, we mustn't kill."

"It's because you were seen with her," I said. Ah, that was better; alcohol in my bloodstream now, coursing through, making me lightheaded. "You didn't have to be seen with her."

"Please, my darling," he said, his voice anything but affectionate. "Please assist her back to a public place, and be discreet about it."

"Me? Why not you?"

"Because I was just seen with her. And because you might have gotten us into trouble with your lack of self-control. Go on, Betty; it won't kill you."

He only called me Betty when he was furious. I changed from my dress into a brown cowl-hood alpaca sweater and dark cropped trousers, a good outfit for discretion and invisibility. Alexander watched me, but he did not really see me, nor did he see the girl who he had just seduced. He was sending me out because he didn't want to leave the room; he had a sudden phobic fear of the swaying hallway of the trains, and wanted to turn down the bunks and lie still and meditative in bed. He needed to concentrate on something, something I couldn't see.

I looped one of the girl's arms over my shoulder, and walked with her carefully, mostly carrying her so that her ankles wouldn't drag on the ground, out of the sleeping car and into the dining car, which was no longer operational this late, but had an empty lavatory at one end. I set her down upon the toilet seat, resting her head back against the wall with her chin tipping forward. Now she just looked like she'd gotten really trashed and passed out trying to take a piss.

I gently tapped her face with my palm. "Courtney-Ann," I said in her ear. "Wake up. We're at Spokane. If you smoke, here's your last chance for the next hour." The girl, still out cold, did not respond. I sighed, shrugged, and walked away, leaving the door wide open for the next person to find her.

When I got back to the room, I no longer wanted any Orchid. Alex had converted the beds and turned out our linens, and lay there, staring at the ceiling. I climbed up and lay next to him in the narrow space, crowding him; he didn't seem to mind. I gazed inward, concentrating myself, teaching myself to do something I had never had to do before. The berth bed was narrow like a coffin, and something about the lack of space soothed me and helped me to gaze inward.

I dreamed of Leland Quary wandering through the aisles of a supermarket. Every time he walked past a sign with a yellow smiley face, he gave the change in his pocket a jingle. He was after a girl that I never saw, and he never increased his slow, ambling pace. I was gripped with dread; I tried to make him change, speed up, leave the place, smash one of the displays, but there was no escape, and therefore, no need to hurry.

I woke up in a cold sweat, the strange bedsheets rough against my ribs and thigh, and Alex's body next to me still and unmoving, but warming up. I wanted to burst into tears, but as Alex's chest flexed drawing breath, I realized that I couldn't cry over a dream so utterly meaningless. Most likely, he had seen that dream, perhaps even shared it, stalking silently along behind Leland in a jeweled canyon of dishwashing liquid bottles. If I tried to explain, he would be within his rights to laugh at me. Instead, I concentrated on breathing, feeling strength return with the air in my lungs.

The train was stopping yet again. I opened the window shade just an inch and peered outside into thickly whirling whiteness. "We haven't outrun the snow," I mused.

"But we did outsleep the sun, thank God." He yawned, scratched himself, and disappeared into the lavatory closet. "Be a pet and bring in the newspapers, would you? They should be just outside the door."

I got my dressing gown out of the suitcase and combed my hair with my fingers. Next to my ankles, the other briefcase rested against the wall. I closed my eyes and turned away, going to the door. I concentrated my mind on Leland, on the unsettling dream, the sound of his pocketful of coins.

There was nothing outside the door except a pair of sneakered feet and the quizzical expression of a child heading toward the dining car. I smiled at the child and went back into our room. "No paper," I said, shrugging.

"Shit." Alex had slipped into the same pair of pants he wore the night before, so I knew he was in a hurry; he had an ex-soldier's distaste for wearing the same clothes twice in a row. "They weren't listening. I shall go down to the dining car and fetch them, and make sure they don't forget the damn things tomorrow. What the hell do they think I'm paying them for?"

I smiled at him. That was a lot of profanity all at once for Alexander Vassilyevich, at least without most of it being sexual. This soft-spoken rant was about as angry as he got, unless he meant to completely destroy something; and even that wasn't really based on anger. I always theorized that it came from that private part of him, and perhaps that was the part itself—a methodical violence as cold and unfeeling as the edge of a knife. But he had no need to hide that from me. I had seen it. I had benefited from it more than once. And I had always been there for him when it was over and he collapsed, invariably coated in blood like some infernal confectionery, appalled and yet somehow proud of himself.

Still, even then, and now, he hid something. Even as he slipped into shirt and shoes, still grumbling about the newspapers, a part of him was veiled. I brought the dream to mind again; it wouldn't be good to be obvious about prying. I resolved to let it go.

"Back shortly. Do you want anything?" he asked.

"Oh, yes, now that you mention it. I would love a cup of hot black coffee."

"No sugar?"

I kept smiling. "Not tonight," I said.

He left. I let a few beats pass before I opened the briefcase and pulled out one of the 200ml bottles. I prayed that the train wouldn't start for a few seconds, dipped my fingernail in, just enough to make a drop of Orchid cling to the tiny spoon shape, and sucked my finger, recapping the bottle and sliding it back into place. It was so minimal, but it was enough. I sat there on the floor next to the narrow bed, stunned at the tension and unhappiness flowing out of my limbs, drifting away even as the train started again with a labored screech. Soon, Alex returned.

He closed the door behind him quietly, the papers tucked under one arm, holding out a Styrofoam cup with his fingertips. Steam gushed from the tiny opening in the lid. "How much?" he said.

"Not a whole lot," I said. "It's probably a triple-ought-four."

He threw down the newspapers. My dreamy voice had incensed him. "Why, Elisabeta? Why? Why deceive me? It's not as though I mind. You can take it if you want. But understand that you're stealing. You're stealing from Ariane, from me, from yourself."

I shook my head. He wasn't making very much sense. "I'm not stealing anything," I said. "She gave some to us. It's ours to take."

"For one thing, I saw what you did—your mind was like a siren. You can't hide anything from me. You didn't take it from what Ariane gave to us; you took it from the bottle supply. That part I don't understand. Are you skimming? Are you cutting it with, oh, I don't know, vodka?"

I couldn't help laughing. It wasn't such a bad idea. "Look, I'm sorry," I said. "I'm sorry. I just took some because I wanted to have it. So I have no self-control. After we're done with this, let's not ever take this again, okay?"

"But I don't *want* to never take it again," he pointed out. "I am not with you on this one. I like Orchid. I like it as much as you do. What I'm wondering is why you feel the need to hide it from me."

"I just had the urge," I said, letting out my breath in a heavy sigh. "I had such a strange dream and I can't get it out of my head. You steady me, Sasha, and when you left I . . ." I let my voice trail away, and closed my eyes. "I don't understand it. I just felt so imprisoned.

Their shops frighten me. Too much color. If I wanted
to see a circus, I'd go to the circus."

He slid down onto the floor beside me, and put the
hot cup into my hand and put his arms around me.
"My dear," he murmured, "my dear, it is anxiety, nothing more. Talk to me about it; that's the only thing that
will help you through it. You're just not used to it,
that's all, all this traveling and adventure. Of course
you'll have tense dreams. It's nothing—just a few
crossed wires, that's all."

I was so glad I knew him so well, and that I learned
quickly. I could protect my thoughts, after all. He
trusted me, and that was the best armor against him
that I could possibly have. That it went both ways, I
had no doubt.

I took a sip of the coffee, which tasted of vinegar,
and stood up to pour it into the toilet. Alexander Vassilyevich laughed. "What I really want is to make love,"
I said. "I think that will help me best."

"I want some Orchid, too," he said. "Remember
when we swam among the stars? I want to try something like that again."

We kissed, and rolled among the tousled bedsheets.
I rested my weight on top of him, and bent to the unlocked briefcase, pulling the syringe free from the
tape. He grinned up at me. "Not too much," he ad-
vised. "I'll hold still."

I held up the syringe to his open mouth, and looked
at the measuring marks with a careful, critical eye. The
train shook gently from side to side, buffeted by the
strong wind, moving slowly and tentatively over icy
tracks.

We might be stranded here, I thought.

I pushed the plunger all the way down, flooding his

mouth with twelve milliliters of Orchid. He coughed and choked, but none of it spilled; his mouth obediently soaked it up and rushed it through his bloodstream.

His expression transformed from shock to fear to sadness in less than a second, but never for a second did he show anger. He just lay back, his shoulders relaxing against the bed, and his head rolling back and forth, one ear touching the bed, then the other. Eventually, even that movement stopped.

"Whatever you do," he said in a ragged whisper, "don't apologize."

"I wasn't planning on it," I said. I licked the end of the syringe, grimacing the last trace of chemical flavor into my mouth. I bent over and kissed his lips, which were deliciously warm, moist, soft.

He moaned faintly. "I want to put my arms around you, but I can't move," he mumbled. "Oh, God in heaven. My little Elisabeta, I wish you could feel this. I suppose you can. You've got hundreds of doses to do with as you wish; you could take it all if you wanted to. Is that what you want?"

"No," I said, tossing the syringe down and tucking myself beside him, folding my arms across his waist, and pulling his arms to me. He shuddered. "I just want to know something."

"You already know my birthday and my favorite color. Oh, but did you know that I dislike sturgeon?" The pupils of his eyes were huge, consuming the blue irises completely; he was as blind as a baby and I wished that he would close his eyes. Instead I closed mine.

"The train," I said. "The accident. Outside Novgorod. When I fell. You remember. Tell me."

He said nothing for several minutes, and if I hadn't been able to perceive the gauzy swirling of his thoughts,

I would have thought that he had lost consciousness. When his voice came, it was faint and resigned. "The accident. There was no accident."

"But I remember, Alexander Vassilyevich—"

"Of course you remember. You remember falsely. There was no accident. You did not fall—I pushed you. I pushed you and I prayed that you would break your neck."

I lay there, stunned into silence, hearing him say what I had never even allowed myself to suspect.

"You broke everything but your neck, it seemed. Perhaps my concentrating on it so closely protected it. As I stood beside you, feeling bullets slamming into my back, I heard you scream. I knew you were still alive, and at once I resolved to protect you. I had already taken three lead pellets in my back that might have hit you instead, and I realized that I would take more, as many as was necessary, but that you must not ever be hurt again if I could prevent it. I loved you. I love you still. For a moment I was a coward. I didn't want to have to protect you and your fragile body, not when my comrades had committed themselves to destroying me and destroying the country I fought for. I didn't feel like looking after you. But I had married you, and not in vain . . . not for nothing. You were my responsibility to protect, your body and your mind. I could bring you with me—I could change you—and we could escape together. I almost let a moment of cowardice destroy the only thing of real value I've ever had. The money, the expensive things—none of that has ever meant a thing to me compared to being with you and bringing you happiness, my precious, my beloved 'Sbeta. . . ."

Now he really was slipping away. He fell silent and his eyes finally closed. His lips had gone pale and dry, and when I tried to move his suddenly heavy arm, his joints were stiff. He wasn't dying; instead, he was sliding gradually into sleep, a deeper sleep than he had ever experienced.

I sat beside him all through the night, as the train shuddered on its route, pausing now and again. I thought of all the places that I had seen and wanted to see again, wondering if the world had changed them so much that I couldn't love them anymore. I thought of all the places that I hadn't yet seen that I had hoped to see someday, and knew that I could never see them as I wished, bathed in heady midday sunlight. I thought of all the kisses that I could never have again, and all the hopes of all the men and women and children that I had killed, vanished into the world like smoke, but, as long as I lived, as long as I contained their memories, never really gone.

I didn't take any Orchid. I fought off the reverie and the urge to doze off, even as I watched snowflakes flash by the window, then suddenly cease, leaving the sky stark black, but alive with stars.

The train stopped as the sky started to pale at the horizon. We had come to a station, and I heard the bustle of passengers gathering their things and exiting the train, too many of them, and too early, for all of them to be grabbing a cigarette break on the platform. I overheard "St. Cloud" and "late as hell; it's ten till six." I looked over at Alex, still unconscious, rigid and peaceful as a corpse, and slowly put on my dress, a cardigan sweater, and shoes. He had never undressed; not that it mattered.

I waited until the hubbub outside subsided, refilled the syringe out of one of the bottles, took a deep breath, and hoisted my husband in my arms. He was heavier than he should be, but that didn't matter to me; I was more than strong enough.

The cold outside on the platform was a revelation. I hadn't felt cold that profound in years, and yet it wasn't the most extreme I had ever experienced, not compared to Novgorod in the dead of winter, so cold, even the snow thought twice about falling. This cold still held some moisture; I knew that a river was nearby, and the cold didn't deter me from going to find it.

I wondered if Leland dreamed of me, of the snow cresting over the tops of my shoes and the freezing wind blowing over my bare legs and Alexander Vassilyevich, shielding me, a barrier against my front side. Would Leland interpret this memory as a nightmare?

I set Alex down on a wooden bench, in a pleasant little park a few blocks down the street from the train station, edged by the river. He retained his slightly hunched position, but showed no signs of waking up. I brushed snow off the bench next to him and sat down, smiling at the ice clinging to my skirt and my skin. On the other side of the river, the violet sky flushed hot pink and tiger-gold.

I rested the edge of the syringe against the corner of my mouth and shot the Orchid in.

Ah, delicious, melting, sugar and butter, igniting, heating my skin—all existence was a treat. I kept my eyes planted on that horizon, staring full into the brightening line until that's all I saw. I was pleasantly surprised. Going blind didn't mean eternal darkness; it was unending light, a tight lentil of illumination. Of course I hadn't seen the entire disk of the sun, but I saw it; the sunrise, cresting over the mighty Mississippi, beside the only man I'd ever loved, who had ever loved me. He would understand.

We did not burn with flames; we smoldered like incense, consumed rapidly, as our human bodies had been at the first fatal touch of the inhuman blood. It happened so quickly that I only felt pain for an instant; then nothingness, a sweet, floating, drifting away.

XVII

You Make It Sound So Clinical

<u>Margaret Williams</u>

I missed a day of work.

I didn't feel sick—well, no sicker than usual, which wasn't bad enough to keep me at home. But I didn't get up. I didn't call in and let anyone know that I wouldn't be there. I just lay there, in bed in the dark, all day and all night, not sleeping, not lighting the candle. I just drifted, never thinking of anything in particular, like I was on hold.

The weird thing was, Ariane didn't seem to have noticed. The next night she never brought it up once. I wanted to mention it to her, but couldn't bring myself to do it.

There was a lot I wanted to talk about that just slipped away when I was around her. It was like having my tongue literally held by gentle but uncompromising fingers. If I wanted to blather emptily about the hot gossip going on in my history class, or about what music I was listening to, or what I'd had for dinner, I could talk myself blue in the face, even if Ariane never responded past a grunt of amusement or a derisive snort. But I knew she was actually listening to me then, even if she had nothing to say about it. But if I tried to mention John, or her past at NCIT, or ask if we were going to continue our original research, my tongue felt thick, and sometimes I had bad fits of coughing, or I'd suddenly be aware of a process finishing across the lab that I had to jump up and attend to. Five minutes later, I'd remember that I was going to talk to her about something, but I could never remember specifically what it was.

I began to concentrate on remembering to ask her about that time she'd showed up at my place in the middle of the night, making a tiny tick mark with my thumbnail on the edge of my desk every time I thought about it, so that I'd remember even if I did get distracted. And all of a sudden there was nothing to say down in the lab. I'd send out some bottles for shipment or load up blood packs into the refrigerators, and not a single word could make it out of my mouth. The edge of my desk began to look like rats were gnawing on it.

It seemed to be hard on Ariane, too, at the same time. She was constantly scrunching her hair really hard in her fists, gazing into space, or grimacing as if she were in pain. When she caught me looking, she'd smile a little, sadly, guiltily maybe. A pretty smile of shame.

I hoped she didn't feel guilty about the poisoning. That was just an occupational risk, and it was my own fault that our antidote kit was incomplete—that was part of my responsibility as lab assistant. I was just grateful that she had gotten me to the hospital. But nobody had seen anything, and nobody could tell me anything at the hospital other than I'd been brought in by Dr. Dempsey, not by ambulance. Which meant that she'd carried me all the way down the hall and up the elevator and all the way to the parking lot by herself. She just didn't look like she was buff enough to lift a woman at least three inches taller and twenty pounds heavier, let alone carry her all that way. She must have plopped me in a wheeled office chair and scooted me along; if I'd been dragged I would have been covered in superficial scrapes and cuts.

When Uncle Stan found out about my trip to the hospital, he got pretty upset, and left a furious voice mail on the office's line demanding a private meeting with Ariane. When I met him for coffee the day after the scheduled meeting, I asked him how it went.

"How what went? Oh, the meeting. It was fine," he said. His eyes were vague. You'd have to know him as well as I did to notice, but it was unmistakable to me.

"It was *fine*?" I repeated dubiously.

"Yeah, why? She gave you a good review. By the way, remember to call your mom; she practically talked my ear off last night complaining that you never call her anymore. You used to call her all the time when you lived in San Francisco."

I was going to retort that I had no *life* when I was there, but found myself silent again, realizing that I had even less of a life here. I mean, I tried; I went out to Tubby's and the Imperial every once in a while, and had a drink and danced a little, but it didn't feel like a life. My life was in the lab. The rest of it was just killing time.

My life was Ariane.

I wanted to quit and go back to Vegas, where at

least the sun came out once in a while, get away from all this darkness and obfuscation; but to be able to quit I'd have to tell her.

Who was I trying to kid? I'd never be able to leave her. There was never any other project but this one.

At the end of the week, Ariane put her hand on my shoulder and looked into my eyes. "I have something really important to discuss with you," she said. "Would you be able to meet me for a drink tomorrow night at ten? I've heard they're closing the Hotel Entr'acte, and I want to have a drink at the hotel bar one last time before it's gone. It's a nice little place, and they're only open until eleven, so I won't keep you long. Do you have plans that I'm ruining?"

"I never have plans that serious," I said, my voice sounding odd in the humming stillness of the office. "Ten? Sure."

She broke eye contact, patted my shoulder, and half turned away. "Don't worry," she said with a forced laugh. "I'm not going to fire you or anything. You've been a great help to me. I don't know what I would have done without you."

I hadn't even thought about the possibility that she might fire me, and it threw me for a minute, and I didn't thank her for the compliment. She arched her eyebrows and gave me a searching look, which I couldn't reciprocate. Now that I wasn't looking into her eyes, I found myself grateful, and dreading the next time she got me. I was prey and my eyes were vulnerable.

"I wonder if—Ariane, what was up that night you came over?" It all came out in a rush, like I'd punched myself in the stomach without even being aware of it. I studied her reflection in the curved glass of the computer monitor; she was looking at me, and she hadn't blinked or gasped or anything of the sort. It was enough for me to feel like a complete idiot for even asking.

She'd make a great card shark in the casinos, with a poker face that good.

My skin began to crawl, my head ached, and I had a sudden urge to urinate. I took a deep breath, and willed these sensations to go away; they couldn't possibly be real, not all of them happening at once.

Ariane sighed, breaking my concentration, but the headache and the pissing urge went away, leaving only a hyper-awareness of my clothing against my skin. "I apologize for that," she said. "I've just been under a lot of stress. I had a fight at home that made me have to leave the house. You know how, when you're so incredibly furious—especially when you know good and well in your heart that it's over something stupid and trivial—you just have to get the fuck out of there?" Her laugh staggered, but I couldn't tell from where I sat if she was shaken with amusement or restrained sobbing. Yeah, probably both. I wouldn't turn around. "And I went out without my coat."

"And you came all the way down by my house," I said.

"Yeah, I was really mad," Ariane explained. "I'm sorry. I promise I won't do anything like that again. It's not like me at all."

"What I don't understand is how I knew you were coming," I pressed on. "Even before you rang the bell. Like, five minutes before. I woke up and thought 'Better get up—Ariane is coming. Better be ready to let her in.' Isn't that weird?"

"Yeah," said Ariane, her voice suddenly flat, "that is weird. I'll see you at ten." Like shutting a book. What had we been talking about? It was late and I was drowsy and my forehead was sore, like I'd been hitting it gently against a wall for an hour. I finished up what I was doing and grabbed my coat and went home.

That morning, I slept marvelously well, like I'd been rolled up in a black velvet curtain.

I had never noticed the existence of the Entr'acte before, as it was in an area of downtown that, while it was only a few blocks away from my apartment, I had never really thought to visit. I might have ridden my bike past the concrete-and-brick edifice half a dozen times without actually seeing it, concentrating harder on avoiding the skinny metal tracks of the light rail line that ran alongside it. When I went through the vintage-furnished lobby to get to the bar, I saw no hotel guests, only sleepy-looking clerks behind the desk who paid no attention to me. The bar had only one other customer, his gaze riveted to the TV screen mounted on the wall, broadcasting a brutal overtime basketball battle. But the bartender said hello to me, and Ariane was already there, sitting alone, smoking a hand-rolled cigarette and staring at her reflection in the mirror.

The sight of her reflection calmed me immensely, and I smiled and sat down. "Hi, thanks for coming," she said. "I hope my smoking doesn't bother you too much."

"I never knew you smoked," I replied.

"I don't know why I bother . . . it's a completely pointless nervous habit. But pointless habits really come in handy sometimes. Would you like one?" She indicated a filigreed silver case next to her glass. "They're definitely the best tobacco I've ever smoked, for what it's worth."

I considered refusing, but agreed and took one anyway. It made me cough. "Sorry, I'm just used to filters," I said. "I'm sure it's really good."

She just looked at me, studying me, smoke hazing the air between us. Her skin was incredibly pale, a translucent honey so light that she seemed to glow. "Margaret," she said, "what I need to tell you is very difficult to explain. But I think that you deserve to know what's going on. You deserve a choice."

The bartender chose that moment to approach. "Evening, ladies. What would you like?" he asked pleasantly.

My blood turned to anxious ice. "Do you have any one-fifty-one rum?" I asked. When he told me they did, I ordered a shot. Ariane didn't order anything; in fact, it didn't look like she had ever ordered anything, as only a glass of ice water sat untouched on a napkin in front of her. "What's going on?"

"I created the pseudo-molifaxone for a reason," Ariane said. "I made it to treat John." I didn't say anything, and she glanced up at the bartender bringing my rum as if he were trampling on a bed of flowers. I took a big swallow of the liquor, gasping as it hit my already rough throat, and relit the stub of the cigarette I had given up on. It was easier on the second try.

Ariane continued, "Because it was my fault that he ended up the way he did."

"What way?"

"Well . . ." She made a face. "Schizotypal. And . . . not human."

I laughed, but quietly. "What are you talking about? Being mentally ill isn't *that* bad."

"Margaret," she whispered intently. "We're not. Human. You've noticed. There's no way for you not to notice."

At the edges of her glistening, wine-red lips, her canine teeth looked long and sharp. No. *Were.* They *were* long and sharp.

She kept talking, although I wished that she wouldn't. "I was changed a little more than ten years ago. John was a few days after me. I made him—I changed him. I had to do it to save his life. He'd been attacked, he was bleeding to death, and I did the best I could, with . . . with the help of . . . of the first one I'd met. But it didn't go quite right . . ."

"The 'one.' 'Made.' 'Changed.' This doesn't make any sense. Are you talking about . . . But that's not real—that doesn't exist. That's not real, is it?" I babbled. To stop myself, I gulped the rest of my rum, and my head went swimmy from the fumes. "That's a fantasy. That's fiction."

"I'm sitting right here," Ariane said, stretching out her fingers to pick up another cigarette. Her fingernails didn't have any colored polish on them, like they usually did, but instead were some dull gray-white color. The bones in her fingers looked as long and fragile as glass straws. I looked up at her face, and she gave me an exaggerated grin-snarl, displaying those canine teeth, top and bottom, maybe a millimeter longer, a few degrees more pointed; but those tiny differences were everything. My throat slammed shut and my eyes burned; I think I would have started to weep, but the smoke had dried me out.

"So why is he crazy, and—and not you?" I stammered.

"He didn't get enough blood," she explained. "We were in too much of a hurry. It's a very precise process, and the slightest error will either cause death or interfere with the re-creation of neural connections in the brain." She gave me a little smile. "It's difficult to explain—let me show you."

I tried to say, "No," but it was too late; I was seeing it in my mind, like I was standing right there, in the past—in someone else's past—and I didn't want to see it, I didn't want to know. Ghoulish, emaciated men with burning eyes and skin like white wax, and everywhere, in everything, sexual and emotional desire beyond anything I could have possibly imagined. Maria and George begat Orfeo begat Daniel begat Ariane; Ariane and Orfeo begat John. Maria was dead and Ariane had never seen her, so her imagining of her was vague, like a blurry photograph. Daniel was dead and she could still remember the touch of his hands like he was there in the bar with us.

"Oh, my God," I whispered. "But I can see you in the mirror. It's not real. I've been hypnotized."

"You *have* been," Ariane said, "but now you're not anymore. I snapped my fingers and woke you up. We have the ability to communicate telepathically and to influence . . . humans." She grimaced. "This ability allows us to survive among humans. We can hide ourselves, make it seem like everything's normal and okay. That ability gets stronger if we ever exchange fluids with one of you."

"Did *we*?" My voice came out as a faint rasp.

She nodded, eyes downcast. "I ingested your blood on two separate occasions," she admitted.

I scoffed at the word *ingested.* "You make it sound so clinical," I spat. "Why don't you just call it what it is?"

She didn't respond to my anger, her face still smooth and sad, like she had been through this so many times in her mind that she was numb to it now. "I offer you the choice now," Ariane said, "to join us. I can make you. I can save your life. The radiation from the heavy potassium's already given you thyroid cancer. You're not going to make it otherwise. I'm sorry, but this doesn't have to be the end of the line."

"What?" I said, jumping from my chair and clutching my throat. Even the guy at the bar watching the game looked over, and the bartender took a cautious step toward the gap between the bottles and the bar.

Ariane slowly, gracefully, lifted her hand and let it drift back down to the table, like a leaf settling onto the ground, and the bartender and sports fan moved back to their original configurations, then sat, motionless, waiting for direction.

I stared at Ariane, shaking my head, trying to gulp away the sticky dryness in my throat, knowing that the overwhelming urge to pee was no longer an illusion. I had no interest in speaking to her. The answer was no. Simple as that. She got her answer; inside my head, I was screaming it. *No.*

The vampire made no move to stand up, just kept watching me, and her expression would have been heartbreaking if she hadn't been a bizarre, impossible, blood-drinking monster. She looked so normal for a second, like a sad, defeated young student, so young, as young as I was, like she'd just been dumped, but knowing that it was because of her own mistake.

How could she? How *dare* she have feelings? *She?* It! Masquerading as a human being so that it could keep me as its slave! The two men just stood there, eyes vacant, on hold.

Just like I had been.

I turned and ran out of the bar, rushing away with my guts churning. Out on the street, the cold air slapped me in the face, and I put my hand against the brick wall next to the glass doors to steady myself as I puked up the rum. It burned twice as much coming up as it had going down, and something about the repulsive and painful action really brought me back to myself. I no longer felt dizzy. I could breathe. The change from how I had felt earlier that day was amazing, from how I'd felt ever since moving to this fucked-up town. The range of her telepathic influence staggered me. She had controlled me twenty-four hours a day since I'd first seen her. She controlled everyone she saw. Except John. It had been obvious that he was outside her control. But of course, he was one of *them*, too. Christ, it all made so much sense.

I ran as fast as I could back home, but it was hard; I was bone-tired, and my legs and arms felt like they had twenty pounds of lead strapped to each one. I needed to get to a hospital and have them check out my thyroid, see if she had been bullshitting me about the cancer. But first, I needed to call the police.

But even more first, before doing anything else, I needed to get the hell out of town. They'd probably be mad that I told on them. I knew where Ariane lived; even though I'd seen no one when I was there, I imagined swarms of them, sliding half-invisibly across the lawn and climbing up from the cellar with mud clinging to their bloodless skins. Once I called the police, they'd go over there with silver bullets and flamethrowers and destroy them.

Jesus, *of course* she had late office hours. She had OMI in the palm of her hand. None of them suspected anything. Stupid academics and their tolerance for eccentricities; who knew how many people had already died?

My hands shook so badly that I dropped my keys four times, once after I'd already opened the foyer door. By the time I was inside my apartment I had started crying; big, thick, rum puke-flavored sobs of sheer terror. I went to the kitchen and poured a glass of water, took a gulp, and cried a little bit more because it felt good to wash myself from the inside. I caught my distorted reflection in the mirrored surface of the water tap; the only thing that was recognizable was the hair. The fucking hair. I resolved to dye it as soon as I was back in Vegas, and if that layered ruby-scarlet couldn't be dyed over, I'd shave it off. To hell with bioscience; I'd work slinging hash in a truck stop. I'd turn tricks. I'd become a hermit. I didn't know if it would help me forget what I'd seen, what I knew, but I'd give it a try.

I drank some more water and went back out to the front room, checking again that the door was securely locked, then waking my computer from its sleep mode and loading an airline ticket sales Web site. The next flight to Vegas wasn't until after five in the morning, and I cursed as loud as I could. There wasn't time for luxury. I'd have to drive. That was fine with me; better inside a car, going seventy, than stuck here, with them.

I actually called Aunty W.; she didn't answer the phone. It was past her bedtime; all the phones got turned off when it was time to sleep. It was just her policy. If there was a real emergency, someone would come to the house, or there wasn't anything she could do about it, anyway.

Uncle Stan and Aunt June were the same way. I resolved that I would go by their houses on my way out of town and force them to come with me. I'd explain to them on the way.

I stuffed as many clothes as would fit into the blue carryall bag and zipped it up. The liquid sound of the zipper reminded me of my bladder, which suddenly yelled for attention. I'd pee and get on the road; whatever had to stay behind, had to.

As I sat on the toilet, I thought of my dub bootlegs. I'd never be able to replace those. Okay, it'd only take a moment more.

Zipper up. Flush. Instinct drew me to the sink and I quickly rinsed my sore, discolored, scaly-skinned hands. I splashed a little water on my face, too, to make sure that I was alert.

Someone handed me a towel.

I dried my face and let the towel fall to the floor.

He was a remarkably small guy, fey and young, but with the kind of granite stillness and heaviness that I associated with very, very old people, ones who spent all day gazing right into the eyes of death and refusing to back down. He was kind of pretty, kind of funny-looking, but his face seemed stuck in melancholy mode.

"Orfeo," I said, suddenly recognizing him. A spike of terror stabbed up into my throat, but it vanished instantly; even the concept of fear just winked out. It was all right. Him being here was all right.

"I love her," he said in his deep, overserious voice, so odd coming out of that little body that it made me smile, since I couldn't laugh. "And I will protect her. I am sorry. You seem like a lovely girl."

From where he stood, his mouth fit very nicely under my chin. It was a nice mouth, with thick, plush lips, a little chilly, like he'd just finished an iced drink. His saliva tingled against my skin. I thought of the last boyfriend I'd had, years ago, back in Vegas, the summer after my freshman year. Jacob had been kind of a jerk, but making out with him was the best thing I'd ever had in my life. He would put his arms around me just like that, and suckle my neck, just like that, even if Jacob had been trying to leave hickeys, and not . . .

It didn't hurt. It really didn't. I felt uplifted.

At first. But after that, it was too late to complain.

XVIII

EXPLAINING DARKENING

JOHN THURBIS

Moments of extreme weirdness.

Ariane and I had agreed to begin lowering my dose of Orchid. Without the drug's buffer, I found that I could hear and distinguish separate packets of radio transmission: staggered blips of mobile phone calls, groaning AM radio, high-pitched hissing wireless data networks. For a few uncomfortable hours before I went to sleep, it was hanging suspended in a jelly made of data, and the thoughts of the others nearby hit my mind loud and ringing with echoes, like shouting in an empty room. I had nightmarish dreams of phone sex chat lines and Empire Auto Glass adverts. But, by the time I woke up next night, I had gotten more used to it. What had been shouting had become a low mumble at the edge of my consciousness, like someone muttering an insult that you're not meant to hear.

It was difficult not to run away, struggling to shield myself from the crowding thoughts of Ariane, Orfeo, and George. It was like the year after Dad died, being the only boy in a house of three women. I was stuck with Mum, grandmother Victoria, and aunt Lydia, all of them ostensibly there to look after me, but so wrapped up in private dramas and priorities of their own that they didn't notice me slipping away, outside of their sphere and into my own. George and Ricari had their bizarre history, Ariane still could not fully blame nor forgive Ricari for all the trouble he'd caused her, and Ariane and George were not speaking to each other. I wanted to have done with it. I reread the Feynman lecture on probability amplitude, and sat on the Rock, watching the waves on the river, listening to the poor humans, forced to use plastic devices, radio transmissions, and wire to communicate with each other at a distance.

I missed Psychward, but was glad that she was no longer unhappy. I missed Mum, but it was best that she didn't know. Maybe I'd drop by someday and make sure she was all right, even if I could never speak to her again.

Family outing.

It was Saturday night, and the weather was shit. The other three walked together behind me, meandering through the city, avoiding major streets. George and Ricari walked holding hands, not in a petting, snogging kind of way, but gripping each other tight, like Hansel and Gretel revisiting the woods. George held a large, store-bought umbrella high over them both. Comical to see the supermodel walking her pet shrimp. She missed me awfully, at least as much as I missed her. Too bad for everybody. Let her walk behind me and give what she'd done a bit more thought, and maybe in time I'd stop feeling a sick stew of anger and betrayal whenever I saw her. And the sight of Ricari made me want to kick him in the windpipe, but that was nothing new.

I could have taken Ariane's hand at any time—she wanted me to—but I couldn't bear forming another coupled unit, just because *they* were doing so. I didn't want to do anything that either of them did, no matter how much it might have made me, or Ariane, feel better. I wasn't ready to provide comfort just yet, even with the dark pall that death had cast over all of us—I was still trying to build the mental structures that would protect my thoughts.

It was odd leading the way and feeling them fall into step with me, no matter how many times I changed my stride, trying to throw them off. They could anticipate me, and did, without even thinking about it. Worse, they *trusted* me.

I ducked into a parking structure, anxious to be out of the biting wind and sleet for a few moments. They followed, silent, up to the second to top floor, and kept close behind me as I sought out the center pylon of the building, furthest from the weather.

Ariane shook drops from the hood of her jacket. "What the hell happened last night?" Her voice came out muffled.

"You know very well what happened," Ricari said. He glanced up at George, and she nodded and closed the umbrella, shaking it dry with one swift, curt blow. "You saw it."

"No, I don't *understand*," Ariane protested, but not in a stupid way; she sounded as though she were really struggling to understand a basic, practical matter. "I'm not talking about what *you* did. Which . . . I guess I understand why that's necessary."

"What do you mean, 'you guess'? There was no other course of action," Ricari insisted.

"Like I said, that's not what I'm talking about. I'm talking about this morning, earlier. Just as I was falling asleep. I saw it, and I heard it, but couldn't do anything to stop it. It's like she wanted us to know. El and Alex. They're gone, aren't they. Really gone." Ariane's face was miserable, and her eyes looked ready to drop more tears. I took her hand then, willing to do anything to avoid seeing that, because if I saw her weeping I'd start up, too, reflexively, like a yawn. I looked into her eyes and shook my head, gently but warningly.

"No one could have done anything to stop it," said George with a sigh. "That was what El wanted to do. None of us could see her plan; probably she couldn't, either, until she suddenly saw an opportunity. But what's important right now is what they left behind in their train car. And that's what we need to discuss."

I looked at George. "How do you know what's in the train car?"

"Deduction," she said. "If you could make any sense of her last scream for attention . . ." She made a face as though the disparagement, though deserved, tasted bad. "One would imagine that she assumed that their belongings would be transferred when the train came to the end of its run in Chicago, and all the passengers who continue on to New York have to change trains and have their luggage carried over. Her emotions were high, and she wasn't thinking clearly. She's been living in a world where she hardly ever has to carry her own things; it completely escaped her that when their train reaches Chicago, their suite will be entered and searched, and the Orchid that you sent with them will be discovered. What they'll make of it, I don't know. At the very least there will be a lot of nonsense about terrorists; at the very worst—"

"They'll be able to trace it back to me," Ariane cut in. "*Greaaat.* I wish I'd been able to send them back to L.A."

Ricari shrugged. "It may take a while for them to piece it all together," he said. "But why wait around for that to happen?"

"Are their bodies going to be found?" Ariane sounded young and scared. I squeezed her hand lightly, then let it go.

"Well," Ricari said heavily, "what's left won't be identifiable. That's a blessing, if nothing else. When we die, not very much remains." He put his hand to his neck, where his old ivory rosary hung, and rubbed his thumb across the crucifix.

Oddly enough, it was George who began to weep, and Ricari viciously rounded on her, hissing, "Oh, save your tears for the living! At least I was there—at least I was with Maria at the end! You forfeited your right to grief. You might as well have pushed her into the fire yourself. Enough of your sniveling—help me help this child. You can't help the dead." Ricari, who had seemed to grow twice his usual size, suddenly deflated, and his face resumed its usual mournful expression. "We have all had loss," he continued. "But our most important purpose is to survive. That is now the matter at hand, and the very reason why your assistant could not be allowed to live. Since you did not seem capable of solving the issue when it was at hand, I took it upon myself to complete the work that you were unable to do."

"I really hoped that I could turn her," Ariane said.

Ricari and George smirked at each other. "You would have known from the start if that were possible," Ricari said. "Did you mean to apprentice her to you, or let her go on her own way? You must think these things through before you commit to such a decision."

"Even though most of us don't, because we're blindly in love," George added. "But that's love for you. Poor planning and assumptions, culminating in hurt feelings and wasted money. And, with us, frequently corpses."

Ricari looked aghast. "George! Not yet."

"Gallows humor should be used as quickly as possible, before the bodies begin to smell." George shrugged. "You've got hundreds of years to really give your intentions toward your assistant a good, solid thinking-over, but why would you want to waste your time doing that? The matter at hand," she said, taking a breath, and staring intently at Ariane, "is that you must leave this life, and the sooner, the better."

"Leave this life?" Ariane repeated. "What do you mean by that?"

"You have to die to this human world," she said.

"But I already did," Ariane replied.

"Not completely enough," Ricari countered, his voice suddenly cold as ice. I remembered the first time I saw him, and heard his voice; it had that same remote, chill tone, and I couldn't imagine what about him had attracted Ariane. How could she be attracted—sexually drawn—to a creature that bore only the slightest resemblance to a human?

The realization came to me suddenly. Any warmth,

friendliness, or affection that was ever present in his voice was a mask, a performance of humanity, a way to give context to emotions that, by rights, we shouldn't have had. We were no longer human; our feelings no longer made any sense, stripped out of their natural settings and placed into the realm of eternity and nightmare.

"Once upon a time, you could simply disappear, and be gone, and as long as you were not a figurehead or politically dangerous, no one would waste the resources searching for you. Things are different now. You have been photographed; you have been published. Students follow your work—both of you," he gave me a slight nod. "But John has already disappeared and is presumed dead. Dr. Ariane Dempsey has existed in two separate places, in two separate forms. We have to conclude your previous identity as completely as possible, now that it seems that it would be impossible to simply erase it. Am I correct in that assumption?" Ariane answered Ricari with her silence. "I'm sorry, Ariane, but you must die, and then you must leave this place and never come back. You have had more than ten years to accept this life. Now it's time that you begin on the life. Ariane, you're not human anymore. I know you'll say that you know that, but I don't think you do."

"Their morality is not and cannot be ours," George spoke up. "It will very quickly make you go mad, and you'll end up well and truly dead in no time at all. You may go mad eventually anyway; most of us do, if we make it through the years, because it is impossible to completely shed yourself of human morality. It is a goal that is not truly attainable, but is no less worthy of pursuit."

"Like trying to be pure of sin," I heard myself say.

Ricari nodded slowly, meeting my eyes. "Yes, John, that is similar," he said, "but you mustn't seriously compare the two—that's blasphemy."

"Of course it is," I replied. "Therefore, isn't it blasphemy for one of us to have affectionate, protective feelings for another one of us? Or for a human being? Or an animal? I mean, is there room in your Christian Heaven for something like us?"

George smiled at me. "Maybe you should write the first book of philosophy for us," she said.

"No, *you* should." I shook my head, finding myself smiling too. "You're the better writer. And you've got two hundred years of thinking about it that you can put into practice."

Ricari lifted his head, listening to the sound of a car entering the parking garage, four floors below us. "We have to move on," he said. "This is extremely serious, Ariane. We should leave as soon as possible—within the week, at the latest. Margaret may not be found for several more days, but if she's reported missing, it could be sooner."

To my surprise, Ariane embraced me for a moment, then gently pushed me away with her fingertips. Her face was as calm and still as an ivory carving.

"Just tell me what I have to do," she said.

XIX

SCATTERING

ARIANE DEMPSEY

Sweet Orchid sleep. Upsetting Orchid dreams.

Red snow fell in thick flakes that melted into blood as they touched the still-warm streets. The gutters were clogged and rushing with sluggish, crimson liquid, all mixed up with fallen leaves, broken glass, mud, and gravel. The limbs of trees dripped red and the air was thick with the ferrous smell. Through a break in the scarlet clouds, the sun emerged like a drill made of white light, and I was pinned on it like a bug, blood-flakes sparkling in the sudden illumination.

When I woke up, though, the sky was dark, as usual, and the few inches of snow on the ground were clean and colorless. The neighborhood was nearly silent, but for a faint sound of a television watched by immobile viewers. Nobody wanted to risk the steep hill that led to my block when there was ice on the ground. This kind of weather was rare here; maybe every other year it would snow a little or glaze the branches with ice, and the city would screech to a halt. It wasn't just the people, either; even the usual flutter and croak of feral animals had been silenced under that frigid, black and white blankness. It felt like a betrayal, like the world was cowering from the sudden slap of cold.

I was alone in the house. John might have slept beside me, but I fell into an exhausted sleep while he was still awake, his calm, dark eyes searching my face. Ricari and George hadn't followed us back from our journey to the Tenth Avenue E-Z Park, claiming that it was for my own safety that they not return with us, instead of being upfront and saying that my house made both of them uneasy. Maybe it was one of those little white lies that they referred to when they talked about human habits; maybe a pure vampire never had need to conceal her feelings, and dispensed with the deceptions of verbal communication.

Great theory, except that they both loved to talk, all the time.

I'd be fine, listening to them lie. I wanted to hear their voices. I wanted to hear George tell a filthy joke, or listen to Ricari's reminiscences about Geneva, as he visited it around every seventy-five years, just in time for the old generation to have died out.

He told me that I probably wouldn't be able to do that, nowadays. Too many cameras watching the streets, not enough dark corners to hide in. We could trick the human eye, but not the electronic one; we showed up on film and tape as well as any other object that reflected light.

It didn't matter where I went; the only thing that was important now was that I had to leave Portland, quickly, quietly, and discreetly. The rest could be determined later, once I was somewhere safe.

I glanced at the clock. It was barely past five, and the sky pitch-black already. Winter solstice; it was going to be a long, cold night. I just hoped it would be long enough. I tried to shake off the prickly sensation lingering from my dream, got up, and hit two of the last four blood packs in the cube fridge. The blood was icy cold, as cold as the snow in my dream, but it solidified me, filling in the empty outline of my being.

I had work to do.

A large carrier bag, already half-packed, sat propped up against the wall of my bedroom. John had put together all the things he wanted to keep, which wasn't much; a spare coat, a pair of jeans, a ragged-edged copy of *The Interacting Fermion-Boson Model*, a figure-eight of nylon rope, a box of razor blades, two black T-shirts, and a wool sweater. I carefully wrapped the last two blood packs in a pair of jeans, and filled the sleeves of my favorite sweater with syringes and small bottles of Orchid. I stacked running shoes and a leather jacket over the top and zipped it all up. I went through the house, room by room, wondering what else I should take, but I couldn't find anything essential, nothing that needed to be taken on a run for my life.

I layered on more clothes that I liked and thought would come in handy, and topped it with the big gray parka and brand-new waterproof boots that I had made Margaret order for me online.

Poor Margaret.

At least I knew she hadn't suffered; if I'd had to keep suppressing her mind the way I had been, she would have had a stroke before springtime. It had already happened to one of my past assistants, and the outcome had been the same, only that time I had to sneak into the hospital to do the task that Ricari had so efficiently performed. It was easier for him to do it; he didn't know her. I guessed that was nice of him. A favor. Yeah, nice, thanks.

As I was driving through the hills to OMI, I noticed that the gas tank in my car was nearing empty. My wallet had a dollar in it. All the ATM machines had cameras attached to them; I almost swerved in horror as I thought of exactly how much footage of me must exist—every convenience store, every department store, every stroll past the traffic cameras in the dead of night. At least I had never killed or bitten anyone in view of those things, but what about the cameras I didn't know were there?

No wonder Ricari had left me behind. My presence endangered him.

OMI was still fairly active this early, with grad students shivering their way from the parking lot into their classes, administrators shivering in the opposite direction. I parked my car and kept my hood down.

The office smelled stale already. I turned on the smallest, faintest desk light, and unplugged all the computers. It was awkward using a fine screwdriver and unplugging wires with my long claws.

Margaret had left a little plush frog toy on top of one of the monitors, and its black plastic bead eyes seemed to watch me dismantle the computers. That would have been a great place to put a hidden camera; who'd suspect a beanbag frog? I started to sweat under my heavy layers of clothes, and hastily scrubbed my clammy forehead with my sleeve. Since my blood was cold, my sweat was, too. Too much Margaret in this room—fuzzy toys, a bowl full of loose change to use in the vending machine, a snapshot of her stiffly smiling parents in a casino, even an umbrella she'd left behind. I reminded myself to take the umbrella and give it to John, to show him that I did listen to him, that I did love him, even with all of my faults. We could always use an umbrella, wherever it was that we would go.

In just a few minutes, I had made a small stack of internal hard drives. I shoved the drives into the pockets of my parka, almost definitely erasing them with my touch, like a rare-earth magnet that reversed polarity with every breath I took.

Ten years of research, destroyed in five minutes.

I put the computer cases back together and plugged them back in. I loaded all of the magazines, printouts and paperwork into a plastic bin and carried it down to the incinerator one floor below, tipping it all down the chute and warming my hands against the sudden, brief flare of warmth. Good-bye, property taxes and department meeting minutes. Good-bye, invoices from the blood product supply company, smudged with red dye fingerprints.

Poor—

Stop it.

Back in the lab, I pulled out all of the Orchid that was still there—about a liter, divided into small bottles—and placed them into an empty backpack, which I had left down there after my last round of bringing clean clothes for John into work. I knew that the backpack would come in handy someday, but I had never really thought it would go down like this. There was one unit of plasma left over after our last synthesis, so I drank it down and put the container into the biohazard bin. The plasma hit my bloodstream like sugar water, and any body heat I'd had evaporated instantly. I promised myself a big cup of hot coffee as soon as I was done, a twenty-four-ounce cup of shitty gas station coffee with five sugars in it, the perfect beverage for the road. Maybe John would want some, too; I'd pick up a cup for him, and drink it if he didn't want it.

Finally, the lab was clean. I shouldered the backpack, took one last look, then grabbed the damn frog off the monitor and stuffed it into my pocket. He was on a one-way trip to the incinerator. The glowing figures on the digital clock read 5:45. I locked the door and turned to go.

They were waiting for me in the hall.

I'd been so busy stripping the lab that I hadn't noticed their approach, or more truthfully, had been ignoring my instinctive warning signs, and chalking them up to paranoia and anxiety. I thought of Orfeo wagging his finger at me, and sighed.

They looked as surprised to see me there as I did them: Stan Williams, in a black suit, his face bright pink above his white shirt collar and his greenish eyes all hollowed-out and red; Coolidge, the co-head of the department, looking nervous and uncomfortable in a suit and tie; some guy I'd never seen before in dark pants and a rumpled brown leather jacket; and a female police officer in black uniform and sidearm. My eyes fixated on the gun for a while. The Glock was loaded and looked very heavy. It dragged the holster belt low over her hips. Still, the cop had muscular thighs and solid, square shoulders; she'd be able to handle the gun all right.

"Dr. Dempsey?" said Coolidge, the pallid spare tire of loose flesh around his neck undulating as he spoke. "Could we speak to you for a moment?"

"Regarding what?" I asked. My voice was so straightforward and calm that I almost laughed, almost threw up. I kept walking toward the exit doors, and they followed me, closer behind than was polite.

"Margaret is dead," Williams replied. He sounded raspy and strangled; it was a weird thought, Stan Williams crying to the point of screaming. He'd been drinking, too, I could smell. He was neatly groomed, though, shaved as smooth as an egg, his hair so tightly combed that it was immobile, the knot in his tie immaculate. "We have a warrant to search your office and your laboratory."

I stopped at the doorway to the outside, turned, and looked at them all. The cop looked stern, but fairly relaxed; she was comfortable with that sidearm, and with her knowledge of her abilities. It wasn't up to her to decide whether or not I was guilty; she was here to do a job. Ex-military. Born-again Christian. The perfect civil soldier.

The man in the leather jacket was more on edge. He spoke before I could respond to Stan Williams. "I'm Detective Aaron Thornton," he said.

"Detective?" I arched my eyebrows. "What's going on?"

"There's no way she died of natural causes," Williams cut in, never taking his eyes off me. "She bled to death, but there's not a drop of blood in the room where we found her, not a mark on her body, no weapon at the scene. Can you explain that to us?"

"That's impossible," I said. "Get a second opinion. Pathologists make mistakes, too."

"When was the last time you saw her, Dr. Dempsey?" asked Thornton.

"You've got a lot of firepower, to ask me a couple of questions," I asked.

"Please, answer the question."

I shook my head. "I won't," I said. "I don't have to." I stared at Coolidge and concentrated on his bladder; the poor old guy gulped and blinked and muttered an excuse, tottering away down the hall. I turned and put my hand on the door's release bar, but the click I heard didn't come from the door.

I put my hand down, and slowly turned around. "She's dead," I said, "and you think it's a murder, but there's not a mark on her, and you just took the safety off your gun. What am I supposed to say? This is illegal intimidation, if I'm not mistaken."

"Just tell us when was the last time you saw Margaret Williams," said the detective. He had a soothing, regretful voice, like he was sorry to always have to be the bad guy.

"I had a drink with her," I said. I wondered how much it would hurt to be shot, whether or not it would slow me down or just be a major annoyance. Daniel had told me that it took about two days to heal completely from a gunshot wound; even if the skin healed completely, the internal tissues would still be chewed up, and it ached like hell to feel them reorganizing themselves. Also, a lot of blood was required. The more blood, and the fresher and healthier, the faster the healing time. My sire had been shot at least a dozen times, twice in the head. Would that ache, too? Brain tissue had no sensory nerves. "Friday evening. At the Entr'acte Hotel bar, at around ten-fifteen. We had a disagreement; she got angry and left. I don't know where she went after that."

"See? That was simple." The detective smiled with coffee-stained teeth.

"Margaret is dead, and I'm out an assistant, and a friend," I said. "It's not that simple."

"You seem to lose a lot of assistants, Dr. Dempsey," Coolidge pointed out as he rejoined the group. "It's pretty dangerous to work with you, isn't it?"

"She's been so sick lately," Williams said, his voice thick. "She told me she's been working with potassium cyanide. And she's been hospitalized for acute cyanide poisoning."

"Cyanide poisoning isn't blood loss," I said. "It's also highly and completely treatable. I took her to the hospital myself. I paid her hospital bills. I didn't kill her."

"Do you think someone did?" asked Thornton mildly. I wished that he was writing on a little pad or something, the way investigators did in the movies. He didn't have to write anything down; he was wired, digitally recording everything we said.

The bottles clinked quietly in the backpack as I hoisted it a little higher onto my shoulder. I tried to find some center of calm inside me, so that I could project it into their minds and make them leave me alone, but I was so agitated I could barely understand the words coming from my own mouth. "I don't, no," I said. "I don't think someone killed her. It's not physically possible, what happened to her. No one could do that. There'd have to be a wound; she'd have to be drained. Without a wound, without a murder weapon, there's no *murder* there. I didn't poison her and I didn't steal her blood." I was babbling. "Please, excuse me. I need to get home. Go ahead and search the office. And good luck."

"You know, that's odd," said Williams. "Shouldn't you be coming *in* to work around now? You always come to work earlier in the winter months, don't you, but this is a little drastic. Now, why is that?"

"I gotta go put gas in the car," I mumbled, and walked through the door into the cold, wet night. I felt like crying. Why couldn't I work on them? They would have just turned around and gone about their business and never remembered me at all. I was rattled and being sloppy. That kind of behavior could get me killed. I needed to get a hold on myself, focus, calm down, be cool.

I wanted a shot of Orchid so badly.

"Uh, Dr. Dempsey," came a voice from behind me.

I thought to myself that I should just keep walking, not turn around, it didn't matter, time to gas up and get out of town, but, reflexively, I looked over my shoulder anyway. First I saw Stan Williams standing in the doorway, his lips white and pressed together in a quivering line of rage, then the cop, outside the door, staring at Williams with alarm, then the detective, only a few feet behind me, smiling at me and holding up a little fuzzy green blob.

"You dropped your frog," he said.

Fuck the car.

I drilled my concentration into the uniformed cop's mind. Still staring at Williams, she drew her pistol, placed it against her own temple, and pulled the trigger.

Oops. Sloppy again. I'd meant to have her shoot the detective and Williams first. Stupid, damn sloppy, stupid. I let myself be rattled.

Stan Williams's jaw had dropped open, and he let out a near-silent hissing that might have been screaming, if he had any voice left. The detective was fumbling in his jacket for his own gun. I didn't let him find it. He was close enough to reach out and touch; my claws gently raked across his cheek, jaw, and neck, opening dark, meaty red lines that exuded steaming blood. The detective clamped his hand against his neck, trying to hold the blood in, but it came faster than he could stop, sliming his fingers and making his grip slippery.

Stan Williams was staring at me, frozen in place, his eyes so wide that there was white visible all around his irises. I met his stare.

Leave me alone.

A bomb blast in his brain, exploding blood vessels, all his neurochemicals pooling together in a psychotic poison.

Instantly, his wild eyes rolled up in their sockets, and he slumped to the ground like a sack of laundry. The detective faltered, too, falling to his knees, a pink, lacy froth of spittle coating the corners of his mouth. He wanted to speak, but his mouth no longer obeyed his will; he was more helpless than a baby.

He'd live. Stan would live, too. Their lives wouldn't mean shit, but they'd make it. But oh, why did I have to physically touch the detective? Well, he'd made me mad, was why.

Yeah, the anger. Like I'd been waiting for it all my life, even though I'd felt it before. Like an orgasm, different each time, but always an ecstasy. It was the reward of a biological imperative, but the need to copulate had been replaced by the need to kill.

Faintly, coming from the building several meters away, I heard, "Dr. Strong. I need Dr. Strong at Building E, west parking lot." It was Coolidge's voice speaking the code, half muffled with a telephone receiver held close to his mouth, shaking badly through his attempts to contain his fear. He'd seen the police officer blow her own face off, seen the detective confront me and then fall to the ground bleeding, seen his colleague Stan collapse. Campus security were on their way, no doubt aware of the investigation, of the warrant for my lab.

Fuck me for not offing Coolidge when I had the chance. I took a few steps closer and concentrated on him through the glass doors until I saw him fall to the ground, spasming and frothing. He probably *wouldn't* make it, but so it went; he was too dangerous to me alive, even though the heat was already heading this way.

I took off running, cleared the fence with one spring, and dashed into the thick woods surrounding the Institute. The bottles clanked once as my feet hit the marshy ground, then were quiet. A patrol car siren rose up out of the darkness, over from the southeast, driving fast over those icy roads. I was glad I had no need to stick to the paved roads, but whiplike branches cut my face as I passed by, and half-frozen ivy threatened to tangle up my feet and yank me back down to the ground.

I tried to concentrate on the beacon of John's mind. He was at the house now, trying to calm himself, wishing for a dose of Orchid to take the edge off his anxiety, settling for a useless cigarette instead. I felt Ricari crowding in, too, filling my head with too much conflicting information.

John said, *Come home.*

Ricari said, *Both of you, get out now, and don't go back there, because that's the first place where they'll look for Ariane.*

John just stood in the bedroom, smoking furiously, irrationally willing the nicotine to work, wishing that Ricari wasn't right.

I climbed through a tree, rather than attempt to go around it. The bark tore the skin on my palms, and I left dark, wet smudges of blood on the pale-gray fabric of my parka. Instinct pointed me back home, not knowing where else to go. If I had to run now—right this second—I would have to start from home and then proceed from there. I felt like crying and John felt like crying, and we both made it worse for each other, and kept each other from breaking down.

I came to an abrupt break in the trees, and found myself suddenly bathed in yellow illumination from a streetlight that had randomly come on. I was on a carless Barnes Road, over by the cemeteries; maybe a mile away, downhill, from my house. I paused to listen closely to the sounds of the environment, and instead got a head full of George.

Orfeo's right. Don't go back there, Ariane. Meet me at Sally's on Sunset. John, you too. Like a trumpet's melody rising up from behind me, her interior voice was brassier and more beautiful than her speaking voice. It made me feel small, but not puny or insignificant; her voice was a call to power, to rise up.

I told John to be sure to bring the carrier bag with him, turned on my heel, and dashed back into the dark, ice-glittering trees. When I made it to the strip mall that housed Sally's Café, it hurt my eyes to come out into the floodlights of the nearly deserted parking lot, even momentarily. I scurried from shadow to shadow until I'd made it into the dark illusion of safety at the back of the long, low brick building. I slid gratefully down the wall, tearing new holes in my already damaged parka and soaking the seat of my jeans with snow, and huddled under my hood, finally letting go of the tears that John hadn't let me release. If it made him break down, too, I couldn't help it.

Oh my God, the look on that poor cop's face.

And I still wanted a big cup of terrible coffee, but I had no illusion that it could warm me up now.

XX

A QUESTION OF HONOR

<u>JADZIA KOPERNIK</u>

"So, you were a model?" The woman chewed on her twist of lime, fine pale-green shreds gleaming against her straight, white teeth, her eyes examining my face, my shoulders, my sneakers, my ears, then returning to my eyes and lowering her eyelashes. She was refreshingly aware of her actions, and assured of their results. Thank God for older women; young girls were too often cute, seductive, oblivious teases. Between the two of us at the bar, there was no ambiguity. I looked forward to removing her clothes and seeing her body bare, perhaps by candlelight. She was interesting enough that I wanted to get her alone and comfortable, not just shove her into the ladies' toilet and wad her jeans down around her ankles.

I was leaving town soon, and heading far, far away. I figured I could take the chance of going down on her, bare tissue to bare tissue. There was no way she could track me, and after a few days, she'd forget what the big deal was about me. For tonight, though, there was a chance I could have a taste, and make a lady fall in love with me for a few hours.

I didn't mind being on the run, and this was one of the reasons why. This one's name was Anne. She was short of stature and generous of chest, with work-roughened fingers and long, curly blonde hair, standing by the jukebox, where her songs had come on immediately. The almost completely deserted bar held just us, the bartender, and a corpulent old man attached to the video poker machine. I bought Anne's drink and provided her with a fresh one.

"I *was* a model, but it's not very fun," I explained, sipping water. "I saved up some money, and now I'm just traveling around, seeing the world." I could get a motel room for not very much, or else we could go back to her place. She was thinking of that, too, mulling over such practicalities as *Are the dishes done?*

I was just about to come right out and tell her that I didn't give a damn if her entire kitchen was stacked with dirty plates, that I really wanted to get her alone immediately so I could sit on her face, when I felt my head jerk up, and my spine pull tight, as if I were a marionette being pulled upright.

Something terrible had happened to Ariane.

Trouble. Ariane had gotten the cops on her. She had killed someone. She had killed a cop, some other guy, scrambled the brains of some others. Bad trouble, so bad it froze her blood and numbed her senses. She was careless with fear. John panicked. Orfeo just wanted to be gone, safe, but his connectedness kept him from deserting her. As far as I could tell, no physical harm had come to Ariane, except that now she was running through the trees like a deer fleeing a forest fire. All of us could suddenly hear all the sirens everywhere, across the city. One dead policewoman, more coming to take her place.

Time to run.

I sighed, and smiled at Anne. "Excuse me," I said, shouldered my bag, and headed toward the toilets. Anne turned back to the bar and began to speak to the bartender, and I carefully and quietly let myself out the back door, glad I hadn't bothered to take off my jacket. Damn, damn, damn.

I focused on John, Orfeo, and Ariane as I walked, driving home a message with every step. Orfeo was trying to restore order, but he approached it like a nail he had to hammer in, instead of air to be absorbed with each breath. Ariane needed a more gentle approach, a caressing, guiding hand instead of a barked order.

I thought of the odd little bistro that I frequently passed by on my way to Ariane's house, and directed her to go there to meet me. I knew that the bistro, Sally's, closed at five o'clock, and the rest of the shopping strip that it shared seemed to close down at around the same time. It would be a good place to converge.

John cleared out of the house immediately and headed toward Sunset. I was grateful that he trusted me. *Just get us out of this,* he sent to me, his thoughts stark and grim.

Ariane had arrived before me. I found her hiding in the back of the building, next to a foul-smelling garbage container, sobbing like an orphaned child. It took everything I had not to break down with her, but I stiffened myself up inside and bent down to touch her shoulder. I'd startled her; her eyes in the shadow of her hood were wild and thoughtless. "You can't let your guard down like that," I said sternly, pulling her sleeve until she stood up. She scraped her cheeks with her hands, ashamed of her tears. "Release it. You've had your moment of giving in to panic, but it's time to get rid of it. Get hard. It's the only way you'll live through this."

"Maybe I shouldn't," she said.

"Okay, you've gotten *that* out of your system too, and we won't hear another word about that from you. We have to run. We all have to run. It's not just about you. Don't make it any worse for the rest of us. Don't punish us for caring about you." I looked over my shoulder at the curve of the road, where John approached from the north. "You've been strong for him before," I said. "You can do it again."

Ariane whispered a thanks and took a deep breath. Already her expression was firming and neutralizing. Yes, she was strong enough to handle this. Orfeo knew this when he saw her, and his whelp Daniel had seen it, too. She could do it for the long haul. I felt a pang of maternal affection.

John soundlessly joined us in the shadows, a stuffed carrier bag slung over his shoulder. As if I had X-ray vision, I could see the bottles of Orchid tucked away inside, and I had another pang, this time of mouth-watering, blind desire. God, a squirt of Orchid would really help everyone out here, especially me. John met my eyes with a strange, twisted smile.

"There isn't any more to spare," he murmured. "It was made for me."

"Yes, I know," I said. "But wouldn't it be nice?"

"I wouldn't know," he replied, without bitterness. "I haven't got a choice."

From a distance, Orfeo suddenly shot a thought into my mind. "He's not meeting us here," I said, gazing up at the clouds gathering over the black sky. "He will meet us in the park at Twentieth and Glisan. He heard a police scanner report about OMI. Three fatalities. They have your description, Ariane. Hair, height, your name, your clothes . . ." Ariane's face collapsed into terror again, and I wrested one of her hands out of her pockets and held it between mine, attempting to comfort her at the same time as I received Orfeo's message. "Well, okay. This changes things. We really need your car."

"What?" Ariane gulped.

"I'm thinking," I said, taking my hand back and pressing the edge of it against my temple. "I'm thinking. We've gotta go."

"Should I change my coat?" Ariane asked, glancing at the black stains on the sides of her parka.

"No," I said. "No, keep it on. I'm thinking. But let's walk while I think."

We had gone a few hundred yards down a minor road branching off Sunset when I spoke again. "I'm gonna go to OMI and pick up your car," I said.

"That's a bad idea," said John.

"No, no, it's not. If we drive, we save our energy and this is no time for a blood break. Besides, we can't let it fall into the hands of the police, right, Ariane?"

"Right," Ariane sighed, handing me a small ring of keys. "There's a lot of DNA in my upholstery, and none of it's mine."

"They don't have an ID on me," I said. "And there's dead people, so your car won't be an immediate priority. Yeah, I'll go get it—you go on to the park and I'll meet you there with the car. Keep your wits about you, all right? No panicking. Just remember that you can disappear to their eyes; nobody else needs to get hurt."

"You didn't even drink from them, did you?" John murmured to Ariane, and Ariane turned her head to spit some sarcastic reply. I turned on my heel and sped away from them before I knocked their heads together. I knew they just did it to tease each other, to toughen each other up because they were both such weaklings underneath, but it drove me crazy. At least when I had fought with Maria, we were fighting about real things that were important in the world, not just incessantly calling out each other's weaknesses. I think that was something else that attracted Orfeo to Ariane; he was prone to doing the same thing. Maybe it skipped a generation.

Still, it irritated me. Sometimes it was best to just be alone. But dammit, I really wanted to hook up with Anne. I wondered if it would have been so critical to let Ariane stew in her mistake while I got my ashes hauled; I might have been satisfied with thirty minutes.

The medical institute was mostly silent and dark, but I could quickly determine which parking lot was the operative one this night. Two squad cars with flashing tricolor lights were parked near the front doors of Building E, and one yellow campus security vehicle took up a handicapped space a few yards away. Men and women in uniform swarmed the area. Ambulances had already taken away the bodies, but a massive smear of darkening blood still spread across the wet pavement. Ariane had not meant to slit a throat, but she had done so, expertly cutting through a major neck vein. What a waste of good, wholesome blood.

Yellow caution tape had been unfurled across a large swath of the parking lot nearest the building, but

Ariane's car was all the way at the other end of the lot, sitting alone in the shadow between two lampposts. I palmed the keys in my pocket, and glanced around me before I unlocked the driver's side door.

Now, I had to remember how to drive.

It wasn't too difficult, once I'd located the turn signals, the windscreen wipers, and the parking brake; it came back to me as they say riding a bicycle does, and I had driven a car much more than I had ever ridden a cycle. I had been one of those early crazy females in a long white scarf and goggles, roaring over poor roads in a rickety horseless carriage. Driving was a fun game of skill. When I turned on the radio, a Blondie song was playing. I grinned and hoped they'd play some Donna Summer when Orfeo was in the car. What a shame our time in Rome was so brief; I never got a chance to turn him onto Chaka Khan or Labelle. Maybe we'd have to stay together for a little while longer.

I controlled my speed until I had left the campus grounds, then gave the engine plenty of fuel and hit the road hard. If we played our cards right, we could be out of the city before eight o'clock, and have twelve more hours of darkness to go. I figured that once we were well out of the state, Ariane and John could go one way, Orfeo and I another. More than anything, I craved mental isolation and rest, with the exception of traveling with Orfeo; it would be all right if I had only to deal with his direct mental interference, but Ariane and John and their immature mental chaos were enough to exhaust me.

I slowed down again as I progressed farther into the city. Only a few cars shared the road with me, and I got to the street bounding the north edge of the park just as my three friends arrived. Their bodies seemed to coalesce out of mist as they came to a stop. Orfeo wore a black leather jacket and beige snap-brim fedora that made him look like a whey-faced teenager dressed in a gangster costume. I became suddenly self-conscious of the fact that *I* also looked that childish, that young. We had both been so young two hundred years ago. I resolved not to be so judgmental of Ariane and John; I'd been new and stupid once, too.

I unlocked the doors, and they all climbed in, John taking the front seat and pushing the seat back into the frowning Orfeo's knees. "I'll drive," I said. "I've got cash for gasoline—we can stop on the other side of town. Ariane, keep your hood up." I eased the car into gear, and drove slowly down Glisan Street toward the highway entrance. On the radio, a Journey song came on, and John let out an audible groan that made Ariane chuckle. "What's wrong with Journey?" I mused.

He gave a little sniff. "If you have to ask, you're already lost to me."

I laughed, too. God, how I would miss that immaculate deadpan delivery. *Love is just a funky moose. Streetlights, people.* I loved this song. I was happy. I asked lightly, "Hey, John, how come you don't ever drive?"

"Killed a mate," he said, staring out the window. "Driving home pissed on a rainy night. Dark out. I'd been too busy with school to replace a buggered headlight. Head-on with a lorry, crumpled the passenger side. My drivers' license was taken away, and I never wanted it back." He spoke in a monotone. "It was odd. He didn't have a scratch on him; it was all on the inside."

"Oh," I said. We were all silent for a moment. "Well, I like Journey."

"That's terrible, John," said Orfeo softly. "I'm sorry."

John shrugged. "Yeah? Don't be. It was a long time ago and I've already paid for it. Gave me an excuse to move to America, so I reckon it all worked out for the best. By the way—George? You have a curable disease. I'd prescribe large doses of the Talking Heads."

He fell quiet, and we all felt our senses snap back into focus after that brief, relaxed moment. "That, there?" John said, angling his head. "That's bad."

On the highway overpass up ahead, a lighted road sign with an arrow compressed the lanes of traffic into a single one, crowned with a duo of police vehicles, lights strobing. As each sporadic car reached the police cars, it was stopped, and an officer leaned in towards the driver's side, checking paperwork and identification with a small flashlight. I felt my stomach pull tight, sick and cold suddenly, and my hands gripped the steering wheel until I heard the brittle polyresin crack.

"Okay, okay, okay, okay," I blew out my breath. "Okay, okay. Now. This is where things get interesting."

On the radio, "Bad Girls" by Donna Summer came on, and sharp new snowflakes began to fall, thickening as they clung together. In the backseat, Ariane gave an involuntary whimper of fear. I kept the car moving forward, toward the flashing lights, which seemed to coordinate with the disco rhythm, and I couldn't help but appreciate the synchronicity. *Beep beep. Hey. Beep beep.*

Think, George, think.

XXI

RUNNING

ARIANE DEMPSEY

"That there? That's bad."

John's voice was as dry and half-interested as if he were pointing out a change in the weather. Sometimes I wished that the British were more like the Italians; a little bit of hysteria at a time like this would have been welcome. Still, beside me, Ricari was just as impassive as John, with the dark pink stains on his cheeks his only sign of alarm.

I could hear the police describing me, describing the car we were in. As far as they knew, I was alone, armed with a knife or a straight razor, and extremely dangerous. Across the way, the other freeway ramp had its own checkpoint in place, more recently established with orange traffic cones directing the cars.

"This can't be happening," I whispered.

"There *is* a solution to all this," Ricari said heavily.

"Yeah," replied George. "It's not pretty."

"Enlighten me," I quavered.

"You have to go out there," George said, not taking her eyes off the road. In the light flashing from the police cars, the snowflakes gleamed blue, then red. We inched closer and closer.

"Give myself up? But that's completely—"

"No, not give yourself up," said Orfeo distantly. I could practically hear the gears turning in his head. "Give them trouble. Give them a reason to shoot."

"And then what?"

"And then take the bullets in front of them and drop," Ricari said. "Give them what they want. Give them a show."

"But . . . but . . ." My heart was caving in and my eyes ached again, trying to draw up moisture for tears, but not having much to spare. I had burned a lot of blood, running from OMI, and then to the park from Sally's, and my stomach cramped. "But what if they get me in the head? Won't that kill me?"

"They won't," Ricari said. "They're not that accurate at a certain range; they don't have sharpshooters here because they're not really expecting you to be here. Besides, even if they do, what of it? Your maker lived through that. You would, too. As long as all of your brains aren't blown out."

"So just be careful," said George.

"That's not really very reassuring," I muttered. Ricari made an infuriatingly noncommittal sound. Up in the front, John was still drilling a hole through the window with his stare. "Don't *you* care what happens to me?" I pleaded.

"More than anything in the world," he said. "But I agree that you won't be shot in the head. And I agree—give them what they want, so that they'll leave us alone. Forever."

"They want a body," said George, her fingers toying with the crack in the steering wheel. "Give them a body."

I shook my head. "No," I said. "I can't do it. One of you do it. Go out there and talk to them. Tell 'em I didn't do it. I didn't kill that cop." No one spoke, and I felt their discomfort at my blatant lie. "Just tell 'em— just tell 'em I didn't do it."

"So that what? You can go back to your job?" John asked. "I don't think it's going to happen. You can't go back there. And you can't disappear now—your picture'd be on every criminal database in the country. Ricari's right. The only way to make them stop hunting you down is to be killed, in front of witnesses. Case closed."

"Oh, God, no," I moaned. "I can't."

"You have to," Ricari said.

I wanted to slap that grave, angelic expression off his face. It was all his fault in the first place! "You don't care one way or the other! You just want me dead! You've always wanted me dead! I'm so fucking inconvenient for you!"

To my surprise, he laughed affectionately at me. "You are such a child," he said, pressing my knee with his. "Listen to what I'm saying. John is dead to them, and now he moves about the world completely unencumbered. I am dead, buried in a mausoleum in Campania with my name carved in marble. Jadzia Kopernik is dead, buried in a pauper's grave in Paris. If you want to live, you'd better provide undisputable proof that you are dead. Does that make sense?"

George giggled way too freely for my comfort, and

bobbed her head in time to the song on the radio. I wanted to punch something until I could see a hole.

"Use that," Ricari said. "Use that rage. Give them something to fear."

All the anger suddenly drained out of me, leaving me sick and clammy with fright, sadness and remorse. It was only right; my life for Margaret's, for those poor people at OMI who had the bad luck to be in the wrong place at the wrong time. Poor fat old Coolidge and his RV and his six grandkids. Poor widowed June Williams, who cheerfully talked to me about New Orleans flowers when I met her at a bioscience department mixer. "What's gonna happen to me?" I whispered.

"You will die," Ricari said. "But only to them. Never to us."

I had been searching for concrete answers, but I could tell that he didn't have any to give. None of them did. It was impossibly high-stakes gambling. Once upon a time, I welcomed such risks, but now that I better knew how much certain things hurt, both physically and emotionally, I just didn't have the stomach for them. I watched John's reflection in the car window and realized that he hadn't been looking out the window; he'd been looking at me, allowing my thoughts into his mind with more freedom than he'd been willing to risk ever since he gained the ability to shut them out.

He was letting me in. He was no longer afraid of what he'd see in my innermost mind. His own self-identity was solid enough, secure enough. I guess he knew once and for all that, no matter what, I loved him, and that nothing he saw in my surface thoughts ever changed that most fundamental fact.

"Will you wait for me?" I asked the reflection.

When John smiled, his fangs were clearly visible, pointed and shiny white against the muted rose of his lips. "I'll be there when you wake up," he said. "Don't take too long."

I almost smiled back, but my cheeks were too stiff. "Is there time to stop, so I can fuck my husband?" I asked, trying to be glib, but my voice came out quivering.

"No," said George. "If I don't get to get laid, neither do you."

"You're a bitch," I said.

She responded with a cheerful, "Mmm-hmm," and winked at me in the rearview mirror.

"But it doesn't have to be as bad as all that," John said, reaching to the floor between his legs and unzipping the carrier bag. He withdrew the closest bottle of Orchid and a syringe, and with deft and rapid movements drew up some of the dark fluid into it. "I can spare this much," he added, handing me the syringe. "Hopefully this will keep it from hurting too much. Maybe you can go and see the sun and the daisies again for a bit."

Ten cc's, the same amount as my very first dose. There was so much of it that the bitter solution felt thick and heavy in my mouth as it seeped in. Orchid tasted more bitter with every dose. I gagged, and when I opened my eyes, my vision had begun to blur. "Thanks," I said.

"I think this is your stop," said John.

The flashing lights filled the interior of my car. We four traded a quick glance, then I turned my eyes to John's and felt myself sinking deep into their darkness. He inclined his head and closed his eyes, holding out his hand to me. I took his hand and kissed the velvety skin over his sharp, bony white knuckles. So beautiful, no matter what.

I opened the door and stepped out into the snow, throwing back my hood, the wind whipping my hair.

My car had paused with two cars and a truck ahead of us. I watched the questioning officer's head arch up, his eyes popping comically at the sight of me. The freezing wind whipped my hair around and chilled my ears until I couldn't feel them. In fact, I couldn't feel a lot of my body, even as my feet carried me forward; it was a strange sensation, like floating five feet and change above the ground.

I leaped into the empty flatbed of the truck. I shouldn't have been showing off, but I wanted to feel near-flight once more, just in case I'd never experience it again. How delightful it was to spring up like a grasshopper and land without a sound; how fun to see the expressions of the police and hear startled shouting.

A woman screamed in the car behind us, and tires swerved in fresh slush as she risked a U-turn in front of a police roadblock. Behind me, three doors on my car opened, and three figures blurred out, the doors whispering shut again without anyone noticing.

I prayed for the falling snow to cover their tracks.

"Stop right there!" cried the cop holding the tiny flashlight, his hand whipping to his side and drawing his pistol. His partner scrambled out of the police cruiser and held out his gun, too, and the cops in the other car babbled information into their radio, requesting backup. "Put your hands where I can see them!"

I held up my arms and jumped down from the truck. The truck's driver was cursing and crying in a panic, struggling to unfasten his seatbelt so that he could get down onto the floor; all he knew was that a cop had suddenly pulled a gun out and was waving it at him. I extended my thoughts and encouraged the truck's driver to jump out of the truck cab instead of cowering on the floor. They wanted a show, did they?

I'd make sure the driver didn't get killed. I was done with that for the night.

"Dr. Ariane Dempsey," called the policeman, "drop your weapon and step forward with your hands held up."

"You can't take me alive, coppers," I murmured, chuckling to myself. The truck driver slowly approached me, his face contorted with confusion and fear.

"What the fuck?" he whimpered.

"It's all right. You'll be fine," I told him, then grabbed one of his shoulders and locked the other arm across his chest, extending my fingers so that my claws nearly grazed his skin. The driver didn't seem to believe my reassurance; his jeans abruptly steamed wet.

Nice one, thought John. He stood on the street a block away, watching the proceedings from behind the thick, ice-rimed green leaves of a rhododendron bush. George and Ricari were hidden to me, but I felt their presence nearby, also watching, their attention focused on the cops at the roadblock.

"Shut up, boyfriend," I said out loud. "You were scared of a street sign."

"Who are you talking to?" whined the truck driver.

"The voice inside my head," I grinned. "He's making fun of me. And I don't like it."

"Suspect has taken a hostage," reported one of the cops to his radio. "Looks like she's holding that knife to his throat. Situation escalating—where the hell's our backup? We've got a clear shot from Fourteenth Avenue."

I closed my eyes, feeling warm and sleepy even while my ears and fingertips twanged with cold, like I was suffering from the final stages of hypothermia. In the theater of my mind, I was wrapped in living, pulsing red velvet, swimming through a sumptuous fabric world.

Was that what El saw at the end?

How about Margaret?

"Drop your weapon!" screamed the cop. "This is your final warning! You don't need to die! We can end this now!"

Oh, they were so right.

I spun the truck driver around and away. He screamed and grabbed his neck, which I hadn't touched with more than my sleeve, then fell to the ground. It was enough for the cops to see an opportunity too critical not to take.

It was like being punched, more than anything else.

Punched in the collarbone, then twice in the midsection of my abdomen, once in my left arm; then I heard the keening whistle and pop of the bullets leaving the gun. As I heard the sound, I felt two more punches in my left thigh, then, coming what felt like years later, the double sound of the gun's discharge. These cops were good shots, unless they were aiming for my head; they'd gotten most of my major arterial groups right away. My blood gushed out, running chilly over my skin. It was creepy, how little it hurt at first; it was more of a spreading, shocky ache until I took a step back and resettled my weight, displacing the shattered collarbone, and then there was nothing creepy about it.

Unbelievable. The world turned upside down.

Even with the Orchid, being shot was so horrible I

would have gladly taken it back and sold out George and Ricari, even John, really; when was the last time John had been shot? Did he have any idea? Orchid wasn't a painkiller; it *amplified* sensation, twisted it, made it into something else. I was falling and my blood jetted out, so cold that it barely steamed in the air.

More screaming, more sirens, more garbled chatter on the police radio. Blood had poured out of me so fast that even the flashing lights on the police cruisers seemed dim. When I closed my eyes, I returned to the red velvet realm, but now I was wrapped tight, paralyzed, unable to move. And it was not red velvet *cloth;* it was blood, the soft interior of a blood cell, all of my consciousness crammed into a single submicroscopic disc.

I decided not to think about whether or not my liver had been punctured, and whether that made any difference in the slightest. I was gone out of this world.

In another plane of existence, John was holding my hand. We were going someplace wonderful. We walked together on a dark, warm, rainy street and had no need to talk, my clever, lovely, hopelessly damaged boy and I. He wanted to walk beside me, and there was no greater bliss that I had ever known.

And yeah, I'd fixed him. I broke him and damned him and I did everything I could, more than was humanly possible, to bring him back, and not for me—to give him back to himself.

Even the vivid redness of the velvet cell dulled now, and I could no longer feel. It was a strange sensation, the feeling of nothing. I thought I'd feel cold, but even that was gone—I was left in darkness, nothingness, oblivion.

Good-bye, everything.

EPILOGUE

THE ANGEL IN THE GRAVEYARD

<u>ARIANE DEMPSEY</u>

Death was different this time.

I couldn't *feel* anything—all my senses were utterly shut off—but my thoughts remained, alternately racing and then slowing to a glacial crawl.

Mostly, I spun through memory. Oh, yes, certainly, sometimes I had visions of being crushed and ground between immense blocks of groaning blue ice, or of being late for the most important test of my life, hopelessly lost in a shifting and unfamiliar city where I didn't speak the language. But I also got a lot of crystal-clear thoughts and impressions from my childhood, stuff I hadn't thought about in decades, thoughts of classes I'd taken ages ago, places I'd lived, murders discreet and outrageous.

I had no control over what I saw. There was plenty that I wished I never had to experience again, but the walls I'd built against those memories had vanished altogether, and I hadn't the strength to look away or the awareness to cleanse myself by crying. I watched, dry and helpless, as my friends died, as my lovers were killed, as I was cold and distant to my loved ones in need, as I was a selfish, arrogant bitch. And no one was there to judge except I myself, stripped of comforting delusions.

I, who had no faith, would have loved to cry out to someone for forgiveness, but there was only me, trapped in the ice.

It was hard to breathe.

There was an immense weight on my chest and throat obstructing the passage of air into my lungs. I grew frustrated and gave a great shove with my arms. I heard a wet, sickly ripping sound and agony tore up the backs of my upper arms. I drew in a breath to scream, and found that the pain instantly dissipated to a level that didn't deserve screaming. I could feel that the skin of my arms had frayed, tearing apart like wet paper, but they were tingling busily, cell building upon cell, the flesh regenerating itself.

I slowly and carefully opened my eyes.

The tissue of my eyelids tore a little, too, along the mucous membrane seams at the eyelashes, which had stuck and fused together with a tacky fluid that might have been blood. Immediately my eyes produced stinging, blinding tears, and at last a sound emerged from my throat—a horrible, ragged gasp like the wind blowing through a haunted house.

Almost in counterpoint, I heard a faint, mellow, smoky laugh.

"Awright, then?" said the voice.

I closed my eyes and then opened them again, and just as quickly shut them, blinded again by the immensity of light. Gasping for breath, I opened one eye just a crack, then both eyes fully. I was drenched in the white light, as bright as noon. The earth lunched under me, but I couldn't fall down, as I was already lying on my side, next to a massive pile of freshly turned dirt.

White blossoms scattered the ground beside the dirt. It was warm, caressing, the air dry and complacent.

Spring.

To my other side, a beefy olive-skinned arm lay, still twitching, faintly smudged with blood. The arm stretched out from a muscular, sweat-smelly male body. The entire side of his neck had been hollowed out, a fist-sized hole in the glistening ribbons of muscle and tendon, still leaking red. Hunger arched my back, and I moaned and put my mouth to the hole. Again. I had already been here. This was all me. The twitching of the arm stopped within seconds; already the veins had collapsed, and I had to suck avidly to get the blood to come through them into my mouth.

That's right; that's what I am. This is what I do.

Only more husky laughter distracted me from my meal. I flung myself back onto the soil and took more deep breaths, gazing fully into the source of the blinding light, a high full moon without a single cloud to compromise it. To my left, a hundred yards away, a white carved stone caught the moonlight and cast a sharp shadow onto the ground, next to the sparse black shade of the still leafless cherry trees, shivering in a very light wind, snowing white petals.

Some of the petals fell onto the bloody neck wound.

The dead guy looked like a football linebacker—at least six and a half feet tall, close to three hundred pounds, with a thick rectangular head with a buzz cut, and hands that were heavy and powerful without being fat. A perfect blood vessel. Ruthlessly and skillfully chosen.

I could easily have another one his size.

But for now, I felt all right.

And *he*—over there—standing, in mud-covered hip waders, black rubber gloves, leaning against a big spade jammed point-down into the earth, the smoke from a cigarette curling prettily around his dark figure. Him? What was he doing here? Was this the embodiment of a faith that had not ever completely died?

"John," I said, my voice cracked and rusty. "You came."

"I promised, didn't I? I even brought you a snack—I thought you might be peckish after five months underground."

"Five months!" I whispered. "It felt like years."

He bent down and reached out one gloved hand to me. "Gently, gently," he murmured. "Your body's still fragile. It's nowhere near as bad as it was when I first got to you, but you'll be all right in a bit. At least all right enough so that we can both get out of here." As I shifted aside, he began vigorously spading the soil back into a deep hole in the ground, inches away from where I and the corpse lay. The wet dirt thudded against a flat wooden surface down below. My coffin, a pine box, unvarnished, unlined. I shuddered and moved farther away, approaching the nearby trunk of a cherry and embracing the scaly bark. How wonderful, sensation; even pain was a revelation and a pleasure, because it was real, not a memory or a delusion.

I was alive.

John picked up the corpse's sneakered foot, dragged it into the hole, stuck his foot in to kick the coffin's lid closed, and resumed filling the hole. I closed my eyes again. Poor linebacker dude. I had needed him, it was true, and it wasn't like he was suffering, but I had so recently come out of that black pit that I didn't want to face anyone else going into it. But it was all right; he was dead. Inside my head John's presence glowed warm, happy perfection, delight, accomplishment, excitement. I smiled. He was just what I needed.

"Thank you," I whispered.

"Thank George," John said without breaking his pace. "She handled all of the funeral shite and kept them from embalming you; I've heard that's *really* unpleasant. She's gone now, of course. Her and Ricari. Went off together, to Iceland or summing. Someplace where they have plenty of discos, I reckon."

"We're gonna go too, huh?" It hurt to talk, and John turned to me and held up one filthy, gloved finger near his lips.

"Yes, we're gonna go too."

"Do you have any . . . Orchid?" I asked slowly.

He smiled at me. "Enough for *me*," he said. "For a while. And after that . . . well, who knows? Maybe I'll go mad again. Least of my concerns at the moment. I've brought you some clean clothes, but you might not want to put them on until you've had a bit more to drink. We're going on foot for a while. We can get far."

I had just wanted to make sure that he had some. Ordinary perceptions were overwhelming enough for me at the moment. "Thank you for coming back for me," I said.

He had almost finished filling in my grave, on that tree-crowned hilltop, in the unrelenting moonlight that my skin seemed to drink in, becoming paler and more luminescent by the second. He bent down beside me, took off his gloves, and held out one of his milk-white, beautiful gargoyle hands. "C'mon, love," he murmured to me, pulling me gently up from the ground, "your redneck mate Leland's got us a place in Tecate. I don't know about you, but I fancy someplace warm right about now."

"But isn't it pretty sunny there?" I murmured back, smiling through the pain.

He smiled back, and caressed the edges of my lips with his fingertips, then leaned in for a careful, dry, tender kiss.

"It isn't at night," he said. "Now let's go."

FIEND

JEMIAH JEFFERSON

In nineteenth-century Italy, young Orfeo Ricari teeters on the brink of adulthood. His new tutor instructs him in literature and poetry during the day and guides him in the world of sensual pleasure at night. But a journey to Paris will teach young Orfeo much more. For in Paris he will become a vampire.

Told in his own words, this is the story of the life, death, rebirth and education of a vampire. No one else can properly describe the endless hunger or the amazing power of the undead. No one else can recount the slow realization of what it means to grasp immortality, to live on innocent blood, to be a fiend.